In the cradle, a small bundle rested. It lay flat on a spine formed of a particularly thorny rose vine; ribs wound and woven of saplings bowed to the center and curled inward to a dried gourd heart. Each limb was carefully bound to the others, arms and legs, knees and elbows, and the head, once turnip purple and white, now carved and dried, then carved some more to soften its rounded cheeks and bring out the peach-pit brown of its eyes. Above those eyes, the wand woman's stars, moon, and symbols spun lazily, set into motion by the rush of air from Clarice's passing, and the rhythmic thrum of her feet as they pounded intricate backbeats across the floor.

Clarice spun to a breathless halt and cocked her head to one side. She drew forth a long, glittering pair of scissors from the depths of her gown and gripped the dark ends of her hair. She worked her fingers, rolling and tugging, choosing her moment, and snipped. The rolled hair fanned out in her grip, and she bent over the cradle.

Her fingers were nimble and supple, trained by a thousand stitches in a thousand shirts, the seams of myriad draperies that now caught sun and moon and stars in windows far away. She had no needle but wet the tips of her rolled hair thread with her lips. She closed her eyes and savored the taste as she drew each strand forth, still rolled, to draw it in, and out, and in again, marking the boundaries of the tiny chest. Each deft flick of her wrist added form.

Macabre Ink is an imprint of Crossroad Press Publishing

Copyright © 2023 by David Niall Wilson
Cover Art by J. Edward Neill
ISBN 978-1-63789-758-4
For information address Crossroad Press at 141 Brayden Dr., Hertford, NC 27944
www.crossroadpress.com

First Edition

THE DEVIL'S IN THE FLAWS
& OTHER DARK TRUTHS

DAVID NIALL WILSON

*This book is dedicated to
the love of my life, Patricia Lee Wilson,
my sons, Zach, Zane, and Will,
my daughters Stephanie and Kat,
and our ever-growing feline army.*

Author's Preface

I have had several collections come out over the last decade, but they were mostly quick, electronic gatherings of stories by theme. Of those, only *The Call of Distant Shores* has a print edition. I've written and published hundreds of stories over the years. My first serious collection, Defining Moments, was nominated for the Bram Stoker Award, and the story "The Gentle Brush of Wings" won the award that year for short fiction. I was okay with losing the collection award to one of my literary idols, Peter Straub. That was a long time ago. Since then, I had a longer collection published by Dark Regions Press, *Ennui & Other States of Madness*. Some of that work holds up pretty well, some of it not so much, but I've never stopped writing and selling short stories, so this new collection is long past due.

My writing, and our world, have changed considerably over the years. I find myself in the midst of a literary reimagining. When you realize you've been writing series novels and publishing other people for too long, and have neglected your career, shifting gears is a little daunting. Thankfully, the writing community, particularly that literary corner where the themes are darkest, and the words cut the deepest, is also experiencing a resurgence. There are brilliant authors filling the shelves with dark, meaningful, and memorable stories. I'm pleased to be a part of it.

When I started writing, the bookstores were overflowing with the works of Stephen King, Peter Straub, Dean Koontz, Jack Ketchum, and Clive Barker. Anthologies were filled with their stories, and magazines, big, small, and in between were everywhere. Then the midlist collapsed, and a lot of the smaller specialty presses went by the wayside. The anthologies sort of dried up unless you could get a big, commercial name tied to them.

That was also a weird time for me personally. A lot can happen in a few decades. Now I see an entirely new group of top-shelf horror and crime authors rising. There are fresh voices everywhere, new themes, new publishers, and I'm here for all of it.

The Devil's in the Flaws & Other Dark Truths is a mixture of brand-new fiction, fiction that has been published, but that I want to draw attention to, and newer works that did not make it into any previous collection. The title piece, the novella at the end of the book, has never been published, and is one of the things I managed to write during the final months of the lockdowns due to the pandemic when my brain and my fingers started reconnecting.

During all that time when we were stuck at home and could have written a small library, it was difficult. Sometimes it was impossible. I completed a few things, failed to complete others, and mostly wished the world would right itself. It hasn't done that completely, but I feel it rolling toward center. I hope you'll enjoy this book.

Let me tell you some stories...

FOREWORD

By Richard Chizmar

If you hang around long enough in this business—nearly 35 years in my case—you get asked to write a lot of these things: Introductions. Forewords. Afterwords. And despite outward appearances, it's not an easy gig. You want to say something insightful and meaningful, conveying a message of substance and depth, all within a handful of pages so that readers can whet their appetite before moving on to the main attraction. After all, that's what they came for.

Ultimately, you end up turning down the majority of these offers due to looming deadlines, bouts of laziness, or a general lack of enthusiasm. Other times, you reluctantly agree out of a sense of duty or obligation. But then there are those rare instances—usually owing to the innate connection you feel with an author and their work—when you find yourself actually excited to sit down and put pen to paper.

This, dear readers, is one of those instances.

David Niall Wilson's short story collection, *The Devil's in the Flaws & Other Dark Truths* is long overdue and well worth the wait. In fact, I devoured it in a single sitting. I can't remember the last time that happened. Three hundred pages, twenty-one short stories, nearly half of them original to this book, and they went down like a shot of top shelf whiskey, scorching my soul and leaving me dizzy. *The Devil's in the Flaws* is a treasure chest of fine storytelling, and I envy you the opportunity to experience it.

Here's the thing about David Niall Wilson: he can do it all. His prose is clear and concise and propulsive. He knows how to hook the reader, make them care, and guide them to the edge of their seat where they are turning the pages as fast as they can. He's a natural born storyteller in that regard.

But he's also something else: a stylish son-of-a-gun; a dark poet. His writing is lush and rich and full of rhythmic layers. Trust me, no one will ever mistake Wilson for a pulp writer (whose work I also happen to enjoy); instead, he comes across as a wizened jazzman, dressed all in black, lurking in the smoky corner of a seedy New Orleans club. If you're lucky, he'll wave you over and play you a secret tune. If you're lucky, he'll hypnotize you with his wordplay. The point I'm trying to make here is that while many pure storytellers—including yours truly—shine the brightest when it comes to moving the reader from Point A to Point B with a minimum of stylistic flourishes, Wilson's talent is such that he is able to accomplish this task with a more lofty literary focus. I only despise him a little bit because of this talent.

I've known David Niall Wilson for going on thirty-five years now. We came up in the same genre trenches together. Back in the day, he published a small press horror magazine called *The Tome*. It rocked, and I still have several issues in my collection. The first Dave Wilson short story I ever published was called "The Mole." It appeared in the pages of *Cemetery Dance* magazine in 1990 and was later reprinted in *The Best of Cemetery Dance*. After that, Dave became a regular in the magazine, as well as in my *Shivers* anthology series. In fact, I currently have an accepted story on file from Dave for a future volume of *Shivers* that very well may be his best effort yet—and that's saying something, folks. It's called "Hickory Nuts and Bones."

It's getting late now, so I'm going to slip away into the shadows and let you enjoy the main attraction. You're in for a treat, readers. For more than three decades, David Niall Wilson has been one of my favorite writers of dark and speculative fiction. You're about to find out why.

—Richard Chizmar

CONTENTS

Unique*
1

The Milk of Paradise
3

A Prayer for "0443"
27

She Mourned*
36

Anomaly
38

One*
54

"You are just like Gods"
55

Interred*
65

Etched Deep
75

His Cold Gourd Heart*
81

Fear of Flying*
91

Little Ghosts*
100

One Off from Prime
116

If You Were Glass
132

Angels
152

Slider
168

Teachable Moments*
180

The Whirling Man
184

The Last Patriot*
196

Wayne's World
207

The Devil's in the Flaws*
217

Original to this collection

Unique

His shaved head and bright blue eyes stood out in the crowd. She saw him coming, repressed the urge to angle her steps away, or to bolt, and watched. His arm was bandaged, wrapped tight in gauze and once-white tape. A dark patch in the center had grown brown and she knew if he pulled that bandage loose, skin and dried blood would accompany it.

She drew her gaze up but did not meet his. Instead, she concentrated on something dangling from a chain about his neck. It was oddly shaped, like a leaf, and had little weight. As he walked, it lifted into the air and seemed to flutter back to his chest, only to lift again.

He was close. She knew she'd have to bolt or meet that gaze. He stopped directly in front of her and, bolder than she felt, she leaned in close to inspect his pendant.

It was thin, like parchment, or leather. On the surface in dark ink was a dragon. Through the center of this a sword. Above the dragon, in a semi-circle, there were words.

"Death before dishonor."

She glanced up into his snake eyes and was caught. She stood, unable to run, trying to make her lips form an explanation, or a question, but barely able to breathe.

"I got a tattoo once," he said. "It was a statement of my individuality."

She breathed a little deeper. His voice wasn't threatening, or loud. He almost whispered.

"Can I see it?"

He continued as if she hadn't spoken. His gaze pierced her and squirmed around inside her head as she heard, and tried not to hear, his words.

"Everyone thought the tattoo was cool. Then another guy got one, and another. I walked in an ocean of tattoos, and I was lost."

She repeated her question, still a whisper.

"Can I see it?"

"You already have. I'm told some men wear their heart on their shoulder. I wear my individuality on a chain."

Her hand came to her lips unbidden. If her legs hadn't been made of rubber and cemented to the Earth, she would have backed away, and away, and turned and run, but she didn't. Instead, she reached out and brushed her fingertip over the dragon. For the first time, she smelled the bandage, ripe and pungent. She gripped the dragon gently and met his gaze.

"You are the only one?"

He nodded.

"It only hurts," he said, "when I dream."

The Milk of Paradise

The flick of a thumb, bright sparks and the faded Zippo lighter with the Grateful Dead emblem emblazoned across its front came to life. The scent of lighter fluid mingled with Sandalwood and hemp. Shadows slid along the floor, wavering and dancing as long slender fingers raised the lighter, bringing the flame to rest beneath a dangling metal ball. The ball was perforated, an old tea ball—an infuser, Art had called it—dangling from a silver chain, suspended about a foot beneath an arching wrought iron frame. Beneath it, glittering and green, sat a glass, half-full of a liquid too odd in coloration to be taken seriously. Art had a name for the liquid, as well. He called it *Flubber*.

Leaning in close, long dark hair dangling over her wrist, Belle watched the ball intently, holding the flame to its base. The heat from the lighter set the chain in motion, buffeting it ever-so-slightly as the point where flame met metal grew hotter. Or maybe it was her breath. It didn't matter—not if the pendulous motion didn't carry the ball beyond the boundaries of the glass beneath it.

The sickly-sweet stench of burnt sugar wafted across the room like the aftermath of a bad caramel, but Belle paid it no notice. She watched the ball spin in lazy arcs over the glass, and, at last, the sizzle of thick brown liquid as the sugar inside melted and slipped through the infuser. Dripping.

Art watched, though not as closely as Belle. He sat back in an overstuffed faux leather armchair with one hand curled around a bottle of beer, and the other held up and to the side. He held a slender pipe between thumb and forefinger, angled carefully away from his face, as if anything could have prevented smoke from burning his eyes in a room so full of fumes. Incense.

Tobacco. The hash that was charring to ash in his small bowl. The sugar in the infuser, dripping, each drop splashing into the green liquid beneath with an odd sizzle as heat met room-temperature liquid.

Art had played a game much like this with his high school buddies. A baggie, a glass of water, and flame. The dripping, molten plastic made a distinctive sound when it hit the cold liquid. ZILCH! He heard that sound now, drifting through memory as he brought the pipe to his lips again.

In the glass beneath the infuser, the green shifted with each zilching drop, growing more amber—less *flubber*. Art grinned at the thought. He imagined the glass rising and floating about the room as Belle, irritated, grabbed for it with long fingernails, trying to keep it from spilling.

"It'll never get off the ground," he said to no one in particular. Belle either didn't or wouldn't hear him, and no one else was in the room. The image of Robin Williams, tiny fists pounding against the inside of the glass as the molten sugar dropped around his head like lava and the glass drifting toward the ceiling momentarily captured his attention, and he snorted, barely containing the laugh. Barely containing the last hit off the pipe. No smoke wasted.

Belle had been at it for hours. Hell, she'd been at it for fucking *days*—maybe her whole life. Chasing the green. To Art she looked like some sort of demented alchemist trying to will her lead into gold.

"It's just a fucking drink," he said at last, irritated by her inattention to anything but the glass. He watched a few moments longer, the silence echoing more loudly as the sound of his own voice faded, ignored. He stood, downed the rest of his lukewarm beer in a single swallow and slammed the bottle on the table.

Belle turned to him for just a second, tilting her head at an inquisitive angle, her eyes deep in some other place. Fevered.

"It's just a fucking drink," Art repeated. He turned away and slipped out through a set of green plastic beaded curtains that separated the room they were in from the dingy kitchen.

Belle turned back to the glass. On the floor to her left a spiral notebook lay open near the center. A pen lay atop the pages where lines were carefully filled with letters and numbers. Many of these were rubbed out, erased, or, in a single instance, scribbled over with such force that the page had torn. There were stains on the page as well. In the dim light, they might have been from tears, or the dripping of sweat—the condensation from a bottle of beer—or the deep green, shifting-toward-amber liquid in the glass.

1885—France—Incomplete

.025 kilograms of dried wormwood
.05 kilograms of anise
.05 kilograms of fennel
.95 liters of 85 percent ethanol
.45 liters of water
.001 kilogram of Roman wormwood
.001 kilogram of hyssop
5 grams of lemon balm

(All original numbers divided by 100)

Let the mixture steep for at least 12 hours in the pot of a double boiler. Add water and apply heat; collect distillate. To approximately half the distillate, add Roman wormwood, hyssop, and lemon balm, all of which have been dried and finely divided. Extract at a moderate temperature, then siphon off the liquor, filter, and reunite with the remaining distillate. Dilute with water to produce approximately 1 liter of absinthe with a final alcohol concentration of 74 percent by volume. AND—SOMETHING—FUCKING—ELSE ...

The lettering grew deep and frustrated at this point, slashing across the lined paper at angry angles. Words were scrawled, then marked out and replaced with other words, also marked out. In the center of the page, about three lines beneath the recipe itself and underlined so deeply the page was scored, the word Peppermint remained. Alone, of a small battlefield of herbs and obscure terms, Peppermint survived.

Belle leaned closer over the glass. She'd removed the flame from the tea infuser and was watching the liquid intently. Where globs of molten sugar had struck, whirling tendrils of yellowish hue spun down into the thick liquid. Belle's hair dangled dangerously close, interwoven with several feathers and a small chain of beads. Her eyes glittered—green eyes so dark they hinted of black. Her tongue slid back and forth across her teeth, touching the cheeks on either side, then swirling.

Belle waited until the peppermint in her mouth had faded to such a thin wafer it threatened to melt over her lips and disappear, then she bent quickly and slipped her tongue into the Absinthe, letting the ghost of the mint slide into the green depths. Her eyes closed, just for an instant, as she contacted that slick, wet surface, then she drew back. Peppermint. Ghosts and hints in books she'd spent long hours poring over hinted that this was the secret. She'd been told it soothed the stomach. She'd been told that slid round and round a lover's cock with the tongue, it could bring hallucinations. She'd been told it belonged in the Absinthe—told by voices long dead, preserved on parchments and the leaves of tattered books. Recipes penciled into the margins of notebooks and tucked into unlikely hiding in diaries and family Bibles.

Absinthe was the key, but it had to be *the* Absinthe. *His* Absinthe. Was it right? Were the caves of ice raised from stalagmites of peppermint? Did they tingle with too-clean, too-bright taste, or would that fail as it blended with the wormwood's bitter kiss? What did *he* see?

The mint drifted slowly, so thin it resembled a coin-shaped shard of ice. Belle watched, waited, as it fluttered down to the bottom of the glass. Fluttered and melted, flew and flown and—gone. The Absinthe had swallowed it completely.

Art shuffled back into the room, but she paid no attention to him. She was staring into the green depths of the glass, mesmerized. He watched her, sipping on a fresh beer and frowning. Her hair dangled over and around the glass, and with the dim candlelight flickering, he could catch green glimmers. The wink of some huge, forgotten emerald. The eye of a great cat. Spider webs of dark hair shimmered around it, slender pale arms braced against the floor.

"Found the flubber, then, did you?" he asked softly, tipping the bottle up again. He tasted the beer, but he remembered the bite of the Absinthe. He remembered her concentration, and how it shifted. He remembered long fingers and curved nails wrapped around a different glass, a slightly different green. He remembered the taste, and the burn. He remembered.

Art turned away and lurched through the room, down the hall that branched left and right. He turned left, not bothering with the lights. Two doors ignored, the third entered and he stopped, tilting the bottle up and closing his eyes. It was there. He knew it was there, didn't need to see to know. Moonlight streamed in the window and glowed on the surface of a canvas, reclining on an easel and watching him in return.

To one side, on a dresser that had been recruited as a workbench, his palette sat, paint dried on the surface in careless blobs, brush dry-tight in the deep blue. The palette itself was a work of art, a reflection of pain. Art stepped closer and tipped the bottle back, gazing at the canvas. He turned, grabbed a candle from the dresser and lit it with a match pulled from ratty jeans.

The light flared. Heineken bottle candelabra gleam lit the surface of the canvas with a dim, yellow glow. Art drank, and stared, and drank again. He reached out with one hand, tracing the brilliantly hued parapet of a domed cathedral, drawing down to rings of fruit trees, littered with bright-colored fruit, rooted in beds of flowers. Ice coated the surface of the cathedral-like doors. Behind, rising, the mountains disappeared into clouds that shimmered with colors, a cotton-candy treat for the gods.

The temple was an entrance, doors swung wide to reveal a jeweled cavern within, lights placed strategically, every brilliant beam reflected and refracted, reflected again, dancing from surface to surface. Ice. It was a cave of ice. Art drained his beer and wished it was something stronger, something with ice he could swirl around in his mouth as he had when he painted. Cold, biting, distant. Footsteps drifted in, quiet and rhythmic, but Art didn't acknowledge them.

The scent of jasmine teased his nostrils. Art felt a small

shiver run up his spine, but still, he didn't turn. It was Sammy. She made little sound. Even when she was in the room, you had to concentrate to realize she wasn't part of one of the tapestries on the wall, or an oversized doll. Sammy was an afterthought to the world, so paper-thin, frail and pale she shimmered and sometimes, if you didn't look closely enough, she wasn't there at all.

"It's like she's made of ice," Belle had said one day, watching Sammy flit about the room. "The ice you see, just after it freezes, so thin on top of the water you know that if a wave rose up from inside, it would shatter."

Art set the empty beer bottle beside the dried palette on the dresser and placed the candle in the top, dripping hot wax around the rim to hold it in place.

"Pretty," Sammy whispered, standing very close to his side and staring at the painting, as he knew she'd stared a thousand times before, when he was there, when he was out. When he was sleeping. Sammy was fascinated with the painting, and when she wasn't playing her music, she was staring at the painting.

At first, Art had been jealous. He liked Sammy, and he loved the painting. Both meant a lot to him, but neither would share. Sammy didn't ignore Art, but she didn't adore him. She adored the painting, worshiped it, and that was supposed to have been Belle. The painting was not for Sammy. The house, its walls dripping thick with images and angst, dreams and nightmares leaking into them, all of it was an extension of Belle. The painting was a failure. Art had failed, and for his pain, a woman he quietly and privately loved had fallen in love, instead, with his failure.

Art turned, pinched the wick of the candle between his thumb and forefinger, relishing the heat as he held tight. The burn. It took his thoughts away, for an instant. He turned and headed to the door. Sammy didn't move. She stared at the painting as if the light had never shifted. As if seeing the same image she'd seen by flickering candlelight. As if she had never seen what Art had seen at all, or what he'd painted, but something more.

Head pounding, Art paced back toward the kitchen for

another drink. Stronger, and more final. Something tall and amber and clinking with ice that would burn his throat as the candle had burned his fingers, numbing the pain.

The night had deepened. There was no light save that of the candles circling the room. On the floor in the center of the patterned carpet, Sammy sat quietly. On her lap, a wooden dulcimer rested. Art sat slumped deep into the depths of his old armchair, cloaked in shadow. Invisible. Occasionally the soft clink of ice on glass could be heard, accompanied by a quick flash of reflected gold tossed between whiskey and candle through a lens of smudged glass.

Belle knelt on the rug before Sammy. In Belle's hand was a crystal goblet, glittering with ghosts of light from the candles. The goblet brimmed with dark liquid. The light was yellow. Shadows loomed. Art knew what was in the goblet, despite the lack of color. He knew the deep, emerald glitter, and the scent, crusted sugar and licorice, the hint of something more. Different, each time, and yet the demon's breath called with the same voice. Words rose unbidden to Art's lips, and he whispered them, then downed another wet-hot gulp of whiskey.

"As e'er beneath a waning moon was haunted
By woman wailing for her demon-lover!
And from this chasm, with ceaseless turmoil seething,
As if this earth in fast thick pants were breathing."

Then he fell silent, afraid of her anger. Belle swung her gaze around, catching Art's eyes as he spoke. She smiled, nodded slightly, then returned her attention to the goblet and the girl before her. Sammy gazed straight through Belle's eyes. She didn't see the glass, or the long, slender fingers that proffered it to her. She saw what she saw, and Art wondered, if his painting had been in the room, if she would have stared into its depths in that moment. He shivered.

"Drink," Belle whispered. Beseeching. Commanding. Neither of them had ever seen Sammy drink anything alcoholic. She seldom ate, and when she did, it was the picking of a bird, the brush of butterfly proboscis over nectar-soaked petals. No substance. Now, as they watched, Belle entranced, and Art aching, half-with the need for this moment to end badly, leaving him the one elevated moment, the knowing he had accomplished where another had failed, even if his offering had fallen short—and half with the need to know. She would drink, or she would turn away.

Art did not share Belle's dream, her deep encroaching need. But he wanted to know. He held his breath.

Sammy took the goblet, staring into its depths as though seeing it for the first time. Her concentration was absolute. She held it reverently, and Art knew the scent that reached her nostrils. He knew the taste that would burn against her tongue, the numbing, intoxicating sensations to follow.

Art had bought plenty of Absinthe since Belle had offered her goblet to him, but his purchases, steadily more covert and in-depth in their inception, had proven themselves to be nothing more than a series of well-crafted lies. They had gotten him drunk. They had similar taste, and, in a few cases, similar effects, but they were miserable recreations. They were the work of a thousand clones, repainting over and over the work of the masters, vending their wares on dingy street corners and dreaming of castles of ice. Belle was a master. Belle might be the last master of a dead art. Art had not painted since the night she had him drink.

Sammy drank. One last second's glance into the depths of the clear crystal, brimming with the green, and she shifted. Everything shifted. The glass tilted, Belle leaned back onto her heels, eyes glittering brightly, fixated on Sammy's face. Her form. Her eyes, now closed, head drawn back and long hair dangling behind as she drained the glass. No sipping. No tasting. No hesitation.

Art expected her to spew.

Sammy only smiled. On her lap, the dulcimer sat silent. Potential sound embodied in curving wood and twisted strings. Gut strings. Strings that had once been the inner workings of a cat or a horse. Strings that had been part of the fabric of some living, breathing being, woven now to the wood, and to her fingers. Sammy didn't speak. She didn't even seem to breathe, though Art stared at her breasts. She fascinated him.

Then she moved. Pale hands tipped by wraith-fingers slid to the strings, pressed against the frets, exploring. No sound at first, only a flicker of fingertips that caused her nails to reflect the candlelight.

Somewhere in the past moment Belle had reclaimed the goblet without insinuating herself into Sammy's motion. Like a snake. A dark snake, swaying in front of the one she would hypnotize, the one who hypnotized her. Art lifted his drink, but it did not reach his lips. Eyes still closed, lips parted slightly, Sammy began to play.

There was a shift in the room. Subtle, hard to pin down, and so complete that every detail was skewed. Art held very still. His fingers trembled, wrapped around the icy glass, slick with condensation, but he didn't risk draining it. He might make some vulgar, slurping sound that would break the spell. It would be his fault. His mind snapped into focus on his painting. It had been his fault that time, not again.

Belle paid no attention to Art and his frozen mime-with-a-whiskey-glass pose. Sammy paid no attention to Belle. The music soared. Pale fingers flew, dancing down chords and melodies with quicksilver speed and liquid grace. The notes didn't fade. Not for Art. They hung before him, pixelating the air. He somehow found the coordination to set his glass on the table beside his chair. He did not see the table. He felt no chair.

The image of his painting grew before him, each color blending to the next, woven from a tapestry of threads that never existed in the center of the room. Incense smoke and candlelight? Too much alcohol and flashback images? Sammy played, and the questions faded to meaningless white noise in the back of his mind.

The painting grew, hers now, his as well, but altered. More vivid. The notes danced along the iced parapets and flowed around the base of each tree, gushed from the geysers, and taunted him with all that had remained just beyond his clouded vision. He heard the birds. He heard the rush of water and the echoes from within the caverns beyond the massive doors. He heard the echo of drums, marching feet, a horde. A heartbeat.

The image shivered, and Art held his breath. The music reasserted itself, and the room flickered into focus. He wanted to shake his head, but he held the urge in check. The notes weren't stopping, merely shifting, and the smoky air coalesced once more. A face twisted and writhed, fighting its way through the gloom, drawing strength from the sound. The eyes flashed with emotion. Anger? Lust? Rage? Desire? Art gripped the arms of his chair and leaned back. The features snapped into focus for one long, lingering moment. The eyes focused, not on Art, but on Belle, who lay back now, knees spread wide and back arched, long hair flowing over her shoulders to the floor scant inches beneath. Her gaze was locked on that face, her lips parted, and her breath came in heaving gulps.

Art stared, the image forgotten, the music lost as the motion of her body called out to him. His body reacted with stunning force, and he gripped the chair arms more tightly still, hips arching, jerking. Her flesh was coated in a hot sheen of sweat. Her eyes were wide, and her taut nipples strained against the loose fabric of her blouse.

A string broke.

The silence that followed this jarring sound was deep, molasses thick and cloying. The scent of the incense flowed in. The dim light of the candles drew back, dragging shadows across the floor and into the corners. The image snapped from existence so suddenly that breath stilled. Nothing moved. The room was a still life, each of them frozen in disbelief. In loss. In pain.

Belle broke first. Her carefully arched body, still stretching to the air above Sammy, curved like a tightly strung bow. Her eyes rolled back, and Art saw her hands slip to her hair. Her shoulders slumped to the floor as she tore wildly at the long, silky locks. Her lips parted, but no sound emerged. Not at first. She drew breaths too deep, too full for any lungs and her jaw worked so fiercely that he feared she'd bite through her tongue.

He started to rise, to go to her and pull her close and bring her back, to be the anchor that bound her to reality, despite the fuzziness in his own head. He nearly made it to his feet before she screamed.

The sound pierced Art to the core of his soul. He slapped his hands ineffectually over his ears, but it had no effect on Belle's tortured wails. The sound vibrated through his skin, seeped into his pores and resonated deep within his senses. His nails dug into the flesh of his cheeks, and he pressed his hands so tightly to his ears that the pressure threatened to burst his skull. He heard her as if he were kneeling beside her, ear pressed to her soft red lips. There was no escape.

Art dropped to his knees, and the screams slowly died to silence. The dulcimer was silent as well. Art eased the pressure of his palms on the sides of his head, and very gently opened his eyes. Belle hadn't moved. She lay back, arched against the floor, eyes closed and hands tightly gripping long handfuls of her hair.

Art leaned closer, slid his arms beneath her, one hand in the small of her back, the other behind her head. He held her there, afraid to lift her.

So quietly that it was difficult to be certain she'd spoken at all, Sammy's voice broke the silence. Art glanced at her, shocked again and unable to react in any way other than to listen.

"A savage place! as holy and enchanted
As e'er beneath a waning moon was haunted
By woman wailing for her demon-lover!
And from this chasm, with ceaseless turmoil seething,
As if this earth in fast thick pants were breathing,
A mighty fountain momently was forced:
Amid whose swift half-intermitted burst
Huge fragments vaulted like rebounding hail,
Or chaffy grain beneath the thresher's flail."

Belle's eyes flickered. Opened. Art turned to her, watching her face. She barely breathed. Her entire frame shook, trembling with the strain of holding the position she'd contorted herself into as she screamed, but she was unwilling to shift. Art held her very still, and very carefully, not daring to speak and break the silence. The air was a miasma of silence. Sammy had returned to her mute scrutiny of things unseen. Her fingers lay limp on the strings of the dulcimer.

The glass, only a short time before brimming with liquid emeralds and alive with promise, lay canted to one side on the floor, a very thin trickle of absinthe feeling its way tentatively over the rim and seeping into the carpet.

With excruciating care, Belle released her grip, letting her hair slide back and down over the carpet. Over Art's hand. She closed her eyes, relaxed, breathed, and very softly, she spoke.

"Help me," she whispered.

Art needed to hear no more. He slid his arms under her shivering frame more fully, braced himself, and lifted. She came easily into his arms, slumping against him, and the nearness of her nearly buckled his knees. His mind shot back to the way she'd arched, the way she'd looked as those eyes that could not have been there, floating above Sammy in the half-light, had devoured her form. Art banished the images and staggered from the room.

Laying Belle gently on her bed, Art sat in a chair beside her. She looked up only once, catching his gaze, holding it, then looking away and curling into a fetal position. Art reached down, drew her blanket up over her thin shoulders, smoothed her hair gently, and stood. As he left the room, he glanced back at her. She was asleep.

With his mind awash in impossibilities, Art walked down the hall to his own room and did the same.

Belle was up, scribbling furiously in her notebook when Art staggered out of his room. Her hair was wild, and he noticed with appreciation that all she wore was one of his own shirts, buttoned about halfway. She was seated cross-legged on the floor.

Belle glanced up. Without a word, she turned back to her work.

Beside her on the floor she had arranged a number of things: a bottle with the latest recipe minus the peppermint and still intact, some vials, a sheaf of yellowed paper, and other implements so familiar Art paid them little mind.

Apparently satisfied with whatever she'd been figuring, Belle dropped the notebook suddenly and grabbed a small mortar and pestle she had set aside. With deft, sure fingers she plucked two peppermints from a bag and dropped them into the wooden bowl. With quick, decisive strokes she crushed them to powder, working well beyond the point where Art would have considered them to be dust. Belle carefully inserted a small funnel into the mouth of the bottle and poured the peppermint through. Art watched, fascinated, as the fine powder whirled in the green depths of the bottle like a small tornado, then faded.

"That was it, then?" he asked softly. "The missing link? The big mojo? Some peppermint?"

Belle glanced up at him, more sharply, and gave her head a shake.

"Not all," she said. "Almost. Very close."

"It wasn't the broken string?" Art asked. "I thought..."

Belle shook her head. She didn't look up, but she replied. "The string broke because it wasn't right. If it had been right, she would not have broken the string."

Art frowned. Strings broke all the time. How could the mixture of a drink have any effect? He might have bought it if Sammy had been trashed, but she had one drink, and only one drink, and she had been playing beautifully. It had been real. Too real, in fact.

"Who was he?" Art asked, shifting subjects.

Belle did not look up. She did not answer. Her cheeks colored, and Art's brow furrowed.

"He wasn't real," Art said at last. "He was a hallucination, Belle. A dream."

She ignored him, but the muscles in her neck tightened, and she leaned more closely over her work.

"He wasn't real." Art mouthed the words but did not breathe them to life. He turned away.

Three deep green sprigs of parsley sat on a napkin at Belle's side. She pored over her notes. There was enough in the bottle for one, maybe two more attempts, and she'd have to start again.

The process was slow and tedious, bringing the mixture back to the point she'd already reached would take weeks. She had narrowed the possible missing ingredients dramatically, but there were still unknowns. Secrets were never easy to steal.

Her mind drifted. She still felt the sharp, tingling intensity of that gaze, probing her, commanding her. She felt the heat rise and drew in a quick breath, gritting her teeth and clamping her eyes closed hard enough to send dancing spots across the inner screen of her eyelids. She curled her leg back and pressed her heel tightly between her thighs, rocking against it for a moment and shaking. The moment faded, and she breathed more slowly, not trusting herself to move for a long moment. Everything she did had a price attached to it, and to spill the bottle, or ruin the mixture, would be more than she could bear. She was so close.

Sammy's voice lingered in the background of Belle's thoughts. She'd heard that voice so seldom, and never the poetry. It was a soft voice, rich in timbre, but subtle. The room had resonated with each verse, but Belle knew that the silence that had been the backdrop was largely responsible for the illusion of volume.

Belle's thoughts were clouded with the memory of heat. Her body had reacted, held and stroked by each note from the dulcimer, bent and nearly broken by the words. She had felt his breath, had shivered with the beat of something so alien, so powerful and erotic that if she had died in that instant, the only thing she would have regretted was the incompletion. She'd been aware of Art, as well, had known his need and felt it funneled through her into the moment. The hint of licorice burned on her tongue, coated in peppermint, and soaked in deeper flavors. So different from where she'd started, the green bottle with the white label, bought at an off-the-street liquor store for too much money and releasing only the slightest hint of the magic within.

That same day, the day she'd found the forbidden drink, she'd found the bookstore. Shelf after shelf of words, coated in dust and forgotten. She'd tasted the absinthe moments after purchasing it, slipping into an alley and taking a too-long draught from the neck of the bottle. With her secret treasure tucked deep in the depths of her purse, she'd run her fingertips along the spines of novels and histories, biographies and collections, leather and cloth, some covered in brightly colored dust jackets, and others with gilt lettering stamped deep.

Then she was discovered as a squat, balding man with one eye much larger than the other suddenly appeared around the end of one bookcase. Belle, too startled to speak, backed away, her fingers gripping the first book that she touched and drawing it free, holding it out in penance for stolen moments of deeply clouded thought. Money changed hands, money she could not afford, and the book was hers, as much a stranger as the man who sold it and she was off with her bottle and her dreams.

Sometime that night, she'd begun to read.

The parsley was more difficult than the peppermint. The recipe was meant for a much larger batch than the single bottle Belle had concocted, and it took her more than an hour of teeth-gritting and mumbled curses to complete the calculations. Even when she had the figure in her mind and on the paper across her knees, she agonized, going over each number one at a time as if afraid they'd shift and rearrange if she didn't pay close enough attention.

At last, she clipped the top of a single sprig of parsley and dropped it into her mortar. She knew the faint dust of the peppermint remained, but it didn't matter. She ground at the leaves with the pestle, pressing tightly and feeling the faint release of juice, the smearing. She made a mental note to be very careful in removing it. Pouring some of the absinthe into the mortar, stirring, and then pouring it all back through a funnel was the best way to be certain. Her measurements were very exact, and if she left anything out, she would not be able to calculate the difference later. She would have to start over. Her shoulders sagged, just for an instant, at the thought. So close.

She worked the parsley slowly to a paste, tipping the bottle now and then to drip a trickle of green liquid over the top, then working patiently to blend the paste to a thick syrup. Finally, wrists aching from the effort, she set the pestle aside on the napkin and reached for her funnel. She inserted it in the neck of the bottle and with practiced grace, she poured the contents of the mortar through. There was no discernible change. Green to green, soft rush of bubbles and the bottle stood, still steeped in mystery. Drenched in dreams.

She corked it carefully and stood, holding the bottle in both hands, and carried it to the altar. It was actually a bar, or had been, but Art had renamed it the altar when Belle began insisting that nothing but her bottle be kept there. The bottle, and the book. Pressed beneath a sheet of glass in an old picture frame, it remained open to the same page that it had been open to for nearly three years.

Belle whispered softly to herself as she placed the bottle reverently on the bar.

"In Xanadu did Kubla Khan a stately pleasure dome decree,
Where Alph the sacred river, ran,
Through caverns measureless to man …
Down to a sunless sea…."

She shivered and the bottle nearly tipped as a moment of vertigo shivered through her. She righted it quickly and stepped back. The book and its frame seemed to watch her as she retreated, as she stumbled among the ingredients and tools and notes, as she tripped, finally, dropping to her knees. She cried out at the sharp contact with the floor but bit the sound off quickly. She wanted no one else in the room. Not yet. Maybe not ever.

This time, she knew, it would have to be her. Art could not paint this moment. Sammy could not draw it from the strings of her dulcimer or whisper it from her half-silent lips. The bottle glittered, and Belle looked away. She fought the urge to drink now, to soar and burn with the deep green liquor sliding through her system. It wasn't time. If she drank now, he might not come. He might never come. He might come and leave her. It had to be the afternoon. She had to be alone.

She stacked her papers as neatly as her trembling hands would allow and gathered her tools. She needed to clean up, and to ready herself. The others would have to be told, warned away and far from the bottle, and the room, when the time came. Belle had work to do.

Without a backward glance, she slipped from the room and into the kitchen. Behind her, the bottle continued to glitter, as if that flickering, captured light dancing along the green glass could watch, or think. Or dream.

Art didn't want to leave, but he knew from the expression on Belle's face that it was not a request. It was her house, after all. It was her gig, her dream or dementia or whatever you wanted to call it. As much as Art liked to see himself as the other half of a couple involving Belle, he knew it was never going to happen.

Sammy only nodded, packed up her dulcimer and donned a long, shapeless jacket before slipping out the back door and into the alley beyond. Neither Art nor Belle knew where Sammy went when she wasn't with them. Just that moment, Art would have liked to know. He would have liked to have been invited to follow, to belong somewhere during the period when he didn't belong in his own home.

It was silliness, he knew, this jealousy he felt toward the bottle. Pointless and foolish. Any other night of the week he would have been up and out and gone without a word, but the thought that he was forbidden changed it all. He hated it, chomped against the invisible bit it implied, and, in the end, he grabbed his coat and stomped out into the streets without a word. As he moved steadily down the street and away, he felt the vague flicker of something familiar and distant, and he stopped frowning. He glanced at his hands, then back over his shoulder.

Very suddenly, he felt like painting. The urge came over him from nowhere, slipped into his thoughts and displaced his anger. He stood, undecided, the scents of oils and canvas wafting enticingly from his memory.

"Damn," he breathed softly. He knew he couldn't go back. Not yet. Not now. Belle wouldn't even open the door, and if he grew more insistent, she might go to his studio and his rooms and throw his things out the windows. Images flickered through his mind. Belle prostrate, lying back across the floor. Sammy, fingers poised near the broken string, speaking softly, her words palpable in the incense-thick air. The green bottle, pulsing, growing, and winding in a coil that reached to circle Belle's prone form. He wanted to capture it, but was forced to memorize, eyes closed, gripping tightly each sinuous roll of what he had seen and refusing to let it fade.

He would paint. Not now. Not tonight probably, but he would paint, and when he did, he would bring that image to life. If he couldn't give Belle her magic, he could record their combined failures. He could make it so real that the music and the lust burned the edges of the canvas.

He couldn't shake the image of the coils.

"Weave a circle round him thrice,
And close your eyes with holy dread."

Art whispered the words, and again he shivered. He pulled his jacket more tightly about himself and headed off for Sid's, a club where the music was dark and dreary, and the lighting was more so. He wasn't in a mood to dance or mingle, but the nightly call of alcohol rang in his ears.

"Fuck it," he muttered to no one in particular. "Just fuck it."

Belle poured the absinthe into a tumbler and set it upon the altar. She knelt before it, trembling, feeling the weight of the empty house heavy on her shoulders. Now that she'd sent the others away, she felt vulnerable, fragile, and inadequate to the task she had set herself.

With a reverence that regularly brought scornful comments from Art, she opened her journal. In the pages of this book, she'd documented her quest, her dreams, each and every mistake and small success. She had also recorded her research, and it was to this she turned for strength. The words that had dragged her into this surreal otherworld. The history of Xanadu.

"The following fragment is here published at the request of a poet of great and deserved celebrity [Lord Byron], and, as far as the Author's own opinions are concerned, rather as a psychological curiosity, than on the grounds of any supposed poetic merits. In the summer of the year 1797, the Author, then in ill health, had retired to a lonely farmhouse

between Porlock and Linton, on the Exmoor confines of Somerset and Devonshire. In consequence of a slight indisposition, an anodyne had been prescribed—here Belle had scribbled a furious note, drawn from other sources—letters and fragments, notes of Lord Byron himself. She had crossed it all out, including the word anodyne, and replaced it with Absinthe—from the effects of which he fell asleep in his chair at the moment that he was reading the following sentence, or words of the same substance, in 'Purchas's Pilgrimage':

'Here the Khan Kubla commanded a palace to be built, and a stately garden thereunto. And thus ten miles of fertile ground were enclosed with a wall.'

The Author continued for about three hours in a profound sleep, at least of the external senses, during which time he has the most vivid confidence, that he could not have composed less than from two to three hundred lines; if that indeed can be called composition in which all the images rose up before him as things with a parallel production of the correspondent expressions, without any sensation or consciousness of effort. On awakening he appeared to himself to have a distinct recollection of the whole, and taking his pen, ink, and paper, instantly and eagerly wrote down the lines that are here preserved. "A person on business from Porlock" interrupted him and he was never able to recapture more than "some eight or ten scattered lines and images."

Belle closed the book. She had read the words so many times she could recite them as litany. She had researched and delved into the letters of Coleridge and Byron, certain she would find the answers she sought. Hundreds of lines, reduced to a snippet of rhyme, and still so powerful that movies had been centered around small quotes from the verse, and novels written in the attempt to finish the work. To close the portal, or open it, as Coleridge had seen it. To present to the world the quality that inspired Byron to insist on the publication of a broken poem, as if it were a key. As if, beyond the inspiration of Coleridge himself, Byron alone could see.

On the altar sat the fruits of years of labor. Belle believed that she knew more of the essence of Absinthe than any living being, and still she quaked at her ignorance. It was a gamble, each time, pouring the essence of each long-dead master's work into her bottles and vials, crashing into the walls of their failures and seeing, just beyond her grasp, the essence, the purity of form that would show her what he had seen, what he would have written. The essence and completion of Xanadu that would make it real.

Art had made it surreal. He had grasped the tenuous threads of all Belle had striven for and woven them into an incomplete tapestry that teased her with its borderline truth. She loved him for his devotion and cursed him for the failure, but she knew that the failure was really hers. Sammy haunted her. There was more to the tiny, frail musician than met the eye, but there was no history, no record of things gone and those to come to measure her against. Sammy was as she was, and she, in the end, had failed as well. This one, also, on Belle.

Now came the test. No conduit. No half-truth or interpretation. Belle, the glass, the deep green magic, and the words. She would find the caves of ice and prostrate herself on their cold, sharp edges until she was accepted, taken, or broken, but one with what had been lost. Dark powerful eyes haunted her, tracking each motion and each thought, seeing through flesh and bone and soul. Waiting.

She took the tumbler gently into her hands. Candlelight flickered about her, and the incense, ever-present, grew cloying and thick, a taste that lingered in the back of her throat, drying her out and reaching to the absinthe for succor and warmth. Belle shivered a final time, so deeply that she shook and nearly spilled the thick green liquid over her hands and the floor. Her knees rattled on the floor, and she gasped.

Throwing her head back, she brought the drink to her lips and upended it. The heat was intense, the burn glorious and excruciating and powerful, all at once, washing down through her in a burst of fire and dripping behind, bringing secondary sizzle to slowly singe her throat. She did not move, fearing it would be too strong, that she might vomit or pass out, that she might fail herself as so many others who had gone before. They hadn't failed because they hadn't been reaching out for anything. Only Belle had failed, and as the hot liquor burned down her throat, she knew it was her courage that had been lacking, not the ingredients, or the mix, not the strength of will of another, presented as her sacrifice. Placing the glass on the altar, she glanced at her book—her notes—in scorn. She had been hiding in the research, hiding between the pages, lacking the courage to see. To know.

She closed her eyes, and the words came unbidden, slowly, then with growing force. She recited in a steady, throaty voice that purred with strength and resolution.

"In Xanadu did Kubla Khan
A stately pleasure-dome decree:
Where Alph, the sacred river, ran
Through caverns measureless to man
Down to a sunless sea.
So twice five miles of fertile ground
With walls and towers were girdled round:
And there were gardens bright with sinuous rills,
Where blossomed many an incense-bearing tree;
And here were forests ancient as the hills,
Enfolding sunny spots of greenery..."

Belle clamped her eyes tightly, her hands out to her sides for balance. The Absinthe leaked into her thoughts and drew her deeper, thickening her tongue as she fought for completion. Images opened in her mind. Art's painting flashed into view, but with details he had never seen. The ice rippled with fire. The ground shook with the marching cadence of a horde of booted feet. The landscape surged with greenery, and huge, spouting geysers splashed into the air and fell to the earth, all in the rhythm of a huge heartbeat, drawing her inward.

Her body arched once more, prone against the floor, the altar before her and her knees spreading wider, inviting. She wore a short, soft linen dress, nothing beneath, but it didn't matter. The sensations that washed through her had nothing to do with clothing, or the room surrounding her, or the world where she lived and breathed and lusted for... what?

"For he on honeydew hath fed..."

The words seeped up from beneath her, hands fashioned of letters that lifted her and offered her…

"And drunk the milk of paradise."

She saw a young man, long flowing dark hair and a broad nose, dark eyebrows furrowed in concentration. In his hand he held a quill, dark with ink. He seemed to see her in that same instant, studying her, every inch and curve, eyes bright. His hand trembled, and a droplet of ink threatened to fall to whatever surface he penned upon.

Beside him a bottle sat, aged and crusted with sugar crystals, the cork removed. A crystal tumbler stood beside it, and Belle felt his fingers as he reached for that drink, felt them stroking her flesh and drawing her up, her hips rising to meet the fall of his lips. His eyes never left hers, and the hand that did not hold the quill slid beneath her, curling into the small of her back.

Belle cried out, trying to close the eyes that had opened when she clamped her own shut, trying to avoid the intensity, the absolute pleasure and terror and impossibility of that touch and that moment, but she could not give voice to the sound, or, if she did, she could not hear it. Nor could he.

He leaned closer, and she knew him, from portraits and descriptions, from the twist of the lips that would one day sneer at his own work, questioning its value and releasing it only at another's whim. Those lips so close his breath, hot-sweet with absinthe, brushed her thighs. Belle's entire being clenched.

The air shattered with a sharp sound. Belle clamped her eyes more tightly still, concentrating, but the moment was shattering around her, falling away. The sound repeated, and she cried out. She arched so violently that her back crackled, spine rearranging to try and compensate. She ground her head into the floor, feeling the tug and tear as the motion pulled against her hair. His face had faded and though the heat remained between her legs, the touch had never come. The ice had faded to molten carpet that burned her as she stroked against it, and again, the sound, and again, blaring and bursting through her thoughts.

Then there was nothing.

Art turned his key in the lock at last, determined, if this was his last night in the house, that he would spend it painting. He could not block the images, and though he'd poured drink after drink down his throat, doubling the shots when the first few rounds failed him, his heart pounded and his head spun, not with drunken stupor, but with the images, drawn from the memory of Sammy's voice and the faces floating in air, the words and the incense, and the failure. He had painted, but now he knew that he had not been true to himself, or the images. He hadn't failed, he'd been a coward. He knew, and he wanted to share that knowing, but the only way to do it was the painting.

He opened the door and burst inside, and he found her, Belle, prostrate on the floor, bent nearly double and writhing against the carpet. The incense was so thick he could barely make out the bar beyond the altar. He saw the bottle sitting there, and a glance at the floor showed the empty tumbler.

Belle was unconscious. He didn't know why, or how, but he knew she was breathing. Art lifted her in his arms and carried her to his room. He placed her on his bed, covered her tortured features with his sheets and blankets and turned away. She was alive. She was safe. He had to paint.

Art never knew when Sammy returned. One moment he was lost in the painting, and the next he realized he was lost in the painting and the sound. She had entered, opened the case, pulled out her dulcimer, and she was playing, matching the notes to his motion, or was he matching his motion to the sound? It didn't matter.

As he neared completion, he was aware of something more. Belle had risen, first to sit on the bed, staring at him in wonder, then to rise and slip closer, molding herself to his body. Other times, other worlds, and he would have worried that she would jostle him, drive him from the images or vice versa, but it was right. Each counterbalance she caused brought the brush closer to perfection, and she held tightly. The eyes glared back at them from the canvas, the ice glistened, and the heat throbbed.

Sammy began to sing along with the tune she was playing, the words distant and familiar, though neither Art nor Belle had ever heard them spoken. The final words of the poem passed, and the milk of paradise ran green in rivers flowing from Art's brush. The eyes of Samuel Taylor Coleridge glistened with longing as he watched them, lost in a corner of the canvas, as they passed. Beyond, seated in a garden, beneath lush fruit trees and near a fountain another sat, also watching. Again, they passed, and as they did, the man's tortured eyes slid over Belle, and he whispered:

"She walks in beauty, like the night."

But they were gone.

The words, so long forgotten, whispered over Sammy's lips, softer and lighter, fading to the sound of traffic passing on the street beyond. The smoke of incense wisped about the room. On the floor, soaked in deep green paint, the brush lay still, leaking its contents into the carpet. The painting was spectacular, image torn from image, blended to other worlds and back.

The room stood empty.

In the next room where she'd left it closed, Belle's book fell open silently. The candles burned low, but the light was bright enough for reading. Leaning low, a long-haired, oddly dressed man gripped the volume, holding it up and apparently marveling at the binding and the lined paper within. The book had fallen open to a page etched with verse, and he read. His eyes filled with an odd pain, then he placed the framed book on Belle's altar.

Before him on that altar, sat the bottle. One final shot remained within. He lifted it, took a whiff of the contents, and smiled. He knew that scent, one thing very familiar in a world suddenly gone mad. Without thought, he tipped the last of the absinthe into the tumbler, closed his eyes, and poured it down his throat.

Lifting the pen, he stared at the paper, mouthing the final words.

"And drunk the milk of paradise."

Slowly, mind awash with images, he began to write.

A Prayer for "0443"

Boz worked as quickly as he could with sweat-slick fingers, teasing the broken ends of wires into place and soldering them with the tip of a homemade iron. The tools were crude, barely adequate to the task. If he made a mistake, shorted a lead to the wrong element, he'd be too late, and "0445 0443" would be lost. Working with his hands inside the tool bag, while pretending to shuffle and inventory the contents, added a level of difficulty that nearly drove him mad. His fingers shook, and he hesitated, breathing deeply. He pushed the last lead into place and applied the heat.

The parts were from a phone, a relic hidden and passed from hand to hand since banned by the Fairness Act. Few components remained and being caught with them would be a serious offense. He might lose his number. Boz knew if that happened, he would have to find a way to terminate, but at the same time he had to take the risk.

There was a soft sound behind him, and he turned. Cherie had entered their shared quarters. She saw him, smiled, and then stopped, standing very still.

"Move," he said softly. "Keep moving. Don't let them notice anything different, or you'll trip the bug."

"What ...?"

"I have to finish this. There are only a few minutes left."

Fear flashed through her expression like dark lightning but recovered quickly. She crossed the room, bent, and kissed him gently on the forehead. Then she turned and headed for the kitchen. He heard her opening and closing cabinets and knew she was making coffee. She wasn't doing it because she wanted coffee, but because she wanted the ritual.

Boz closed his tool bag, concealing his creation in one hand as he tugged the straps tight with the other. Then he turned in his seat and pressed a button on the console in front of him. A tray slid out of a recess in the wall. He laid his fingertip on the scanner and the screen lit. An image filled the monitor, just for a moment, with the familiar HAS logo (he had been taught that this stood for Human Access Screen but had long suspected the acronym had other meanings). A bright, generically cheerful voice welcomed him.

"Welcome, 9628356."

Boz said nothing. At home, he was Boz. With Cherie, and a few close friends. To the world, he was 9628356. To the system. Moving slowly, keeping his actions as casual as possible, he reached for the music controls. At the same time, he slipped his fingernail into a panel on the side of the tray and tugged. It popped open, and he held his breath. No warnings. He had not been discovered.

The music would start soon. He leaned casually to the side, palming the device he'd created, glanced at the panel, and saw what he was after. Two wires protruded slightly, not far enough to catch on the tray as it slid in and out, had been carefully stripped, a bit at a time, so that bright copper shone through their plastic insulation. He had seconds.

Two curls of wire protruded from his device. He hooked them over the bare points in the wires, let the small circuit card swing down, and out of sight, and leaned back. He watched the screen expectantly.

Anyone monitoring his actions might have believed he was merely anticipating the music. No warnings appeared on the screen. No lights flickered. Sound rose slowly from the speakers in the walls. He recognized the first strains of "0443" and his heart nearly stopped.

He wanted to lean down again and check the connection. He wanted to know if it was working, but he knew that if he did, it would be lost forever. They would see. They would send someone to yank him out of his life and his home. They might erase his number and take his words. They might take Cherie, change her number. He had to trust his skill, the things he'd remembered, and those he'd learned.

He knew there were others. He'd found the clues they'd left. He'd collected and passed on the artifacts. Forbidden secrets. Lost science. It passed beneath the radar of system like a network of spirits, a dimension of its own. There had been a term in the past—*darknet*—for a network of secret, private things hidden from the government and other prying eyes. Boz's darknet consisted of small caches of antique tech, stolen bits of wire, components slipped in and out of pockets and left where others could find and access them. Folded bits of paper with schematics and designs. Even snippets of verse, lyrics, prose, and occasional drawings. Signed drawings, not with numbers, but names. All forbidden.

There might be ten others—there might be a thousand. Maybe all of them—every single number in the system—had something hidden away, something special that they were scared to death to share or pass on. For all they knew, the system was fully aware and allowed their small indiscretions to keep them in line—the illusion of individuality.

Somewhere out there was a singer. Her voice called to Boz in ways that the endless streams of music he'd been fed from the console's speakers had not. Her song had begun its cycle one year to the day in the past, and the very next day Boz had started gathering parts.

Musical compositions were allowed only a single year of existence. They were played in a steady, repetitive cycle, no one piece or artist granted a moment longer than another. Books and stories were the same. You could write, if the urge came upon you, but you couldn't save it. Once you typed it into the console, it was part of the system, stamped only with your number. It would be there for a year, but no one could read it twice. If you were caught singing or reciting things that you'd read, your access was cut off until the next cycle, so that you would forget.

The only things that were constant were the histories, and the laws, and every citizen jacked into the system knew them by heart. The rules existed to protect. The histories existed to remind them of all that had gone before. Equality was the only true hope for survival. Total equality. Stories came and went.

Songs sifted through the collective consciousness, and then faded, replaced by new voices and new tunes. Nothing but numbers differentiated them one from another.

Boz knew the mantra. No one would be worshipped. No one would be held above any other, except, as it had always been—someone was. Rules only exist when they can be enforced. Men and women were kept equal by people who believed in their own right to make that decision. Boz and his peers knew them only as The Noble—a title that, in itself, denied the truth of the equality it purported to serve. The rules were so simple and calming on their surface.

Music is for entertainment.

Writing is for sharing and moving on.

Names and labels only encourage pride and inhibit equality.

We are one. Except, there were those overseeing that unity, and so, it was false.

The song started. The urge to close his eyes, lean back, and enjoy it was almost overwhelming, but he was afraid to react. He'd heard the song three hundred and sixty-four times, and this was to be the last. To react to that—to show emotion at the passing of one work while ignoring the others—would send up a flag.

He heard Cherie moving around in the next room. There were times they could talk, places where it was allowed—between couples—to share in private. He wanted to go to her and explain himself. He wanted, more than anything else in the universe, for her to understand, for *any* other to understand, but he had to wait. She had to wait.

Sweat had beaded on his upper lip, but he didn't brush it away. He concentrated on the music, letting it draw him out of the moment. It was a complex piece, starting softly with a smooth melody and moving into sequences of more powerful notes. There were no lyrics, but the voice was high and sweet, finding vocal tricks and subtle shifts that somehow conveyed their message without words. He had been surprised since the moment it first drifted through his console that they hadn't cut it. Too controversial. Too different. But then, music was a very subjective experience, and sadly, he knew, most of those who heard it wouldn't even notice.

The last strains of "0443" died away. He felt the muscles in his arm twitch, but he forced himself to remain still. He let the next song play halfway through, and casually opened the screen to the story he'd been reading. It was a disjointed ramble, fantasy carefully wound around a thin plot without deep meaning or serious intent. It was a very safe story, and he skimmed the text without really seeing it as the music continued through three more forgettable songs. He leaned forward and saved his place in the story.

At the same time, he bent slightly, flipped the small device up and off the wires, and palmed it. He turned off the music, and the console slid slowly back into the wall. He held his breath, afraid he might have dragged the wires out too far, and that they would catch, or short, without their cover in place. He couldn't lean down to retrieve that yet either, but he knew he could in a few moments. He leaned back, stretched, smoothed his pants, and managed to slip the small, solid-state recording into his pocket as he did so.

He rose and left the room, heading into the kitchen for coffee. Cherie sat at the table. She had the kitchen console open and was watching a vid of fish swimming placidly through a coral reef. Such calming uncredited programming was always available. There were other shows—films and serials—but like the music, and the books, they were available for a set cycle of time and gone forever. Never the same actors in any two programs. There were no names. For all the viewers knew the people in the dramas *were* those characters. It was difficult to discuss any particular program with others because the numbers that differentiated them were long and intricate, worse by far than the music, and they did not run at the same time or in the same sequence in all homes at once.

Everyone had a purpose. Skills were valued. All the education one might desire was available and encouraged. In isolation. Boz worked within a pod—a group of individuals with disparate abilities. They completed tasks that required their combined efforts, sometimes supplemented by a new member, or in smaller groups as they were called away to collaborate with others. There was no competition between artisans of the same skillset. There was no way to know if you were as good as or better than others performing the same duties. There was no impulse to excel, no fear of falling short. Work was completed, for the most part, in a state of utter stagnation.

Now he had a purpose, though he was not certain what it would lead to. He had the song. He had no way to listen to it, but it existed. He wondered if there was another, somewhere, who had been equally driven, but driven to create a device to play music or display stories and essays, words and thoughts. He wondered if there might be an entire society hovering just beneath the surface of the system, feeding ideas from one to the next, building something unique while the world rolled bleakly onward. He thought about writing about such a network, thought about what it might be like to create that world in his mind, write it down, and submit it to the system... but he knew that he would not. If they were out there, he'd be doing them harm, and he'd likely disappear from the grid forever. If he was wrong... he might disappear, and the idea would die as well. And there was the song. Now it wasn't just his own thoughts he protected, but the work of another. Something with meaning. Something worth saving.

He took his coffee to the next room and sat down, sipping slowly. The carcass of the phone he'd used to create his recordable drive had been built into a section of a console he'd been called to perform maintenance on. It wasn't the first time he'd found something that didn't seem to belong. He'd learned not to react. The first time had been years earlier—a coil of wires wrapped around components not connected in any way to the system he'd been servicing, tucked in behind a large transformer. He'd yanked it out and stared at it stupidly, and moments later men had appeared, calmly taking it from him and disappearing back into the halls of the complex.

It wasn't until later that same night that the implications had hit him. It had been put there to be found, but not by the system. He'd allowed something precious to disappear from the world. Somewhere out there was another person he had failed.

When he'd found the phone, he'd calmly worked around it, giving no indication that anything was different. Since none of those working with him had his expertise, and it was secreted into the case of the machinery, there was little likelihood another would notice. It had taken his entire day to work the instrument free while calmly going about his normal duties, and a heart-stopping moment of near panic as he palmed it along with one of his tools and slipped it into his bag.

Not long after the confiscation of the wires and components, he'd begun working at the seams in the bottom of his tool bag. It was constructed of double-layered canvas. Over time he was able to cut a slit from one end to the other, very thin. This left a pocket where something could—if it was thin enough—be slipped beneath the inner lining. Unless the search was very thorough, which it usually was not, it was possible to smuggle small items in and out of each workspace.

Boz had done this exactly three times. Once for the phone, and once each for bits of wire and a tiny roll of tape that had been unrolled from the end of a spool and stuck to the underside of a circuit board. The number who had left it must have unrolled it, rolled it back up without the tube, and turned in the empty tube for a new roll. It was clever and inspiring.

The phone had come home in the lining of his bag and remained there for months. He'd worked with it, always inside the bag, during the time he normally spent organizing and inventorying his tools, careful not to spend too much time at any one point. What was left of the phone he intended to install in another unit, in another room, along with his recording.

There was no way he would ever be able to build a player. Probably, he was never going to hear "0443" again, though the strains of the song were currently playing in an endless loop through his mind. He knew, over time, it would fade. Memory would warp the melody and rob him of the haunting tune bit by bit until it was nothing but a ghost of itself.

But it would exist. He intended to leave the drive in an inconspicuous circuit, the two wires necessary to hook it into—something—dangling free but tucked up where they could not be seen. One day, he knew, it would be found by another tech. If he was lucky, it would prove interesting enough to be passed on. If a time came when it was possible to resurrect the things that were being cast aside in the wake of the world, "0443" would remain, ready for a rebirth. Maybe the woman who had sung it would remember. Maybe she would be alive to know that someone, somewhere, had heard her and loved the music.

Cherie sat across the table from him. For a moment or two they sat in silence, sipping their coffee. Then, on impulse, he stood and circled the table, wrapping her in his arms and leaning in to whisper in her ear... but instead of whispering, he hummed the melody of "0443."

She didn't tense up, as he'd feared. Instead, she opened her hand very slowly. Inside was a small scrap of paper. On the paper, in very fine print, he saw lines and words. He couldn't make them out, because tears welled in the corners of his eyes and blurred his sight, but it didn't matter. The words were preserved. They were secret, and sacred. They were hers, and she'd shared them, and somehow, he knew that she would pass them on. She closed her hand, and he turned her face to his, kissing her deeply. Without another word he led her off to the one room where they were absolutely alone. Already, he was dreaming of the next thing he would save—the next thing that would matter.

He had a momentary flash of vision, lines intersecting other lines, secrets reaching out to other secrets, like fingers grasping, or a tapestry that had been unraveled drawing back in on itself. It comforted him. As he slid the door closed on their bedroom and lay down beside Cherie, he closed his eyes—just for a moment—and sent out a silent prayer to the voice behind "0443."

He knew he'd begin his search the next day for something new. Something to believe in. In the back of his mind, the Noble's laws echoed and pulsed, and he tried to ignore them.

Music is for entertainment.

Writing is for sharing and moving on.

Names and labels only encourage pride and inhibit equality.

He only hoped that wherever the words, and the music, the technology and the art, lay hidden, others would continue to pass it on. He hoped the cleverness of his recording would bring someone a smile, and that the music would live again.

He thought that when he hid the recording, he'd sign the case. Not 9628356, but Boz. No one would know who he was, but that didn't matter. It wasn't just the art, he knew, but the artist. He wished that he knew who had sung "0443" because he could have added her name to the cache. It would have to be a collaboration.

Then he drew Cherie close, and they began a collaboration of their own—a creation that the system had not found a way to control or deny. He put his heart and soul into their coupling, sharing himself fully. The lie in the system was that they were all one. The truth of the moment was that if the lie ever became truth, as it did for the two of them in that moment, it would set them free.

She Mourned

The man died, and she mourned. Money stolen from the fallen, leeched from the poor, paid for her grief by the hour, bought tears and pain and screams. She learned their faces and their names, took their money, and drew them close. Her mourning was a show for those who remained, but for her it could not have been more real.

She sat by candlelight, recording their lives and loves, their deaths, and those they had caused. Rich men, all. None who would have given her the time of day, their families so numb to the world they brokered the grief of his passing through her, rather than experience it.

Her rooms were paid for by the deaths of men whose passing left fortunes and fame, and nothing else. Portraits on the covers of forgotten magazines. Brass plates removed from doors and recycled. Possibly to bullet casing that would end others just like them. Empty men, drained of life and inflated by greed, forgotten by anyone they ever claimed to love, except in dry-ink signatures on checks.

She sat before her one window and stared out at the skyline with its spires and flickering lights, teeming masses of rats running mazes for masters they did not even understand that they served. She shivered. She felt them dying, slowly. She sang softly to prevent the chattering of her teeth.

She sewed. Tears trickled down her cheeks, dampening spools of brightly colored thread in her lap. She'd unraveled it carefully from garments worn by the dead. She'd stolen it, bartered for it, bought it from relatives who thought she was motivated by the same greed that fueled their lives. They were light, she was dark. Life, and death, were rainbows.

In a casket across from her a dead man had lain, face on display. Family, colleagues, enemies, all had offered charms to attract his shiny, empty luck to themselves. Then they'd walked away, and she'd sat alone with his empty shell.

They'd given her one of his scarves, assuming she would sell it on the street. It had unraveled easily. Now she watched the stars, and the city, and she worked her needle in and out, tight, intricate stitches. Sometimes one color, then another. As she worked, she dreamed. She drew the dead man's soul in tear-stained thread.

He'd owned the poor. Entire neighborhoods sucked through middlemen and women, had fed his wealth. They spoke to her and guided her hands. Their lives were colors, some bright, some dim. She was paid to mourn the rich. She mourned these others for free. Their pain burned her veins. She stitched them into patterns and wove their sorrow into a memorial to one man's ugly life. That theirs would not be wasted, she preserved them. She worked until they grew silent.

She would find a child in need, cold and poor. The pillow she created would cradle their head and feed their dreams. It would drink their tears.

They died, and she mourned.

Anomaly

Roberts stared at the screen above his workstation. Sweat crawled down his spine and dampened his armpits. His hand rested on the base of a compact electron microscope. The screen depicted the contents of the slide currently under the lens. The sudden realization that he was touching that instrument, and the instrument was touching the—thing—on the screen cut through his lethargy like a white-hot blade.

With a small cry he withdrew his hand and jerked back from the workstation. What writhed in the pink, jellied solution he had used to prep the slide could not exist. He worked in a clean lab. The samples he worked with were genetically pure— proteins and enzymes. The entire workstation was cleansed three times daily, as was Roberts himself. All of this flashed through his mind and speared his brain with a single word: No.

He should already have hit the large, red, mushroom shaped button that rose beside his keyboard. The button would set off alarms, flashing lights, and galvanize a dozen men in pristine white lab suits into action. He should have sealed his workspace until the cleansing unit arrived. He did none of these things. Instead, Roberts sat down, forced his reluctant fingers to the controls, and increased magnification on the microscope.

In the back of his mind, he knew that the alarms should be sounding, with or without action on his part. The spike in his own nervous system was detectable. In the white, clean world of EXOTECH, it was an infestation. As much as he hated the word for all its science fiction connotations, it was an anomaly.

The thing moved. Tentacles shot out from either side, seeking sustenance. Roberts blinked, glanced at a small graph display on his desk, and swallowed. The thing was twice the size it had been when he first spotted it and appeared to be growing exponentially. Roberts calculated from what he'd observed, whistled, and backed away again. Too fast. It was growing too fast, and if it continued, more than just his workspace might be compromised. Still, he hesitated. There was something in the slow, sinuous motion, something with a barely concealed pattern. He tried to place the sensation but failed.

He reached out his hand to smack down on the contamination alarm and froze. He stared at the perfect image on his screen and bit back a scream. The thing—the anomaly—was gone. The slide contained only the standard "control" base he used every day. In his mind he still felt the tug of spiraling tentacles. He tasted the bitter bile in the back of his throat brought on by the thought of the cleansing to come, the quarantine, and the silence. He blinked his eyes, but the screen remained clear.

Trembling, he sank back into his seat. Soft leather formed about him, separated from his clothing and his skin by slick plastic. Roberts reached for his control panel, stopped as his hands were gripped by an intense trembling. He closed his eyes and breathed deeply until his nerves calmed.

When he glanced up, he saw that the roving security patrol had stopped outside his "pod" and was staring in at him. Roberts raised a hand to signal all was well. The guard didn't move. He pressed his shielded face close to the window and stood, watching.

Roberts reached out for his controls. This time his hands were steady. He lowered the magnification back to its standard level and began his process. The guard watched for a few moments longer, then moved on down the corridor. If it hadn't been for the built-in gauges and fail safes, Roberts was sure the guard would have questioned him.

He focused on his work and tried to press the disturbing hallucination from his mind. There was no room for error. The proteins and genetic material he worked with was brought in from Earth in small quantities. Supplies were limited, and it was months between deliveries. A single small error could cost millions.

His work, combined with that of a team of more than two

hundred other scientists, each working in a similar environment, formed the backbone of EXOTECH'S prime technology, a process Roberts' colleagues termed genetic cleansing, and that was marketed to governments and the masses as *Exotechnology*. The term had no serious meaning. EXOTECH'S earliest work was in the field of exoskeletal human enhancement. When they slipped over into the realm of genetic manipulation, they used the company name as a smokescreen. The scientific community as a whole did not endorse what they were doing, which was another reason for the off-world facility.

Roberts never gave it much thought. He was a technician, and the pay for this project would allow him the freedom to complete his education on his return to Earth, or to retire. Twenty-four months of isolation in an absolutely clean environment. The compound, a space station locked into orbit around Mars, was a hive of separate quarters, workspaces, and routines. Each and every person assigned had volunteered for the work and only been accepted after strict background investigations were complete. They were joined at the brain via the main computer bank when off duty, able to converse, share ideas, and retain their sanity, but in the workspace even this weak umbilical was cut.

The isolation had begun even before they left earth. Biological, emotional, and mental examination, testing, and monitoring cleared their minds and their bodies to interact with the super-clean environment of EXOTECH'S lab. The training was simple enough; memorization of sequences and codes, and a thorough grounding in procedure was the core. The experiment itself, and the results gleaned from the research, had been outlined and was monitored every step of the way by technicians on Earth. Roberts had only to provide his data in a constant flow and to maintain vigilance against contamination.

The rest of the day's work proceeded without incident, and Roberts closed his workstation with a heavy sigh of release. There were no more incidents with contaminants that didn't exist, and the guard passed him by without notice on all rounds subsequent to what Roberts now termed *The Anomaly*. He sealed his results, began the decontamination sequence. He stepped into the bio-suit he wore between his workspace and his quarters and stood motionless inside the door of his pod until scanners had checked every inch of his protective clothing for the slightest hint of anything outside the strict parameters allowed on the station.

Roberts would be back in the pod in 16 hours. He would eat, read for a while, spend a little time on the computer system trying to find something to talk about with the other technicians, and then he'd sleep. His vital signs would be checked and monitored as he slept, and when he woke any deficiencies that might affect the quality or efficiency of his work would be addressed by supplements added to his breakfast, which would be delivered to his quarters through a thirty-minute decontamination process and a tri-level lift system that would not proceed from one step to the next until the preceding level was sealed.

A claustrophobic person would have gone insane in an hour, but Roberts was very self-contained, and after four months barely missed the distractions of the world he'd left behind. He did miss sex, but there would be plenty of time for that when he got back. He told himself over and over that he'd managed to make it the first seventeen years of his life without it, and a few more months wasn't going to kill him.

In fact, nothing but very random chance could kill him until his assignment ran his course. His health was monitored and pampered constantly. There was no illness on the compound. There was little or no discomfort. There were no germs. He felt like he worked in a dream state. Only the short periods of conversation with the others broke the illusion. They had little to talk about after the first couple of months. Each of their jobs was very similar to the next. They monitored the effects of certain chemical and sonic reactions on gene structure. Each change was infinitesimal, the results carefully recorded and transmitted, but none of them knew the exact purpose of their own part in the greater puzzle that was EXOTECH. There was speculation, but it fizzled under the weight of apathy. It was more stimulating to talk about what they would do when they returned to Earth, and that is what filled most of their on-line hours.

Roberts logged off early that night and sat staring at the white, blemish-free wall of his quarters. His mind painted the writhing tentacles across the smooth surface. He still felt the itch of something just beyond the reach of his memory, or his perception. There was something he should know, but he couldn't bring it to the forefront of his mind.

The walls dimmed from luminous white to blue. Roberts rose, went through the familiar rituals of cleaning his teeth and washing his face. None of it was necessary, and all water that contacted his skin was immediately purged from the station to be recycled, cleansed, and purified off-station before returning to the system.

As the walls faded through shades of blue toward deep purple, Roberts lay on his cot and drew his thin blanket up to his chin. He didn't need it. The environment was programmed to respond to minute reactions in his nervous system. If he got cold, the small bedchamber would simply become warmer. The blanket was another old habit that had refused to leave him. Too many such rituals could disqualify a person from service with EXOTECH, but some ritual was encouraged. It made transition back into life on Earth simpler.

Roberts closed his eyes and wiped the last of the writhing image from his mind. The air was slowly infused with a mild sedative. The deep purple glow of the walls soothed him. The world dropped away to darkness, and he slept.

EXOTECH INTERNAL MEMO 1009-53-0

Step one of the key accessed. Source genes human, as prophesied. Trigger is acoustic. Subject Roberts activated. Standard sensor array disabled; decoding sequence initiated. Subject is stable.

The first sensation was helplessness. Roberts could move neither arms, nor legs. His head was gripped on either side by padded braces. His eyelids would not close, and when he tried to blink the pain was excruciating. His fingers were individually banded to a cold, hard surface. Someone moved, and the motion sent a soft breeze rippling across his skin. He was naked.

He scanned the periphery of his limited vision. The walls were bright, luminous white, like those of his bedchamber. A painfully bright light glared down at him from above. He heard the sound of voices; at least they seemed to be voices. He could make out none of the words. He tried to speak, but his lower jaw was clamped in place. His tongue was so bone dry it crackled when he moved it and a wave of thirst so excruciating it knifed into the base of his brain and caused his entire body to go rigid stung his throat.

Someone moved close by, out of sight. He tried so hard to see them that his eyes actually cramped from the effort of trying to twist them sideways. Something hummed. A large, polished metal bar slid into view above his toes. It stretched across from one side of the table to the other. The whirr repeated, followed by a loud THUNK! And the bar swiveled. A whine rose, like a turbine firing up, the sound louder and louder until it became painfully piercing, beating at his eardrums with insistent, malevolent pressure.

He heard more mechanical movement to either side of his head, but he saw nothing. Moments later he felt soft pricks of pain just forward of either ear. The pressure increased slowly; something long, thin, and very sharp slid through his skin. He wanted to scream and could not. The effort brought the thirst again, and he nearly blacked out.

Then the bar glowed bright blue at the end of the table, shifted to white, and a solid beam burst from the base of the thing, bathing his feet in its glow. The pain was incredible. He trembled, fought to scream, and fought the urge to scream because it brought the thirst. The bar moved so slowly down the length of his body that he only knew it was moving at all by the burning, searing pain of its passing.

Ice cold pricks of sensation formed where the long, thin probes had pierced his flesh, behind his ears. He started to shake, and then...grew still. The pain ceased. He still followed the progress of the scanner up his calves toward his thighs, but the burning, searing pain was gone. He floated, detached from all sensation. In the back of his mind, something itched. He wanted to watch the scanner move over his form. He wanted to think about how he would remove the icy probes from the sides of his head. He wanted to scream, but he had no more control over his lungs and vocal cords than he did over his arms and legs.

In the air above him, particles joined, separated, and joined again. They swirled. He watched, fascinated, as they formed an image similar to the thing he'd seen on his slide. It pulsed. Tentacles stretched out to either side, probing. It whirled slowly, and he followed each motion, picking out the pattern as it moved. He wanted to speak, though only to seek a certain word. The thing was like a letter in an arcane alphabet— something he'd known and forgotten. It meant something important and was communicating that thing to Roberts, but he could not understand. Tears formed in the corners of his eyes and rolled down, sliding around the probing lengths of metal piercing his skull.

The scanner passed over his torso and reached his neck. There was an unpleasant ripple about an inch beneath his skin. His jaw ached, and as the scan rippled over his face and up to his cranium whatever the icy pain relief that had flooded him had been, it was overmatched. All thought ceased and the blinding white of the light wiped away the room and the machinery, leaving him silently, motionlessly screaming into a luminous void.

The walls pulsed from deep purple shades up into shades of blue. A light mist of stimulant, laced with the scent of fresh coffee misted the air. Roberts sat up slowly. Wide-awake in seconds, as always, he slid his legs off the side of his cot, leaned his head into his hands, and fought the urge to vomit. His skin tingled. The dull throb of the memory of machinery echoed in his head and his ears were filled with a buzzing, ringing sensation.

If he didn't move, sensors would alert the central control. Roberts stood shakily and began his morning routine. For once, the absolute monotony of his existence worked in his favor. Synthetic coffee and breakfast slid up through the multiple airlocks; he ate and drank quickly, and the tray disappeared. Next, Roberts stepped into a clear tube. It closed around him. He shivered, as always, as the chemical and sonic cleansing removed any and all impurity from his skin. He stepped clear of the tube and straight into the bio suit that now hung in front of the tube.

At the door he stopped again, moving through the air-lock sequence and the careful scan of the exterior of his suit. His heart pounded. What had become a simple routine terrified him. What if they saw it? What if there was something left on his skin, in his blood? What if he hadn't been dreaming? Had they done that to him—EXOTECH? Was it possible? If he asked, his time here would be over, along with his dreams of retirement. If they were behind it, they'd silence him. If not—well, then he was going crazy, and they'd ship him out on the next freighter home with a partial pension.

He stepped into the hall and headed for his pod. Once he was inside, he could drift into the mechanics of the job and try to forget this. The quicker he wiped it all out of his mind, the more likely he was to relax. He passed none of the guards and made it into his workspace without incident. Once he'd passed through the safeguards and left the bio-suit behind, he set to work quickly.

He worked methodically. He would get no extra pay for extra output, and EXOTECH frowned on hurried results. If his standard time parameter for a particular task varied too much, they would light a warning on his control panel and withhold samples. Too many variations and he could be called out for examination. They allowed this to happen one time during the tenure of employ. Any variation beyond this was considered an unacceptable expense, and that technician was replaced.

Everything went smoothly, and within half an hour he had several slides prepped and had set his "control" data carefully. All that remained was to submit the slides to a set of sonic pulses. In his time on The Compound, he'd been through several batteries of tests. Each time the control was identical to the last. Only the slight variation in sonic pulses changed, and each time the test ended, the results were whisked off by the sensors and monitors to the central memory banks to make way for the next batch of data. Clockwork.

Roberts liked to think of the pulses as notes. Each vibrated differently, and over time he'd fancied he could detect the minute differences himself. It was ridiculous; they were far too subtle for anything but very sensitive electronic equipment to monitor, but he couldn't help toying with the notion. Maybe the pulses were affecting his mind, as well. Maybe they caused the hallucination that had invaded his screen the previous day. It could be that familiarity with the sonic patterns was what he'd been unable to put his finger on when he saw the waving tentacles. A similarity in patterns.

Roberts shook his head. He swapped the first of the slides out and replaced it with another. He studied the chart beside him on the bench and performed very minor adjustments to the sonic equipment. He pressed the toggle that began the sequence of pulses and watched as the invisible lines of force interacted with his slide.

The back of his hand itched, and he glanced down. In the valley formed behind the knuckles of his index and middle finger he saw a tiny black dot. Roberts stared. The itch continued, and he knew he wouldn't be able to stand it long. What in hell could it be? Not an insect. Not here. No dirt. Had he slipped up somehow in prepping the slides?

Very carefully, he reached down with his free hand and flicked at the dot with the back of his fingernail. He felt nothing. Whatever it was, it was flush with his skin. He leaned closer, but still couldn't make out what the offending spot could be. The itch grew more intense with each passing moment. Roberts flicked his gaze back to his screen, grunted, and reached for the slide. He could barely grip the edges as he slid it out, deposited it in the disposal slot, and clicked on the button that transferred his data. Gritting his teeth, he ignored the itch on his hand and grabbed the next slide. He managed to get it into place without mishap, changed the setting on the sonic pulse, and flipped the toggle for the next sequence.

Just for a second, the itch on his hand abated, and he leaned back. Then it hit harder and faster, a sudden stab of pain. He stared, horrified, at his hand. Tiny tentacles branched out from the perimeter of the spot, groping across his skin. Each touch burned like fire. Tears in his eyes, frantic, Roberts glanced up at the screen. Everything looked normal, except...

The settings. He'd changed them. He ran back over the past few moments in his mind. There was no way to doubt himself, despite the distraction of the pain in his hand. He'd moved the pulse settings to the next combination in line, but now they'd changed back. He hadn't touched the dials, and yet there it was. The previous settings had been restored, and the test was running a second time. On the screen the mirror image of the spot on his hand stared back at him. Under the lens of the electron microscope, it was so large it threatened to writhe off the edge of the slide.

Roberts cried out and flipped the toggle, ending the test early. He backed away from the workstation. The image on the screen faded. His hand stopped burning. He glanced at the slide, and at the disposal slot. He knew that somewhere in the complex, alarms were sounding. Lights flashed on security desks and in medical to warn them of an "anomaly." Still, he stared at the slide. He could return the settings on the switch to the position they were supposed to be in and finish the test. He might get on to the next setting before anyone arrived, and he could always claim that the glitch was in the machinery, and not himself. No one needed to know of the spot on his hand, stretching out and groping across his skin, or the way it had burned. No one needed to know that the slide had been contaminated, because all sensors indicated it was as clean as any before it.

Roberts decided quickly. He'd get away with it, or he wouldn't. He had nothing to lose by trying. He flipped the controls to the next setting again, double-checking, and held them there. With his thumb he flipped the toggle. There was a small jerk in the controls, as if they wanted to twist back again, but he held them firmly, and after a moment, the pressure subsided. He was just sliding the finished test slide into the deposit slot when the guard's faceplate pressed against the outer window of his pod.

Roberts ignored the man. He grabbed a third slide and slipped it into place. He fought to keep his hand steady, and it only trembled a little. He made the adjustments to his controls and flipped the toggle. The settings remained intact. There was no flip back to an earlier position, and there was no spot on his hand. He felt the weight of the security patrolman's gaze on his shoulders, but he didn't turn. If they wanted him out, they were going to have to reach him. He wouldn't give them the satisfaction of admitting he'd screwed up. If they didn't catch it, what harm could one slightly irregular slide in half a million make?

Finally, unable to endure the strain, he slowly turned his gaze to the window. The patrolman was gone.

The day finished in a blur. He worked through his slides,

secured his equipment, began the cleansing sequences right on time and sweated bullets through each, expecting bells and whistles and flashing lights, and getting nothing more than the hiss of the inner pod door sliding open, followed by the clinging security of his bio-suit, and, finally, his room.

He knew it was a risk, but after eating, he didn't log on to the main system. He didn't want to risk the temptation of asking questions. Had anyone else noticed the anomaly? Did they know about it? Were they readying themselves to remove him, even now, or worse yet, to study him? The calm, glowing walls took on a sinister aspect and the strictly structured life and world surrounding him felt like some strange kind of prison.

The wait was interminable, but eventually it was time for him to sleep. He lay back on the cot, pulled the blanket up to his chin as always. His heart raced. His skin was clammy. He knew the sensors would pick it up. Was it fever? Had he managed the impossible, becoming ill, or infected, in a place devoid of illness or infection? No alarms sounded. The lights shifted through their color spectrum and the misting sedative tugged his eyelids closed, despite his best effort to keep them open. Roberts slept.

EXOTECH INTERNAL MEMO 1009-53-1

Subject appears to be near the key. Mental stability questionable, but motor skills normal. Sensor readings indicate partial solution. Initial scan incomplete. Risk of damage to subject in second scan acceptable. Sonic pulses, even at reduced control rates, caused reactions in multiple workstation pods, despite shielding. Subjects cleansed. Recommend commencement of pulse ray construction. Next scheduled flight to Earth in fewer than sixty hours.

The pain was immediate and excruciating. Roberts felt the cold metal table against his naked flesh. His limbs were secured as before, eyes clipped open, and the two long, slender needles were already in place just forward of his ears. He felt the numbing icy touch of whatever they dispensed, but it wasn't enough. The pain shot through him and despite the danger, and the additional pain, he fought to force a scream through immobile lips.

The walls glowed white. He heard whispered voices, but, again, could make out no words. The ringing in his ears, accompanied by a sizzling, chemical hiss each time he strained to move, gave the voices a rhythmic, hypnotic quality. Like a chant in some foreign tongue. He wanted to call out to them. He wanted to beg them for mercy.

The metal bar slid into place just beyond his toes and the balls of his feet. Roberts' eyes rolled up into his head in panic as the turbine sound returned and the scanner kicked to life. It wasn't a steady beam this time, but a pulse. It flashed so brilliantly he felt as if his eyes would boil from the heat of it. The flashes recurred at a steady rate, like a hideous strobe light. The bar began its excruciatingly slow ascent of Roberts' body and he shied away. He couldn't move, but his skin drew back, and up, and every muscle in his body was clenched. Though he fought against it, perversely, his penis stiffened, stretching up obscenely as the scan made its way slowly upward.

Something was different. He grasped this thought and clung to it. Maybe it was important, maybe not, but it was something. If he sat and watched and waited for that pain to leave his toes and ankles and work its way up to…

What was it? The pulse? He tried to blank his mind. He couldn't close his eyes. He couldn't look away from the inexorable ascent of the bar and each time the light pulsed, his nerves screamed with pain, blanking thought. Between those pulses, he fought to think. There was something he should be seeing, something just out of reach. The pulse came again, radiating his upper thighs and teasing at the edges of his groin with fiery tendrils of agony.

He held that thought. Hairs, sticking out at angles, brought the image of the anomaly to his mind. The pain flashed again and thought vanished. When it returned, colored dots swam before his eyes. He knew he was nearing unconsciousness, but as he slid away, the dots formed patterns, like motes swimming in his eyes. They whirled into small circles, each with strands of something—tentacles? —trailing from their perimeter. His skin crawled, though the next pulse had yet to fall. Something deep inside detached, moved slowly from a point directly above his navel.

FLASH and the scan reached that same point. His thoughts

extinguished like the quick flash of a camera, and all was darkness.

EXOTECH INTERNAL MEMO 1009-53-1. B

Subject stabilized, scan complete. Sonic pulse settings verified as key. Construction of pulse ray reported in stage four with expected completion in thirty-two hours. Freighter conversion complete and ready for installation of Pulse Generator. Test subject's transformation terminated at various points, not to exceed safety parameters. Final solution imminent.

The walls shifted color, and the stimulant misted the air. Roberts blinked. He stared and blinked again to convince himself he had control of his eyelids. His body was on fire with a burning ache that permeated muscle and nerve endings. He moved his toes slowly, and then bent one leg. It hurt, but the pain was bearable. He slid his legs off the cot and stood.

Everything was as it had been every single day of his time at The Compound. Roberts forced his aching body through the motions of his daily routine. Something was horribly wrong, but the central control team didn't appear to be aware of it and lacking any other form of defense against his world crumbling, he decided to delay their awareness as long as possible. If he were sick, they would have come for him. If his synapses fired erratically, they would note this too, eventually. Everything was monitored. Everything was clean.

He managed to make it into his bio-suit and into the hall without incident. Normally he didn't pay much attention to the other pods he passed. When he'd first arrived, he'd been fascinated, staring into each and trying to imagine what kind of person the other technician was, where they'd come from and where they were going when all of this was just a memory. Then the novelty faded, and he paid them no more attention than he did the walls or the floor. Now, he glanced from side to side surreptitiously. Everything looked much as it had the last time he'd bothered to check until he got within two pods of his own. He knew they had technicians assigned. He also knew both should be at their stations. The work was scheduled on a cycle so that none of them hit the passage at the same time, and the two pods directly before he reached his were on an earlier start schedule. They were empty. No lights flashed. There was no indication that anything was amiss, except for the missing technicians.

Sweat slicked his skin. The bio-suit was suddenly very tight, warm, and restrictive. Roberts forced his steps to remain steady, and when he reached his pod, though the desire to be free of the suit was overwhelming, he fought it back. He stood quietly through the layers of decontamination and moments later stepped free into the workspace.

Inside, he stared. The Electron microscope seemed alien to him, the chair something from a bad dream. The row upon row of blank slides awaiting his attention gleamed, and he thought of their sharp edges. He wondered how his blood would look under the microscope, and how long it would take the system to sedate and remove him if he tried to find out.

He wondered where the missing technicians had gone.

Mechanically, Roberts grabbed a slide and began to prep it. The work took little of his concentration, but there was nothing else to focus it on, so he stared blankly at his hands as he worked and ran through the past few days in his mind. The screen flashed on, and he cringed, nearly dropping the slide in his hand. The flash of light had triggered memories of the scan. His skin itched and his bones ached. He managed to get the slide into place and focused.

He glanced at the chart beside his workspace. He stared. Each day when he came in the chart had changed. He wasn't allowed control over keeping track of his tests because this allowed for error. The system itself made the shifts, always slight, in the control settings.

Except the settings were the same. He forced himself to visualize each knob position, as he'd set them the day before. It was hard to concentrate. His fingers, while not broken, were stiff and did not want to bend to his will. The date on the chart was new. All the information was as it should be except the first setting. It was identical to the previous day's setting.

Roberts' hand shook, but he didn't hesitate. If this was a test to see if he would deviate or become a problem, he was up to the test. If they were using him in some way for a separate study, he had no doubt he'd be compensated for it. He flipped the knobs into position and hit the toggle. The pulse bombarded the slide with its subtle pressures and "tones."

The shift was more immediate than before. He saw the thing tug *itself to the surface of the slide. It was larger, still, than before. If it got any larger, it would not be contained on the slide, and all he'd see was a black splotch. Roberts felt a stabbing pain in his hand. He glanced down and screamed. The black mark he'd noticed the day before had grown. It was a splotch, pressing outward from inside the skin of his hand. He could clearly make out the outlines of tentacles, reaching down the length of his fingers and groping toward his wrist. It throbbed and each throb ground the thing into his bone.*

It was too much. Roberts lurched forward and smacked his hand down hard on the alert button. If they were going to cleanse him and deport him, fine. He hoped they would hurry. He reached out with his free hand to flip the toggle down and stop the pulse. At that moment, the thing burst through his skin. He whirled and stared in horror as it oozed out of his vein and gripped his arm, tugging itself along, and growing. In its trail his hand shriveled and sank in upon itself.

The screen had gone dark. Whatever pulled itself free of the slide had completely blocked the lens.

Gas hissed through nozzles set deep in the walls. Roberts clawed his way upright and used his one good hand to drag himself toward the object they'd piped in. He hoped it was a sedative, or a pain killer— some sort of antidote. He never reached the nozzle. Whatever sprayed from its tip solidified, like a bubble. Within that pale surface he saw a familiar swirl, and he screamed again. His arm no longer existed below the elbow.

Grinding his teeth against the pain, he turned to the window. Nothing. There was no one there. He turned to the table along the far wall, and the row upon row of blank slides. The thing passed his elbow and gripped his bicep.

With a hoarse, maddened scream he gripped one of the slides, dragged it free of the rack, and drove it into his shoulder. He sliced, drawing a long, bright red burst of blood. The sensation was warm and almost comforting in the face of the agony in his lower arm. He ignored the screen, and the microscope. With desperate, slashing strokes he worked the slide through skin and muscle, tears streaming down his face as he fought to reach the bone.

There was a searing flash of light and everything in the room went still. The light filled the pod, glaring from the windows. Smoke rose from the screen and the equipment. Where Roberts had stood, there was nothing. On the floor the clean, broken shards of a glass slide gleamed like forgotten crystals.

EXOTECH INTERNAL MEMO 1009-53-1.c

Subject terminated. Test exceeds parameters. The key is functional and programmed. Installation is complete. Launch for Earth is one hour. Remaining subjects terminated. Destruct sequence engaged. Pulse ray primed and programmed for release upon achieving Earth atmosphere. The key functions exponentially, as expected. Projected annihilation of host cells twenty-four hours. Rebirth achieved. Ia Cthulhu.

One

Michael sat quietly, staring through the plastic bubble surrounding Thomas. They hadn't touched in nearly a year. The few short conversations they'd managed were broken and distant. On the surface of the plastic, Michael had affixed an intricate design. He stared through it and Michael's features fractured into memories.

They'd met in the 90s. Everyone was young and beautiful. T had fronted a band of thin boys with incredible hair and tight pants. Michael had been a waiter. He'd delivered a drink to T that another man had paid for and couldn't help flirting. He'd met T's gaze and they'd tumbled together into the wild years. Carefree. Too loose with money and flesh.

T was diagnosed with AIDS in 2002 and started a slow decline. Michael learned to cleanse everything, to isolate if he became ill, to snap around at the sound of a sneeze or cough. But he'd had T. They were one. That was the design. He'd started drawing it the night they met, kept it secret and hidden, added to it with numbers and symbols, dates, and emotions.

When Covid-19 hit, they'd put T in the bubble. Michael had had the design tattooed on his chest that same day. Dr. Nicholson said he thought T would pass any moment, so Michael stayed.

T's body shivered, very suddenly. His back arched, and in that same moment Michael rose and stepped to the bubble. He pressed his chest to the symbol on the plastic. A bright flash, like luminous smoke, swirled from T's mouth. He turned and met Michael's gaze. They spoke a single word in a single breath. "One." The smoke shot through the symbol and Michael's skin felt suddenly white hot. He stumbled back, closed his eyes, and saw T smiling. Under his breath, he whispered... "One."

"You are just like Gods"

Myoshi felt his foot slip on the slick, moss-covered stone, and he gripped the rocks above him more tightly. The sharp, hardened lava cut into his fingers, but he caught his balance and remained still, letting his breath and heartbeat calm. The sun rose slowly, warming his back as he climbed. Birds cried from the peaks above, and from the depths of the trees. Myoshi brushed his fingers across his brow, wiping away the sweat.

Fuji rose above him, grim and imposing, but no more so than the formidable drop behind. Myoshi had begun his climb at first light, and he'd made good time. On his back, his book bag bulged with supplies. There was a souvenir shop at the edge of the forest, but he'd wanted to avoid prying eyes.

He carried some well-packed fish and rice, and two small packets. One was his schoolwork, graded and banded carefully to be saved and shown to his parents. The other was a packet of letters. Letters from Myoshi's grandfather. Letters Myoshi's father had kept, wrapped carefully in rice paper, and bound with a silken ribbon. Letters that one day would be missed.

The mountain leveled off for a time, and Myoshi was able to walk normally, sweeping his gaze along the trail that wound up and up until it was lost among trees and clouds. It was a wonderful day for a climb.

Far below, beyond the ocean of trees that was the ancient forest of Aokigahara, school was in session. Myoshi's father had been at work for two hours, and his mother would be home, cleaning and organizing. Nothing in their small, neat apartment was ever out of place. Myoshi's father would not have permitted it and his mother would do nothing that shamed her in her husband's eyes. Perfection. Myoshi yearned for that. In everything he did, he fell short.

In school, his mind wandered. His grades were not bad, but neither were they good. In Myoshi's household, mediocrity was not an option. Other children excelled. Some were athletes, others could calculate in their heads faster than Myoshi could press the buttons on his calculator. Myoshi could write, some, but even in this he fell short in his father's eyes. His marks in penmanship were less than satisfactory, and his grammar was erratic. His teachers said he lacked focus and discipline.

Myoshi's grandfather had known about discipline. He had understood about being different, as well. It was all in the letters. Letters written by a man who died before his own young son could bring home grades or books of letters. Letters that were Myoshi's father's one link to the past. A fragile link, built of memories half-forgotten and fantasies long rehearsed. Myoshi had heard those fantasies. He had met his grandfather through his father's words. He had seen the glint in dark eyes, and the shining leather of the uniform. Myoshi had heard the roar of engines as great birds of war took flight.

"You are just like the Gods," Myoshi breathed, "Free of earthly desires…"

He slipped under the umbrella of tree-limbs and continued up the mountain. His father's voice echoed through his mind. The mountain slipped away, just for a moment, replaced by white, billowing clouds. The soft cries of birds and the chirping of insects gave way to crackling static. He sensed the others, tightly formed squadron of death, moving as a single unit with the sun blazing above. Myoshi could feel the sweat beneath the flight helmet. He could sense the symmetry of the squadron's practiced motion. One great bird. One bolt of lightning aimed at those who opposed the emperor.

"To fly as one bolt
From the crossbow of a
Victorious light."

A tree root protruding from the mountain's rough hide sent

Myoshi tumbling, and his mind returned to the moment. He caught himself on both hands, scraping one palm, and fighting the urge to cry out. The weight of the pack pressed him more tightly to the earth. Turning, he seated himself on a rock and caught his breath. The sun was bright, and as he looked back the way he'd come, he saw that the trail had disappeared, the winding course cutting off his entrance to the tree line completely. Nothing below but the green tops of the trees, obscuring the forest floor, and the rocky peak above rising on a gentle slope above a second line of trees. Myoshi could just make it out, and he smiled.

From his pack, he pulled free a rice cake, and the packet of his graded school papers. Carefully, he unwrapped the bundle, plucking out the sheets one by one. He laid them on the stone beside him, tracing the even lines of his script with a critical eye. He had been doing well on this one. Line after line of formulas strung together in the proper patterns. Then the error. One figure out of place, another line used to scratch the mistake from the paper and the continuation—flawed. Beside each figure, a corresponding red character in the elegant script of his teacher. Corrected. Berated. Imperfect.

Myoshi had done well enough to pass from this class to the next, but with no honors. No fine words from teacher to parent. No pride. It had taken him hours to complete that assignment, painstakingly forming each character. He had wanted so badly to please his father that the old man's image had formed in Myoshi's mind. The words, and the stories, and lectures slipped in to distract.

Myoshi traced the scratched-out characters with the nail of one finger. He whispered to himself.

"You are just like gods."

The figures mocked him. The red letters, so bright in the sunlight, glittered like the eyes of serpents. His father had not seen them. Myoshi had kept the papers, folded and tied. Bound and under his control. He could not control the characters, or the formulas, but he could control their outcome, for a time. The birds did not threaten to expose his secret and Fuji beckoned.

Myoshi glanced at the second packet of papers. He slid his

hand into his pack, stroked the silk bindings, but he did not open the letters. Not yet. He quickly packed the wrapper from the rice cake, and the schoolwork, and rose, turning to face the mountain once again.

"Free of earthly desires," he said softly.

Free of his family. Free of school, though it tugged at his heart. He would be a disappointment to his father this final time. Myoshi had not missed a day of school in five years. The only desire he could recall in all those years was to please his father. The most wonderful moments of his life had been spent at that great man's feet, listening to stories of emperors, and wars. Stories of his ancestors. Stories that filled his heart and mind with dreams of other places, and other times. Times and places where he was not a clumsy young boy, but a hero. There were ways for those unworthy of honor to regain it. There were answers to the loss of pride.

The good times with his father had grown fewer and further between as Myoshi had grown older. As the piles and piles of papers, just like those in his pack, had stacked themselves against his future, and his honor, his father's eyes had grown distant. They still saw Myoshi, but not the same Myoshi they had seen before.

Myoshi rose once more, his gaze sweeping up the winding trail to where the peak of the mountain slipped through the clouds. Eagles soared through the highest branches of the trees, circling slowly. Myoshi screened the sunlight by cupping his palm over his eyes and watched them. The brilliant light glittered on a bit of mica imbedded in the mountain, diamond glimmer nearly blinding him. Myoshi squinted, cocking his head to one side to listen.

He could hear his father's voice as the mountain faded. Could sense the shift and welcomed it.

"We watched from the decks as the pilots swarmed to the sky, a black horde, synchronized and dangerous. It was not our time. We were too far from the enemy, and these would return, but they were majestic in flight.

"I remember standing very still on the flight deck, watching them shrink to fly-specks on the horizon, and knowing, when it was my time, that speck would be me. Shrinking to nothing. Here, and then, no more, a bright spark in the emperor's eyes—a memory in my family's heart. Just like the Gods."

With his eyes squinted so tightly, Myoshi saw the aircraft shimmering against a darkened sky, saw them bank and circle against the clouds. Saw them focus. Eagles. Eagles were like the Gods, as well, but a different sort of God.

Myoshi picked up his things and started up the mountain once more, suddenly eager for completion. He could feel the wind on the wings of the eagles, and that same wind shivering through his hair.

There were few letters. Myoshi's grandfather had not served for years in the military, or even for a year. Months, only, and he had never returned. He had not been a precision pilot, nor had he been blessed with the blood of the Samurai. Still, he had soared.

Myoshi had read those letters again and again. He had begged his father's indulgence to allow him to watch over them. To guard them. He had seen in his father's eyes the struggle this had been but those words, those images, were ingrained in his father's mind. That great man no longer required the letters and so they had passed to Myoshi, who had cherished them as no other possession.

His grandfather's penmanship had never faltered. There were no red characters or strikeouts. There were clear thoughts, worded in poetry stretched to prose without loss of continuity. It was his grandfather's words that inspired Myoshi's own writing, unworthy as it was. It was the images of his grandfather's death that stole those words and distracted him from his own honor. His teacher said his mind wandered. Myoshi knew it soared.

The trees had begun to thin. All that stood between Myoshi and his goal was a ragged backbone of rock. Far above him, farther than he could have climbed in such a short time, patches of snow were visible. The air was noticeably cooler, and Myoshi was glad, very suddenly, that his mother had insisted on the sweater he wore, though it had been too hot less than an hour before.

"The higher you go," Myoshi's father's voice, "the colder it gets. The harder it is to breathe. It is always dark. We don't fly by day, and those few of us who get to practice at all are very sparing with our fuel. We are not trained to fire at the enemy. We are barely trained to land. It is not expected of us.

"We study the great maps daily. We listen to the inspirational words of our leaders. I have meditated more this span of two weeks, my son, than I have in the last two years of my life. Things I have never thought of become clear. Your mother. Your face, watching over me in my dreams.

"My face reflected
Bright smile, shining eyes, dark
Like the twilit sky."

Myoshi's eyes were dark, as were his father's. He knew that he resembled both men, third generation to bear that visage, first to fail. There would be no medals hanging on the walls of Myoshi's home. Not unless he inherited them. He would not write wondrous letters to a son yet unborn, telling tales of glory and darkness, blood and fire.

He stopped again, shielding his eyes and glancing up toward the mountain's peak. The eagles had roosted, leaving the sun to beat down on a desolate slope. Myoshi planned to be across the ridge and safely on the plateau on the far side before the afternoon sunlight waned. He considered stopping for another snack, but there wasn't much shade until he crossed, and he wanted to reach the ledge with enough light for reading.

Not that he needed light. Not that every word in every letter wasn't ingrained in his imagination, every image fully formed and captivating. He stepped out onto the bare stone. The wind whipped up and nearly toppled him from his precarious perch, no longer blocked by the trees. Myoshi fought for his balance, regained it, and took a quick step forward, then another. It was easier once he was moving, and he concentrated on the stone at his feet.

Myoshi did not want to think about the side of the mountain, or the lava fields, obscured by the forest below. He dislodged a tiny avalanche of dust and stone and stopped, waiting for his heart to grow still.

Myoshi thought of Cherry blossoms. His grandfather had often mentioned them, as had his father. One of the other pilots, younger even than Myoshi's grandfather, had written a poem that Myoshi loved. The haiku, so simple, so profound, and complete in that simplicity.

"If only we might fall
Like Cherry blossoms in the spring
So pure and radiant."

Myoshi contemplated the mountain. The distance to the base. The remaining climb. There were no cherry trees on the mountain, and somehow, he was glad. He didn't want to think about the ground littered with their petals. He didn't want to walk over so many great souls.

As the sun warmed his back and the wind chilled his face, Myoshi climbed.

The sun dropped fast beyond the horizon and Myoshi leaned in close, trying to catch enough of the dying light to finish the letter. It was the last of them. Eight, carefully penned slices of life; all that remained of Myoshi's grandfather. When he had read the last familiar word, he carefully folded the paper, painstakingly matching the folds and tying the ribbon as it had been reverently. Myoshi tucked the bundle under his shirt, close to his heart.

Next, he pulled free a single sheet of blank paper, and his pen. It was getting more difficult to see, but it would not matter. There would be no red glaring characters to mar this piece. Nothing to correct. No figures, only a promise. A single promise.

Myoshi wrote slowly as his mind wandered, for once allowing the words to be absolutely his own. He didn't watch the paper. It was getting too dark for that. He had to depend on his instincts and luck. He knew his teachers would not approve, but for once, he was beyond that as well. He was not writing a lesson. He was writing a history. He was encapsulating his life.

"Since I was very young," he began, "sitting at your knee, my father, and listening to your stories of grandfather, I have loved the cherry blossom. I read the haiku, and in my dreams, the blossoms grew to men. In the words of those who died gloriously, taking the paths of falling stars to the hearts of their enemies, I found dreams. As I failed in my life, they gave me hope."

The mountain faded around him as shadows lengthened. The moon had yet to rise, but only the last rose-tinted hints of the sun licked the skyline. Stars glittered like diamonds. Like petals. So many petals.

Myoshi continued to write, but his mind closed out the reality of mountain and paper, the pen slid silently, marking the trail of his thoughts, but not carefully. Not with the painstakingly rigid strokes of the school, now empty and silent, like the mountain. Not with the measured rhythm of his grandfather's even script. With Myoshi's heart. He penned each character as it felt, and he paid no more attention to it than he did to the breeze. He mouthed his grandfather's words and shivered.

"The air was cold on deck. We were allowed only minimal equipment. Nothing, really, to prepare for the weather. If we grew ill, we would find our release. If we were cold, we had but to think of the flame, and the glory to come. Each brow was covered with a single strip of cloth, white, with the rising son emblazoned.

"I remember last night. I went, alone, to the flight deck. The Oka—cherry blossom—stood before me, silent and empty. I tried to picture the skies, the enemy, the waves. I saw a coffin. I saw an end and a beginning, etched in flame. My heartbeat quickened, fanned like a flame by the wind as it whipped across that dark, empty deck. I stood there a very long time and when I returned to my bed, I could not sleep. Instead, I turned to the pen, and the paper, wanting you to share the moment.

"Waves lapped gently at the sides of the ship, rocking us like babes in the arms of our mothers. It is the last night we will spend in the arms of any mother, cradled by the earth. I want to sleep and let it slip away. I want to awaken to that last day as I had so many others. I know I will not. I cannot sleep.

"Now the sun is rising, and my handshakes as I hold the pen, my heart races. The others have tossed and turned all around me. None found the peace of deep sleep, and those who did sleep are round-eyed with visions and final dreams.

"I will close this now, so that I may seal it and put it in the Commander's hand. He will see that you get this letter, and the others. Tonight, I die, but part of me lives on. I have a son, and I am blessed.

"I remember the words of Admiral Ohnishi, by whose grace I have this chance to die so well.

'In blossom today, then scattered,
Life is so like a delicate flower.
How can one expect the fragrance
To last forever?'

"May I honor you. May I honor our Emperor. May the gods embrace me.

"Farewell."

Myoshi's pen did not stop scratching at the paper as his grandfather's words ended. He could feel the deck swaying beneath his feet. He wrote on until the paper was filled, and turned, and filled on the opposite side as well before he set it aside, unsigned. Only the weight of the pen held the paper in place against the stone, and the edges flapped in the breeze, like the wings of a great moth reaching into the moonlight.

The takeoff was rougher than usual. The waves had risen higher, and the deck slanted one way, then the other, great sweeping rolls that skewed the skyline and stole one's balance. Myoshi blinked, the strobe effect easing his nausea. A thousand butterflies had risen to flight in his breast, and his hands shook like those of an old man.

All around him the roar of engines. Each coughing to life, sputtering drowsily, then roaring with barely contained life. Life. That is what pulsed through Myoshi's veins, pounding so loudly he thought of the surf, and the ocean. The air was cool, but he felt a fiery heat building, felt the glorious binding of man to machine to air as they launched.

The air whipped against his face, and he felt the exhilaration, the pure joy of release as the deck/earth/world slipped away. His breath was stolen and though he fought against that breathlessness, he could not quite force the words past his lips.

Myoshi's body tumbled, falling freely from the ledge of stone, arcing out from the stone and whirling, head over feet over head again and crashing through the upper branches of the ocean of trees, swallowed whole by the ancient, silent forest.

Far above, the clouds opened for one second, and the silhouette of a single plane was outlined—then gone.

A group of teenage boys, on a hike, came across bones, picked clean and whitened by the sunlight, slipping through the trees. They turned in horror, ready to bolt, but one stopped.

A packet of papers, mildewed and rotting, lay to one side. It was bound by a single ribbon of silk. Forcing his eyes from the bones, the boy reached out and grabbed the packet.

They ran. It wasn't until much later that the papers were carefully opened. Most were very old, but a single page of newer script was tied atop the pile. On it, this verse.

"White blossom, broken
stained petal, crimson, gliding
Lost in the moonlight"

Interred

The moon was bright enough to read by, and Allan did just that. He sat in the middle of a semi-circular grouping of headstones. Tree branches blocked some of the moonlight, but for the most part he inhabited a chiaroscuro world, shades of white and black. He read aloud from a newspaper article, turning first to face one of the headstones, and then to the next.

"Convicted murderer Jonathan Richter has died in prison. Having murdered his wife, and three of his four children in 2002, he passed in his sleep of sudden heart failure. Prior to his conviction, Richter and his late wife, Audrey, purchased a family plot at Shady Grove Cemetery in Lavender, California. Despite protests from several local church groups, and his son Allan, the sole survivor of his murderous rampage, Richter is scheduled to be interred in the family plot. Protests are expected, but officials say there is no legal precedent to prevent it."

Allan laid the paper in his lap. He stared at his mother's grave-stone, then turned to those of each of his siblings. No one commented.

"Well," he said. "Isn't this some shit. I mean…sure, he paid for the plots. Everyone is dead, excluding me, of course, but what the actual fuck?"

The silence didn't break. It hung heavy in the air, mingling with the early morning mist. Allan folded the paper so that the article faced front. He leaned it against his mother's grave and rose.

He was tall, six-foot-three in black Doc Martens. When his father went to prison, Allan had been a gangly teenager. Now he was a slightly less gangly adult with long dark hair, a closet full of jeans and band shirts, and a job peddling CBD oil and occult paraphernalia in a small shop downtown. On the side he read tea leaves, Tarot Cards, and palms. An entire wall of his apartment was lined with every esoteric resource he could get his hands on. His computer setup was impressive, if eclectic, a tower case housing a very fast Linux server and a terminal with a thirty-two-inch curved monitor. It looked like a gaming system, but Allan didn't play. Not on the Internet, and not in life. He'd left the games on the shelf in his bedroom the day they shipped him off to social services.

He spent a lot of time in the cemetery. He'd planned a thousand punishments for his father while daydreaming by his mother's grave. He'd tried spells and incantations. He'd buried daggers in voodoo dolls, carved symbols into every imaginable substance, attempted to summon demons and angels, and so far, all he'd managed was to watch his father, already interred in the walls of a maximum-security prison, die of natural causes.

What a crock of shit.

Allan was alive, and exactly one of his close family members had died of natural causes. The wrong one.

He'd brought more than the newspaper with him. His backpack was stuffed with books, papers, bottles, and vials. He had scribbled notes on old napkins, spiral notebooks, and printouts from obscure websites with his own thoughts and changes sketched into the margins.

Shady Grove, once you drove in past the ornate wrought iron gates and the cheaper, brand-new plots, stretched into a forest near its rear border. Very old graves could be found, half-crumbled among the trees. Families who'd come out in the gold rush, Spanish immigrants older than the nation. It was a like a history book written in bone and stone.

Jonathan Richter had wanted something special. Just inside the borders of the thicker forest, younger trees had begun to grow. Much of that space was already spoken for, but he'd found this spot, circled by young oaks, and laid out a sizeable amount of cash to secure the small clearing for his family. Allan's father had been a successful investment counselor and money wasn't really an object. The cemetery also had a checkered past, and the truly rich of San Valencez and Lavender, California avoided it. The Richter family had laid claim to their small portion of the place nearly twenty years in the past. The oaks had grown tall and strong, and they ringed the plot, leaving one wider opening to serve as an entry. A dirt path led out to the main trail through the cemetery.

Seated inside, Allan felt closed off from the world. He visited often, sometimes reading stories aloud by the graves of his siblings or telling his mother's spirit about his days and weeks, the people he met and the things he hoped to do. It had become a special place for him, almost sacred. When he'd begun to feel the draw of the occult and mystical, he'd studied the trees first. Then the lore of spirits and ghosts.

There was a particular oak tree, nearest to his mother's grave, that he loved to lean on. The roots had provided a sort of natural seat, and if asked, he'd have sworn that over the years, that seat had refined itself, shifting to fit the contours of his body.

As he studied, he added bits and pieces of the knowledge to the grove. Slips of paper with the proper symbols, and a drop of blood buried just so. Witch jars all around the perimeter. He'd performed rituals, left hidden objects among the roots of the trees to be absorbed and swallowed over time until they were all part of a single web of—something. He sensed it when he was there. He never took anyone with him. He didn't want to appear foolish or have his quiet place invaded. He didn't want the trees to reject him.

Now all of that was in danger. There was one large spot left near the rear of the grove where they would dig his father's grave. It was directly beside his mother's plot. The tree where he liked to sit was a couple of yards back but centered between the two spaces. The trees could not be too close. They were already sending roots in toward the graves and digging through those was going to be a chore. It was undoubtedly why the groundskeepers had chosen oaks.

Oaks grow their roots in balls. They don't snake out like those of other trees. A bad storm, where the ground gets too damp, can blow one over, a huge mess of roots and soil clinging to the base after it topples. This had made it possible for them to be reasonably close to the graves. There was little threat of them unearthing something unpleasant as they grew, and they offered shade and seclusion. In the middle of the day the sun shone directly into the clearing, as it did now, with the full moon rising high above.

Allan pulled several vials from his pack and began to walk back and forth across the clearing. As he did, he hummed to himself. Each time he reached the perimeter he tossed a bit of the contents of one vial, or the other, and spoke a single word. The words were not in any single language, as the pattern was not from any existing sigil or grimoire. The design was his own. He'd pulled bits and pieces where they seemed to fit, joined cultures and belief systems. All of the charms and wards he'd already placed were a part of the overall design. Allan believed that the purpose of ritual, and spells, was simply focus. No single system was better than another if the practitioner believed in the outcome, or the impossibility of one. He'd made this his own, and though the few "experts" he'd consulted had warned him that he was making a serious error, it felt right. One old fortune teller had made the sign of the evil eye when he'd explained what he was doing. He was pretty sure the woman had hissed at him.

As he crossed back and forth, he felt a tickle, and then a crackle of energy. When his boots touched the ground, it strengthened. He ignored it, concentrating on the scripted words, blanking everything else from his mind. He had a vision. Literally. It had come to him over many nights of deep sleep and been recorded in a small mountain of journals. More than once he'd questioned the simplicity of it all, the way it had simply come to him, but it didn't matter. Overlaying every concern, doubt or warning screamed by voices in the back of his head was the certainty that if he saw it through, his father would never be buried in the family plot, and that was more than enough.

You must stop.

The words slipped between his thoughts, but he pushed them

away. He recognized the voice of a professor of anthropology he had consulted.

You do not know what you are dealing with.

Another familiar voice, this time from the old fortune teller who had hissed at him.

It will be the end of you. Nothing comes without a price.

Allan did not care about the price. He cared about his family. He cared about the sanctity of the grove. He cared that his mother's spirit would not spend eternity beside her murderer. He was happy to offer his life, since he didn't really have one, and all that mattered was the circle, and the trees. A shifting energy rippled beneath the Earth, lifting him and settling him carefully back into his pattern. It didn't matter what the voices said. He was locked in. The moon hung high and bright, and he felt his mother, and his sisters, calling to him. Reaching out to join their voices with his from beyond death.

He smiled. His sisters, Ada, Melanie, and Cynthia had all been younger. It was hard to grasp it now, them never growing older and his life moving on. He'd hoped to terrorize their dates for years and proms to come.

A sudden jolt nearly caused him to falter. Something warm had slapped lightly against his left calf. A few moments later he felt a similar sensation on the right. There was tension, and resistance. It felt as if the air had thickened. Where the energy touched him, warmth spread out and up. A third touch, and a fourth attached to his hips, a fifth and sixth to his shoulders. He continued to walk, and as he did, slender ropes of light followed, bringing the pattern to life and glowing. He had one final crossing of the grove to complete his ritual. When he was done, he flowed past the perimeter and turned, holding his hands up in wonder as filaments of light, parting with brilliant sparkles, released him.

"That," he said to no one in particular, "was fucking cool…"

Between the trees he saw the pattern from his journal. Lines of light were joined, like a giant illuminated dreamcatcher. Then, drifting like a fallen leaf, the pattern settled onto the ground, blinked, and was absorbed. Allan stood very still.

"Sacrifice," a voice said. Nothing more.

And suddenly it was over. He stood very alone in the small patch of trees. The lights were gone, and the moon had slipped beyond the tops of the trees, no longer lighting the graves. Allan gathered his things, touched each gravestone in turn as he whispered goodbyes, and headed back through the main body of the cemetery toward his car. The funeral was set for the next day. He had no intention of attending, but he wanted to be awake, and aware. He wanted to be ready, though he had no idea for what.

There were no friends or family at Jonathan Richter's funeral. Despite that, the minister on site was in full regalia, and there were cameras everywhere. There was also a large gathering of locals, come to see the infamous killer put away forever. There was a small contingent of protesters, hand-painted signs held high. "Let the family R.I.P." "Dignity for the Family," and others. They were passive, but very present, vying with the protective detail, the minister, and the plain wooden coffin for time in front of the TV cameras. Everyone said they were outraged, but none of them would care beyond the end of the ceremony. It wasn't their family. It was just their moment of fame.

Crews had come in overnight to dig and prepare the grave. Neat corners, exactly the right depth, and the coffin arranged above, ready to be lowered slowly and dramatically for the entertainment of a crowd with no skin in the game, but an appetite for the dramatic.

A couple of screeches of feedback from the microphone, a fake-humble foot-shuffling apology from the minister, and it was underway. He spoke of the victim's long life before his crime. In grave tones he described the lives of the three daughters, cut off in their prime. He told the crowd of Audrey's community service, and her devotion to her children. He mentioned Allan in passing, that he'd never lived up to the potential he'd shown, how he'd dropped out of college. No one who heard him listened or cared. They were there for the finale.

The Eulogy ended, and everyone stepped back. The funeral had been paid for at the same time as the plot, so there was a full crew on hand, dark suits, and solemn expressions, ready to lower the body into the earth. The process began, and the coffin dropped a slow inch at a time toward the ground. As it slipped beneath the surface, very suddenly, it stopped. There was a moment's confusion, and then the coffin was raised once more. The crew gathered around the grave. The crowd angled for position to see what was wrong, but there was no way to get a good view.

One of the men by the grave rose and turned. He waved to the funeral director, who hurried over, listened for a moment, frowned, and nodded. He walked quickly away from the grove, pulling his phone from his pocket, and dialing as he went.

About ten minutes later a work truck trundled down the narrow lane to the gravesite. Two men got out. After climbing out they each lifted something from the bed of the truck. One had grabbed an axe, and the other a chainsaw. As the startled gathering parted to let them through, the second man yanked on the short pull-rope and brought the saw to life. Other men shifted the coffin off center to make room for them to access the grave. Pulling a set of safety goggles down over his eyes, the man with the chainsaw knelt beside the hole and set to work. A spray of wood chips and sawdust rose, flying in all directions and moving the crowd back yet further.

Allan was carrying a cup of steaming hot coffee to his chair in the living room when it hit. He'd been watching the funeral live on a local news station. The preacher had been talking about Allan's family as if he'd known them, but Allan had no idea who he was. The funeral parlor had made the arrangements. They'd sent him a sympathy card, and an invitation. Included in the package was the schedule. There were no questions about what his wishes might be. Despite being the only heir, the plot and the burial arrangements had been bought and paid for before he was out of junior high school.

He was just turning into the living room, catching the odd roar of a chainsaw from the television, when his right calf simply gave out, and he stumbled forward, screaming. The coffee splashed up and out of the cup, soaking his shirt and the front of his pants in a scalding wave, but he barely noticed. He crashed into his chair, catching himself on the nearest arm.

Searing pain drove into his leg, and it was all he could do to bite back another scream. From where he'd fallen, he could see the TV screen clearly. Tears blinded him but he managed to raise his left arm and wipe them away with his sleeve. Someone was talking, but he couldn't hear them over the grinding screech of the chainsaw.

The pain stopped suddenly, and he gasped. He rose on his good leg, turned, and dropped into the chair, ignoring the burns from the coffee. He'd barely hit the cushions when his right arm jerked like it was caught in huge hands. Pain drove into him once again, and this time his scream was more of a howl, winding up and up and falling away in waves. He tried to pull free, but before he could react his left arm was also gripped, held, and pulled. He gritted his teeth and concentrated. The energy that had bound him to the grove the night before was yanking him in all directions, and each point where he felt its touch white-hot pain drove in through his nerve endings, biting deep. Slowly, but inexorably, his limbs were drawn apart. He rested precariously on the chair, legs now spread painfully, and arms dragged to either side.

"No!" he screamed. He drew every bit of his remaining strength, every synapse of conscious thought, to that moment, and pulled back. He felt the bindings falter and pulled harder. His arms trembled and his back arched. Once again, he opened his mouth and screamed. "No!"

There was a pounding on his apartment door, there was nothing he could do to answer, or stop whoever might come in. Allan pulled again and something snapped. He dropped into the chair again and there was an audible crack as whatever force he'd opposed released him.

He fell back, sobbing, and turned once more to the TV.

A man stood in the center of the now partially cleared grave, the chainsaw roaring. It was impossible. Long, thick roots had formed a solid barrier at the top of the grave. They had to have come from the oaks, but they had not been there at the start of the funeral. When the coffin was readied to be lowered in, there had been nothing but an open hole. What he'd cut away had filled the entirety of the opening. He was barely halfway finished clearing it. The saw was powerful, but the roots seemed to resist, pressing back against him and refusing to part.

People had gathered closer, peering in over the edge. The funeral director and his men tried to keep them back, but there were too many, and it was too strange. The saw dipped and roared again and there was a horrible screech; the chain bound and slowed. The worker gunned it, gripping the trigger as tightly as he could and, just for a second, it spun free. Then, with metallic twang, the chain parted. It swung back up and into his face before he could move. His arms jerked, but the saw was stuck. The roots slammed back across the opening as if he'd never touched them, erupting from the soil on the sides of the grave as if they'd been launched.

Before he could utter a sound, he'd been pierced, the roots driving through him, joining with the torn bits on the far side. Within seconds the saw was completely obscured, and nothing of the man remained but his head. The neck was mostly severed, and blood leaked and spattered across the dirt-encrusted roots.

The crowd backed away in shock then, like a wave of dark suits and inappropriate gowns, turned and stumbled out of the clearing, screaming. A few brave souls, mostly those too far back to really know what had happened, were still catching it all on video. The preacher, getting a clear view of the ruined mass of flesh in the grave, turned as if to say something, took a step, and fainted.

Allan felt a sudden release. Whatever had bound him to the pattern and the spell parted, and he sat, drained and shivering, sweat drenching his shirt and trickling down the back of his neck. He stared at the TV. The image that remained, broadcast from a stationary camera that had continued to run when its operator fled, was that of a man's head, lolling to one side, eyes wide in shock. Beneath and around him, roots twined and snaked. Impossible roots.

Allan could only see one of the man's eyes. The angle the head was cocked at aimed its gaze down toward the ground.

Allan flipped the switch on the remote and turned the TV off. He took a deep breath and rose on shaky legs. He needed a shower, and a beer. He was certain that grave would not be reopened, except maybe to extract what was left of the worker. He knew he should feel guilty about that, but all he felt was relief, as if a huge weight had been lifted. He'd been told that the funeral was not his responsibility. He considered this an extension of that.

As he grabbed clean clothes and headed for the bathroom, he wondered if it was too soon to call the funeral home. He had no intention of helping them figure out what to do with the old man's body, but he was going to take great satisfaction in reminding them that it was all paid for, and that it was not his problem.

Then it would finally be time to get on with his life. When things died down, he'd visit the graves, the ones that mattered, and say his farewells. He would take a book to read to his sisters and leave it by their graves. He would leave chocolate and wine for his mother, sharing a glass and telling one of her favorite stories. He had protected them, and they would understand.

There was a big world out there. He had what was left of his father's money. Time for the sole survivor to move on. He thought, wherever he went, he would do his best to avoid oaks.

Etched Deep

Ethan sat back in his rocker and propped one booted foot on the porch rail. He watched the sunset dribble down behind the trees. Trails of color streaked the clouds. The steady creak of the rocker emphasized the silence. Now and then he heard one of the animals shuffle in the barn.

The shotgun lay across his knees, barrel angled out over the yard toward the tree line and the butt nestled close into his waist. He reached down to the cooler at his side, lifted the rusty metal lid, and fished out a bottle of beer. It was cold. Ice water dripped onto his hand and his pants as he lifted it and twisted off the cap.

A loud, muffled thump sounded inside the house. Ethan paused, cocked his head to the side, and listened, but the sound wasn't repeated. He took a pull off his beer. A few feet to his right Jake sprawled in a mass of wrinkles and fur. The dog watched Ethan sleepily. Ethan leaned back, closed his eyes, and let the cool evening breeze brush him back through the years.

He couldn't remember a time when he hadn't owned a dog. His father gave him a puppy for his second birthday. Casey, they'd called her. Ethan's sharpest memories of that dog began with the warm, comfortable scent of her fur and the deep, trusting gleam in her eyes.

There were other memories as well. He remembered the scent of the forest in the early morning when the dew still dusted the grass and the shrubbery that lined the trails. He remembered the sour smell of oiled gun metal and the acrid tang of powder. He remembered Casey, baying and thrashing through the trees, his father's heavy footsteps and slow, careful voice.

Ethan's father lived and died in a cut and dried, black and white world of absolutes. There were no gray areas. There were no shades or demilitarized zones. A thing was what it was, a man did what he had to, and a boy listened to his father.

Casey grew faster than Ethan, and by the time he was six, she had given them three litters of fine dogs. Each grew to either hunt at their mother's side, or to be sold in the town and hunt with another man's family. It was what they were born to, and she dropped them like clockwork. She carried the small, furry bodies into the crates Ethan's father prepared for her, lined with hay and scraps of cloth. She bathed them until they were glossy and when they were hungry, she rolled onto her side and offered herself without question. When there were no puppies, she slept with Ethan, and his father allowed it.

When Ethan was twelve, Casey was getting a little long in the tooth. She hadn't had a litter of puppies in over a year, but then she got pregnant. Ethan worried over her, fussed with the crates himself, and waited. The dog grew nervous and restless, but they chalked it up to the coming litter. The days came, and went, and then the final litter was born.

Another loud thump drew Ethan from his daydream. He glanced at the house. No one appeared in the doorway. He heard muffled voices, but they died away. There was a third thump, and someone cried out sharply. He thought he heard a low wail after that, but the breeze kicked up and the sound was lost. He set the empty beer bottle on the porch floor carefully and extracted a second icy, dripping bottle.

Casey carried that last litter, only three pups, into the crate, just like she'd done all the times before. She washed their tiny heads until their fur shone bright and she nuzzled them close to her when they whined. She fed them and watched over them, and they grew, even the sickly, smaller one that Ethan had resigned himself to losing. They grew, and as they did their hunger followed suit. Their teeth sprouted white and sharp, and they grew insistent when it came time to eat.

Ethan had seen Casey wean her whelps again and again, nipping them and driving them away, rising to run off in a shiver of loose skin and swollen teats, nudging them toward the bowls of milk-soaked food his father provided. She had always been patient and careful. This time she snapped. One of the pups lingered too long when she growled at it, and her jaws closed over its tiny head in an instant. One flashing moment of blood and sound, and it was over.

Ethan remembered that moment with a clarity he'd seldom experienced. He still saw Casey, whining, nudging the dead puppy with the tip of her nose as if in apology, wanting it to stand and come to her, to feed and grow strong. Her eyes had been so full of misery and emotion–so human–that Ethan wanted to scream every time the memory surfaced.

His father took the other two puppies away after that. They were ready to eat solid food, and he kept them clear of Casey until they were old enough to take care of themselves. She never went after them again, but something inside her had snapped.

Two weeks later, Ethan's younger sister, Jenny, walked too close to Casey's tail. The dog turned like brown lightning. Her eyes were crazed with mad anger, and she snapped. She only caught the material of Jenny's skirt; the girl was also quick, but it was enough. Ethan's father beat Casey near to death that day, and everything in Ethan's life shifted. Sometimes you grow up slowly and learn over years of trial and error. Sometimes it's a snapshot in time, one moment a boy was young and the next as old as the hills.

A wail rose from the house and Ethan half turned in his seat. He saw Benjamin, his eldest, press his nose to the inside of the screen door, but the boy didn't come out. He watched his father through that screen, followed the arc of the beer bottle as it was tipped back again, and then the boy disappeared. The sound of someone crying softly joined the eerie voice of the breeze.

Ethan drifted back one last time. Ethan always hunted with his father. They gathered the dogs, strode slowly off into the woods that lined their pasture, and walked together in silence. They hunted for food, and they shared the hunt for companionship. It was the strongest bond the two forged over many years, but the night after Casey snapped at Jenny, Ethan's father went alone.

His father had spent extra care on his shotgun that night. The barrel was cleaned and oiled, the stock polished. Each load was pulled from the case and examined before disappearing into the many pockets of the old hunting vest Ethan knew so well. He knew the scent of that vest from sitting on his father's lap. He knew the places it had been torn and mended. He knew where things had been spilled on it, and the exact point on the collar where a drop of blood from his own first kill had soaked in and stained the material a dark brown.

Ethan had carried his own gun to the porch that evening, but his father had just shaken his head.

"Not tonight, son," he'd said.

No explanations were ever offered or expected. As the sun set, his father headed off toward the woods. Ethan sat on the porch, watching. Casey trotted along at his father's heels, and this was odd. She was old and she rarely accompanied them. When she did, it was always with some of the others–faster, younger dogs that could run an animal down or tree it. Casey had grown slower and generally kept close to home. Ethan watched until both man and dog were out of sight.

He remembered the sunset glinting off the oiled barrel of his father's gun. He remembered the way that same light shimmered off Casey's fur. Hours later, when all hint of the sun had left the sky and the night breezes set tree branches dancing in the shadows, his father returned. Alone.

Ethan remembered that lined face, the vacant stare that presented itself in the pale light of that long-ago moon. His father walked up and sat on the porch. He didn't say anything at first. Ethan wanted to scan the trees. He wanted to ask about the dog, but something hung in the air that clotted in his throat. He kept his silence and eventually, his father spoke.

"Sometimes things change. There are things inside that guide us and no matter how hard we work to keep them whole and safe–sometimes they break. They snap like dry twigs and even if you're very quiet about it, people will hear that sound. Things you try to avoid come back to stare at you and to see what happened.

"Casey was old, son." His father spun to him then and held

his gaze. "She was a good dog, but that last batch of puppies was too much. She was broken inside and there's nothing you can do to mend such a break. She killed that puppy–that was the start. She would have killed your sister if she hadn't missed–or you–or taken a chunk out of my leg. She couldn't help it–the thing that kept her steady was gone. The broken thing inside poked and prodded at her until she snapped, and it would have done it again."

Ethan remembered the burn of tears in his eyes. He remembered the cold clutch of invisible fingers around his heart, and the way his breath caught in his chest and couldn't get free. He said nothing. His father turned away and fell silent, staring out over the distant trees. His gun rested beside him, barrel leaned on the porch rail. Ethan remembered it as a giant finger, pointing somewhere he'd never go again. He thought of Casey's warm fur and her huge, soulful eyes. He'd seen the lines in his father's face differently for the first time, recognized them for what they were. Pain had etched those lines, deep pain held inside for too long. It was a lesson, the sort left unspoken, yet never forgotten.

The screen door creaked, and Ethan drained his beer, half-turning toward the sound. Rebecca pushed the door open just far enough to slip out and let it close behind her. She stood, staring at the interlocking boards of the porch floor. After a moment of silence, she spoke.

"Jimmy's arm is hurt. He…"

Ethan held up a hand, and she fell silent. He lifted the lid of the cooler, drew out two more bottles, opened the first, and offered it to her. She stepped forward slowly, as if dazed, and took the bottle from his hand. He opened the second bottle and took a long pull. He still heard the quiet sobbing from inside and he felt the press of Benjamin's face to the screen, though he didn't turn to look.

"Beautiful night," he said.

Rebecca turned and stared at the blood red drip of the sun as it melted beyond the trees. She nodded and sipped her beer. It was warm, but she trembled. Ethan reached out and touched her arm, remembering other nights–other times. She was still beautiful. He watched the dying daylight play over the dulled highlights of her hair. She still had the old defiance in her stance, the spark that had won his heart, but now it was cockeyed. She stood just a little off balance, as though waiting for some unseen thing she kept in the periphery of her sight to strike.

They drank in silence. When the bottles were empty, Ethan rose. He turned to her, gave her a quick hug, and leaned in close.

"Walk with me?" he said. Not really a question.

She nodded again, setting her still half-full beer bottle on the porch rail. Ethan slid his arm around her shoulders, and they stepped off the porch together. He kept the barrel of the shotgun angled down and away, the weight comfortable in his hand.

Benjamin stepped onto the porch. He held the screen half open.

"Papa?" he said softly.

Ethan stopped and turned.

"You want me to come?"

Ethan shook his head. "Not tonight, son," he said.

Benjamin stood on the porch and watched them go. He saw the sunset glinting off the oiled barrel of his father's gun. He remembered the way that same light sometimes shimmered off his mother's hair. He watched until they were out of sight, then watched a bit longer, then turned back to soothe his brother's tears.

His Cold, Gourd Heart

In the kitchen, steam rose from a pot of water on the old electric stove and tiny bubbles whirled and bounced off the surfaces of several glass bottles. Cleansing. Nearby, steamed and scrubbed sanitary, a row of nipples dried in the fading evening sunlight. On the burner behind the bottles, a smaller pot simmered, releasing the scent and life from gathered rose petals, herbs, and spices, permeating the air with the sweet, cloying aroma of potpourri.

Lace-edged doilies dangled from the handles of kitchen cabinets, and in the window, a single yellow lily hung limply over the edge of a glass half-full of water. The last red and gold ray of sunlight winked past the window and refracted through the water, clipping the center of the stem neatly. A black, bulbous spider slid down the side of the window on a thread of silk, stopped short of the rim of the glass, and swung deftly to the wood frame. Scuttling upward, she dropped again, weaving her web.

Down the hall, past a large living room and through another short hall, lights played in the growing gloom. They were multicolored, blinking and dancing. Behind it all, candle flames flickered. A soft voice chanted into the silence and joined the breath behind the words with the scented smoke of four candles. Clarice's shadow slipped past the doorway with rhythmic precision; her voice rose and fell as she approached, and receded from, the door.

The back room, smaller than the others that branched off of both halls, was adorned with more strings of festive holiday lights, the sort that chase one another in circles, blinking so quickly the sensation of waves of color is unmistakable. Bond had called them chasing lights, but Bond was lost, had been since, well, since he was last *found* of course. For Clarice, the lights were dancers.

In the center of the room stood an odd structure of branches and vines, twigs and leaves, ribbons, blankets and more. The center resembled a bird's nest, but at each corner stouter branches stood sentinel, supporting the whole like a rounded cradle.

At the tip of one of the four branch supports, a glittering metal woman rested, like the angel atop a Christmas tree. Her gown was hollow, meant to diffuse candlelight through the many moons and stars cut into the sweeping folds. The gown was creased four times. A long wizard's hat rested on her head, cocked back over one shoulder as if caught in some cosmic wind. In her left hand, she held a wand. In her right, she dangled a mobile of stars, moons, and silver-plated symbols.

Clarice circled it all, her aspect mirroring that of the metal woman. Clarice's hair was dark, tied back and looped through the scarf so that it ran between her shoulders. Her ice-blue eyes glittered in the dim light, reflecting the dancing Christmas tree bulbs and the wavering of the candles. Her skirt, long and dark, was pleated and creased knife-edge sharp with starch and steam. Droplets of her sweat had dripped into the fabric each time she ironed the creases. The Starch spread out to flatten the geometric planes between pleats. The hem formed a perfect square about her dancing, slippered feet.

When Clarice turned just so, and you stood perfectly still in the proper corner of the room, she was the image of the metal woman with the wand, though Clarice held no dangling mobile, and the wand woman could not sing.

In the cradle, a small bundle rested. It lay flat on a spine formed of a particularly thorny rose vine; ribs wound and woven of saplings bowed to the center and curled inward to a dried gourd heart. Each limb was carefully bound to the others, arms and legs, knees and elbows, and the head, once turnip purple and white, now carved and dried, then carved some more to soften its rounded cheeks and bring out the peach-pit brown of its eyes. Above those eyes, the wand woman's stars, moon, and symbols spun lazily, set into motion by the rush of air from Clarice's passing, and the rhythmic thrum of her feet as they pounded intricate backbeats across the floor.

Clarice spun to a breathless halt and cocked her head to one side. She drew forth a long, glittering pair of scissors from the depths of her gown and gripped the dark ends of her hair. She worked her fingers, rolling and tugging, choosing her moment, and snipped. The rolled hair fanned out in her grip, and she bent over the cradle.

Her fingers were nimble and supple, trained by a thousand stitches in a thousand shirts, the seams of myriad draperies that now caught sun and moon and stars in windows far away. She had no needle but wet the tips of her rolled hair thread with her lips. She closed her eyes and savored the taste as she drew each strand forth, still rolled, to draw it in, and out, and in again, marking the boundaries of the tiny chest. Each deft flick of her wrist added form.

Clarice stepped back and admired her work. A soft smile crept down her lip and curled at the end. She stepped forward, and then again, more quickly, until she was skipping around the tiny bed of dreams. She did not stop until she'd circled thrice. Then she held a hand to her lips, the heel to her chin and the fingers pointed toward the tiny, hollow heart. She breathed and closed her eyes. Clarice mouthed words so soft they could not be heard, yet powerful enough to vibrate over her tongue and shiver through her cheeks. She did not open her eyes but saw the breath like stardust floating away from her fingers and down, whirling through the tiny mouth and snaking deep to the cold gourd heart.

Then she turned and left the room, her four-cornered skirt wheeling to one side, and then back around her ankles and her passing setting the tiny arcane trinkets dangling from the wand woman's stick to spinning and dancing, catching colors as they blinked on and off and reflecting them back between the rhythm of the chasing lights.

The bottles, now scrubbed and cleaned, stood like hollow sentinels on the cabinet, the nipples aimed skyward and capped with plastic to keep the germs out. A teapot had replaced the pot of boiling water, and it whistled in melancholy discord to the bell tones of the wind chimes on the porch.

Clarice bustled slowly about the kitchen, dropping cubes of sugar into a China cup, measuring tea into the diffuser, spreading fresh, half molten butter onto a warm sesame muffin with the flat, shining blade of a polished silver butter knife.

The sun had disappeared over the horizon and the moon bathed the yard beyond the windows in brilliant light. The flower gardens were a chiaroscuro wash of vines and blossoms, leaves and shrubs. On the table, in contrast, a vase overflowed with lush color and green accents.

She had stopped chanting, but she hummed softly as she worked. Every few moments, she glanced over her shoulder at the doorway. The candlelight still danced, but the glittering, colored lights had been extinguished. The breeze from open windows in the hall and in the kitchen flicked the leaves and twigs beneath the cradle, and the dangling charms of the wand woman's mobile into motion. Their shadows chased one another across the far wall.

Clarice sat at the table and ate her muffin, dipping bite-sized pieces into the hot pungent tea and letting the soggy bits slide warmly down her throat. She kept her head cocked, as though listening for something, but the only sound was the soft whisper of the breeze, the chimes, and the light clink of the spoon on her China cup. Just for an instant, a frown flickered across her soft features. She rose, poured the crumbs from her plate into a small trashcan beside the stove and placed the dishes in the sink.

She grabbed one of the bottles, and turned it first one way, then another, watching the light play over the shiny surface. Clarice removed the nipple and crossed to the far side of the sink. A spice rack hung on the wall, small shaker-topped bottles held in place by dried, looping grape vines. They appeared to have grown in clusters straight out of the wall, and the sight of them always made her smile.

She took down three of the jars, and then opened a cabinet to the right and grabbed two small vials. Her fingers were quick and nimble, choosing first a bottle, then a vial, counting drops and carefully shaking powders in a rhythmic pattern that matched the tune she hummed. In the bottom of the bottle, greenish syrup formed from the mixed ingredients, and, after adding a single drop from a final vial, she held the bottle under the sink and ran in six ounces of tap water. She screwed on the nipple, added the plastic cap, and shook the mixture thoroughly, turning toward the back room once more with a bright smile.

The lights leaped back to life at the flick of a switch, and with night fallen beyond all the windows, they gleamed brightly in the semi-darkness of the room. The candles had burned lower, and Clarice was careful not to brush them with the four-cornered trailing hem of her gown. The creases remained sharp, and when Clarice glanced down and caught sight of them, her smile returned. She swiped four fingers of her free hand through the air and whispered a soft prayer to the number four, a symbol of completion.

She stood beside the cradle and tipped the bottle up. She brushed the nipple across the front of the turnip head with a giggle, letting some of the greenish liquid drip and run down what might have been tiny cheeks. Her soft laughter melted to words, teased and whispered through the branches as she lifted the bottle and drew it down the length of the spine, across the ribs, and shook its contents over the leaves. All the time she spoke and sang; her words were rhythmic and continuous, matching the pattern of lights shifting around her.

It took time. The tiny holes in the nipple dribbled and dripped the liquid, which was thicker than water and thinner than milk. Quick flicks of her wrist rained green droplets over the rose spine and the gourd heart. Her voice sent words and sounds to mix with the bottle-spatter in the cradle, born of branch and limb, and all the while she walked in slow circles, round and round.

She nodded to the four corners and glanced up, now and again, to where wand woman's mobile spun lazily in the opposite direction to her own steps. On the wall their twined shadows waltzed, one large and one small, four-square skirts, one dipping and swaying, one stationary and punched through with arcane symbols that wrote themselves on the walls in refracted light.

The door to the hall was behind her, and from that portal came a different sound. She heard boots on floorboards, but though she cocked her head and smiled again, she did not pause, nor did she glance in that direction. Time for everything and everything in time to her voice. She sprinkled, and she danced, and when the bottle was dry, she drew it close to her, hands pressed to the smooth glass as if in prayer and held it to her chest as she turned, flicked off the dancing chasing lights and stepped into the hall.

He sat at the table where she had eaten her muffin and drank her tea. He stared out through the window, searching between the waving branches and clinging vines that groped their way up the frame and outside of the glass. Potted plants that hung in braided vine macramé harnesses dangled spider-like and brushed leaf tipped fingers over his hair. He didn't notice that subtle touch, but when Clarice entered, he glanced up.

"Bond," she said. It wasn't a greeting, but instead a statement of fact, placing him in the grand scheme of the room as she might have placed the teakettle, or a teacup. He watched her enter and she had the sudden urge to reach out and brush back the wild tufts of his hair to free his eyes. Her fingers yearned for pruning shears, or a tiny fine-toothed rake.

"Clarice," he replied. He rose and stepped closer, and she wound around him, brushing very close; their scents mingled. She stopped behind him, placed her hands gently on his shoulders and leaned up on tiptoes to whisper through the soft strands of his hair.

"You must come see."

He shook his head gently and leaned back against her. He turned slowly and placed his hands on her hips. He saw the bottle then, clasped in one long slender hand.

"It's no good," he whispered. "You need to come out, into the light. You need to come and breathe the air and feel the earth beneath your feet."

"I'm growing," she laughed, "my feet touch the Earth, and

my breath brings him forth. You must come see."

He tried to shake his head again, but Clarice pressed her palms to the sides of his face. On one side the cool glass bottle rested against his skin. He felt a single drop of moisture drip down his neck toward his collar. His skin tingled, and he gasped. He held very still, and then slowly backed away. He didn't touch his neck, but he wanted to. It wasn't a burn, exactly, but at the same time his skin felt hot and very cold. Something tickled the lobe of his ear. Her eyes danced.

Clarice turned to the sink. She rinsed the bottle carefully and placed it in a rack on the counter to dry. She turned, and she watched him stand in the center of the small kitchen, watching her in return. He was more haggard than she remembered. His beard was a tangle of matted snarls. His eyes were sunken and dark, lined with the feather brush strokes of fatigue and worry. His hands trembled, and she knew what he wanted.

He wanted to touch his neck. She watched, fascinated, as the single sprout wound out through his skin and stroked itself against the lobe of his ear. He closed his eyes and before she could step forward and breathe the sprout to further life, it grew still, wilted, and fell away.

He opened his eyes, and she felt the draw. She saw the sun dancing in his wistful smile. She saw roads winding off beyond the curling ends of his lips and sensed the stories, just beyond her reach—other voices, otherwheres and otherwhens almost forgotten that they could share.

"You must come see," she whispered, and, as she stepped forward and reached out a hand, he took it and nodded in resignation.

They crossed the living room and the short hall, their steps out of sync and Bond like an anchor, dragging against walls and the floor, turning to peer into doorways and to click his tongue at dust bunny colonies burrowed in beneath the tables. Clarice flicked the switch, and the lights danced.

Small green stems had sprouted beneath the woven hair she'd left behind. Roots sprang from the sides of each tiny vine, digging in deep and forming a tighter web across the bowed framework of ribs. The dried gourd heart, so open to sight and sound short hours before, was obscured, and the crude knotted joints of knee and elbow grafted themselves into singularity with the creeping certainty of growth.

They stood, Bond drawing back and away, and Clarice leaning close, her eyes alight with wonder and her breath quickened at the sight of new life. She arched into the soft material of her blouse and knew a new fullness of breast. Soon green syrup drips would wet the cloth and she shivered in anticipation.

Her shiver slipped through her fingers to Bond, where it grew to a shudder. He shook as though caught in the grip of an icy wind, and his haunted eyes darkened further.

"You know it isn't real?" he asked. It was a hopeless, half-question, half plea.

"It grows," she ignored him eloquently.

He glanced up at the wand woman, really seeing her for the first time, and Clarice shifted her hip subtly, so the squared hem of her skirt brushed Bond's calf. There was a soft rustle from the cradle, and Bond backed away. He turned, flipped off the light switch and ran from the room.

In the dark, Clarice danced. There was enough light from the nearly dead candles and filtering down the hallway from the windows and Mother Moon to keep the shadows whirling. The cradle had begun to swing on its vine supports. Now and then, leaves brushed against one another, or crawling, sliding vines, like sinew, snapped and rustled.

When the candles had burned to the floor and guttered out, she stopped. The wand woman dangled her shiny baubles in anticipation. The breeze that had blown so strongly from the windows down the hall no longer teased Clarice's hair or shifted the wand woman's toys. A tiny sound rose from the cradle, and Clarice leaned close, cooing the arcane words of a soothing song.

Bond sat on the porch and rocked. His eyes were closed, and his heart hammered. The chair was formed of looping bent-wood slats and thick, ropy vines dried and coated in resin. The rockers curled up in front like snakes and back to tie in place as arm rests. He heard the voice of the wind, and he felt the soft touch of it on his skin, teasing through his long hair and beard like cool fingers.

Behind him, the door hung half off its hinges. It clapped against the wall disconsolately with each small gust of the breeze. He timed his rocking to coincide with the sound so it would be less jarring, and so it would not remind him of what he'd seen inside.

His mind strobed with images like an old projector, missing cogs but playing on gamely, stutter-stepping through frames and blinking cockeyed images in rapid-fire succession.

He saw the kitchen, dry as a bone and empty. He saw the hall and the furniture, coated in dust and overgrown with plants half-withered and groping through dust toward windows and doors—and sunlight. He saw her, wasp thin and gray, teetering steps and wispy breath, eyes rheumy and her lips dry and thin.

He saw the crude cradle, and what lay within. Bond bit his lip until blood trickled out at the corner and pinched his eyes until he squeezed out tears, but he did not open his eyes. He heard her footsteps in the hall, so light—so weightless—they scraped like sand across the once polished wooden floor. He heard her, and knew she drew near.

Clarice held the tiny, squirming bundle to her breast and smiled. Beneath the crack of the front door, she saw the first traces of dawn sliding in to greet her. She heard the creak of the rocker on the porch, and she knew that this time Bond was not quite lost. Not quite. Fern hair draped over her arm, and she felt the groping, propping brush of bruised bark lips on the skin of her breast.

"Bond," she called. "You must come see."

Clarice turned, then, and danced toward the kitchen, kicking up dust clouds in her wake like low-flying clouds.

"It's not real," Bond whispered, and opened his eyes.

Arching and purring, flexing ropy sinew, something flashed into his lap. He remembered the cat. Bond reached out instinctively and ran his fingers down its back. He brushed bark, and with a yelp of pain, he drew back his finger. A small sliver of wood protruded from his skin, and he glanced down.

Raisin eyes and corn-tassel whiskers, sapling boned frame and a cattail brown and puffed with seed, the truth stared back at him and purred. A rough leaf tongue stroked the skin of his hand, and Bond trembled.

Clouds banked in the sky, black with silver rims that spread sunlight in all directions, diffused. Large drops of rain spattered the ground, and the dust, dripped from the eaves and washing in dark rivulets down into the soil. Behind him, leaves rustled in the wind, and he heard her voice, chanting softly as the teakettle whistled, and something cried in answer.

Bond rose, glanced at the clouded sky, and slipped back inside. In the kitchen, down the hall, he could make out her dancing form, dark silky hair washing out behind her, and the lush, green leaves of the vines through the far window.

As he passed through the hall, he glanced into the back room, where no candles burned, and no lights blinked. He caught sight of the wand woman on her perch, and, in the glimmer from a sudden flash of lightning, he would have sworn she winked. He shivered again and felt the chill through to the center of his dried gourd heart.

Fear of Flying

She stood in the center of the room and stared at the window. It was several moments before the others noticed. Mindy seemed to be daydreaming, and there was nothing very odd about that. All of them were between fifteen and eighteen years old and the future loomed like a huge, out-of-control video game with no instruction book. In the face of that kind of pressure it was not difficult to understand if a girl was daydreaming.

Except that she wasn't.

Mindy stood so still for so long that Janice Wilkins walked over and waved a hand in front of the girl's eyes. Janice smiled, but the expression faded through perplexity to a frown as Mindy ignored her and continued to stare. Janice shook Mindy's shoulder and got no response. She leaned in quickly, glanced around the room to be certain no one was staring at the two of them, and whispered.

"Mindy," she said. "Earth to Mindy."

Mindy's receiver was broken, and she did not respond. She stared at the window. Janice stared at Mindy.

In a dark clearing surrounded on all sides by trees and broken by the entrances to four paths that led off into shadow, Mindy flew.

The clouds above were silver with moonlight, and below her the trees fell away to a single dark shadow as she soared. Mindy arched her back and banked into a dive. She saw the trees more clearly again, growing larger and closer. Wind whistled past her ears and dragged her hair behind her like the tail of a kite. Her heart raced.

Then she was through the upper branches and sliced cleanly between trunks and limbs, diving so close to the earth that she saw the shadowy, grey-shade flowers and shrubs that lined the clearing. She shot across, then back up again in a spiraling loop. She was afraid to stop moving—afraid because she didn't know what she was doing to keep moving—afraid because she was so high above such a dark, unfamiliar place—afraid because someone whispered in her ear, breaking through the wind, and it was the wind, after all, that held her aloft and kept her safe.

"Earth to Mindy," the voice whispered.

Mindy fainted.

They brought her ice water and a damp cloth. They told her to elevate her feet and wrapped her in a warm blanket. They stood in a circle around her, wrung their hands nervously and watched the clock. In an hour it would be 3:30 and Mindy's mother would take her home.

They were gathered in the gymnasium. Brilliantly colored streamers burst from the center of the high ceiling and drooped in curling loops to the walls. A ball of silver mirror chips spun in the center. Afternoon sunlight shone through the windows and sent sparkles of light dancing over the walls and floor.

Mindy sat on the bleachers with her feet elevated, wrapped in the blanket with a glass of ice water at her side and watched the lights. She didn't speak to anyone around her—she was too embarrassed. They said she'd been standing in the middle of the room, staring off into space, but she remembered none of it.

Whispered voices roamed through the back of her thoughts, plucking them one by one so she could concentrate on none. She thought of trees, slicing up into the sky and of birds. The breeze from an open door caught the hairs at the base of her neck and lifted them gently; they settled as the door closed. More voices echoed, external this time, and Mindy turned her head.

Her mother huddled close to Coach Reshard, who had an arm protectively around her shoulder. He whispered in her ear, and she nodded in time. The two matched steps as though the moment were choreographed. Someone whispered in Mindy's ear that the two were talking about her, but when she turned there was no one there. Only the reflected glimmers from the disco ball in the center of the gym ceiling dancing on the wall met her gaze, and they said nothing.

"Are you okay, dear?" Her mother asked solicitously.

Mindy noted that Coach Reshard's arm was still about her mother's shoulder, and that her mother did not object. She didn't scan the gymnasium to see if others had noticed. Of course, they had; teenagers miss nothing. They understand little, they hate everything, but they miss nothing.

"I'm okay," Mindy replied. Her words were so soft she could not hear herself speak. Her mother heard, or read her lips, or didn't care, and it was all the same.

Mindy rose, and Coach Reshard reluctantly stepped aside as Mindy's mother took her arm.

"Coach Reshard?" a soft, lilting voice spoke timidly.

The three of them turned. It was Sandy Preston, a tiny wisp of a girl who wore sundresses and braided her hair. Her slender ankles were wrapped in the delicate straps of Greek style sandals. Her eyes were wide.

"What is it, Sandy?" Coach Reshard's voice was stern. He leaned toward Mindy's mother, as if to offer more support.

"It's Todd," the girl replied. "Have you seen him?"

Todd was Sandy's older brother. He was Mindy's age, tall and nearly as slender as his sister. He had a hooked nose like a buzzard and thick-framed glasses that added to his bird-like qualities. His eyes glittered behind too-thick lenses, and they burned. He watched Mindy's legs until she felt sunlight focus through the glass and burn her flesh. Sometimes she watched him burn holes in others.

"No," Coach Reshard replied. "I haven't seen him in about half an hour."

Mindy's mother led her toward the door and away. Coach Reshard leaned in their direction, as if some physical connection had stretched, and then broken. He snapped back to Sandy; Mindy and her mother snapped toward the door. A few heads turned. Mindy was glad that Todd the buzzard would not be watching her legs as she left. She wondered if he would have watched her—or her mother. She knew which of them Coach Reshard watched.

The drive home was silent. Mindy climbed out without a word to her mother, grabbed her things, and ran to her room.

Her mother ran to the kitchen, then to the television, and the phone. Mindy's dad wouldn't be home for another two days, but Coach Reshard...

Mindy threw her book and gym bags onto her bed and sat at her desk. Her window faced the back yard. She stared out past her old swing set, the chains rusted now and the plastic seat half-cracked in two. Beyond their yard and across a churchyard there was a band of trees that lined a golf course. It reminded Mindy of the forest.

The phone rang. Footsteps approached and Mindy heard her mother's voice in the hall. The words were soft, but Mindy heard.

"Oh my god, John."

Coach Reshard's name was John.

"When...are you sure? Oh my god..."

As her mother prayed, Mindy drifted. The chair fell away behind her. She dangled her arms and used them to balance on the breeze. Subtle shifts lent altitude and angle to her flight. The sunlight shimmered and died as she soared above the trees and circled.

Far below her mother's voice echoed.

"Oh my god."

Mindy dove. The trees spiraled inward, starting as a thick wall and thinning as they wound toward some unseen core. She followed the spiral and wondered who had planted it. She dove lower and skimmed the upper branches, dipped and flashed between trunks, slid sinuously over branches and back up again. She flew like dolphins swim, and always she wound inward. Tighter. Like the spring of a clock, her passing drew the trees behind her and held them taut. As she neared the center of the coil, the tension eased. The line of trees flowed behind her, swayed upright and then whipped back in a line, never touching one another as they snapped first one way, then the other, and finally came to rest.

In the center she turned up and flew toward the sky through a tunnel of green leaves and dark limbs. Just as she turned, she caught a flash of color, and it stuck with her as she rose, reached a peak, and flipped, dropping into a graceful swan dive toward the center of the clearing. None of it was powered by her thoughts. She moved. If she stopped moving, she would fall. She knew this but did not know how she kept moving. She didn't know how not to fall.

In the center of the clearing a new sapling had sprung from the earth. Colored streamers were hung from its tip. They flowed up and out and fluttered in a breeze that Mindy couldn't feel. She was moving too fast, making her own breeze. She wondered how the streamers had gotten here, so far from the gym, and where was the disco ball? She cut to her left, broke into a sweeping spiral that brought her very close to the ring of trees, but not touching. She spun down at dizzying speed.

The sapling took form and thickened, sprouted dark hair. She pulled out of the dive to flash inches above the ground and turned directly toward the intruding growth.

She pulled up from the earth to launch herself skyward once again, turned short of the sapling and slipped up its length. She passed the center where a root wound round and round and protruded at an obscene angle, hard and dripping with sap. She gasped and, in that instant, passed face-to-face with Todd the buzzard. He glared at her through too-thick lenses and ran his fat, wet tongue over his lips.

Mindy cried out and arched, hurtling toward the trees. She closed her eyes, and...

"I have to go out for a while, dear."

Mindy's mother's voice cracked and ran in myriad directions at once. It dripped concern. It was flushed with excitement. It hid secrets but held no real concern for Mindy.

Mindy nodded.

"There's frozen dinners," her mother continued. "I shouldn't be too late. They still haven't found that boy—you know the one, Todd..."

"Preston." Mindy finished, hoping the finality would paste itself to her mother's departure and drive her away.

"The buzzard," Mindy added. Her voice was very soft, not really meant to be heard.

"Excuse me?" her mother asked.

Mindy said nothing. She turned to the math textbook on her desk and put on a character-actor performance. She portrayed a student. Her mother clucked her tongue, spun on heels too tall for searching for lost boys and too short to scream impropriety. Moments later the door shut with a loud Click!

Alone, Mindy closed the math book, shoved it aside, and walked to her bed. She wasn't hungry, and she loathed the microwave dinners her mother kept piled in the freezer. When her father was home, the freezer held ice cream and neatly stacked packets of frozen vegetables. Some mothers were talented at bringing complex five course meals to the table, all warm and fresh and ready to serve. Mindy's mother could plan the freezer space to allow for three tightly packed rows of microwave meals the same day her father left on business.

Mindy wondered if Coach Reshard ate microwave meals. She wondered if his freezer was the antithesis of theirs, full of vegetable packets and ice cream only when Mindy's father was out of town.

Mindy lay back on her bed. The soft feather pillow her father had given her for Christmas formed itself to the shape of her head and slid up to cover her ears. The down muffled all sound but a roaring in her ears. Mindy closed her eyes.

The feathers in the pillow were restless. They remembered the sky, wind whistling through and beneath them, ruffling them and driving them aloft. Mindy felt them buoy her up, head and shoulders first, until she floated over the bed. Then the bed, and the room dropped away. The pillow tore and the feathers floated out around her. They tickled her arms and legs and teased over the back of her neck. Two large, grey and white feathers drifted across her eyes and dimmed her vision.

The room dissolved into fluffy white clouds. The feathers coated her skin, slick and smooth. They rustled in the breeze. Mindy turned and knifed through the clouds. Moments later she broke through into a gray sky and soared above the trees. Lights winked at her in the distance.

From her vantage point the forest was a great whirling Nautilus shell of greenery, winding inward to a hollow center. Mindy remembered flying that spiral, and she smiled. This time she cut to the quick. Darting straight down, she drove toward the center of the woods. She was an arrow; pillow feathers flocked the shaft of her body. The clearing rose through the branches, a tall cylindrical column with branches and leaves for walls and at its root?

She dove, oblivious to the ground below or the sky above. In the center of the clearing the sapling had grown taller. It had grown more disgusting. The root jutted from the center of the young tree's trunk nearly back to the ground. Sap dripped obscenely from its tip in a string that bridged the short distance to the tips of the blades of dark grass. Mindy ignored it and dove. She stopped so close to the Earth that grass tickled her, even through the coating of new feathers. Knees dropping first, she pressed into the earth at the foot of the sapling and trailed her gaze up its length. She was careful not to get too close to the dripping root.

When her eyes locked onto twin knotholes above a beak-shaped broken branch, she saw that they met her gaze with hunger. Black dots of intensity floated in their depths and trailed down her body. A worm, unaware of her presence, stuck its head from a crack in the bark, just beneath the broken branch beak. It lolled to one side, then the other, as though dampening bark lips. As though hungry.

She dropped her gaze and watched the root ooze new sap.

She rose to her feet and felt her feathers ruffle. The black dot eyes followed her motion. She reached out with thumb and index finger and plucked the worm from its crevasse. The sapling shivered. Moisture leaked from the twin knotholes, but she didn't care.

Mindy raised her eyes to the sky. She gave a great cry, mournful as an owl and predatory as any falcon. She raised her foot, kicked it down, and snapped the root off at its base. She felt the slick, viscous fluid on the ball of her foot and wiped it in the grass. She kicked off and caught the breeze. She rose in a spiral, gathering speed until she burst free of the trees and banked off toward the distant twinkle of city lights.

Mindy woke to the sound of crunching gravel. She sat up when she heard the kitchen door open, and then close stealthily. She clutched her pillow tightly and found the seams intact. One sharp shaft pricked her arm, and she gripped it, drawing it out through layers of cloth and pillowcase to rest in her palm.

She heard steps in the hall, saw shadows shift, and her mother stood in the doorway to her room, looking in.

"You're awake," her mother said.

Mindy said nothing. She tried not to imagine the scent of leaves, and of sap. She tried not to feel the weight of wood and root cracking against the ball of her foot. Her skin tingled.

"They found that boy," her mother said. The tone of the words indicated compassion, but it felt forced.

"He was in the woods. Alone. He ..."

Mindy turned away.

"He'd been through a lot." Her mother concluded. "He's alive, but his mind..."

"Snapped off at the root," Mindy whispered.

"What?" Her mother's voice was sharp and brittle. The concern in it snapped like glass and was gone.

"How is Coach Reshard?" Mindy asked.

Her mother's shadowed form grew rigid. Mindy heard long, pampered nails dig into the wooden frame of the door. Her mother's indrawn breath was a sudden hiss.

"He found the boy," her mother said at last. "He brought him back."

Mindy nodded. "You too, mother? Did you bring him back?"

A soft, impatient stamp of her foot and Mindy's mother shifted the subject. "The boy was found with feathers. Can you imagine? Buzzard feathers. He had them in his...clothes. He..."

"Do you ever dream of flying, mother?"

Silence.

"Do you think Coach Reshard dreams of flying?"

"Honestly," her mother said softly, spinning on her heel and escaping. "I don't know why I talk to you."

Silence fell again, and Mindy laid back on her bed. She placed the single loose feather against her cheek, pressed it into her pillow, and she slept.

In the dark, with a colored spotlight trained on the spinning, mirror-shard-coated disco ball, the gymnasium was a fairyland of whirling lights and dancing couples. Long tables with cookies and punch bowls lined one wall near the door, far away from the dance floor. Mindy stood at one end of the table.

She stared up and out a high window. The window was a flat pane of darkness. Mindy didn't see it, and nobody saw Mindy. She stood alone with her cup of punch and the crowd milled around her, lost in a myriad of tiny, two and three person worlds of which she was no part.

Mindy's mother had volunteered to chaperone. She stood in the doorway, staring out over the parking lot. Then she turned and came to stand beside her daughter.

"What are you staring at?" her mother asked.

Mindy said nothing. She gave no indication she'd heard the question.

"Why don't you dance?"

Mindy's mother stepped in front of her daughter and stared deep into the girl's placid, far-away eyes. Her stomach shifted and she thought of the downside swing of a Ferris wheel. She heard something. A screech of feedback from the DJ? The cry of a bird.

"Have you seen Coach Reshard," her mother asked softly. "He was here, and then..."

Mindy stared out the window into the dark night sky.

Her mother turned away, moving back toward the door. In turning, she missed the flutter of white, glittering feathers dropping from the mirror-light splendor of the gymnasium sky.

Mindy soared.

Little Ghosts

**"Nathaniel David Winslow—2004-2004
survived by his parents Eliza and Alan Winslow."**

– Old Mill North Carolina *Daily Trumpet* obituaries

Lacey was old. Years had creased her skin with wrinkled valleys. There were lines of sorrow in her cheeks, and there was laughter in the crow's foot patterns at the corners of her eyes. Those eyes had weathered the onslaught of time, bright and fierce, deep, and wise. Hawk's eyes, when she was angry and a doe's eyes when the lights were low and soft music filled the air. Magic eyes, she had been told.

The oak rockers of her chair stroked the hard-pine porch floor in a rhythmic squeak that blended perfectly with the voices of the birds and insects that called to her from the swamp. Inside, the embers of her fire burned low, but they were hot. The heat was an extension of her strength. It would hold, waiting for the next chance to burst into flame and dance up the sooty walls of the chimney toward the stars. The coals smoldered. Lacey rocked, and the moon rose to glory, bathing it all in soft, white light.

It was a night for thinking. The town, miles distant beyond swamp and road, fields, and hills, glowed faintly, but it did not intrude on Lacey's world. Not this night. It melted into the white glow of moonlight and diffused, lending an eerie pallor to the skyline, and sending hosts of shadows to stretch and grope across the earth.

She stared into the mottled sky, read the edges of cloud etched in silver moonlight, and worry lines at the corners of her ancient eyes grew taut. Bats whirled and danced across her vision, and she cursed them silently, willing them away and knowing they would not heed. Something deep and powerful called to her. Its outline, even its name, was written in those silver-lined clouds, but the bats whisked it away each time she thought she would have it. Then the wind rose and erased it all like cotton over chalk-etched slate, and the moment passed.

Lacey closed her eyes, and her lips moved in silent prayer. The night was lonely, and at times like these, she yearned for another to read the signs with her. She wanted someone to carry some of the burden that weighed on her shoulders and pressed down on her soul. She wanted a voice to break the silence.

Lacey rose, turned from the swamp and the moon, and entered her home, pulling the door tight behind her and latching it. In the sky, far above, the bats continued their dance.

Eliza stared out her window along the road leading away from the town. The moon was full in the sky, and it shone through her window and danced down the long, silken tendrils of her hair like droplets of liquid silver.

Behind her, sleeping quietly, Alan dreamed. She liked to watch him this way, with the lines of worry the day brought to his face smoothed by the darkness, but this night she was drawn to the window. She couldn't sleep. She couldn't get the image of Nathaniel lying so still before they took him away. Before they sealed him in the tiny coffin that bore him to a better world.

The moonlight illuminated their yard, the gnarled trees lining the swamp, and the white gravel of the road leading out and away, curling toward the highway and the town beyond. Nothing moved, but everything stood out at sharp angles, shadows and white moonlight clashing and breaking like shattered glass.

Eliza glanced up at the silver-lined clouds and followed the trails of bats, winding in and around them, writing their arcane symbols across the sky. A sound tickled at the far-reaches of her senses, but she couldn't place it. It seemed, at first, as if the bats carved the sound with their wings, but after a few moments of listening, her head tilted to one side, Eliza realized the rhythm was off. It was steady, the shifting of soft silks and the brush of cotton on cotton, or cotton on flesh. She heard the light crunch of gravel. Lights danced among the trees. The bats were too chaotic to be involved in such a sound.

Eliza's heartbeat sped. Her mind shifted down older roads than those she watched by moonlight. She had heard such footsteps before. She knew what they meant, even as her mind rushed through other possibilities, discarding them as quickly as they arose.

Long shadows appeared in the center of the road and stretched closer. She watched the shadows lengthen slowly, ushered into sight by eerie, rhythmic sound. Eliza closed her eyes, and an image of her mother's leathery, wild-eyed face leapt into focus with such clarity that she cried out softly and stepped back from the window. She knew these women. She didn't know which women they would be, only that they would know her, and her mother, and that she would know them.

Alan stirred in his dreams but didn't wake. Eliza kept her eyes closed but shook her head to clear the memories before they could fully take hold. She returned to the window. This time, she managed to keep her gasp silent.

In the road, just beyond their fence, staring at the window from which she watched them, three shrouded figures regarded her. They were stooped and old; skirts billowed like lace wings about their legs, faces hidden among the dark folds of deep cloaks. Eliza could make out none of their features save their eyes. All three sets caught the moonlight at once, flashed gray-green—the color of the swamp or sloshing pools near the edge of forever. That was how Eliza saw them.

With a soft cry she backed away from the window. The moon shifted across her vision as she fell, unable to catch herself on the footboard of the bed, though she grasped it desperately. She came down hard on one hip, cried out again and toppled back. As her head caught the floor and sparks leapt to sting the backs of her eyes, she heard Alan's groggy voice, calling her name. Then she heard nothing at all.

"I don't want you to go," Alan said softly.

Eliza leaned back in their bed, propped against a small mountain of pillows he'd fluffed for her, still staring at the window. She didn't want to glance the other way, through the open door of their bedroom and into the empty room across the hall.

In that room, the walls were striped in pink and blue. There was no furniture. The windows were bare of curtains, and there was no rug on the floor. They had only gotten as far as the walls the last time. Nathaniel had been the third of their children to die before seeing that room. She tried to think of it as the nursery, but it seemed such an empty word.

Late afternoon sunlight filtered through the trees and layered the floor and the bed in long shadows. Alan's face was striped as well, one single band of shadow cutting him in half. Eliza thought of yin and yang—black and white. She thought of the white face of a harlequin, and she could only see half of the warmth of his smile. She couldn't even give birth to half of one of her own.

"They didn't ask me to come," she said. "There is no asking involved. Some things just happen, Alan. You should be glad."

"Glad?" He spun to her, gripped her shoulders tightly and stared into her eyes. "How could it make me glad? I would be happy if I could do something—anything—but …"

She reached up to caress his cheek. Tears spilled from her eyes and down her cheeks. She shook her head, a quick jerk, and no chance for words to waver or break. No chance for her heart to falter and offer promises she wouldn't keep, just to wipe the pain from his eyes.

"You can't do anything. I can't do anything. The doctors and their tests can't do anything."

"But…" She cut him off with another jerk of her head, tearing her gaze from his. She bit her lip hard.

"They can," she whispered. "She can."

Alan turned away and stood framed in the window. His features melted to shadowed silhouette as he blocked the sun. Eliza lay back in exhaustion. Her eyes burned with tears. She clutched her belly and drew her knees up to her chest as the trickle of tears grew to a flood.

Rays of sunlight shot out at odd angles from her husband's still form. Through the tears it gave him the rainbow-lined aspect of an angel.

Lightning lit the sky, as she lay alone on the firm, single mattress of Lacey's bed. Her sheets were soaked in sweat, and the curtains shifted and curled around the window frame, though the window was closed. The wind found its way in through cracks in the ancient wood. Those walls were like her skin, she thought. They were solid in the daylight, but when the shadows fell and the moon was high, they weren't quite able to separate the inner world from the outer.

She drifted, trying to sleep. It would be time, soon, but not yet. This night she would dream. The lightning flashes strobed more evenly, and her eyes closed. The dream images passed through her mind—a 16mm film reel gone staccato and surreal, blinking in time with the brilliant electric flashes beyond her window.

– A shadowed doorway with a single dim bulb spilling soft light into an empty alley.

– A face, hidden in shadow, as arms handed small bundles, one for each blink, one for each dancing streak of lightning, into waiting arms. Different arms each time.

– Closed wooden boxes. Empty boxes, buried.

– The slick green surface of the swamp shimmering with discolored moonlight.

– Slender, liver-spotted fingers sliding ragged bundles into those waters, and the thick, pungent mud, drawing them down.

– Lights dancing, deep in the swamp, blending with lightning streaks and softening as her sleep deepened and the night slipped into the past with the same soft, smooth motion of one of the tiny bundles, sliding into the mud. She felt the warmth of that embrace and sank deeper. All around her, small voices sang, whispered and called out to her.

Tiny hands stroked her withered cheeks and curled in her gray hair. There were so many, and she could help so few.

Outside her window, the storms abated. Against the silver and black backdrop of moon and cloud, the bats renewed their dance. Lights danced among the trees. The sheet that covered her rippled, like the curtains had rippled, but there was no wind.

The dream was so real Lacey smelled the rot of the swamp and felt the soft ground squishing moist and slimy beneath her feet. Three others stood to one side, watching. Each held a candle in gnarled, white-knuckled hands. Eyes peered from beneath dark hoods, but no features were visible. They never were. The women were always different, and always the same. Voices chanted low and deep, but the words dissipated in the moist air and lost coherence. They didn't matter.

Lacey held a swaddled bundle in her arms. The material was robin's egg blue. Lacey couldn't see this in the silver drip of moonlight where the world melted to shades of silver and gray, but she had seen it in the brilliant light spilling from the back of the clinic. It had flashed blue as it was placed in her arms.

She tried to lean quickly to the smooth, mirrored surface of the water. She tried to slip the bundle from her arms, as she had done so many times before, so very many... but this was a dream. She moved too slowly, and the blanket folded back.

She saw tiny, still features. She saw herself, just for a moment, reflected along with the moonlight on the glassy surface of eyes that would never see again. The skin was puckered and grey in the dim wash of moonlight, the limbs so small. There was no breath. There was no hope.

The bundle slid from her grasp, and she reached for it, crying out. She raked her hands frantically through the air, but the blanket unraveled. She fell to her knees beside the tepid water and stretched prone, her gown dipping into the swamp and her fingers scrabbling at the slime. Too late. Always too late. The small form slid into the muck in slow-motion. The water cupped and rippled, rising up and out and the sucking back over the tiny form.

Just before the muck rolled back in, she saw the tiny, shriveled body, no blanket to protect it from that dark embrace, cradled in a cup of mud and moss—angelic in a halo of moonlight. Then it was gone, and she fell forward, hands outstretched, the blanket fluttering aside forgotten. She saw her reflection; fell into herself, and ...

Lacey woke shivering and wet. She reached her hands up reflexively to wipe away the swampy water, but her fingers brushed only sweat and damp hair. Her sheets and pillow were drenched, and tears rolled suddenly from her eyes. Not trickling, pinched tears, but a steady, salty flow, draining from her soul.

She drew her blankets up and over herself, wrapping them tightly over the aged frame of bones and wrinkled skin that her body had become. She shook in the grip of tremors she could not control. Turning on her side, she drew her knees up to her chest and buried her face in her tear-soaked pillow.

When sleep took her a second time, there were no dreams.

Beyond her window three figures stood watching her walls breathe. They were hooded, stooped and old. Behind them, along the trees, lights danced.

Alan sat alone in the empty, half-finished nursery. He didn't turn when Eliza made her way to the doorway and blocked the dim light from the hall. She reached a hand toward him, started to speak—then didn't. She was afraid he wouldn't answer.

She turned and slipped away, tears burning the corners of her eyes. As she stepped into the cool night air and closed the door behind her, he remained still, staring at the striped walls, his head cupped in his hands. He trembled, but he didn't rise. In the far corner of the room, a single teddy bear leaned drunkenly on the wall. Its head was cocked to the side and one small, fuzzy hand rested across its chest. The room was empty, but it felt so oppressively full—so dense with its own uselessness, that Alan barely had the strength to breathe.

They met her at the road and placed her in the center of their triangle. Eliza had to slow her steps and measure each pace to keep from stepping on their robes or entangling herself with their feet. She wanted to speak. She wanted to beg them, to explain—something—she didn't know what. She wanted to be strong and to have faith, but all she had was legs that were suddenly too long and too clumsy and too weak to bear her weight and cold, trembling lips without the ability to form words.

She thought about the empty striped room.

She thought about her husband and could not see his face, but only the stripes.

They skirted the swamp, not sticking to the road, but cutting off at an angle into the shadows. Eliza saw that it was a trail, overgrown on either side with vines dangling from the branches overhead. They reached nearly to the ground, teasing over her cheeks and tangling in her hair as she walked. She had walked and driven past this trail a thousand times over the years of her life and never suspected its existence.

There were sounds all around her, but she could place none of them. Trees cut off the moonlight, and the shadows deepened, but the three who walked before and to either side of her did not slow their pace. None of the sounds emanated from the three, beyond the wisping of their robes and the soft shuffle of their feet.

There was a break in the foliage, and Eliza glanced up. The bats danced again, weaving across silver-edged clouds. Then she was led beneath the trees once again, and that silver light strobed in her mind, reminding her of the previous night's lightning.

Lacey stood in front of the mirror on her nightstand brushing her hair slowly. Sixty-seven strokes. One for each time she'd been called. It wasn't part of the ritual, but it was part of hers. It was a way to put a bit of herself into something she barely understood. If she stood there again on such a night, she would stroke sixty-eight times.

On the chair beside her a dark robe was folded over the seat. Lacey unfastened the buttons at her collar and let her soft cotton dress fall away, exposing her thin frame and aged form to the dim light. She lifted the robe over her head and slipped it on, the intimate touch of soft material over naked flesh as familiar as a lover. Her skin tingled.

There was still time. She opened the top drawer of her nightstand and pulled out a slender leather-bound album. Caressing the deep brown cover, she lifted it free and placed it beside a worn leather bag she'd laid out earlier. Each of the items the bag contained had been carefully checked, counted, stroked and re-packed. Another bit of the ritual that was hers alone. She knew what was in that bag as well as she knew the lines of the face that watched her from the mirror.

She flipped open the album. The pages were yellowed and growing slightly brittle. Lacey turned the pages, one after another. There were hundreds of entries. Each represented a death, or a birth. Miscarriages, stillborn children, lost children, so many their names blurred as Lacy flipped the pages. She ran her finger gently down the lines of the old newspaper article on page one.

It was a short, one sentence obituary, the dates of birth, and death, identical. Died in childbirth. The next page showed a smiling-faced girl of nineteen, the arms of her husband wrapped tightly around her as she cradled a baby against her breast. The baby had been a boy, Lacey remembered.

It was the same throughout the book, stretching back so far into her past she could scarcely put names to the faces. The buildings in many of the earlier photos didn't exist any longer, but the swamp was the same. The winding road and the trails leading off to that tepid pool were constant. She closed her eyes and white, dancing lights whirled and blinked through the memories, scattering them like so much dust.

Was it really only sixty-seven? Hadn't she seen the mud suck them down every night of her adult life, followed their tiny forms deep into that primordial embrace in a thousand dreams?

On the wall opposite her bed, a portrait hung. It was a tin litho photograph of her mother. The picture was very dark, and her mother's features and dress had been so severe she looked like the headmistress of a Victorian private school, thin lipped and without humor. Lacey knew where the humor had gone, knew what it had looked like as it slipped from her mother's groping fingers into the mud.

Lacey could still see her mother's withered, veined fingers as they'd unpacked the bag, one item at a time, laying the contents out across this same bed. Each new thing had been held, placed into Lacey's fingers, explained and learned, and then returned to its place. The only new things in the bag were the candles, short, squat, colored with the hues of the swamp and scented with gathered herbs. New for each calling. She would collect what she needed for the next time this very night.

Of course, Lacey knew that Charlotte had not been her true mother. Charlotte had never had a husband. No man had ever lived within the walls of the cabin or leaned back in the rocker out front. No male eyes had watched the bats write their arcane symbols across the clouds. It had always been so, and Lacey accepted it. If she found no one to pass the secret to, then the lights might well dance for eternity through the trees and reeds, and the cabin might fall into disrepair and then to dust. It would be the same for her.

She closed the album with a snap and ran her fingers along the leather binding. She turned and stared at herself in the mirror a moment longer, then slipped the book back into the dresser drawer and grabbed the bag. She had heard the first words floating on the breeze, wafting in her open window. The last red touch of sunlight had left the skyline, ushering in the darkest moment of the day.

Lacey slipped out into the night and set off toward the tree line across the road. She clutched the leather bag tightly and it slapped against her thigh as she walked. She ignored the cries of the bats overhead—the moon leaked down through the clouds, but she was in no mood to be entertained by the leather-winged authors of the night. Without glancing back or hesitating, she stepped between two trees and wound her way into the swamp.

Eliza stood trembling beside the waters of the swamp. The images and thoughts crowding her mind whirled in time with the bats overhead, clearly visible now that they had come to the murky, moss-choked bank. The three who accompanied her had not spoken. As on the trail, sound surrounded her, the voices of small animals, the fleet steps of creatures skittering off into deeper, undisturbed shadows. The cries of the bats. Something sloshing in the water off to her right.

And the lights.

Eliza had noticed the strange lights shifting through the trees since they'd left the road. She wanted to say something, to ask what they were, but she held her silence. When she turned her head to get a better look, there was nothing to see. Each time she focused on the trail ahead, the periphery of her vision filled with soft glowing spots, until she grew dizzy from their constant dance.

Then, the lights were gone. She saw nothing but the murky water and the dark hem of the women to either side. She knew the third stood somewhere behind her, but there was no sound to mark her location.

Behind, and to her left, footsteps approached. They were light and accompanied by the soft brush of some sort of material. Not like the dark skirts of the old women that rustled like brittle gauze. This sound was the brush of wind over leaves, or her hair when she flipped it over the back of silk nightdress. The moonlight caught a line of trees in dark stripes of shadow, painting them on slick wet surface before her. She closed her eyes and saw Alan, staring at the striped walls of an empty room. Her heart clenched with an ache that made her gasp.

Lacey saw them, but they didn't turn. Even the girl, trembling like a freshly bloomed lily in the moonlight, stared across the water in silence. Lacey walked to the water and stopped. Kneeling in the wet, loamy soil, she placed the leather bag before her and opened the strap. From within she pulled the candles, five in all, and placed them behind her. "One to draw heart," she whispered, placing a reddish candle directly opposite the water. To the left, she placed a lavender scented candle and said, "One to draw mind." She repeated this, one to each side in a widening arch, and completed the words as she remembered them. She felt the mud clutching at the base of each candle, grasping and hungry.

"Spirit," "Strength," "power."

The final three candles were placed and lit. Lacey rose. She reached into the bag again and pulled out a long, silver chain. On the end of that chain an oval pendant dangled. It was dark, onyx with a hollowed center that was even darker, a shadow hole in a shadow. It seemed that a stone should rest in that central cavity, but there was nothing, and Lacey showed no dismay at that emptiness—nothing had broken free of the setting. She slipped it over her head and let it rest against her breast. Then, as easily as she had let it slip on over her head, she released a tie within the robe, and it slid off and back.

She stood poised on the edge of the swamp. Long, twisting roots groped from the bases of trees, and stretched claw-like into the muck. There was a sloshing sound to her left, something slipping from the bank, finding the silent grace in the water it lacked on land. Lacey ignored it.

A light slid from the trees and slipped around her ankle, leaving a tingling line of ice like a manacle. Another transited her waist and flipped up and away, blinding her momentarily as it slid past her eyes. Lacey stepped forward. Trance-like she entered the water, not stumbling at the cold, cloying grip of the mud. Sight fell away. She heard whispered voices without language whirling about her and cutting her off from the world. The water reached her thighs, and her feet had sunk to the ankles, but she moved steadily. All around her the lights danced, drawn to her like the antithesis of insects to light, the dark pendant in her hand made darker by a brilliant halo of darting lights.

When the water reached her breasts, buoying them gently, she turned. The girl stood on the bank, transfixed. The dark forms to either side and behind were blurred from where Lacey stood. She saw shadows. The girl's robe was removed, and she stood glistening in the moonlight, pale, naked, and frightened. So softly the word nearly lost itself in the wind, Lacey spoke.

"Come."

Eliza watched the old woman slip into the water. It was hard to follow the motion, because the lights, so bashful and sub-tle only moments before, flashed about the slender form in a brilliant whirlwind glow. They darted in, then away, then in again. The woman—Lacey, her name was Lacey. Eliza knew that; everyone knew—Lacey was like a magnet to the lights, but the polarization was off. Just as they should have made contact, teasing along her ancient skin, they darted away. By the time Lacey stopped, the water lapping at ancient nipples and wetting the tips of her hair, the lights had grown frenzied, a swarm of glowing wasps sizzling and diving through the air, angrier each time they were denied contact.

Eliza's arms were gripped on both sides, thin, bony fingers digging deep to prevent thoughts of escape. The air crackled now with the lights, blindly rushing at Lacey's still form, standing in that brown, slimy water and holding something out toward shore. The dark object hung on a chain about the old woman's neck. E even in the blinding brilliance of the furious maelstrom of light, that single point of emptiness caught and held Eliza's gaze. She shook free from the hands on her arms and felt them draw back.

She stepped into the water, shivering in the chill air and gritting her teeth at the icy embrace of the water. The mud slid between her toes and worked its way up over her feet, teasing her ankles. There were things in that mud, hard gritty things, soft, sliding things. Eliza ignored them and stepped forward steadily, leaving the bank, and the three old women, behind.

Lacey watched her through the whirling lights, and Eliza was certain she saw the older woman's lips curl into a soft, sad smile. She moved slowly at first, then more quickly, dragging her feet from the clinging mud and fighting for balance. She didn't want to pitch face first into the swamp, but more than anything else, she wanted to touch that light. She wanted to fall into it, to reach out and join her hands with Lacey's and feel them swirling around her as well.

The distance wasn't as great as she'd thought. The murky water was more pungent and pleasant than she'd have believed. It was a smell of decay, but beneath that decay, there was something else—something urgent and powerful.

A final step and she locked her gaze with Lacey's. Without looking down, they joined hands. Eliza wrapped her smaller, younger fingers around Lacey's, holding the amulet—she could see it was an amulet now—cupped in all four of their palms. The crackling Eliza had heard, or sensed, when she stood on the shore resolved itself with sudden, horrible clarity.

Voices.

She heard voices and saw faces. Eyes gazed at her from dream rooms she'd never visited. Hands reached to her, beseeching. The world tilted on its axis as the voices multiplied again, and again, leaving her mind a confusion of pain and loss, grief and... something. She grasped it. It shone from Lacey's eyes and glistened in the tears rolling down the old woman's cheeks.

Together, they raised their arms and held the amulet aloft. The cloud of energy tensed—it was palpable, a hesitation in sound and purpose. The dark, empty center of the amulet, black like the back of a closet, or the depths of a cavern with no entrance, black like space or the place inside you go when there is nothing left, and your mind runs further than even your body can take you.

A sigh of release, air slipping from a tire when the valve stem is pressed, or a balloon nearly expired releasing its air. A vacuum suddenly filled at the twist of a jar lid. Darkness.

It happened with a snap of such power that Eliza fell to her knees. She felt the water rise to her throat, beyond, fought to close her mouth and didn't completely succeed. Lacey stood with her arms, held up, so solid she might have been carven of stone, and she held Eliza afloat.

Eliza's muscles were jelly. She tried to speak, but her mouth moved in slow motion, and she tasted the rot of the swamp. She spat and coughed, but could not get a good strong breath, because her hands were still held tightly over her head.

The lights were gone. She stood, facing the old woman in the mud and the mire, the cold water suddenly gripping her and wringing deep shivers from her frame. Then Lacey lowered their hands and pressed the amulet toward Eliza. There was no way to stop it, no protest to be made as the dark stone with its glittering jewel was pressed hard into her chest and held there tightly.

The jewel bit deep, deeper than it was possible for such a

small stone to bite. Eliza cried out; her back arched and her hands slid free of the old woman's. Lacey did not back off. She pressed forward, driving the pendant between Eliza's naked, shivering breasts.

White light pulsed behind Eliza's eyes. Her frame grew rigid, and she toppled backward, falling into the waiting arms of the three old women who had come up behind her, still robed and nearly throat high in the water. They held her by her arms and backed to the bank, where they drew Eliza out prone on the soft ground and dried her carefully. Wrapping her once more in the robe, they gently woke her and got her on her feet. No word was spoken, but somehow, she was moving, a shoulder under each arm, and moving away from the water.

Her last glimpse of that place, as she turned away, slipping in and out of consciousness, dug deep into her memory and stuck. The image was of Lacey, still standing in the center of that dark pool. There were no lights, and she held the amulet out before her like a shield, her eyes down and her long hair, somehow loose from its tie, draped over her like a shroud.

Sunlight filtered in the window, lanced across the hall through the open door and illuminated the brightly striped wall. Eliza shook her head groggily, slipping the covers back and sitting up propped against her pillow. Tiny wailing cries called out to her, an ache deep inside that nothing could ease, and then grew silent.

Alan stepped into the doorway with little Grace curled in his arms. She watched them, her husband cooing softly and rocking his arms as he carried the baby back into their room, and the tiny hand, groping for her father's cheek.

Eliza closed her eyes. She heard the voices every day now, very quiet, deep inside, but she heard them. She saw the eyes and felt their gaze on her in everything she did. They couldn't come—not all of them—but they lived a little bit now, through Grace. Eliza thought of Lacey, standing alone in the swamp, thought of the frenzied little lights, fighting to be free of that place. To be chosen.

As Alan sat on the bed, she opened her eyes and took her

daughter, eyes filling suddenly with tears. Alan leaned in and kissed them away. He thought they were tears of joy, and they were, but there was so much he could never know.

She held the baby and leaned back again, drawing the child to her breast. Alan retreated, giving her the moment. Tears and milk blended on little Grace's cheeks and lips, salty and filled with love.

"Twins, one male, one female, born to Eliza and Alan Winslow ..."
-- Torn, scribbled portion of a discarded birth announcement

Lacey sat on her porch, and she rocked, watching the skyline give birth to the sun. She was wrapped in a shawl, and the creak of wood on wood was heavier than it had been, the rocking motion slightly slower. She glanced down.

From her lap, tiny bright-dark eyes watched her in fascination. So much like Eliza's eyes when she'd met that gaze across the waters. So much like little Grace. So much like sister and mother that the events of that night, not so long past, played over and over in Lacey's mind. Her heart nearly skipped a beat when the child smiled.

She glanced up at the morning clouds, rimmed in gold as the night clouds were in silver. Birds whirled in sudden flight, dancing across the scudding line of cloud, and Lacy smiled. She could almost read the promises they wrote.

Closing her eyes, she whispered, "Thank you," then rose and turned into the doorway of the cabin. The birds whirled off and away, lost in the brilliant light of the sun.

One Off from Prime

The walls of the shelter were dingy and gray. The paper was white or had been white. Too many hours stuffed in the bottom of Angus' bag had dampened the sheets and marred their sheen. Most of the pages were empty, windows and doors to places the words hadn't yet taken him; even doors need a new coat of paint now and then—a hinge, or a knob replaced. Angus' paper, as his mind, remained unhinged and without knobs or slots, collecting flecks of dust and smears of sweat and blood.

He wasn't alone in the room, but he might as well have been. Angus stood adrift in a whirling miasma of images and words so thick they obscured the bland walls and walking, talking worlds that orbited him.

A thin, wisp of a woman sidled up sneakily and glanced sidelong into Angus' vacant eyes. She eased along the table, trailed her bony fingers over its surface and watched with bird-like intensity for any reaction. Angus didn't flinch. The woman's dry, pale lips curled into a cruel grin. Like a striking snake her hand darted past the sheet of paper Angus held flat on the table and gripped the strap of his old, green duffle bag.

There was a blur of motion, and the woman screamed. Between her fingers, gouged into the surface of the table and quivering, stood Angus' pen. It didn't touch her skin, but it prevented the sliding of the duffle across the table. The plastic shaft of the pen was shattered, but the inner plastic tube and the ballpoint were intact, quivering from the impact.

Without a word, Angus worked it free of the table. The woman fluttered back and away. She sputtered words that died in strangled bleats of sound and a yellow mist of spittle. Angus paid no more attention to her departure than he had to her approach. He stared at the paper in front of him and willed the words to stop spinning and sort themselves. He had to capture them and bind them to the paper to get them out from in front of his eyes and behind his ears.

He thought—no, he knew—that there was one word among them that could set him free, if only he could unravel the rest and place it properly. He vaguely remembered others who had once helped with the placement, but though he knew there had been three, he couldn't recall names or faces.

None of those around him saw the words. They saw a thin, emaciated man of thirty or so years with thick black hair that dropped over broad, muscular shoulders, their strength belied by thin, protruding shoulder blades. They saw wide eyes that stared at everything except what was directly in front of them and long, slender fingers perpetually wrapped around a pen, or a pencil, or a paintbrush.

One time the counselors found Angus in the alley behind the shelter with a piece of charcoal in his hand. He'd covered half the back wall with a single long, rambling sentence.

A young woman, thinner still than the insectile Angus, stood midway along the wall, reading. Her slender, beak-like nose was pressed so close to the wall that its tip was black from accidental encounters with charcoal and brick. Her hands were filthy from trailing along behind. She wore thick cats-eyeglasses that slid down her nose and had to be pressed back into service every few minutes. This action streaked her face with more of the charcoal.

When the counselors led the two back inside, she looked ready for a combat raid, camouflaged and intense. Angus looked confused and on the verge of saying something he couldn't quite remember. He'd written it down, but she'd caused it to blur. She'd taken the words into her pores or her skin and the ridges of her fingers. The counselors took the charcoal, and by the time anyone thought to try and read what Angus had written, the words had faded and smudged.

Angus didn't remember the wall. He remembered that there had been words, but not what they'd been. He remembered the young woman's face. He remembered the dark swatches of charcoal embedded in the pores of her skin. He remembered her expression, and her eyes. He'd wanted to reach out, brush his fingers over her cheeks and drag the black, dusty smudges back into the proper order. He'd memorized her features in an instant and imagined them covered in letters, the words merging to one long statement encompassing everything he was unable to say. He thought she was more beautiful without the words but had no way to be certain.

Now he stared at the blank paper, clutched the shattered pen and tried to bring her face into focus and transfer it to the page. He imagined the lines of letters, like soldiers, or the bricks on a wall. His lips moved, but before he could record the wispy words they slipped away and new ones took their places, always a step ahead. His hand trembled, but he didn't touch the pen to the paper.

The girl sat in the corner of the room, huddled in a severe chair of hard wooden slats. She clutched her knees to her chest and her chin rested between them. She gazed in unwavering concentration at Angus' profile. She saw the paper clearly, and the pen. She knew the tremble in his hand and the nervous shake of his head. She'd seen both so many times they'd become a part of her.

She didn't have to huddle in the shelter. She didn't have to watch this skinny man stare at his paper and chase the words flitting through his head. She had a home and a name, a family who wondered where she had gone, and friends—acquaintances, really—who noted the empty spaces she would have filled in their own small worlds. But none of that was real. They knew the thin, wispy shell of her, but her connection to Angus was much deeper. Given time, she'd fade from their minds as surely as Angus' words had faded from the alley wall.

Angus knew she was there. He felt her. He sat and he tried to imagine the lines of her face on his paper, but he refused to turn and watch her watching him because it was no good. The face smudged with charcoal had been cleaned. The words, if they were still there, were hidden too deeply for him to recapture. If he looked at her now, the earlier image of her would dissolve, and be lost. He would still have her eyes, of course, and that was a temptation. They were eyes that had watched him without guile, and without judgment. They were hungry eyes as eager to see him find the order in the words, or behind them, as he was to provide it. They had seen the words, if only for a few intense moments.

Others watched as well, but not for long, and not with much interest. An old Italian man in a faded army uniform shirt covered in colorful patches shuffled by. He looked like an ancient, rotting parody of a boy scout. He wore two pairs of pants and had a variety of odd items tied to his belt, protruding from his pockets, and slung about his neck. His hair, which would have been a fine blend of white and gray had he bathed, was dark and greasy and clung to his liver-spotted scalp in sparse patches. The man glanced over Angus' shoulder at the blank page and snorted.

"Shouldn't write it down," he said. His voice was weak and formed of shrill, reedy tones that shattered in the air like thin icicles. "They'll read it. They'll know. Never write it down."

Then he shuffled off with his hands covering his pockets as if afraid the things he carried would leap out and escape. Angus didn't look up. He sat with his hand hovering over the page expectantly.

Some spoke as they passed. Some stared at the paper, or at the back of his head. Some made faces behind his back and then walked on. A tall black man walked around to the far side of the table, directly across from Angus and stared down at the point where the pen had slammed into the tabletop. His lips moved constantly. Now and then his shoulder dipped, or he shuffled his feet. His hips swayed to music no one heard.

He leaned in and inspected the table. A small pile of dust and shattered plastic circled the point where Angus had slammed his pen into the wood. The black man studied it. He cocked his head, checking perspective, and then seated himself in a chair. Angus didn't look up. The black man reached into his pocket and pulled out a small pouch. From this he extracted a razor blade. The cold steel glittered like fire in the dim light, catching stray flickers from the bare, yellowed overhead bulb that illumined the room. It was the kind of blade used by artists and carpenters, braced on one edge with a rounded shield to protect the fingers.

The man's hand darted out. He smacked the blade loudly on the table and drew it toward himself. The razor swept the plastic shards and dust across the surface, his fingers nimbly dropping and dragging, scooping the remnants into a pile. He was careful and he missed nothing. When he had it all in a heap in front of him, he raised the blade and chopped at the pile.

Everyone in the room except Angus and the girl looked up sharply. The man brought the blade up, and down, up and down; his fingers flew and quickly pulverized the larger shards of plastic, cutting them to dust, reshaping the mound, and cutting again, each run through making a finer powder. No one in the room spoke. The black man's lips never stopped moving, but if he spoke, there was no sound to accompany it, and if he was answered it was not from within the room.

When the plastic was reduced to glittering dust, the man stopped and studied it. He drew the blade through the center, split the pile, and then split those piles. He cocked his head again. His shoulder dipped. He squinted with one eye and shivered, as if a particularly beautiful rhythm had rippled through his long, lanky body. The ripple ended at his fingers, and they danced.

When he was done, there were six lines on the tabletop. Three of them were broken lines. Each of the six lines was of equal length; all were perfectly parallel with one another. The man carefully returned his blade to its pouch, rose from his chair, and did a careful quickstep in place, dropping his hip and throwing his hand out to one side. He turned and walked away.

Angus looked up. The girl rose, came to stand beside him, and stared down at the lines.

Behind them, the door to the room opened and the world poured in. The sudden shift in air pressure sent the dust whirling off the table and away, erasing the trigram.

A voice called out, "Angus Griswold?"

The room they put him in was white-walled. The table at which he sat was covered in white Formica. There were windows, but they were the kind that was only transparent in one direction. On his side, they were mirrors. Angus stared at one for a long time, intrigued by the lines of his own face staring back at him. He wondered briefly if, on the far side of that mirror, the words made sense. He had the odd sensation that he recognized himself, and then it was gone.

They had the girl too. She was in another room. He felt her presence, though he hadn't seen her since being closed off. He hadn't seen anyone, in fact, since a very stiff-backed young man in a white jacket had brought him a white cup. He half-expected it to be filled with milk in the colorless void, but it was coffee. Angus loved coffee, but he hadn't touched it. He wasn't afraid of being poisoned; he was concentrating. The room was white, but the coffee was dark, like the words, and it distracted him. He watched the white walls and day-dreamed that ink might sweat out through hidden pores in their surface and flow into words and phrases.

In another room, not so bright, and not so white, the girl sat. On the desk in front of her was the remnant of a day planner. The spine had cracked and worn away and the pages were loose. She kept them bound in a pair of large rubber bands she'd stolen from the post office.

She glanced up as the door to the room opened. A tall black man in a dark suit entered, closed the door behind him, and crossed to the far side of the desk. He took a seat and placed a folder on the table in front of her. His eyes were dark brown, so dark they seemed black, and she saw that the cuticles of his fingers were meticulously groomed. He steepled his fingers.

She glanced up at him. He wore thick framed glasses. The wrinkles at the corners of his eyes looked as though they might be accustomed to humor, but in that moment his gaze was flat and serious.

"Why am I here?" she asked.

"I think you know the answer to that," he replied. "I am Mr. Johnson. You don't know me, but I believe you are very familiar with a former associate of mine, Mr. Griswold. You may also have heard of my employer, Mr. King."

"I don't know anyone named Griswold," she said.

"His first name is Angus."

She didn't answer.

"Do you have any idea what Angus did when he worked for us, Miss Prine?"

Her head jerked up. She had not known that they were so close to knowing her name. She smiled, but she tucked her head to hide it, and she didn't answer.

"That's unfortunate. It seems that Mr. Griswold has also forgotten."

Johnson fell silent for a moment, then flipped open the folder on the desk.

"Angus Griswold was a financial analyst. He was very good at his job. Possibly too good. He and his team had the task of scanning pages and pages of computer data and...anticipating."

"Anticipating?"

"I think that's the best way to word it. Angus had a way of seeing a very large amount of data at once. This ability of his allowed him to anticipate trends, predict problems, and circumvent inefficiency. One thing my company loathes beyond all else, Miss Prine, is inefficiency."

"I don't..."

A sharp jangle of sound cut off his reply. Johnson slid a thin cell phone from his pocket.

"Yes?"

She watched his face, but his expression never changed.

"You're sure," Johnson said. "Four hours, then? I see."

He flipped the phone closed and turned back to her.

"There's not much time. Mr. Griswold has been working on something very important for a very long time. He indicated to us that he'd discovered something big—something profound. That knowledge could prevent a very large disaster from taking place, and Mr. King is very interested in obtaining it. Mr. Griswold told us the nature of the disaster, and even gave us a rough idea of when it might take place. Unfortunately, we did not immediately see the importance of what he told us, and at that point his behavior had become...unstable. The file he left behind is incomplete. The single data point he failed to mention before disappearing into the streets was how to stop it."

"He doesn't know," she said. "He's been trying to figure it out. He believes that he will be able to write it down."

"How do you know?"

"He wrote it on the wall. I read it. It was too much to take in at a single reading, and they came and took us away. The words were gone, smudged and ruined. I had them...but they slipped away."

"Do you remember?"

"No. Not all of it. I've written some of it down, but it's not perfect. There was a design."

"Design?"

"Six lines. It was a trigram, like in the I Ching. I drew it."

She fumbled at her ruined day planner. Her hands shook, and she had trouble spreading the pages. When she found it, she slid it free and turned it to face Johnson.

"What is it?" Johnson asked.

"It's a Hexagram. I looked it up at the library. It means Obstruction. Stagnation."

"He wrote this?"

She shook her head. "No. He caused it."

Johnson stared at her a long moment, then made some unspoken decision.

"You have to help us. There is not time to explain the entirety of what is at stake, so I will be brief. I believe that you understand a lot more than you let on."

She held her silence.

"If we do not find the answers we seek, a few tiny calculations in a very large algorithm will return bad data. At first, no one will see. It won't even matter. Over time, the errors will multiply. There is a critical point after which, even if we were to discover the original error, nothing we could do would halt its progress. That error is embedded deep in the database behind the world's largest finance and credit system."

"What can one tiny error do?"

"One error is incorporated in a thousand calculations, the results of which will fuel a hundred thousand more. The integrity of the data will be compromised within minutes. When the world gets the first hint that we do not have control of the system—that their millions of dollars are suddenly in question without even a good direction to point their finger, there will be anarchy. Mr. King believes that within only a few moments, automatic fail-safes and security protocols will shut down everything."

"Everything?" she asked. "Surely there are backups? Contingencies?"

"Also corrupt. We do not believe we will be able to pinpoint the entry point of the error. We believe it is possible that Mr. Griswold can, or already has and has forgotten. We believe, in fact, that he's been trying to put what he already knows in words that others can understand. Even if we found the error and returned the system to its current state it's likely trust and confidence will have eroded sufficiently by that time to cause worldwide panic."

"Where is he?" she asked.

"He is safe, for the moment. As safe as any of us can really be."

She stared at Johnson for a long moment.

"I need to see him."

"Why?"

"He needs to remember. He believes that I can help. He won't look at me, and I think this is because, in his mind, he will either find what he is looking for in the lines of my face, or will find that it is lost forever, and he's afraid."

"I see," Johnson said. "We will give him time, then. The room we put him in is one giant blank canvas. The walls are made of dry-erase white board. The windows are mirrors. The table is white, the floor is white. Soon he will be given markers. We have, at the best estimate of those who have an inkling of what Mr. Griswold has seen, about four hours. If he can't write it down before then; if we get so close to the deadline that there is no hope, I will take you to him. You may be that hope."

She continued to stare at him. Johnson remained unruffled.

"Coffee?" he asked.

She nodded, and then looked away, trying to see through the walls to where Angus was seated. She had visions of her own, had been having them since the first time she laid eyes on him so very long before. In her dreams, the angels warned of fire. They warned of destruction. Each of them wore a very large, ticking clock on a golden chain, and the clocks were winding down. In those dreams, men worshiped idols made of shifting symbols and scrolling numbers, falling away to dust.

Johnson slipped out of the room without a sound. The door closed behind him, and she stared at it, just for a moment. He had not hesitated, or fumbled with the knob, but she knew it was locked. Less than four hours. The room didn't even have a clock.

Johnson stood behind a row of three chairs. The chairs faced a bank of huge monitors across which columns and patterns of numbers shifted and scrolled. Each screen was divided into terminal windows, and different events triggered flashes of color. In the chairs, a young Asian woman, an old gray-haired man, and a boy of about sixteen sat. On the backs of their chairs, the names Meshe, Shad, and Abe had been scrawled across white nametags. They watched the scrolling numbers, working keyboards, trackballs, and a bank of peripheral controls without once glancing away from the screen.

Johnson wanted to question them, but he knew that either they would ignore him, as per their instructions, or he'd likely cause a new set of problems by his interference. When Angus had worked with them, there'd been a fourth chair. Mr. King had removed it when the prodigal walked out.

Johnson watched the numbers for a moment, but they meant

little to him. When they had been sifted down to spreadsheets and balanced equations, he'd understand them well enough. In their current raw state, it was beyond his ability. That was fine—it wasn't his job. His job was to be certain that the numbers did balance. In the upper levels of the company, they joked that every transaction since the beginning of time flowed across those screens—that the Templars had kept records, and the Egyptians had been meticulous

The woman, Meshe, gasped suddenly. She didn't stop working her controls, and she didn't look away from the screen, but he knew that she'd caught something. Her distress passed, and he knew it couldn't be what Angus had seen. These three were very good. There had once been more than two dozen "watchers" working in shifts, and they had all been good. None of them had borne Angus' singular gift—or his neuroses. Now there were only three, and though Angus had spoken to them before leaving, none of them could find the fault, though they would no doubt remain vigilant.

Johnson turned away and left the room as silently as he'd entered. He headed down a brightly lit hall and entered a glass-doored office at the far end. An elderly man, grey at the temples glanced up from where he'd been scouring reports on his desk.

"What has he said?" the man asked.

"Nothing. He's confused and barely coherent. The girl isn't much better. I think it's time to put them together and see what comes of it."

"It's our last shot. If they can't get it back in time…"

"I know," Johnson said. "Don't think I haven't considered walking out, buying a bunker in a survivalist camp and stocking up. We haven't got much time. For all we know we don't have any time at all. We have to try it now."

"Take her in," the man said.

Johnson turned, hesitated, and looked back.

"It's been good working with you, Ezekiel."

The older man smiled. It was a fleeting expression that looked lost in the patchwork of stress-fractures that made up his face. Then he turned back to the papers, and Johnson slipped into the hallway, closing the door quietly behind him.

When the door opened, Angus didn't look up. The girl entered and the door closed behind her. She sat opposite him at the table. He stared at the white surface, refusing to meet her gaze.

"You wrote it down once," she said. "In the alley. You wrote it down, and it was all there."

Angus twitched but did not look up.

"I knew you'd get it. I knew you'd find the words. It's why I watched, and why I read. "

"They're gone." Angus said.

She shook her head. She rose, circled the table, and stood directly beside him, but still, he did not look up. She reached out and stroked his cheek. He didn't pull back, but she felt the inner struggle. He quivered as if unable to decide whether to press into her fingers, or to lean away.

"The words are not gone. If they were gone, you'd be at rest. They are there, buzzing and crackling with energy, and you need them to stop. We both need that. The world needs that. You started it, and only you can finish it. It's up to you."

She stepped behind his chair, pulled it gently away from the table, then slid around and straddled him. With one hand on each cheek, she raised his head until he stared directly at her.

"It's time," she said.

Angus shivered, but he didn't look away. She leaned closer, and her features blurred. At the end, he saw her lips, red and moist, and crisscrossed with tiny veins that shifted and rearranged. They kissed and those crooked, wretched lines clarified. Angus pulled back, just for an instant, but she held him fast.

His mind flooded with memories. Lines of figures flashed past on mental monitors so fast it should have been dizzying, but he already knew them. He felt each ripple and saw the tiny bugs nibbling away at the heart of the pattern.

He was vaguely aware when she began stroking her hips up and down. He rose to meet her and wrapped her in his arms. He was so close. He had walked so long in a world that buzzed and whirled that the clarity was painful. The haze beckoned. He itched to hold his pencils, or a piece of chalk. The white walls streamed with row after row of symbols and numbers, and he wanted to fill them in and trap them. He felt her unbuttoning his shirt and then the hot touch of her flesh and then...he let them go.

Johnson and Ezekiel stood before a huge video monitor. On the screen, Angus stood, disheveled, and coated in sweat, before one of the white walls. He held a dry erase marker in his hand, poised. Behind him, the woman lay back across the table, spent. It was difficult not to stare at her; something in the aspect of her pose gave her a sensuality her street-urchin attire and schizophrenic actions had hidden. She did not look at Angus, but instead stared back at them through the monitor, as if well aware her naked flesh was on camera and reveling in the attention.

"My God," Ezekiel said. "Who is she?"

"You know who she is. You know what she is. What neither of us knew was how profoundly ... real ... she would turn out to be."

"She calls herself Prine?" Ezekiel asked absently.

"I think we may have been mistaken. It sounded like Prine, and we have assumed that to be correct, but upon closer examination of the original document, I believe she is called... Prime."

"It's her last name?"

"It's her only name."

"My God."

"Not exactly, but...wait! He's writing."

On the screen Angus reached out with the marker. He started drawing horizontal lines. After only a few seconds work the hexagram was complete. "Obstruction." He stared at it, and then turned.

"There is no new flaw in the numbers," he said.

"It's not a question, but it's directed to the girl."

"Of course not. There is only the one flaw. You knew this once."

"I know it again," he said.

He dropped the marker on the floor, and it rolled under the table. He walked to the table and lifted her to a sitting position.

She smiled into his stern gaze. Angus leaned in and kissed her, and then turned toward the cameras.

"Numbers are pure," he said. "The system by which you calculate them is a language, and it is the closest to perfection man may ever come, but there are flaws. There have always been flaws. You have built a world on numbers, filled in the cracks when the foundations shifted, and applied new paint, but the central flaw was always there. It's eaten at the foundations since the first dollar was saved and reinvested. It's the root cause of all the tiny cracks I patched for you, and the thousands more rising to the surface."

"Tell them about Schrödinger's Cat," she said.

He turned and frowned at her, and then the frown cracked into a crooked smile.

Ezekiel turned and started to ask Johnson a question, but Johnson held up a hand. He focused intently on Angus.

"I spent my life looking for flaws in the perfection of the data. No matter how many times I found and fixed a problem, the imperfection screamed at me, and I had to go on. All I was doing was plugging holes in a sinking ship. There was never any perfection to mar, only a crumbling façade."

Johnson stepped back from the monitor. Behind him a red light began flashing slowly, and then another. Alarms sounded. Ezekiel turned and glanced at them. He touched Johnson on the shoulder, but Johnson shrugged him off.

"It's too late, Ezekiel," he said.

Johnson reached out and pressed a button. He leaned down and spoke into a microphone on the desk beside the monitor.

"Angus," he said.

Angus turned and looked directly into the camera.

"I cannot speak to you," he said. "I have a message for Ezekiel."

The old man stood very still. Johnson turned to stare at him, and then pressed the microphone button again.

"Ezekiel is here."

"Now is the time, old friend. You must remember. Mr. King and his minions have built this false idol of greed and gold, this mountain of numbers. You know what will happen should it crumble, and yet, the choice remains yours. Worship, or be taken by fire."

"Your name is not Angus," Ezekiel said. His voice was soft, as though he was forcing memories from somewhere deep inside.

"What are you talking about?" Johnson said. He shook Ezekiel hard. "What do you mean he isn't Angus? Who is he?"

"Call the main office," Ezekiel said, ignoring the question. "Get Nebbu…get Mr. King on the line. Tell him … tell him that we choose the fire."

The blinking lights and alarms lit the wall behind them like a holiday celebration. Johnson ignored them. He stared at Ezekiel, and then turned back to where Angus still stared through the camera and into his soul.

"Who are you?" Johnson asked. "Who, in God's name, are you?"

"Names are only patterns," Angus replied. Then he smiled. "I am many, and I am one. I would tell you that I am the way, the truth, and the light, but she—pointing at the girl—would tell you I am Hermes, or Mithras, or Odin, and she cannot lie. It does not matter who I am. What matters, and what has always mattered, is who *you* are, and what you will become.

"The numbers have failed. In the beginning, there was the word—and that is all there has ever been. Plurality is divisive. Heaven isn't a chord, it's a single, pure note. Go, and learn to sing."

The monitor went dark. Power in the building flickered, and then dropped. For a long moment auxiliary power tried to kick in and bring it back to life—and then died. Ezekiel had gone. Johnson sifted through unfamiliar memories. He thought of the three in the other room, staring at blank screens that had been filled with numbers only moments before. He mouthed their names, and almost laughed.

"Shadrach, Meshech, and Abednego," he said softly. How had he not seen?

It didn't matter. Without a backward glance he turned, left the room and the building and walked out into the world. Behind him the monitor blinked to life without external power. Angus and Prime stood, wrapped in a tight embrace. Dark flecks danced up from the floor, peeled off the walls, and began to whirl. The flecks grew, diving and dancing through the air until they enlarged to numbers and words, letters and symbols. The cloud whirled faster and darker until the room was obscured by a tangle of dark images and shifting patterns.

And then it was gone. All that remained in the room was a battered spiral notebook and a number two pencil. On the top sheet, the Hexagram symbolizing "Obstruction" had torn down its center. On the streets beyond the building, men and women stepped out into bright sunlight...so bright, it burned.

If You Were Glass...

Ice. It coated the shelves, dripped columns of crystalline light down from cabinet to counter, smooth and constant. Frigid air hissed into the room through small valves protruding from the wall. Light from the lamps flickered from surface to surface like will-o-the-wisps or dancing diamonds. Jacob watched through a fogged window and smiled. His smile held no warmth.

The room where he sat was barely warmer than the icy palace beyond. The frost on the window showed the slight rise in temperature, but his breath, white puffs of frigid air, belied it. Jacob wore no gloves—no jacket. His black turtleneck sweater was thin, tucked tightly into black jeans that seemed too small to fit. The cuffs were frayed, and the frayed threads were frozen where they'd dragged across the rain-swept walk as he entered. Frost glistened on the smooth black of his ponytail. His lips were nearly blue, but there was no tremble to his hands. He held a glass—vodka—and ice.

Clay caked under his nails, dark now—hardened and flaking. Falling away. Dust to dust, ash to ash. Jacob lifted the glass to his lips and took a long swig of the clear liquor, letting it slide down his throat, ice—and fire. The flames from the kiln still danced before his eyes. The heat and the scent of baking clay permeated his lungs and lingered in his nostrils. He could never quite flush the fire from his mind or spit the sour stench of the clay from his lungs. The icy vodka dampened the flame.

In this outer room, the temperature was a steady thirty-eight degrees Fahrenheit. Not quite freezing, though closer to the windows, the temperature dropped dramatically. The joining of two worlds.

Once, it had been a dining room. Now it was a gateway.

There were three doors. One led to the world beyond, the other two doors leading inward. Two wardrobes, and two sets of tools in matched, black leather bags.

His numb fingers itched, but he steadied them and took another long sip from his drink. He couldn't hurry the process. If he began too soon, if his *other* world leaked beyond the frosted glass …

Jacob shook the thought from his mind. The ice clinked against the tumbler in his hand. Something in that sound jarred him deep inside. He stepped closer to the glass.

Directly across from the window, a long table stood against the wall, ice cascading down the front, water in static pseudo-motion, captured forever like a long-forgotten candle left to melt and puddle on the floor. He had designed the room so that the AC vents were placed high enough on the wall that the mist would not obscure his view of the table. Jacob stared intently at the object closest to him.

The gnomish creature glared back at him, eyes filled with malevolence, one hand raised behind itself, as if preparing to throw something in Jacob's face, or to slash with the claw-like nails of its too-small hand. Frozen. The sculpture glistened, brilliant and dancing with light from the cool overhead fluorescent lighting.

Jacob studied the sculpture, but his mind was drifting. He felt the heat of the not-quite-frozen air at his back warming him, and he stepped closer to the glass. His memory resurrected soft words, whispered in his ear from far too close. Words riding warm breath and lingering on his throat. His cheeks reddened in a sudden blush. Heat invaded other parts of his body.

His drink sloshed as the tumbler hit the wall with a soft clink. Icy vodka dripped over his hand and left frost-trails running between his fingers. Jacob laid his cheek on the cold glass and closed his eyes, trying to clear his mind. He needed to work, but not like this.

It's lovely, she'd said. Too close. *Too warm. It's lovely, but wouldn't it be exquisite if you'd used glass? If it magnified? If each of those wonderful angles glittered like a diamond?*

Glass. The glass on the window in front of Jacob's face

fogged, and the sculptures shimmered. He blinked. Focused. Everything faded. He saw her eyes reflected in the frost, felt her long, too-slender fingers teasing his hair. Felt transparent.

He pressed off from the window with a shudder. Just for a moment, his skin adhered, frozen in place. Joined to the glass— to the ice—to the frost.

"Not glass," he murmured. "Never glass. They could take that away. They could have it and hold it and..."

His mind whirled, and he pressed his hand flat on the window to steady himself as he let out a breath that nearly reached a growl.

It would be so COOL!

Her words echoed in Jacob's mind, and he winced. Cool? Cool wasn't enough. Never enough. Cold. A moment frozen. That was art. Fragile, fluid, and transient unless given one's full attention. Not timeless. Not to be hung in some huge, faceless building to be ogled by students and professors, would-be's and has-beens, critiquing what they didn't understand, judging experience that had never been their own by perception that could only, by definition, fall short. That was why Jacob had the clay. When he worked with the clay, it was for them. All the others. Let them stare. Let them wonder. God—let them stay away.

Glass.

Jacob shivered. His fingers itched to grip his tools. In the corner stood a small, faux-wood-grain refrigerator. Inside, he kept the chisels, the knives—a small and a large mallet. He kept them at twenty-eight degrees. Any colder, and it would take time to be able to handle them. Some had metal handles. Any warmer, and he would have to stand with them, watching the ice, not *working*, until they reached a temperature where he could place them on the frozen surfaces of the room without fear of damage. Lessons learned.

Jacob gulped the remaining vodka and felt it burning its way down his throat. There was fire, but without the heat most fires elicited. Without the danger.

He staggered to the small refrigerator and slapped the now empty glass down on top. He opened the door, grabbed his tool bag, and spun toward the room beyond the frosted glass. The refrigerator swung shut behind him with a soft *snik!* And he hurried to beat the encroachment of the heat.

He pressed a black inset switch in the wall, and the door to the gallery slid open, allowing him just the amount of time he needed to step inside before it closed on an automatic timer. Forty-five seconds. The point beyond which Jacob couldn't guarantee integrity. Two entire degrees of heat would gain entrance in the vicinity of the door, but the room was kept at a very steady fifteen degrees. Nothing important was kept too-near the door. Nothing would be lost.

As he turned to his work, Jacob was suddenly very aware of the window at his back—and that the window was made of glass.

The gallery was quiet when Jacob pulled over to the curb. It was early. They weren't scheduled to open for a couple more hours, but he'd wanted to give himself plenty of time. In his mind, he could hear Michael already, strutting around the gallery with the single, too-long curl of auburn-tinted hair bobbing against his cheek.

"Everything is *important* darling. Everything. The angle, the lighting—everything. You have *got* to give me time to work with things, Jacob." It was very early, and at that moment in time, Michael wouldn't be there to work his magic. Jacob would have to do his best—he tried never to leave anything to chance.

He was sweating. It was seventy-two degrees, and he stood in the shade of the gallery's low awning, a cool breeze tickling through his damp hair. Jacob had run the AC on high in his low-slung Mercury Cougar. The Freon had been recharged only a month prior, but he was considering taking it back in. The climate-control seemed unable to provide an environment much under sixty-nine degrees. Too hot.

With a quick press of the remote in his pocket, the trunk lid popped up, and Jacob reached inside. All of the work slated to be shown was already inside. Jacob hadn't counted on this newest piece—hadn't even meant to work on anything new—but it had come upon him in a frenzy, and he'd worked through most of the night. It was rough—just the clay—this piece—but what he'd done after—what waited in his gallery he was excited about.

As he lifted the sculpture from the trunk, his hands shook. His palms were sweaty, and he wanted to wipe them on his pants, but it was too late. He gripped the piece so tightly his knuckles grew white from the strain, and he turned too quickly, nearly tripping on the curb.

The sculpture was wrapped in black canvas. Covering the work in cloth helped him to steady his nerves. It wouldn't slip. The sweat soaked in and left him feeling clammy, but not slick. His mind wouldn't quite accept the logic of it. His hands were like quicksilver, and at each step he felt things shifting, the impression that he was losing balance. Jacob leaned on the door frame of the gallery before entering, closing his eyes and trying to calm his nerves.

Closing his eyes was a mistake.

He could still smell the kiln. Metal so hot the scent of it permeated the air. Moist clay, baking, all liquid draining out into the air, shriveling from the heart out and hardening. The glaze had left a cloying, sticky coating in his nostrils. It itched, then ached—burned into his skin. His hands had formed the image so clear in his mind, wet clay gleaming, glistening— almost like red ice. Almost.

Jacob remembered the heat, and in that instant, he felt it again, flowing over and around him. He imagined the liquid evaporating from his body. Imagined his eyes drying up and shriveling, sucked inward, skin pitted with the thousands of tiny imperfections the glaze could cover, but never truly heal.

Jacob clutched his package tighter and lurched through the door. He opened his eyes, just in time to see them reflect in the front window of the gallery. The image strobed through his mind. Captured. His eyes had been captured in that glass—not shriveling or melting. Not dry empty husks.

Jacob shivered and was thankful for the air-conditioning. The sculpture in his arms seemed to pulse with heat, and the stench of baked clay caked in his nose sickened him. It was cloying, reeking of a world too mundane and static. As he walked under the jetted air of one of the air-conditioning vents, Jacob closed his eyes again and willed his mind back to his work room. To the ice.

If it hadn't been for the necessity to earn money, he never would have come to this place. It was like a mortuary to him, his dreams, his visions baked into clumsy bricks and lined up for the curious. The room was lined with pedestals, shelves—displays of all types. Each was designed to set apart a particular piece, or group, of his work.

"This is *my* art, honey," Michael said, each time the subject was broached. "You *are* you; I *sell* you."

Not quite true, Jacob thought, steadying his nerves. The clay wasn't Jacob. It was close, a "rough" imitation of his art, but nothing more. The images he allowed Michael to present were imperfect. They were solid, clunky shadows of what was to come.

He placed his burden on an empty pedestal and caught his breath, then unfastened the drawstrings and drew the black cloth downward. Slowly, the sculpture was revealed. Tall, slender, with long hair trailing behind in a ponytail, Jacob mocked himself. The glaze was a deep brown, fading across the contours of the clay, darkening to pitch in the crevasses and sharper angles. Portrait of the artist. Hot. Too-hot, too-dry. Not real.

Jacob didn't know what had come over him. He didn't do reality. He didn't put the world that surrounded him, the super-heated, dry-to-the-bone images that bombarded him each day, into his work. He worked from his mind, from some recess that reality had overlooked, spiny lizards and serpentine dragons, gnomes and fairies, angels—demons. Among the pieces surrounding him, their hard-clay eyes glaring from shadows and splotches of sunlight slipping in through the windows, the new work was out of place. Though he'd stylized the piece by adding long flowing robes and giving himself a beard he'd never been able to grow, it was too close to mundane. He stared at himself, and he felt his tongue drying out like a piece of crumbling sandstone. He wanted vodka.

He lifted the sculpture from the pedestal and slid the bag

from beneath it, replacing it with a solid thump. Club-footed, half-finished crap, he thought. The eyes continued to stare back at him, eerie in their detail. Like staring into a mirror, reflected from glass. *Glass.*

At that precise moment, his mind registered that he'd heard another rhythm competing with the heavy backbeat of his heart. Footsteps? Fingers closed over his shoulder gently, and he felt hot breath on the back of his neck. Jacob froze, afraid he'd stumble and knock the statue from its base. Afraid he'd turn and find himself, staring back, an endless reflected hallway dragging him into an Escheresque nightmare.

"Perfect," she said softly. Her words brushed him physically, the air dancing over his clammy skin. "Who did you make yourself, Merlin? Moses? I like the beard."

Jacob didn't turn. He stared at the statue, acutely aware of each point where their skin touched. He hadn't thought about the source of the image in that way. He hadn't seen the wizard, or the prophet in the flowing robes—until that moment. He'd wanted the beard because it was a symbol. It was unattainable, like perfection in the clay, something he couldn't have, but that he could create. It was the *point* of it all.

"You don't think it would be better in glass?" he asked, his voice unsteady. There was something in her heat—the nearness of her flesh—that was unnerving. The sweat that coated his skin trickled in a thousand Chinese water torture rivulets, but he controlled the urge to shiver.

She hesitated, considering.

"If it were glass," she said at last, "I could see through you. Somehow," she turned him slowly, drawing him back and closer to her by her grip on his shoulder, "I don't think you'd like that very much. There's too much you don't show."

Jacob met her gaze, just for a moment, as he turned, then blushed and looked away. She reached out with one finger, long nail pressing up under his chin, and turned him back to face her.

"I don't want to see through you," she said softly. "I want to see inside. I would love to look out from there, to see what *you* see. If I looked through you, all I would see is something on the other side, and you wouldn't exist at all—or would you be my lens?"

Jacob heard the words, but he couldn't concentrate on them. She seemed to be talking for the sole purpose of blasting the sweet-hot scent of her breath across his face. He had the intense urge to spin and run, hit the door and never look back. The draw of his workshop was stronger than he'd ever felt it, the need to feel the soft hiss of Freon-cooled air washing over him near-overwhelming.

As if she sensed his thoughts, she tightened her grip slightly.

"Don't," she said softly. "I'm sorry. You don't even know me—not really. I'm Sylvia—Sylvia Mathers. I'm studying at the University, Visual Arts major. I've been to every show you've had in the last year."

Jacob's mind whirled back. January—at the beach. He vaguely remembered her, colored streaks in her hair, which had been braided then, but her eyes the same. He remembered. He'd put those eyes into a fairy, smoothed the shaved ice and diamond-bright chips away carefully. He'd molded them in clay and dried them for the world to see. He'd put the hair on an angel, as well, though the clay hid the colors.

Jacob's glance shifted to the right, and she followed with her own bright eyes. The fairy stood in one corner, half-shadowed. Sylvia's lips curved upward in a smile. Did she know? How could she know? It was only her eyes.

"I... I've had a lot of shows," he mumbled, trying to draw her attention away from the corner. What had she said? *Would you be my lens?*

He couldn't be a lens. He couldn't be seen through. He was dry, caked and solid, glazed and fired. Flesh / clay / all the same. Static. As she watched him, trying to read his eyes, he felt as if he'd put himself on display—not the clay statue, but something more. Something solid and permanent that could be viewed, and judged, criticized and misinterpreted.

"I have to go," he said quickly, drawing free of her fingers.

"The show?" she asked, eyes showing a bit of the hurt his rebuff had spawned. "Your show will be starting."

She was right. Jacob heard movement in the back of the

gallery, and the lights would be on soon. Perfect lights. The lights that made these clay mockeries of his work seem more than they were, that caught the perfect angles and showed just why each was placed as it was. Michael was not going to be pleased at seeing a new piece he hadn't had the chance to display properly. More reason to be absent.

"They don't come to see me," he mumbled, turning toward the door.

She called after him. "That is exactly what they—I—come to see. There is no separating it. The art is you."

Jacob heard her words trailing away behind him. Fading. Echoing.

"Not this art," he whispered.

Would you be my lens?

He slipped behind the wheel of his car, jammed the key into the ignition and fired the engine. Tepid air instantly poured from the AC vents, cooling slowly. Sweat ran freely down Jacob's arms, down his back and under his collar. His hands shook and he couldn't fix his mind on the act of putting the car in gear and pulling away from the curb. His head lolled onto the steering wheel, and he barely avoided setting off the horn.

The impossible sound of the passenger door opening brought him upright. Before he could speak, or act, she was sitting beside him. Her eyes were wide with fear—with the expectation of—what? Rejection? Anger? Jacob couldn't speak.

Then she had closed the door behind herself, leaned closer and slid her hand slowly up his thigh, one finger trailing along the inseam from knee to crotch. Her touch was hot, and as she pressed her lips suddenly to his ear, her tongue slipped out to tease his ear lobe.

"Show me," she whispered. "Take me where you work, the clay—the fire. Show me how you stole my eyes."

Jacob glanced to the latch of his own door, but he knew there was no way he could run. There was nowhere to go, and he couldn't leave her in his car.

Her hand pressed more firmly between his legs, palm rocking up and back, and he felt himself molded, felt her re-forming him with heat. Jacob shivered. There was nothing else to do but to pull into traffic and hope a shred of concentration would be left to keep them from plowing into the side of a building or painting a still life on a canvas of asphalt with the body of a passing jogger.

Jacob had never allowed a living soul into his workshop. Neither clay, nor ice. His payments were sent to a post office box at a post office miles from home. His utilities were in a dead cousin's name, and he had never had a phone. He had spent time with others, but never in his own space.

He had even known a few women—fans, mostly—rich older women with too-much makeup, expensive clothes, and leopard-skin heels—art students hoping something would rub off of his flesh—but not many. Time was too precious. His art was a fever that burned brighter and more painfully if he denied it, and his art left little room for the world beyond his walls. Eat. Sleep. Work. Anything else was an intrusion.

She was different. "Sylvia," he whispered softly.

He felt the zipper of his jeans sliding down and held his breath, afraid of the biting metal teeth. Afraid, suddenly, at how far and fast he'd pressed down on the gas pedal. The Cougar lurched through traffic, speeding, slowing, and Sylvia began to laugh softly, her hand fully inside his pants now, cupping him as her thumbnail stroked up and down the length of his erection.

"I have to work," he gasped, trying not to hit the brake and the gas at the same time. "I ..."

"I want to watch," she replied immediately, ignoring the panic in his voice. "I want to see how you do it—to see it *really* happen. Could you sculpt me? All of me, not just the eyes? Like you did with yourself—maybe an angel?"

Jacob closed his eyes and shuddered, despite the danger of driving blind. Then he forced them open and swerved, narrowly avoiding a parked Jeep.

He was panicked, and he hoped it wouldn't show in his eyes. He was too hot. The heat washed through him and burned in his cheeks. It rose to her touch. It seeped into the Cougar, battling the steady flow of cold air from the AC. Winning. He felt as if his skin would crackle and curl up.

Jacob gritted his teeth, not wanting to embarrass himself by releasing in her hand—in his pants. Not knowing how the fuck to react or to regain control. Not sure at all that he wanted to regain either as long as she kept her fingers working, slow and steady—as long as he didn't kill them both.

Miraculously he held on, pressing his spine so tightly into the seat back that he thought he'd warp the framework, shifting side-to-side in his seat each time the pressure threatened to bring that final release.

He made the final turn down the alley behind his home and wondered what the hell he was doing. He couldn't take her here. No one came here. Her hand curled around him and slid slowly in, and out—and he gasped a sharp little bark, gritting his teeth and cutting the engine, hand sliding down to grip her wrist and pull her back.

"What?" she asked, watching him, half smiling, half-worried that she'd committed some horrible offense and ruined the moment.

"Wait." he said. "Not here."

Her smile widened, and she nodded.

With a deep breath, Jacob opened his door and climbed out. He hesitated a moment, then moved to the passenger side door and opened it. Sylvia slipped out and Jacob pushed the door closed behind her, leaning on it a second to try and regain control. He felt his erection pressing tightly through his jeans and the heat that pulsed through his veins. He pushed off the car and lurched past her to the door, still unsure what he was doing—what he would do once they were inside.

He found the key and forced it into the lock. Sylvia pressed tightly to his back, and he shivered. With a quick twist of his wrist, he opened the door and pushed it wide, nearly falling inside from the pressure of Sylvia's body against his back.

At that moment, Jacob panicked. No one had ever been inside. He'd kept this place sacred, kept the silent promise of secrecy with his work. Now she would know. She would see what no one else had seen, and he would truly be transparent. Glass.

Jacob was afraid he might shatter.

Regaining his sense of balance, he turned and pressed a hand against her eyes, wondering what she'd seen.

"Wait," he said. "You asked me to show you—let me do that." He hesitated for a moment, then added, "No one has ever been here. Ever. You are the first. Let me be your guide."

"My lens," she answered, her words barely a breath of too-warm air, sweet-scented and tempting. Misting in the air. She shivered at the room's cold. The slip from outside into the constant thirty-eight degrees was a shock, even when you were used to it. Without a word, he turned her, and led her past the small refrigerator and through the second door.

It was hot. Stepping from the cool room to the heat, their clothing matted to their bodies within seconds. Jacob spun Sylvia slowly, hands on her shoulders, one turn for every four steps. He wanted to keep her off balance long enough to come to grips with what he'd done—what he was doing. Somehow, she had not seen the window. The secret—the real secret—was safe. Still, here she was, and as she spun, Jacob's attention caught and hung on the swell of her breasts and the small "o" of her tentative smile. Sylvia had very full, red lips.

Jacob stopped her suddenly, slipping in closer and wrapping his arms around her to steady her if she stumbled. Sylvia gasped, and as she did, he covered her lips with his own, teasing his tongue over even, white teeth. He pulled his hand away from her eyes, and she met his gaze with hunger, pressing into his arms.

The kiln loomed to their left, and behind her was his bench. Bits and chunks of clay littered the surface. Below the bench and lining the walls were metal cabinets—damp and cool, they held the huge plastic-sheathed bricks of clay. No shape, just block upon block of his future, stacked in pyramids and palisades of grey gook.

Unlike the cold room, there was no work on the table. When work was finished here, he glazed and fired it as quickly as time permitted. This wasn't a gallery; it was where he created. Where he worked with heat and clay, molding the rough work that the world shared. Jacob's work was born in fire, and at the moment, the fire worked within him as well.

Letting his hands slide down the small of her back, Jacob lifted Sylvia easily and stepped forward, letting her come to rest on the edge of his bench. She leaned back for a moment and watched him. Sweeping the room in a gaze filled with wonder, curiosity, and desire, Sylvia's smile widened. The kiln in the corner beckoned like a great, silent beast. The air was so warm that breathing was a conscious act.

Jacob saw the sweat sliding down her neck and disappearing beneath her blouse, and very suddenly he wanted to know exactly how it would continue downward. He wanted to know the final destination of each drop. As if linked to his thoughts, Sylvia gripped the bottom of her blouse and lifted, sliding it up and over her head and tossing it away behind her, where it landed atop a small mountain of clay blocks.

Jacob moved closer, but she held up one hand, her eyes challenging.

With practiced ease, Sylvia slipped from the remainder of her clothing, tossing each piece away without releasing Jacob's gaze. He watched and waited. His eyes watered from the salty sweat that drenched his hair and slid hot droplets down his cheeks. He sensed the heat of her body, but he respected the moment. Something hung in the air, something he couldn't define.

Jacob stepped forward again. Sylvia didn't move at first, her gaze locked on his eyes. Then her hands rose, pressing into his chest—stopping him just before the bulge of his jeans brushed between her thighs.

"You promised," she said, holding him with the soft pressure of her hands. "You said you'd sculpt me."

"I will," Jacob said, breath ragged and eyes suddenly wild with the need she dragged from him so easily. "I will."

"Now," she said. Her eyes flashed. Jacob knew she wanted him, knew that she was as hot as he was—Jesus, as hot as the kiln—but her eyes told him she was also serious. She leaned back against the bench, hands pressing down to lift herself up and back. Her thighs dropped to each side, and she slowly collapsed back against the wall. With one hand, she reached out and grabbed a glob of grey clay, lifting it and squeezing, letting it slide through her fingers, her gaze locked on Jacob.

He moved to the bench, but not to Sylvia. There was a space just to the left of her, between her thigh and the door of the kiln. Jacob moved to that space as if in a trance, walking forward, but watching Sylvia. He found the bench by running into it with his hands outstretched, and he stopped.

Jacob took in her features slowly. He let his gaze slide down her form so that every contour of her naked flesh etched itself into his mind. Then he closed his eyes and the image remained. Taking a deep breath, Jacob leaned to the cabinet beneath the bench, opened it and grabbed one of the blocks of damp clay. He reached for a second, then a third, before he was satisfied.

Sylvia watched him, eyes wide, sliding her fingernails up and down her naked thighs, leaving damp clay trails. Jacob shook his head and turned away from her. The room was hot, the temperature ten degrees higher than it needed to be. That is how he worked. This was different.

Sylvia's proximity shifted the dynamics of his universe. Jacob's pulse undulated slowly through his throat and pounded against the inside of his temple. There was a loud roaring in his ears that distracted his thoughts. He plunged his hands into the damp clay. Clutching the slick mass, he lifted his hands upward, drawing the clay into shape. His fingers kneaded convulsively, matching the hammering of his heart, and he forced the control that usually came so easily. He had to be gentler—had to remove all the bits and pieces of slimy gray clay that did not belong on the form. At the heart of every slab of clay his demons waited. If he didn't concentrate, they would not be freed, and the alternative was something Jacob didn't want to contemplate.

His thumb brushed down the center of the piece, forming the cleft between Sylvia's thighs and he started as she moaned. Jacob let his gaze flicker to Sylvia, then back, then again. He did not stare, not at her, and not at the clay. Jacob didn't work from models. He worked from memory—from his mind and vision. He knew if he looked too long and too hard, he'd lose the piece completely, and it was already difficult to concentrate with so much of his blood draining below his waistline.

He felt the heat of the kiln. The moisture drained from him

slowly, sweating out to run down his neck, his arms and legs, dampening his shirt. Sylvia was sweating as well. Jacob tried not to think of that sweat, trailing down the curves of her body. He grabbed a tool from the bench beside him, flicking a bit of clay loose, rolling it on the bench—returning it—rolled and smoothed, a tiny rivulet of sweat, the woman beside him taking form in miniature beneath his hands, the heat working its way into the mix as his nimble fingers formed flames that licked and tickled from the ends of the statue's hair. He worked hot coals into the base of the piece and more flames, sliding up her flesh, baking the liquid from her body. Hardening.

He was hardening.

Sweat burned his eyes and his pants, too tight to begin with, clung and chaffed each time he moved. The burning in his eyes blurred the room around him and he couldn't shake the image of steam. Moisture escaping.

The basic form was complete, and Jacob's fingers moved in the rhythm that set them apart from the fingers of a thousand other men. Each flick of his wrist sent a bit of clay flying, or pressed a shape into another shape, all so rapidly it was difficult, even for Jacob himself, to understand how such exquisite precision was possible.

Sylvia watched. Her lips were parted in—what? Wonder? Awe? Anticipation? Maybe pure hunger. Jacob couldn't be certain in the strobed flicker of images that was her face, the clay, her torso, the clay, his fingers molding as his mind recorded, and shifting it—each bit of it—to fit the fiery, molten creature he was transforming her into. A demon. A succubus.

And it came to him—to his touch and his call. He watched the clay, no longer needing the quick glances to the side to bring forth the magic. Her image was supplanted by the image of his creation. It was Sylvia, and it was not. She might as well have not been present.

Everything in the room was surrounded by a prismatic, multi-colored aura to his sweat-stung eyes. The statue gleamed, clay still wet, though it was slowly drying, the moisture seeping into the heat, misting and rising. It was hardening, and as Jacob's fingers gently stroked the smooth thighs, the long tresses of delicate hair, his own erection throbbed.

Then he felt her. Sylvia had moved, slipping down and off the bench to shadow him, pressing in from behind. She was careful. She didn't move in until his hands were back and up, away from the work, and only slowly.

"Hey," she whispered. "Where'd you go, genius?"

"Jacob shook his head, trying futilely to maintain the concentration.

"I ..."

He couldn't speak, and her hands were working now, much as his own had been, drawing the heat to each touch. He felt her breasts brushing the damp back of his shirt, felt her hips grind into him and her hand sliding around his thigh to grip him as he pulsed and lifted into her touch.

"It's wonderful," she said. "But you were—I don't know—gone. You didn't even know when I stood up and moved."

Jacob closed his eyes and leaned back into her for a moment, then he pressed up and off, hands on her thighs as he drew away.

"I can't leave it here," he said. "It has to be fired."

"I have some fire for you," she replied. Jacob heard the light disappointment in her voice.

Stepping to the kiln, Jacob reached over and turned the valve that would release the natural gas to the burners beneath. There was a soft *WHOOF!* as flames blossomed inside. The heat swelled. Jacob spun, walking to the workbench and sliding a tray near to the statue.

This was one of the trickiest parts. He had to get the piece onto the tray so that it could be slid into the kiln, but if he tilted it too far, or moved too quickly—if the sweat dripped into his eye and he staggered, it would be gone. All of it. There would be nothing left of the inspiration but a ruined blob. Already, it was drying.

Jacob slid a plastic paddle carefully under the clay base, lifting very gently with his free hand and working slowly. There was a particular danger of shifting the hair, and the flames, the tips of which were rolled very thin.

He didn't notice the quick burst of cold air as the door

opened and closed.

The heat was palpable, permeating the air as Jacob slid the paddle / shelf into the kiln. He took a last look at the work, nearly reached out to touch it through the searing heat, then pulled back. He slid the door closed and he closed his eyes as well, letting the last image of the un-fired clay linger.

It was quiet. So very quiet that it itched at his mind. Opening his eyes and spinning, Jacob realized with a start that he was alone. He vaguely remembered brushing Sylvia off before placing his work in the kiln. He'd been so engrossed in that work that he'd not noticed her leaving.

"No." That single word and he was moving, muscles aching from prolonged standing and work in the high heat. The sudden motion made him dizzy, but he managed to reach the door and tug it open, slipping into the room beyond.

She wasn't there. Jacob looked around frantically, but there was no sign of Sylvia, other than her purse, which lay on a small table just inside the door. Not gone—then where?

His heart sank. He glanced at the frosted glass, and he saw a flash of dark where there should have been only crystal and light. The door to the ice room was closed—but she was inside. The timer had sealed off the heat. His heart clogged his throat in a sudden spasm of disbelief.

"No." he said again, leaping toward the door to the gallery. He was too hot, he knew that, and the clammy sweat that clung to his limbs and clothing would freeze to his flesh within moments of entering, but no options remained. He had to get her out of that room, out of his home and his life. Had to compensate before her heat, and the heat of the room she'd unleashed unwittingly damaged his work.

As he slipped through the door and pressed the button to close it, not waiting for the timer, he leaned back into its frigid surface to get his bearings. She turned. Her features glowed. Her eyes sparkled and her fingers, he saw at a glance, rested atop the head of the gnome at the end of the row. Hot fingers. Hot flesh. Melting—releasing the moisture. Drying it away.

He stepped away from the door, and she turned to him,

clasping her arms about herself. For the first time, Jacob noticed that she was still naked. She'd not removed the clay that had clung to her thighs as she stroked herself, and her nipples were taut—frozen. Her skin had a bluish tinge, and her breath smoked through pale lips. She was trembling.

"We—you have to get out," Jacob said.

Sylvia shook her head slowly, either in negation or disbelief. She stared at him, but she didn't really seem to be seeing him at all. Her movements were slow, and Jacob realized with sudden clarity that she'd been in the room too long. Hypothermia was setting in.

"You have to get warm," he said. *You have to get OUT!* he thought.

He stepped toward her, and she turned away. Her limbs were clumsy, stiff from the cold, and her feet had frozen to the floor where her flesh momentarily melted the ice, then held still long enough for it to harden.

Jacob realized with sudden clarity that he was still hard. Throbbing. She was more like ice than any warm flesh he'd seen. She was turning to ice for him, heat, clay—then ice. His art, hard, cold, and smooth. Enticing.

Then she was falling. It was very sudden in contrast to her sluggish motion. She tripped, tilted forward, and staggered a single step before giving up hope and raising her arms to protect her face.

The long display bench stood directly before her, lined with his work. Lined in ice and sculpted carefully. Beside the gnome, the crystalline image of Jacob, bared and frigid, gleamed, its arm outstretched to her toppling form. Jacob was moving too slowly.

Sylvia's arms struck the bench sharply, twisting her and she fell with a dull thud, the sound dulled by the heavy mist in the air. As she struck, her head whipped back, striking the bench with a sickening *thunk*.

Jacob slid to his knees at her side, crashing into the table in his haste. There was a crash, like thunder, and Jacob felt his own head crack into the ice-coated wood of the display table.

Cold misting air hissed through the vents on the wall.

The wizard-Jacob toppled.

Jacob reached out to try and catch it, to right it on the bench, but other works were falling as well, and he twisted, confused and disoriented. The ice-sculpture toppled over the edge and down, its outstretched arm striking directly between Sylvia's naked breasts.

Jacob's question was answered, then, as the ice pierced her skin, and she screamed. She was alive. The statue leaned, caught now in her flesh, based tilted at an angle against the table behind. Sylvia arched, trying to rise, to push away, to move. Failing.

The room spun. Blood dripped down the side of his head where he'd struck the table. The tinkling crash of ice breaking echoed in his mind. Fallen, all but the gnome had fallen, some breaking, some shattering completely, others canted at odd angles.

Jacob staggered to his feet, gripping the edge of the table for support. He wanted to help her, but his mind reeled. Blood dripped into one eye now, and the room shimmered as the warmer air of the room beyond dragged mist from the slowly heating ice. His work was a wasteland, and his breath came in shallow gulps.

Out. He had to get her, get out.

Jacob turned, too quickly, and his foot slipped. Again. His knees struck hard, and pain shot up through his body—paralyzing him before he could brace himself against the fall. His face struck the back of the wizard. His weight forced it down, deeper into Sylvia's arched, too-still form. Through skin gone blue and cold. The second impact on his head was too much, and his knees felt as if they'd been shattered.

Jacob tried to rise, but he found that his arms would not move. Nothing would move. Nothing. He stared.

The statue was clear and brilliant, stained in red below but pure and glistening between them. He saw Sylvia, her face drawn back as if to continue her long-silent scream. He saw her through the ice, through the image of his own body—the blue of her lips magnified—the clear depths of her eyes gone pale and empty.

"Be my lens."

The words whispered through his mind as thought faded and the numbing cold stole through him.

In the room beyond the room beyond, the fire burned bright and hot. The moisture melted and boiled from the clay. Earthy and hard. Drained.

Lips, cracking with cold, froze in a smile.

Angels

Cynthia didn't talk to angels, but she saw them. She never mentioned them. She didn't watch them directly, only out of the corner of her eye, and only because they were always *there*. It wasn't like she had a choice. They haunted the periphery of her vision, watched her world from the shadows, but they never watched her. Synthia saw the angels, but they didn't know she was alive.

When Syn had been ten, she'd tried to tell her mother. She'd sat down at the kitchen table and asked to share the oddly scented herb tea that filled her mother's afternoons. She could still recall the heat of the cup as she wrapped her small hands around it, and the way the mint and herbs had sifted up through the mist to tickle her nose.

She'd felt very grown up that day, as if a page in her life had turned, or a cycle had shifted to the next ring. Her mother had had very deep, brown eyes, and long hair teasing down over her shoulders. Syn remembered the way the morning sunlight had filtered through the blinds, striping the refrigerator like a surreal, oblong zebra. She remembered her mother's odd little smile, the one that caused the shift. The one that made them friends, in that moment, and not mother and daughter. Deceptions were realities on all levels. That smile had drawn her in, and Syn had spoken her heart.

She had told her mother then, about the old woman on the landing of the stairs, white hair wisping about her face and eyes wide in pain, or fear. She told her mother about the two boys who mirrored her steps as she walked to school, books clutched tightly to her chest and eyes to the ground so that they would not catch her attention. She told her mother about the girl in the shower at school, the one who was there, always, naked and cringing in the corner, and the shadowy, half-seen figure who hovered over her. She even told her mother, for the first time, why it was that when they went to visit Grandmother's grave, Syn had clutched so tightly to her leg.

Throughout that dialogue, Syn's mother had not said a word. She'd nodded, sipped her tea, and listened. Silence is golden. Right. The liquid that had slid into the syringe had been golden. The doctor's eyes had been a deep, golden brown. Her mother's smile had been as sweet as golden honey. Nothing. Syn's mother had believed nothing. She'd called a doctor, and Syn had told her story again. The drugs had followed. One drug, another, and another still, in quick succession, each chemical attack trying to drive out the demons. Trying to drive out something that was just *there*, not illusion but frightening reality, made more frightening as the drugs robbed Synthia's control. There was no way to make them understand; only silence had helped. The silence had stopped the drugs, but by then two years had passed. Cynthia had passed to Synthia irrevocably, awakening as a junior in high school with barely passing marks and no friends with a future. Through it all the angels had watched the world in silence, and she had watched them in turn, never speaking.

Now they were multiplying. No matter where Syn turned, she saw them. When she closed her eyes, she felt them. When she slept, she dreamed dreams populated with their shadowy forms and empty eyes. She didn't even know why she called them angels. They looked more like ghosts, but that wasn't a place she felt comfortable. Angels would never hurt her... ghosts might not care. Ghosts might have laughed when Momma and the doctor brought the drugs. The angels had paid no more attention to the drugs than anything else.

Since the night Brandt had left the band, the ghosts had slowly overrun her reality. She knew it was foolish to dwell in the past. She hadn't spent enough time with Brandt when he was with them. She had teased him, promised him, but she'd never let him get close. Now he was gone, and that music—that last night. How could she reconcile herself to the reality that was the band

and the memory that was Brandt and feel anything but loss and regret? How could she live her life walking through a mist of angels? Brandt had noticed her. Without that notice, the weight of his eyes and the soft sound of his voice, the nothingness of the angels' presence weighed on her like a shroud.

Syn rose, pulling the sheets up around her, automatically shielding herself from the prying eyes of those who didn't even watch. She blinked and shook her head to clear the cobwebs. She needed to hurry and shower. Shaver would call soon. He called her like clockwork, every afternoon at four. It gave her a minimum number of minutes to shower, paint herself to perfection, and gather her wits. It gave her a chance to push aside the visions and focus on herself, and her life. Angels didn't pay the bills, and though the band wasn't breaking any records, since Brandt's drunken ass had carried itself so dramatically down the road, they had been doing well enough to get by. They might even break out of the bar circuit and cut a CD soon. If Syn could keep it together. If Shaver didn't lose his heart. If the new guy, the pseudo-Brandt they'd hired, Calvin, with his long, long hair and his long, long eyes, and his constant sniffing; no way to ignore the chemical base of *that* subconscious habit. Calvin could play. Calvin could sing. Calvin was barely aware that he could do either. He was helping the band in ways that Brandt never could have, but… he was no Brandt.

Synthia felt Brandt's loss in ways she'd not been willing to admit possible. He had always just been *there*. Now there was the band, and her life, and the angels. Nothing else. Nothing that touched her on a deeper level than a mild sunburn. Not that Brandt had ever seemed so important. Synthia had spent more time cursing him than talking to him, and though she'd felt very comfortable in his presence, she'd not spent as much time there as she might have. No reason to. No reason to believe the opportunity would not present itself in its own time.

Now he had marched off down the road, right through the gathered ranks of angels who had actually watched him go, not ignoring him, as they did Synthia, as they had *always* ignored her. Brandt had left her to watch his receding back, looking somehow more appealing in the tight, faded jeans than she'd remembered him. And he'd left the memory of the music. Brandt had always been good. He'd always been just able to pull it off, no matter how drunk or out of it he might have been.

The music had meant more then, though it had taken the vacuum of Calvin and the "new" sound to drive that reality home. Even through the thick white makeup, dead-clown pretty-boy attitude, and sneering lips that sugar-coated a frustrated heart, Syn had sensed Brandt's talent. Each time Syn had been ready to kick his ass out on the street and demand he be replaced by someone who would at least show up for practice, he'd pulled something out of his ass and tugged at her heart strings with it.

Synthia remembered the night she'd convinced him to take her out, to the carnival. That night Syn had nearly told him about the angels. Then the old witch lady had turned over that card, and Brandt had flipped out. The moment, and the courage to speak, had slipped away.

Everything had been so right that night. Syn had felt so close to him, so special to be with him, though she'd have never said so. None of the others ever seemed to get it, but Brandt did. During his rare lucid moments, he was the only voice she trusted to answer her in the same language she asked a question. That night might have been the beginning of something special, but she'd seen that damned tent, and the past had intruded once more. There had been a single old angel, kneeling by the door in prayer, or sorrow. Brandt, of course, had seen nothing. The old angel's hands had scratched what seemed at first to be random lines in the dirt. The random lines had formed a word.

"Remember."

Synthia had read the word, turned from the angel, and her vision, and the only straight path had led through the doorway of the tent, toward the cards and destiny. Synthia's words, the whispered confidence she'd meant to share with Brandt, had slipped a notch back down her throat, and the night had done the rest. Stolen moments were often taken back. Rules of the road in the game of Life. Brandt had staggered out of the tent, drunk, tripping, and he'd fallen. Syn had followed, but the chemicals had robbed her of her strength, her ability to help him. She had tried, *God* she had tried, but the act of *trying* had pumped her blood more swiftly and the drugs more powerfully, and they had nearly *both* ended up lying together in the dirt, staring at the huge Ferris wheel instead of just Brandt. At what? She'd never asked him what he'd seen.

They never watched her. They never saw her. She saw the angels, but they ignored her. That was her pain. Her mother had seen her, but never really *seen* anything. Her father hadn't seen her at all. Boys, men, all had seen her body, her heat. None had seen beyond it. She had her own silent chorus of angels, mocking/accompanying her dirge-like song of life.

That was why Syn played the bass. The deep, droning tones. The vibration straight through to her soul and back again. Even the angels wavered when she played. When the deep intonations of rhythm and resonant power rippled through the air, it took on a deeper acuity. The angels did not listen to her bass, but they felt it. The universe was one giant chord, one universal vibration. Syn longed to find her niche in that unity. Her heart was a rebel... fighting her desire. Her playing was dissonant, deep, wild, and passionate, but it seldom blended. Instead, it forced the blend to her... forced her to become the eye of the storm, and every eye to seek her form. The only time she could forget that the angels ignored her was when no one else did.

She'd never asked Brandt why he staggered out of that tent, or what he'd seen, stumbling into the midway. She had stared into his eyes as he stared up at the Ferris wheel, far above them, and she'd seen... something, reflected in his eyes. She couldn't remember what, or who.

The phone's ring ripped through the silence. Syn gripped the blanket around herself more tightly, willing the world to silence. Failing.

She rose, the blanket trailing away behind her, gripping the phone's receiver tightly and drawing it to her ear, concentrating.

"Yeah?"

"Rise and shine, Princess." Shaver's voice was edged with caffeine and fueled by that bright, inner fire that set him apart from every other being on the planet. Lead notes rippled through the tones of his voice if you knew him. The taut, corded muscles of his arms spoke of an inner fury, a driving need that only the guitar could sate, and then, apparently, poorly. Shaver had been, if possible, even more intense since Brandt's revelation and departure. His leads were faster. His eyes wider and more incomplete in the perfection of his motion. A technical marvel with etched tears tattooed on cheeks of granite... muscles drawn so tight they could turn bullets aside. The angels didn't watch Shaver either.

"I'm up," she said. "I'll be there."

"Coffee is on me," he said, and then the click/buzz/tone of the phone and silence again. Somehow it was less perfect, less intimate.

Syn let the blanket fall away with a sigh and rose, moving to the bathroom, the shower, hot, soap-scented mist, and the grit of the past swirling away, sliding over the lip of the drain and into oblivion. The clock ticked. Rhythm of reality. She needed to get in and out of that steamy heaven and down the road to the coffee, Shaver, and the club. If things worked out, this could be their last night at Sid's. The "right" people would be in the audience tonight.

Calvin had managed it, somehow. Calvin and his drugs, his mediocre, good-enough-for-record-company-work guitar, his scratchy, cigarette-ravaged voice. His "Rod Stewart stars in the *Day of the Living Dead*" perfect look. Calvin had the package that sold. They should change the band's name to Pretty and Empty. The angels wouldn't care. The angels didn't even listen, no matter how hard Syn played, or cried, screamed, or lied. They stared into the nothingness of eternity and Syn was left to watch them as they watched. Alone.

Quick paint job at the mirror, pointedly ignoring the figure in the corner, a stooped old man staring out the window as if he'd been watching the city grow for a hundred years. Syn worked the mascara and blush carefully, practiced flicks of her wrist painting the hard, brittle edges of her eyes, first defense against the crowd. First defense against Calvin. If they didn't get the recording contract, she would have to do something with or about Calvin. The latter made her nauseous, and the former scared her like nothing in her life had scared her before.

The record execs had been around before. She'd seen them tossing back expensive drinks and slumping in corner booths, watching and smiling like they cared. They didn't listen any more than the angels, most of the time. Maybe recording contracts had nothing to do with what they heard. It didn't matter. Somehow Syn knew that if they didn't listen tonight, she was gone. No plan, nowhere to go, but she was out. Shaver would be fine. Caffeine and high E would get him a ticket anywhere he wanted to go. Calvin? Fuck Calvin. He would probably be signing copies of his tenth gold record within a couple of years, with or without Synthia. With or without Shaver. With or without a meaningful thought or moment in his long, tired existence. As he signed, the ghosts would stand around, oblivious. Synthia needed to hear them sing.

Brandt had done it. Fucking Brandt with his drunken-ass lyrics and his so-natural-the-fucking-alcohol-couldn't-blunt-it talent. His sad, out-of-date clown-face paint and words no one else had understood, but that everybody had loved. His beautiful guitar and tenement apartment. His voice, clear and transcendent when it didn't slur and spout the wrong words in long litanies that meant as much to the crowd as the real words—nothing at all. Brandt and that magic night he'd left, when the angels had played, and sung, and danced. The crowd and the band had watched Brandt. Syn had watched the angels, and on that single night, they had watched back, not just her, but Brandt, and the band… the crowd. They had spoken, and joined the song, making it something more than just Brandt's song. Brandt had flowed through the notes, but Synthia had felt them in her heart, and those of the others who heard. Brandt had played, and the world had gone still.

But Brandt was gone. Syn shook her head. Coffee. Club. Music. Those were the only things that could bring even temporary solace. If she closed her eyes, let her fingers draw the rhythmic, pulsing notes from the bass and her voice join with Calvin's, it formed a barrier. The angels didn't listen, but at least they seemed remote, part of the audience and the energy. They were less depressing as backdrop to the sound.

The coffee did less than Syn had hoped to raise her energy

level. As she sipped the Americano, a tall iced-tea glass of black coffee with a shot of espresso, she'd been preoccupied by the young girl at the window. The girl's back was to the world outside, her gaze locked to the back of the bar. Not exactly a bar now but a bar in the past. Syn knew this as truth, though she had no way of knowing *how* she knew. She also knew that the angel... the girl... knew it. The world the girl watched was different. In that world, Syn did not exist. It hurt. Alone in the crowd and singing to nobody, that was Syn's story.

The coffee had burned her tongue, and it rolled around inside her, the caffeine waking her body, but the empty ache of no food and too much sleep fogging her mind. She couldn't get Brandt, or his angels, out of her mind. She drank the bitter liquid down quickly, hit the street, and headed for the club.

Sid's wasn't too busy for a Friday night. There was a small crowd of regulars gathered near the bar and the pool table, but nothing to write home about. Synthia moved past them all, oblivious to the stares and soft catcalls. She was used to it. If she could stand the empty gazes of the myriad angels populating the vacant tables and leaning against the dingy walls, a few Goth-Punks and losers weren't likely to cause much stress. No sign of the record company, but no surprise there. Too early for anything serious. If they showed, it would likely be somewhere mid-third set, when the band was catching their stride, or stumbling to fall on their faces. Either way, it eliminated the gray areas.

Syn slipped through to the back, closed the dressing room door behind her, and leaned back against it to catch her breath. Something was different, something in the air, the taste of the evening on her dry lips. For once she was alone. None of the others was in the back room, and there were no angels. Syn turned to the mirror, watching herself watch herself and thinking.

When she exited the room, turning toward the stage in silence, her face was white. Ghost white. She'd found an old tube of Brandt's makeup. None of the black he'd used to darken his eyes and accent his lips, only the white, blanking out all that was unique, all that made her stand out from the crowd. She came to the stage as a blank page and lifted the strap of her bass over her shoulders with a quick shrug.

Brandt had always told her that the bass was the backdrop, the canvas across which the music was painted. If she faltered, the image was skewed. If she lost the rhythm, the lines would waver, and the notes fall to discord. Shaver would shift off into a discordant shiver of steel-strung notes with no stable support. Face white, ready for the music, she became that canvas. Shaver stared at her for a long moment, his brow furrowed in concentration, then nodded and turned away, tuning. Always tuning, a nervous habit, fingers molded to the keys. Calvin's jaw dropped. He started to speak, started to make a bigger fool of himself than life had managed, then clamped down on his tongue.

What crowd there was grew silent. There was no one there who'd not heard the band before. There was no man in that bar that had not, in some way, come to share a moment with Synthia. To steal a fantasy from the supple curves of her body, the taut strength of her wrists and forearms as she played. The deep, purr-growl of her voice when the words were hers and the higher-pitched backdrops she laid for Calvin's throaty, grinding vocals. The white-empty face changed everything. Synthia's arms cradled the bass, but her face was... blank. No one knew how to react, so no one did. The angels didn't even notice.

The lights dimmed. Some bright-boy behind the bar found a single black-light spot and focused it on the stage, on Syn and her white-makeup, now brilliant and glowing. The eerie blue illumination removed even more definition from her features, a purple-haloed ball of captured moonlight floating above the glistening sheen of the sunburst finish on her bass. Energy. Synergy. Sound and motion blurred to wipe her from their sight and minds.

Syn couldn't see this. She felt it. The sound started, at first no different from a hundred other nights. Soft shimmer of cymbals, rippling to snare and back to cymbals. Dexter, the one constant in the band, the rhythm behind the rhythm. Dexter and his "skins," who never said word one to anyone but Shaver, who just showed up, played, and left. Syn's fingers moved to the strings of the bass, slipping into a slow, pounding thud of notes, overgrown-heartbeat rhythm rippling from the strings, winding down the wires and out through the speakers to shimmer through the air.

No one moved in the audience, no hips matching the swaying pulse of Syn's own, no feet shuffling. She knew they were watching her. They always watched her. It was different. She felt them seeking her face, her eyes, trying to pierce the black-light glare and the blinding white of the paint to meet her gaze. They seldom let their attention roam that high when she played. They were usually too occupied with their own fantasies to hear the lyrics, and too ashamed of them to let her catch their gaze. Tonight, they were denied, so they sought the reasons in her eyes.

The band followed her lead. Calvin found a way to make his following seem like leading. That was his way, but everyone knew. The bass wrapped its notes around the music and wrestled it to submission, and beyond. The rhythm drove the melody. The lyrics hung from a backdrop of resonant harmony so deep and soulful that the air/floor/room shook with the power of it. The angels shimmered around the edges of the bar, stood nonchalantly in doorways, staring into eternity. Nothing. They were everywhere, and nowhere, and Synthia felt something inside her slip hard, falling away. A layer of—need, closer to the raw pain beyond. Her fingers had begun to ache, but she twisted the notes deeper. She played to the angels, the room slipping away, and the band towed in her wake.

She played the usual songs. The band knew the chords, the rhythms. It wasn't like when Brandt had just taken over the stage and silenced them all with his pain... their pain... the world's pain. She didn't change the music fundamentally. It was the subtle shifts of emotion, the infusion of her frustration, and her hunger, that drove the notes deeper into the minds and hearts around her. Somewhere in that crowd were the record execs, or not. It didn't matter anymore.

Surrounding them, filling in gaps in the crowd, the angels stood, impervious, and the tears flowed down Syn's cheeks as she aimed her notes at their ethereal hearts.

She had never played to them before. She had watched them, all her life she'd watched them as they ignored her. Now she needed to know. Who were they? What were they watching that was so damned important they couldn't see her... hear her... comfort her? Who the *fuck* were they and why wouldn't they *hear*?

The songs shifted, one to the next. Syn caught short glimpses of Calvin's eyes, begging her to slow, to stop, to take a break. She turned to the side and saw that Shaver's fingers bled. He ignored it, as she ignored Calvin, but the music could not go on indefinitely. She felt as if she could play forever—close her eyes and drift into the music and not return. Syn didn't look at her own fingers or think about them. The pain was there, but it didn't matter. The crowd shifted.

A figure wound slowly through the eerily quiet crowd toward the dance floor. Syn's eyes were half-blind from the spotlights, and the black light. She saw strobing, half-formed images, the one moving closer and the others that surrounded it. She concentrated. She couldn't tell if it was a man, a woman, or an angel, but she played to that figure. It was the last song of the set, maybe the last song of her life, and she played it with no remorse. The sweat and tears blurred her sight and she blinked, fighting to see, to know who would share that moment.

There was something achingly familiar in that swaying gait. Syn could make out long hair, but no features. She played. She felt the resonance of the bass through to her bones, felt the growing fire that was her fingers, and the strings, and the slickening of both, but the notes did not falter. No way. Not this time. There might never be another chance, and the face became clearer with each step, narrowing the gap between them, and the years. Syn's voice wavered, just for a second. Between verses, when she should have breathed, she spoke.

"Mother?"

For that eternal moment, the band sustained her. Those she had dragged swelled up behind her, Shaver's notes, still crisp and rippling, so technically perfect they seemed magical, and Calvin, his usually weak rhythm crunching suddenly, as he sensed her near-falter. Dexter, solid, bolstering the rhythm and jumpstarting her fingers. They sacrificed themselves to that moment, held together, bonding and transcending the bar, and the mediocre, blues-cover melody to join in something more powerful. Syn breathed deep and sank to her knees on the stage... staring as her mother's form moved closer. Her fingers moved with the sound, her arm shifting, the bass a part of her, held close and tight.

The notes were winding down, but it no longer mattered. Synthia had no idea how she knew, but the thrumming of the notes slowly gave way to the thudding of her heartbeat, and the bass, still clutched tightly to her chest, grew silent. The room receded, sucked into a vacuum that left nothing but Syn, white-faced ghost girl and the angel/spirit of her past, faced off in a duel of eyes and silence.

Somewhere in the distance, the music continued. Syn knew it wasn't the band. The crowd was silent, staring. The magic of the band's moment was fading. She couldn't tell if they saw, finally fucking *saw* the angels, but they knew that she saw... something. Someone. Why now?

Her eyes raised to meet the milky-white, cataract-glazed gaze of yesterday. Syn felt something lift free of her soul, but it did not make her feel better. She felt bare, naked before the crowd, nasty secrets and mother's love dragged to center stage in black-light synapse-strobed images.

The angel reached out dim-white hands, veined in deep blue, as if to stroke Syn's cheek, but falling short, always falling short. Syn nodded. Just like all those years before. Just that much short of all right. Syn held still, strained forward inside, and gritted her teeth, rigid on the outside. No way she leaned into that touch. No way.

The moment passed, and a soft sigh escaped the angel's lips, first sound, only sound, Syn had heard from one of the apparitions other than the music, Brandt's music. That sigh, nothing more. No apology. No words could have mattered. No touch could have mattered. Syn lifted her gaze to her mother's, held it for a long moment, and watched through a sudden flow of salty tears as that face, so long gone from her life, melted once more, as the lights haloed. Syn's lip quivered.

Syn slithered back and away suddenly. Her head drooped and her eyes closed. She clutched the bass and she rose in a stumbling lurch. She felt the drums topple as she backed into them, microphones tilting and stands trapping her feet. Somehow, she remained upright as her world crashed in a metallic heap. She was vaguely aware of the others, cursing, calling out to her, and touching her shoulders. She shrugged them off. She heard the voices of those who'd watched from the audience.

She moved through them, away from the stage toward the door. The crowd parted. Some of the braver among them stretched out their hands, brushing her skin, tugging at her clothes. One woman stepped into Syn's path and tugged at the bass, as if she would take it for her own. Syn rocked her hip forward quickly, and the woman stumbled back with a soft, surprised cry, coming to rest against the wall beside the doorframe as Syn slid sideways through and into the night, careful not to crack the bass on the wooden frame.

She knew they were calling out to her. The others: Shaver, Calvin, the bartender, maybe Sid himself. A hand grabbed her suddenly by the shoulder as she turned away from the club and started down the walk. Syn spun in a daze, meeting a set of too-bright eyes. Her own turned down to where his hand held her arm.

"...wonderful," he was saying. "Exactly what we are looking for, what the scene needs, you know?" His voice was too fast, the words slipping from sincerity to business to sleaze in increments so obvious Syn could barely follow the progression. "... just sign, and of course the band, though they aren't a *deal breaker*, you know, because I can *see* who the talent is here..."

Syn pulled her arm back violently, glaring at the man. "Get away from me."

The man held her arm a moment longer. He blinked, as if struck, as if there was no possible way in the universe he could have heard what he just heard.

"You don't understand," he said more slowly.

Carefully, not wanting to break his fingers... yet... she gripped his wrist and yanked his hand free of her arm. "Get the *fuck* away from me."

He started to say something. He even reached for her again, but something in Syn's eyes must have warned him away. The man stood, looking very foolish in his power suit and expensive jewelry, Rolex gleaming under the soft glow of streetlamps and a small crowd gathering at his back, pouring from the mouth of the club in a slow, curious stream. Syn turned without a thought, bass sliding to her hip, dangling from the strap. She saw the angels, lining the streets. They did not ignore her, nor did they speak, or move. They watched, and she walked, steps as steady as her heartbeat.

Behind her she heard Calvin's shrill, whining voice, begging the idiot in the suit, selling what little soul he had left and trying to include hers as if it were his to sell. It meant less than nothing. So close, she'd been so close to letting the answers slip away. She wondered if the angels would have faded if she'd signed that paper, if she'd never seen her mother, and the music had carried her in a different direction. She wondered if Calvin would ever understand. She wondered where the music was coming from that dragged her on.

She moved through streets of dim light and scattered shadow. No one else moved, slow-traffic parade, coming and going in a rise-to-fade shimmer of sound and headlights. Synthia passed no living soul, but the angels lined the road, translucent sentinels tracing her motion with their eyes. She felt them as she never had before, and the sound, the music, swelled up around her, gripping her heart and twisting. It was her. The music was her song, her pain, and she felt the march of angel after angel, ghost after ghost, not speaking to her, but acknowledging, each moment where they'd slipped away silently brought back in a wash of images, and pain.

She reached 37th Street and turned, winding down Elm, knowing what was ahead and shivering. Her arm snaked down, drawing the bass to her like a lover. The music was louder, and she knew. Somehow, she knew who it was. There were the sweet-soft strains of harmonica, the soul-deep song of a lone guitar. A thousand voices sang deep harmony in soft, half-whispered tones that led her on. Syn felt like the star in a bad horror flick, angel choruses leading her home.

Then the voice sounded, so close to her ear she couldn't understand why she didn't feel the warm brush of breath.

"Ain't no angels, sugar," the voice grated rough and sweet as the whiskey and honey cough remedy Syn's Grandma had given her when she was a child. "Just those dead and gone, and those just dead. You come to sing, you come to da right place, little one."

Synthia trembled, but she didn't turn. She knew that voice. She'd heard it once before: the night Brandt had disappeared. For the first time in as many days as she could imagine, she wasn't concerned with the angels. She followed the guitar, stepping through the entrance to the graveyard and feeling the gravel crunch beneath her feet. The gates were open. No security for the dead.

Syn wound down familiar trails, through a maze of white-stone markers and pretentious monuments to those beyond caring. White marble angels watched her progress, and the moonlight patterned the trail with crosses, shadows from the graves that lined the way.

She didn't stop until she reached a familiar plot and a dingy, off-white stone, rectangular and low-slung. Insignificant. One forgotten bit of granite in a garden where memories grew—this bit forgotten.

Synthia fell to her knees in the soft earth, letting the bass rest against her thigh. Tears trickled down her cheeks, but she wiped them away. The words were still clear, etched in stiff, final precision across the stone. Syn reached out, long black-painted nail tracing the final tribute to her mother's life.

She half-expected her mother's angel to appear again. Or ghost. Or whatever. She expected to hear the scolding tones of her mother's voice. Out so late, and in a graveyard. It's what comes of hanging out with no-goods and playing *that* music. What happens to girls who talk about seeing things that couldn't be. Angels. The tears streamed, and the gravestone rippled, but she stared, stubbornly, blinking against the salty pain.

"She loved you, you know." The voice rippled with her vision, slipped through her senses, and gripped her heart.

Brandt. His fingers still worked the strings of the guitar, the strings of her heart.

"Fuck you," Syn said through her tears, voice tearing roughly from her throat. "She didn't even know me."

"That is why it didn't work," Brandt said. "Doesn't change the love, only the outcome. She saw them too, you know."

Syn whipped around, finding Brandt lounging back over a mausoleum to her left. His fingers moved as he spoke, stroking the strings. The soft melody echoed the bittersweet march that had led her to the graveyard, to the stone and the memories.

"What do you mean?" she asked, knowing the answer but praying it would not come.

"She was afraid too," Brandt said. "She saw them, knew them. They even spoke to her. She knew one thing you didn't."

Syn gripped the bass more tightly, gazing into Brandt's eyes, searching now. For answers. For peace. "What?"

"She knew they weren't angels," Brandt said softly. "She didn't want you to know."

Syn's chin dropped to her chest, and her tears trickled down and off her cheeks, wetting her blouse, the ground, the white makeup running to a thin film. Brandt's fingers picked up the pace, drawing the moment around her and pulling tight the drawstrings on her soul. Her shoulders shook, her mind blanked, and deep inside, she drew her mother's angel tightly to her heart, holding and breathing apologies into the soft chorus of the blues.

Slider

The old man had been staring at the showcase so long that Ted couldn't stand it. He walked over and stood on the far side of the glass enclosure and gazed inside.

"It's amazing, isn't it?" He asked at last. "There has never been another ball like it."

The old man glanced up at him, and something flashed over the weathered features–some emotion Ted couldn't make out. The guy was older than he'd thought, weathered and dried up, as if he'd spent too many days standing in the hot sun. His hair was gray and wispy, thinning on top and standing in random tufts that moved gently in the grip of the overhead fans.

"Never," the man agreed. "Never before, or since."

They both stared into the case. On a tripod stand, enclosed in an acrylic case, which was itself displayed behind glass and protected by multiple alarm, sat an aged baseball. The stitching was rough—and there were scuffs on the horsehide surface. There were also scrawled signatures, slightly faded, but clearly legible. The auction lot number sat beside the ball, a folded bit of cardboard proclaiming "Lot #65."

There was another mark on the ball. A dark smudge feathered out from one line of raised stitches. It was dark brown, lighter at the edges. One of the signatures cut across the edge of the stain with bold strokes.

The old man reached out and brushed the tips of the fingers of his right hand lightly across the glass. Ted was about to say something about fingerprints, or smudges, but the man seemed to realize what he was doing and pulled back.

"It's not real, you know," the man said softly "This isn't the ball."

Ted stiffened. He hadn't seen it coming, and he cursed under his breath. He'd thought he was facing off with an aging fan, or someone trying to relive a past moment of glory. Instead, it was something all too common and irritating.

"I assure you sir," he said stiffly, "that you are mistaken. We have absolute provenance on this item. A private collector consigned it, and we can trace this ball through three sales and four owners to the day it left Jeb Rabinowicz's hand and returned, care of Kevin "knock it to Heaven" Smith's bat. This item is absolutely genuine, and I'll have to ask you not to spread stories to the contrary before or during our sale."

The old man glanced up at him sharply, almost like he was only then realizing whom he was speaking with. Then he returned his gaze to the ball and shook his head. "I won't queer your deal, son," he replied. "Wouldn't do any good for me to try. I'm just telling you what I know. That's not the ball that killed Jeb Rabinowicz, and I ought to know."

"Why is that sir?" Ted asked, glancing around for security.

"Because" the man replied, looking up once more, "I was there."

Ted contemplated his options. He could humor the guy and see where it led. As long as no one overheard them, and no doubt was cast on the auction lot, there was probably little harm in it. He took in the stranger's stooped frame and slender, weakened form. One thing was certain; the guy looked old enough to be telling the truth.

"This ball," Ted explained slowly, "was pitched by Jeb Rabinowicz on June 3rd, 1939. The count was three and two, and Jeb had a strong arm. He was used to blowing his fastball past every batter he faced, and that was what he intended to do that day. They didn't have radar guns back then," Ted continued, "but experts guess that "Rocket" Rabinowicz's fast ball closed in on ninety-five miles per hour. It was a little wild, but things were different back then.

"Some say he was trying to dust Smith off the plate with that pitch, and his bit of wildness steered him wrong that one time—slid the ball right over the center of the plate, hot and fast. Me? I think he just thought he was too fast to be hit and served it up straight. I've read everything there is to read on Rabinowicz, and that seems more his style than the duster. It might have been different if it was some other batter, or some other out, but Smith was hot. He'd already singled and doubled in that game and the bases were loaded. If Smith got a hit, it would have driven in the tying run. A double would have won the game, but a strikeout? That would have won it for Rabinowicz, and the only way through the batter was through the batter, as they say. That pitch was a point of honor, and if he'd grazed Smith with the ball, he would have lost on a walk."

The old guy had remained silent through his speech, and Ted wasn't certain, for a moment, if his words had even been heard. Then, without turning his gaze from the case, or the ball within, the man spoke.

"It was a slider. They didn't really call it a slider then, and it wasn't the pretty dipping fastball they throw today, but it was slider, all the same. Rabinowicz never intended to hit him with the ball. It came in fast, slightly high and inside, and then it jerked out over the center of the plate at the last minute like it had hit a bumper on pool table. If it had come inside, Smith would have popped up, or missed completely, but that pitch dove for the strike zone, and it found the bat. I'll always believe that. The swing was straight through the heart of the plate with no thought given to the pitch, the curve, or anything else. That's where logic said the ball would have to come. No one throws a ball when the bases are loaded, the count is full, and the game is on the line. It was pitcher against batter, and the swing took nothing into account but that confrontation.

"A fastball would have snuck past. A curve would have left Smith swinging on his heels and spun him around like a fool. Any pitch but that one and everything would be different now."

The man's voice trailed off.

"I don't know about the slider," Ted said, "but I know about that ball. Smith cracked it straight down the pike. It came so fast that Rabinowicz was still sideways in his motion when it caught him just behind the right ear. He spun halfway around and dropped, and he never got up. That smudge," Ted pointed to the deep brown stain on the ball.

"I know," the old man snapped. "I know what happened to Rabinowicz. I know what you think that smudge is, too, son, but I'm here to tell you, whatever it was that stained your ball, it never leaked out of Jeb Rabinowicz. That's a pretty convincing setup, with the doctor's signature, and the papers that come with it. I see it's signed by the catcher, Randy "Big Dog" Sherman, and Smith, too."

"And I have certificates of authenticity on all three signatures," Ted cut in. "I've had this checked and rechecked, valued by more experts than I can even remember. I don't know why you came here, or who you are, but I know that ball. I think I know more about it than any man on the planet, just now."

"You don't know the first thing about that ball, son," the old man said softly. "But I'm here to tell you, if you'll listen. What do you have to lose? No one is going to question all those signatures and letters, why should they? You say it's the ball, and as far as the world is concerned, it is, but I'm here to try and set some things straight."

Ted was willing to do just about anything if it would get the old guy out of the auction house where no one could overhear the conversation. Besides, it was getting late, and with the sale the next day he'd have to be up and in early.

"I'll tell you what," he said. "You buy the beer, and I'll listen to what you have to say, but not for too long. I have to be up and back here early."

The old man smiled thinly. "That's fair."

Ted nodded. "Let me get my jacket. There's a bar right down the street that isn't too loud for a quiet conversation, and they have most of the league games on. It's a sports bar."

The old man did smile then, and he held out a gnarled hand. "It's still a great game," he said. "No matter how hard they try to kill it."

Ted shook the man's hand, and then hurried off after his coat, wondering what he'd gotten himself into, and how difficult it would be to extract himself if it started getting crazy.

They sat beneath a TV where the channel was set to a Yankees vs. Red Sox game. It was the fifth inning, and the score was tied. Nothing spectacular, but Ted was a Yankees fan, and, as it turned out, his companion favored the Sox, so they were able to crack the initial ice with light game-time banter.

Finally, though, the old guy just stopped talking for a minute and stared off past the televisions, and the bar into the mirror behind the liquor bottles. He stayed like that for so long Ted thought something must be wrong, but just before it was time to break the silence, or break for the door, the man turned to face him and started talking.

"That game happened a long time ago, son. I may not look it, but I'm coming up on my eighty-seventh birthday. I've seen a lot of baseball in my time, and I don't have so many innings left to go. Still, there're times when it seems like only yesterday I stepped up to the plate in my first little league game and faced off with Big Matt Scharf. He was the tallest kid in the league, and the meanest. He had a fastball that made your knees knock—particularly if you knew just how accurate he wasn't. Strong memories, but my time in the little league isn't important. The thing that *is* important is this. I was there the day Jeb Rabinowicz died. I saw it with my own eyes.

"I know another thing about that day," the man said, turning his eyes down to the beer in front of him, "that ball was never supposed to be hit. Smith was supposed to strike out. It was the pitch that did it, that damn dropping curve." As if talking to himself, or to his beer, the man added, "Why couldn't he have just thrown the fastball?"

Ted decided to ignore the odd mumbling and stick to the point. "The ball is signed by a lot of people who believe what *they* saw as well," he said. "The doctor who pronounced Rabinowicz dead signed it, a guy named James Bradshaw, and he was there as well. The catcher, Sherman, signed it. There can't be much doubt unless you're accusing one of them of faking the ball. Why would they do it?"

"There's a lot more to it than that, son," the old guy said. He downed his beer, signaled the bartender for another, and went on.

"There was a lot of money riding on that game. In those days, almost nothing happened without some money laid down, and the people who bet that money didn't like to lose, especially when the stakes were high. Rabinowicz was supposed to win easily, but it didn't work out that way. That meant the people with money needed a backup plan. What I'm trying to tell you here is, that backup plan was Kevin "knock-it-to-heaven" Smith. He brought the count to full with the bases loaded, but he wasn't supposed to hit the last pitch. He was supposed to swing from his heels, miss, and never say a word."

The old guy turned away for a moment then and took a long pull at his beer before he spoke again. "It isn't a pretty picture, young man. There were men back then who didn't live by any rules but their own, and the police were picky on who they backed, and who they backed off of. I'd like to tell you that the mom, apple pie, and baseball myth is gospel, but it just isn't so."

"He was going to throw the game?" Ted asked dubiously. "How in hell would you know that? And what happened? I mean, I can understand if he was supposed to WIN the game, and missed, how that could happen, but how the hell do you accidentally hit a line drive straight down the gut?"

"I told you," The old man said, turning to meet Ted's gaze, "it was the pitch. It came in high and inside, and then it dropped. Kevin Smith saw that ball and he swung straight down the middle of the plate. It should have been a clean miss. That kind of swing always looks good from the stands, strong follow through and the slap of cowhide when that ball hits the catcher's glove is unmistakable, even from the top seat in the bleachers. An ending with finality. A closed book. Except..."

"Except the ball dropped and he hit it?" Ted's words were formed as a question, but the inflection was tainted with something more. This old guy didn't seem to be making up stories, and for the life of him, Ted couldn't see an advantage to be gained by doing so. Ted wasn't even paying for the beer.

"Exactly. The ball dipped and shot in over the plate. Smith couldn't have missed that ball if he'd tried; it was like it dove for the bat. Fate. Kismet. Call it what you want, that ball should have hit leather, and instead it hit Jeb Rabinowicz."

"And killed him instantly," Ted added, finishing his beer. "This is all interesting, fascinating, to tell you the truth," he said, readying to rise and head on home. "I still don't see it disproving the authenticity of the ball in my showroom. It's getting pretty late."

"Just a few more minutes, son. Humor an old man, if nothing else. I'll buy you one more beer, and if I haven't convinced you by the time it's gone, I won't bother you again."

Ted hesitated. He really wanted to get home and get a good night's sleep, but so far this hadn't been such a bad evening, and at the very least he'd walk away with a new story tucked away in his memory.

'Okay," he agreed, sitting back down. "One more beer, and I promise not to guzzle."

The old man smiled, just for a second, and Ted caught a twinkle in his eye that looked like it had winked at him from very far away. Years, he thought suddenly. That had been across time, not distance.

"It isn't a question of whether Smith killed Rabinowicz that day," the man went on. "It isn't a question of whether the ball is marked with resin, blood, dirt, or catsup, for that matter. It's a matter of possibilities. That ball you have can't be the ball that killed Jeb, because this one is."

The old man slid his hand into the pocket of his jacket and pulled out a baseball, carefully wrapped in plastic. It was easily as old as the one in the case they'd left behind. There were a few smudges on the white, cowhide surface. Ted leaned closer and saw that there were also three signatures on it, and one smeared, dark splotch. That was the biggest difference between the two balls, he saw. The ball he had, back in the glass case, had a dark, rusty smudge. This ball had something clotted on its surface, like a scab. It looked eerily like the ball itself had been cut, bled, and healed. Ted reached out as if to touch the bag, then pulled back at the last second. It had an unclean aspect, and even though they were indoors, he felt a sudden chill.

Ted glanced at the old man and the man returned his gaze evenly.

"Go ahead son," the man said. "You can check it out. I'd be careful if you open the bag, it's easy to smudge a ball this old."

Feeling silly for having pulled back the first time, Ted

took the ball in its plastic wrapping and turned it over in his hand, inspecting it carefully, but skeptically. Cosmetically, it resembled the other ball a great deal. The signatures were the same, Kevin Smith, the catcher, Randy Sherman, and the doctor, James Bradshaw, whose signature was impossible to make out if you didn't already know whose it was. That same scrawling chicken scratch graced the bottom of the death certificate. Ted had studied it a thousand times, and he couldn't tell this signature from the one in his show room. His gaze kept sliding back to the raised, clot-like smudge, the one difference. He wanted to scoff. He wanted to toss the ball back to the old guy, laugh, and tell him it was a good fake, but that he knew what he was doing. Except it was true. He did know what he was doing, and something about this ball felt—right. Or wrong—maybe that was it—the ball felt somehow more the way he expected a death ball to feel, if such a feeling could be defined.

"Tell me why you brought me this." Ted said at last. "Tell me how you came to own it, why I should believe you. For god's sake, that other ball has been authenticated for more than fifty-five years. The doctor, Bradshaw, first owned it. He died young, heart attack I think it was, and the ball passed to his son, who sold it at auction. The next owner was a big-time collector out of Los Angeles. He paid two hundred grand for it at that first auction and put it in his collection. He was robbed soon after that, over a million dollars in signed cards and memorabilia were taken. He was shot and killed during the robbery. Somehow, they overlooked this ball and the associated paperwork—or maybe they couldn't figure out how to unlock the safe. In any case, it went back to auction just last year. The new owner consigned it to my auction house. We expect it to sell for over a million and a half, what with the crossover of baseball and morbid death collectors involved. Now you walk in with this in your pocket and tell me it's all a lie? Why?"

"That ball you have isn't the one from the first auction," the old man said, studying the beer in his hands. "The ball was not left behind by the thieves in Los Angeles, it was stolen and replaced with the one you have. This is the ball they took."

There was a long moment of silence, and then the man

continued. "No one was supposed to get hurt."

"Who are you," Ted asked, scooting his seat a foot further back and staring at the old man. The ball rested on the table between them.

"That isn't important," the man replied in a very tired voice that, for the first time, showed the age he had mentioned. "What is important is that the ball you have isn't cursed. No one will die if they give you a million dollars for it, and no one will ever know. No one but you."

Ted gulped his beer and slapped the glass on the table.

"You're crazy," he said, rising. "You're a certifiable nut."

"You know I'm telling the truth," The man said, glancing up. "I've had that ball with me ever since it was stolen. It hasn't killed me, like I thought it might. I figured if I got my hands on it, I could put an end to the curse—to the death and find my own way out at the same time."

"Who are you?" Ted whispered.

"My name is Smith," the old man said softly. "Kevin Smith. I should never have agreed to throw that game. I should never have signed that ball, after Jeb died, like it was a souvenir instead of the cause of a man's death. Now it's taken others, and I'm a very tired old man. I don't have the strength to carry the secret, or the curse any farther.

"I burned the bat. I scattered the ashes of it over home plate in the stadium where Jeb died. I intend to do the same with the ball. It will be the last thing I do. I'm going to put an end to it, once and for all."

"But why are you telling me?" Ted asked again. "Why now? Why me?"

"I didn't intend to tell a soul," Smith sighed. "When you came up to me earlier and I saw the gleam in your eye as you looked at that other ball, I knew I had to tell someone. I had to explain why, and how, and to let you know that it isn't a trophy. It isn't a thing to be collected and polished and revered."

He held up the ball and shook it in Ted's face. "It's a cursed, black reminder of something that should never have happened. If I ever had a soul, it's bound up in this leather ball, and I signed the contract over the blood. You sell your ball, and you keep my secret. The world will forget both soon enough; it's the way of things."

"But..." Ted had a million questions. If this was really Kevin Smith, there were so many stories, so many things the man had seen, and known, and done. It was too late. By the time Ted had his thoughts even half straight, the old ball player had picked up the ball, turned, and wound his way through the bar toward the street beyond.

Ted dropped a bill on the table, since neither of them had paid yet, not even looking back to see how much of a tip he'd left. He rushed toward the street, but as his hand touched the door handle, the air was split with a screech so loud and violent that he pulled back and let the door close. There was a crash, the sound of rending metal, and then he was moving again.

He took in the scene in seconds. A delivery truck was canted over on one side. It had plowed into two parked cars, and streams of gasoline poured into the street. It wasn't possible to tell which tank had been punctured, but the smell of fuel was strong. Ted ignored it and raced to the street. He saw Smith sprawled under the fender of the truck, face down in the road. The old man lay in a pool of gas and blood, one hand outstretched before him as if he were reaching for something. Ted followed the line of the groping fingers to the gutter, and he saw it. Still safely in its plastic wrapper, the ball lay wedged against the curb. It had rolled or bounced beyond the reach of the gas.

There was nothing to be done for Smith. The man was crushed. His neck was twisted at an odd angle that brought his face into plain view from where Ted stood, and blood trickled from between his lips. He was gone. Ted sprinted to the curb and picked up the ball. He ignored the scent of the gasoline, ignored the screams of others as they saw what had happened and yelled at him to move, to hide, or to get out of the way.

Ted stared at the ball. The brown smudge had shifted. He looked more closely, and in that instant, his own scream was born, catching in the back of his throat, and constricting over the sound before he could force it to life. The clot had been knocked free of the ball. Inside the bag, as he held it up near his face, the tear in the ball had begun to ooze dark, red blood. The seal on the bag was not broken.

Ted flung it from him as if he'd touched a corpse. Turning, he lurched toward the door to the bar, diving heedlessly into the metal and glass frame and tumbling through as the explosion rocked the street. He was pressed to the glass by the force of it, then through. He felt his flesh tearing, but then he was through, rolling to the floor of the bar among a jumble of running feet and screaming voices.

Somewhere in the moments that followed, he was noticed, and towels were wrapped around his arms. Sirens wailed in the background. He closed his eyes, and he was there.

He stood, facing the mound with a bat dangling limp in his hand. Sweat trickled down his neck—or was it blood? On the field before him, a man lay sprawled in the dirt, one hand flung up and over his face, his limbs at a crazy angle. Around him, the crowd roared, whether in terror or approval he couldn't say. Then, slowly, the man on the mound moved. At first it seemed his arm just fell free of his face, but a second later the man planted his palm firmly in the dirt and lifted his head groggily. Then, with an unbelievable effort, he rose to his knees, and then his feet. Without looking up, the man brushed off his pants, straightened his shoulders, and placed a hand behind his neck, rotating it to snap everything back into shape.

Then, glancing up and raising his finger to the bill of his cap, Jeb Rabinowicz winked at him and turned, walking into a mist that had risen slowly from the grass at his back. In seconds, the man was gone, and the darkness rose to claim Ted. In that darkness he heard the distant slap of cowhide on oiled leather. The roar of the crowd returned, and then faded gently.

And he was lifted carefully, slid onto a rolling gurney. A young paramedic with curly hair and wide eyes leaned over him, shaking his shoulder gently. The young man held Ted's wallet and was calling his name. Ted smiled and opened his suddenly very dry, parched lips. He spoke so softly that only the boy heard him, then he relaxed and let the darkness carry him away.

He said, simply, "strike three," and he was out.

In the street outside the wind caught the ashes of the million-dollar ball and whirled them up and away. It was a long way to the pitcher's mound, but the count was full, and it was a glorious night for a ballgame.

Teachable Moments

Basil stared in through the window from the shadows beneath a tall willow tree. Bob, the husband, sat at the table, nose pressed to his phone, frowning. Jeanne, the mother, loaded the dishwasher, stopping now and then to rinse off some stubborn bit of food. The twins, Annie and Dale were watching a movie. From the muted sound that reached him, Basil guessed it was one of the Marvel Universe superhero sagas, AC/DC ushering Iron Man onto the scene.

Upstairs, the older brother, Simon, was gaming on his computer. Everyone was accounted for except the older sister, Eileen. She was on a date. Basil knew Bob was staring at an app on his phone, tracking her, because Basil had been jacked into Bob's phone, Jeanne's phone, and every device in their lives for weeks.

He'd used their electronic doorbell to hack into their home wi-fi, installed backdoors on all of their computers, and scraped their passwords. He knew what they browsed, what they bought, who was chatting secretly with whom, and he watched. He kept meticulous records and filed them carefully.

When Basil had been just a boy, he'd had a toy that first belonged to his father. It was a black ball with a small window, designed to look like the eight-ball on a pool table. If you turned it up so the window was on top, what basically amounted to a twenty-sided die pressed into the glass and offered answers. Like, would his father hurt his mother? Would they let him out of his closet soon? Would they remember to put food in his lunchbox before sending him to school?

It sat, dried up and answerless, on his desk. But he had learned a lot from it. After Social Services had finally pulled him out of his home, locked up his mother and buried what she had left of his father, Basil had discovered computers. Ones and zeros. Logic that neither judged nor forgave. Never a "Reply hazy, try again."

The problem was that people took it all for granted. They had the power of the known world in their pocket and used it to share pictures of their dinner, or their cats. They trusted it with their names, bank accounts, stocks, bonds, photos, and text-based romance.

Basil broke it down into a familiar mathematical formula. Twenty answers. He worked part time at a security company, and also at an Internet service provider. He removed viruses and malware, and occasionally added his own back doors to the systems of his clients.

Sometimes a family caught his attention. Usually, at least one person would try to protect information, or would know enough to use a complex password on their wi-fi. Sometimes they had a firewall and changed their passwords regularly. When Basil found a family like that, he secured their Internet without their knowledge. He removed anything harmful and made sure they received regular emails suggesting security updates.

"There is always someone out there wanting to take you down."

That was something his father had said. "You have to watch them. Don't let them play you. There are wolves, and there are sheep. Don't get eaten."

His mother had taught him things as well, but they were *different* things.

"They say the Lord helps those who help themselves." she'd told him, "But that's a bunch of crap. He doesn't help anyone. Keep your eyes open. People who try to do the right thing? You help them."

Basil did what he could. But when there was a family like the Willets, Bob, Jeanne, and the kids, ignoring all security and safety, inviting the Internet into their world as if it were their friend, Basil felt the need to create teachable moments. That was what his father had called beatings, or extended periods locked in the closet. It was even what his mother had called that last night, when she'd slammed a cleaver into Basil's father's forehead and left him bleeding on the kitchen floor.

Basil clicked a small eight-ball icon on his tablet. He'd taken images of the Willet's and photoshopped them into tiny triangles. Two for each family member, one green, and one red. Green triangles were positive responses, and the red were negative. That left four blank positive triangles, and four negatives.

Basil had created twenty-eight versions of his app. Each family he chose for his special security curriculum had six members. Each time he'd created the triangles with images of their faces–importing them into an interface that emulated the window on a Magic Eight-Ball. Now he had completed the ball for the Willets, and he had chosen this night to ask his question.

A car pulled up to the curb outside the house and Eileen stepped out. A boy also exited from the driver's side. He hurried around the front of the vehicle and drew the girl close for a long, slow kiss. She returned it, pulling free before his hand could cup her ass.

Once she was inside, he tapped the 'play' icon in the eight-ball app. A liquid-filled video shimmered on the screen, and Simon's face, rimmed in red, appeared on the screen in a tiny triangle. The liquid looked like blood.

The boy, then. Basil would teach the boy, and the lesson would spread to the family. That was how it worked. Sometimes, to get through to someone, you had to provide the proper example.

Basil fingered the hilt of the hunting knife on his belt. He knew "teachable moments" were important, but it always brought an ache to his heart. Had to look like suicide. He would have to dox the boy's chats with his hot young English teacher, and the images they'd shared. He'd have to send a message to Bob, letting him know about the breaches in his security. He pressed on the image of Simon's face, and it melted slowly to a pool of bright, red blood. Then he closed his phone and headed for the tree that stretched to the upstairs window. He hit send, and a variety of ads, links and offers went out to the rest of the family to distract them.

He wondered briefly if he was doing the right thing, but an image formed instantly in his mind. A black square with a triangle and white lettering.

"Yes, definitely."

He reached the tree and began to climb.

The Whirling Man

The little man spun, whirling forward and back, trapped in the center of the rubber band between Mason's fingers. The two little handles could be pulled further apart—tightening the twist, speeding the motion. Just as the molded plastic features would come into focus, materializing from a red blur, Mason's wrist would flex, and the dance began again.

His apartment dripped with a thick coat of suggestive shadow. The small shaft of moonlight slicing beneath his drawn shade pooled in the contours of a discarded food wrapper. Down the hall the soft glow of a single lamp shown from the crack beneath the bathroom door.

On the wall, the slightest shiver of shadow reflected from the whirling man, its efforts to gain recognition competing with the plastic man's chances of escape in a battle of futility.

Mason's mind was a million miles away. Another time, another life, rooms with sunlight and garbage that made its home in cans, not strewn across the horizontal surfaces like a rotting carpet. A world with sound and color, voices and faces whose names he knew from more than the evening news or a stolen magazine.

The words wouldn't let him go. Jesse's face haunted each corner of his mind and prevented him from escape. Her lips moved—were always moving—but her voices were myriad, blending and warping to those of others and back.

"It's not you," she whispered, "it's me."

Mason yanked violently on the rubber bands, spinning the whirling man into a frenzy.

"Your brother needed the money for grad school, son," she explained patiently, in his father's stolen voice, eyes dead and not really watching him at all. "Maybe next semester we can get you in...but he does so well...Bud down at the garage is looking for someone..."

The room spun, the little man danced, and Mason could feel the paper tearing, again, and again could see the words art and school splitting down the center. The two halves floated beside Jesse's haunted half-smile, held in mirror sets of Mason's own hands and torn, multiplying, and tearing again until his mind rained confetti and he jerked the whirling man into another helpless jig.

In the shadows to his left, the one ordered space in his personal chaos, were the notebooks and the sketchpads that chronicled his life. Each was different—either the size or the color, the binding, or the paper. They were lined up like a demented too-thin regiment—one notebook for each sketchpad. Words and form. Life.

Mason's mind flickered into the present and he glanced down at the pad sprawled in his lap. He could just make out the carefully etched text. Uniform. What had his father said so often?

"Each thing has a form. Each form has a perfect state. Each time you recreate the form, you redefine the thing."

His father had been full of shit, but the words still haunted Mason. He couldn't form a letter or a complete word, without painstakingly comparing them to those that had come before. The words were his life, and he couldn't bear the thought that as he wrote them, he was recreating himself. He didn't want to recreate the insanity, only to explore it, and record it. Exactly as he lived it. Exactly as it happened.

The notebooks he remembered best were those filled with pain.

"We build a world of walls that surrounds us," he'd written. "They keep us happy, safe, and oblivious. Pain ignores the walls and re-arranges life to suit its own ends. Nothing is ever as it seems."

Jesse was the latest notebook. Deep purple in color, bound in steel coils that spiraled out to sharp ends. Mason had filled every line with her, the magic, the heat—each scent and sound.

Each moment. His fingers had stroked those spiral bindings and the coils had clenched his heart with each caress. The metal was smooth and cool, like her skin. Like the lying surface of her eyes, rippling with a love and compassion that faded—like a screen of smoke—to ice and boredom.

In the end, that is what Mason had symbolized, her boredom. Jesse bounced from man to man, occasionally to another woman, time and again. Nothing captivated her. She found someone with real passion with a vision that drove them, and she latched on, leeched the "high" and moved on when the thrill faded.

Mason had been a three-month binge on the thrill scale. She had loved it when he drew her—preened as he posed her to paint, laughed and blushed at his showing of the work, more of her revealed to the world in those lines and angles and colors than even a nude walk on the beach could have shown—all in his art. All from his passion and gift—curse—of insight.

If only he'd stopped while she was still smiling. If only the art didn't mean more to him than the rest of life combined. If only he hadn't seen through her.

The painting stood in the corner, draped with dark cotton and coated in dust. He'd had offers for it—solid offers—but he could no more sell the painting than forget the expression of shock and betrayal that had washed across Jesse's face when he'd unveiled it.

The image was as clear in his mind as the first moment he'd lived it. Jesse was a tall woman, slender and sharp-angled. Where some women had soft curves formed of circles and smooth skin, Jesse had classic, sculptured beauty so sharp it could cut. That is how he had painted her, in the end. Line upon line forming angles and honed edges, eyes bright like diamonds. Tubes extended from her heart, thousands of snaking, tangled tubes, whirling toward the edges of the canvas in a spiral and at the end of each, a face. A person known, or yet to be known.

There were tiny colored droplets beaded along the lengths of the tube, sliding through the centers and back toward her heart, but never would that imperfect vessel fill. There was a drain at its base.

Jesse's head was flung back, those diamond-chip eyes beseeching—someone, something—above. Her hand, long, slender fingers curled back, as if to stroke the base of her breast, or to unbutton an unseen blouse, held the plug to that drain, a self-assured, self-induced lack of fulfillment echoing through the chambers of her heart.

At the lower corner of the painting, Mason himself hung suspended from a deep, forest green tube.

There were twists in the tube. Twin, winding clots in the artery attempting to drain his soul, held thus by wooden handles. Each handle was held in a hand, and those hands Mason was intimately familiar with. Each line, each hair, vein, and knuckle, had been copied with the same, exacting precision as the words in his notebooks—as each letter mirrored the last. Mason had wanted her to see them, the same hands that had teased her hair and cupped her breasts, crawling hungrily over her flesh—those *same* hands were what had saved him.

The painted image of Mason was a blur. Whirling up and back, backward, and forward. The tube was caught mid-twist, trapped in the moment of his painting the image at the point where nothing could flow between the ends of it. Cutting her off.

That painting was the one he'd saved for last—the end of the exhibit. There had been others at the showing, others who appeared in the painting. Tall, lean Lydia with her metal sculptures and metal piercing jewelry and cold, gun-metal eyes. Lydia, who'd done Jesse in cold steel.

Robert, the poet, whose career had nose-dived after Jesse had twisted his gift for angst and despair into a sappy string of words defining unrequited passion. Only the devastation she'd left in her wake had saved Robert. Robert's tube was pale yellow, his features drawn and taut.

There were others, some that had sprung to life only in Mason's mind's eye – potential. Still more hovered, like Patrick. Patrick was a concert violinist. His hair was feathered back like something from an Armani commercial, and his style matched it. He watched Jesse constantly. Mason could see the man undressing her with his serpent eyes, tongue lashing the corners of a too-dry too-thin smile.

Patrick wasn't undressing her to linger over what Jesse's body might offer. He was undressing her to rebuild her in the image of his perfect fashion accessory, and more and more Jesse's glance had begun to shift to the rings, and the gold chains, the expensive suits where others wore Levis. More and more she had looked elsewhere when Mason talked, her enthusiasm slipping away.

The painting had a home for Patrick, too, in the intricate framework that surrounded Jesse's form. His tube was blue—blue blood—blue for the pain he caused as he tried to draw on Mason's green and Robert's yellow to encase Jesse's heart and display it on his shelf. He could not. She was his failure—his perfect prize denied, and he would never match her with any other. Fashion was his passion, what was that song?

The words faded again, and Mason drew the handles in his hand apart once more, sending the small figure dancing.

He glanced down the hall. The bar stood against the wall outside his kitchen. There were colored bottles lined across the top. Mason didn't buy his drinks for their taste, or out of habit. He had a rainbow of liqueurs, whiskeys, mixes, and gin. He could see none of the colors in the dark, but he knew them. Each stood in its place. He had arranged them the day after that last show. The colors matched those in the painting. The bottles were full, stoppered, and safe, and Jesse would not be dropping by to drain them. Not anymore.

She'd stood in front of that painting for what had seemed an eternity. Mason had pulled aside the covering and stood back to watch.

The others had crowded around to see, but as they caught full sight of the piece, and of Jesse's face, they'd given her space, backing to a safe distance. Not too far. Everyone wanted to see. Those who found themselves in the frame had glanced at Mason, astonished. Some miracle allowed them all that long moment without the taint of anger. The anger had come later.

Jesse had stood, and stared, and then she'd just been gone. One quick spin, like the whirling man, only she'd jumped off her rubber band at half-twist and launched herself at the door, scattering those who'd crowded too close, and who flowed into the gap she'd left without even glancing at her back.

Mason caught one kaleidoscopic flash of light from Jesse's eyes as she spun. Colors whirled in those depths, captured colors, and for just a moment he could see the tubes, see the flowing creativity, the heat and the joy, the pain and the maniacal laughter. A hot pulse of—something—flowed between them in that instant. Green and snaking. Mason's wrists had flexed, and the world spun away. He'd staggered, nearly falling, and when he snapped his eyelids open once again, Jesse was just gone.

Mason had left Gwen and "her boys" to close the show. He'd covered the painting, ignoring the cries to leave it—and the offers to take it—ignoring everything but the words and the images and the pain. The muscles of his heart whirled inward, spinning tight and releasing, sending him stumbling into the night, the canvas in a death-grip clutch against his chest.

Now the painting was just another shadow in a dark landscape, shrouded and catalogued. Mason had put the image in the front of the purple sketchbook in black and white, carefully recreating each line—the colored droplets chrome-bright in their stark lack of pigmentation. This time there had been no room for distraction. Jesse's voice haunted him, and his father's voice haunted him through Jesse's image. The words and pictures he had so carefully locked away in the notebooks leaked at the edges, threatening to spill over and infect those he was recording. The letters fought him, g warping to q and back – the l's crossing themselves into t's.

Still, in the end, Mason had finished the sketches, and the words. The Jesse he'd first met. The Jesse he'd manufactured in his mind. The Jesse from late-night drunken stories of her childhood. Nude, alive, sleeping. Every aspect that had joined them, one to the other. Every angle that crossed had been penciled in and recorded. The pages were bound in the spiral metal loop that so signified Mason's life.

The whirling man spun and suddenly, it was too much. Too fine a mirror of his own soul. Mason flung the toy against the wall violently. Still spinning, it crashed loudly against the windowsill and clattered to the floor. For a long moment, that sound echoed unchallenged, then, with a tired squeak, Mason rolled forward, closing the notebook carefully and leaning to place it on the shelf beside his chair.

There were no lights burning, but Mason knew the well-worn track between chair and bed too well to trip. Oblivion beckoned. Beneath the window, the whirling man lay in a tangled, twisted heap of plastic limbs across the remnant of weeks of fast-food wrappers and soft drink cans. Maybe months. The days had been blurring for so long it hardly mattered.

He knew he'd have to call out eventually to find out if he was poor yet. He'd made a lot of money on that final show, more money than he'd ever expected to see in his life, but he knew it wouldn't last forever. Some things had to be faced—time was one.

He passed the doorway to his studio and paused. As he scuffed to a halt, dust rose from the polished, wooden boards of the floor to nearly choke him. Too long. He couldn't remember the last time he'd felt he could paint. In the center of that room his easel stood, blank canvas facing the window beyond, so light that never shone through too-dark shades would illuminate its surface and guide him from synapse to shadow, angles and deep shades of gray. Everything was gray since Jesse had stormed out of the show, despite the array of colored tubes that haunted his mind.

In the hall stood a small table—more a desk—that held his phone and had once held his mail—when he still checked to see if he had any. Momentarily, his mind hung on this. How long would the postman continue to pile mail in a box before it was all carted away and returned to sender? How much mail might be waiting for him outside his door?

To the left of the phone, where the mail had once lain in careful piles, was a wooden case. This case had been special ordered, made to Mason's specifications. The wood wasn't important, nor was the carefully tooled latch, though it had cost more than it was worth. Mason lifted the lid and peered inside.

Lined from one side to the other, separated by thin slivers of wood, were the straws. Green, blue, red, and yellow, every color of the rainbow and then some. Each was carefully categorized by color, circumference, and length. Each had come into the house with a meal, sometimes four drinks with one burger, or a pizza with five sodas.

It had taken a long time to find the colors, to learn which restaurant served what with their drinks. Each straw had been cleaned and stored, and as the patterns had emerged, Mason had woven them carefully, making certain he had equal numbers. Tubes. He couldn't get them out of his mind.

With a soft click he let the lid close and turned toward his room slowly. No time. Too sleepy to put them together carefully, and he didn't want to turn on a light. Without the light, the colors blended and leaked. Like the words in the notebooks, reforming and blending, changing what he knew to be the past and confusing what he knew to be reality.

With a quick lurch he stumbled into his room and turned to sit on the edge of his bed. He was facing the window, and the shadows played light and dark games on his ceiling. Spinning. Neon lights below flashed, strobing against the white backdrop of his ceiling, shadows from the power lines outside the window dancing. Whirling.

The little plastic man whirled before his mind's eye, trapped, spinning, not releasing its energy down the rubber bands, but unable to reach out. Unable to use that energy itself. Trapped.

Jesse had trapped him. Bound and whirling, he sat and stared into the night, guts clenched tighter than any rubber band and head pounding in time with his pulse. He couldn't paint. He'd kept her from stealing that from him. That had been the essence of his painting, of *her* painting. That was the essence of the whirling man. She had gone away unfulfilled, but she had left him stagnant, filled to over-flowing with images and pain and unable to draw the least bit of inspiration from any of it. He'd kept her from stealing it, but what good was that if he couldn't release it? Who had won, in the end?

Laying back across his rumpled bed, Mason clutched the sheets close to his chest, not bothering to undress. Even as his head met the stack of sweat-stained pillows, he was drifting away. He had been up far too long, too many hours of nothing but going over and over and over the words and the images, staring at the tiny plastic man whirling his life away in effigy. The straws and the bottles, and always that painting, hunched in the corner, watching him with eyes that didn't exist, and never closed.

The walls melted to darkness, then unfolded like heavy velvet curtains. Mason sat up, though some inner sense of balance and propriety told him he had not. The room had elongated, the ceiling had dropped lower, and the window was an endless row of slats, striping his world in black and neon-strobed yellow from the streetlights beyond.

Shadows flickered beyond the door to his room, as well, but they were ill-defined. He couldn't tell if someone were there, or if something flapped in an impossible breezed. There should have been no light to cast the shadows, and yet they danced.

As if in counterpoint to the impossible motion, a murmur of voices slipped in and out, around and about the bed, confusing his senses. Mason thought he recognized some of them, though it was hard to tell. They were too low and indistinct to make out, and each confused the other. Each slid over the walls and blended with the shadows, and with a gasp Mason saw that each shadow had taken on a hue of its own, dim at first, like a halo around the perimeter of darkness, then brighter.

Yellow. Pale yellow, snaking and thrashing and held tight by some unseen pressure at its base. Red, bright, and running, loud and breathy – so bright that the sound almost worked its way free into words. Almost. There was Blue, and silver, violet and beige. An insane rainbow to shame sixty-four color crayons with its complexity. Whirling.

The bed shifted, and Mason tried to roll to one side. His limbs were too heavy, veins running with lead and his eyes stuck open, held as if with super-glue beneath each lid. He tried to lean back, but the bed folded neatly in the center, mattress re-creating itself in the form of a chair with rests for his arms and a rounded pillow at the nape of his neck to hold him stiff and upright.

He should have been able to stand. His feet brushed the floor, but when he tried to lean forward, needle-sharp bindings bit into his throat and shoulders, knees and thighs, and he shrunk back with a small cry. He felt tickling trickles along his skin. Blood? Insects? Fingernails?

A sudden flash of memory blinded him, and Jesse was

there, long, crimson nails caressing the underside of his chin, pressing into his throat, sliding back through his hair as her lips pressed closer. She always whispered to him at those moments, questions, endless questions about the art, the colors, what he was feeling and how he would work the two together. Like a leech. She wanted to know the paintings before they *were* paintings. She wanted it for her own, even though she knew that if he could give it to her—if he could make her see it, deep within her soul—it wouldn't matter. The paintings were not hers, never would be hers.

Mason's vision cleared or shifted. The bed that was a chair now had spun toward the door, and he could make out the shadows beyond more clearly. Long, slender shadows, like the antennae or feelers of some giant crustacean, shivering along the walls. They glinted with light, translucent. Each left a glimmering light dancing in its wake against the wall ... each was a different color.

Sweat oozed through every pore in Mason's skin. His hair matted itself to his brow, but he couldn't lift a finger to straighten it, nor to flick away the trickles of blood and sweat teasing his wrists, and his nose, sliding around the curve of his lip and down to dangle maddeningly from the tip of his chin.

The chair flattened at his back. Not like the mattress, not exactly. Taut. It was taut like the skin of drum—like the skin of his face as he tried to work the droplets of sweat free, quivering with the effort. His arms stretched, legs widened and extended to toe-curl against the backdrop. The canvas. Sweat trickled deep forest green down his cheeks and arms.

The shadows drew closer, swirling. At first, they brushed against the wall, whispering sandpaper touches just loud enough to keep the voices in the back of his mind from reaching coherency. Then the tendrils of color began to cross, and re-cross, rainbow-hued blending, twisted and untwisted, very slowly. It was mesmerizing, and Mason felt something deep within his chest growing tight, drawing outward. He fought it, fought to twist his head to the side, but he could not. The canvas behind him grew tighter, and the colors whirled faster. He could not close his eyes.

His heart clenched so tightly it felt as if it would burst. Mason gritted his teeth, shivering wildly, but before he could brace against the pain, it released, and he felt his head dip forward. Fast. The floor rose to his dropping gaze and passed, inches only, his hair brushing the solid wood of the floor and up in back—over and again.

He whipped around, faster, and faster, skin stretching and twisting, grinding into his bones. He wanted to scream, but he could not. The only sound was the voices. Soft, sibilant voices. Hungry voices. Then he stopped. Just for an instant. Long enough to see. Long enough for the world to coalesce into a single solid image.

Long enough to see the endless lengths of straws, joined end to end, groping through the doorway and across the floor toward his feet. If he could have moved his eyelids, they would have shot wider, just as he whipped backward, away and down, and up again. Whirling.

The last sound Mason heard was the clink of colored glass. He didn't know how he knew, but each color had a distinct tone. A voice. Each cold, empty bottle cried out to be filled.

The tubes slid nearer with each passing breath. Joined and separate. Each in its place.

"Each thing in its place," his father whispered.

"What do you feel," Jesse crooned in his ear, her voice like the passing horn of a vehicle on a long, lonely stretch of road. Passing too quickly, high-to-low-to high. "What do you feel, just when you first ... touch?"

He whipped back and the tubes, cut to sharp tips, drove into veins, deep, following his motion and wrapping around him.

Mason clenched his heart, but the colors flowed. He felt them, draining slowly, then more quickly, then more slowly. Pulsing. He whirled, back and forth, heard the soft, chuckling laughter as the handles were pulled. Tighter, released, and tighter still.

Then it was gone.

Mason woke to the scents of old sweat and fresh coffee. The blinds had been rolled up to allow far too much sunlight access to his room. He the drumbeats of music just loud enough on his stereo to make out and not loud enough to hear. He heard the clink of glass—or cups.

Rolling to a sitting position, he crossed his legs and wrapped his arms tightly around his chest.

Footsteps approached softly, and in the periphery of his vision, he could just make out her shadow.

Jesse entered the room on cat-feet, sleek and smiling. Her hair was brushed back just so, tied with a deep green ribbon, and in her hands, she carried a tray. Mason didn't ask where the tray had come from, where she'd found coffee in a home where only the remnant of last week's fast food should remain. The tray held two cups, steaming.

It also held a notebook. A brand new, spiral-bound green notebook, and a pen. Wrapped tightly around the pen, rubber-bands twisted so tightly they should have snapped, rode the tiny plastic man.

Already the letters were forming in his mind. He could see them, lined up like soldiers, even and ordered. Words and images—images and words.

He could see the gleam in Jesse's eyes.

His father's voice whispered through her breath as she leaned closer to his ear. "Each time you redefine."

Her lips brushed softly at his skin.

"What do you feel?"

The Last Patriot

PAGE 1

The Last Patriot
Script for pages 1-22
Written by Eustace Grimes
Illustrator—TBD

Splash Page

Exterior shot of a synagogue.
Focus is on the front doors where vermin crawl in and out of this cesspool. They stop and chat, hug one another, wear their devil hats. The parking lot to one side is filled with high-end foreign cars, sports cars, and sedans.
The Sign out front reads Talmud Torah followed by evil Hebrew characters. Our POV is the front seat of a 1961 Dodge Dart. Behind the wheel, watching the temple, is Eustace Grimes. His hand grips the wheel so tightly bones show through.
1/CAPTION: The unclean swarm from their nest, but he is vigilant. Soon there will be a cleansing.

After this, the line "A storm is coming," has been scratched out. Droplets of sweat splatter the edges of the page. The ring from a soda can marks the uppermost right corner. The rusty old single-bulb lamp on the desk bathes the notebook in brilliant light.

The walls are covered in posters, articles, stickers, and banners. It's hard to make most of them out in the gloom, but directly above the desk hangs the Nazi flag Billy's father gave him when he was eight, mounted clumsily with nails pounded into old, crumbling plaster. The lamp's light is directed downward, so most of the banner's red, bright near the center and the white circle, darkens through scarlet to a dried-blood brown at the edges.

Billy McFarland is concentrating. His bulky, six-foot three form, too tall for the small desk he'd owned since middle school, is hunched forward. His close-cropped reddish hair nearly brushed the desk lamp, and the pen is lost in his tight, fleshy grip. A small patch of sweat stains the back of his black t-shirt, but in the shadows, it is all but invisible.

He could have worked on the computer, but the screen is taken up by an Internet based talk show. An angry commentator explains how the deep state has aligned itself with Israel to infiltrate the purity of America. The commentator is black, proving there is no racism involved. He wears thick glasses, and his hair is cut high-and-tight like a marine. Billy received the link from his uncle, who sends such things regularly.

Uncle Bob is the only family Billy has left. Bedridden, his body collapsing in on itself from years of drinking, smoking cheap cigars, and research. Uncle Bob knows things. A lot of what he knows hadn't made sense when Billy was younger. It wasn't until later, after his father died, and his mom took off with that preacher, that Billy buckled down and started paying attention. Things happen for a reason. The world is stacked against God-fearing white men. It's important to understand what's happening, and to stand against it.

Uncle Bob can no longer stand against it, but he is jacked into the Internet in every way imaginable. He has one of those hospital beds that you crank up straight like a chair. He's bought swing arms for either side that hold monitors, and he has a 75" LCD TV on the wall a couple of feet in front of him. It's connected wirelessly to his home network, a server with an array of hard drives, and a wireless router with a seriously well-maintained security system. Uncle Bob doesn't mess around when it comes to security. Since they started inserting the vaccination chips, no one who's had that shot is allowed within range of his router. Billy isn't sure how the router detects them, but he isn't going to question it. There is serious business to take care of. Freaking DNA manipulation, blood impurities, probably aliens, and you couldn't trust the government to protect you from any of it. They were already infected.

He needs to finish his script. He knows it's irregular to record history before it takes place, but he has few illusions. He is a soldier. He's not clever, like Uncle Bob, and he's not rich. When he takes his stand, there isn't much chance he will escape.

The Last Patriot is his memoir. His legacy. He needs to finish it before he makes his move, and he doesn't have a lot of time.

PAGE 2

Three Panels
On the interior of the temple. Worshippers gather in groups. Focus on one shifty looking man holding a door open. Visible is a stairway leading down.
2/1/CAPTION The guilty gather to mask the truth. Below, the catacombs await.
2.2
A man slips past the one holding the door. He has a large, wrapped package over his shoulder. Both men watch the room as he slips through into the darkness. Protruding from the end of the bundle is a child's shoe, and an ankle.
2.3 Bottom of the stairs and the bundle has been unrolled. There is a young boy lying on a rug, eyes wide. The two men stand over him, grinning. To the right a tunnel leads off into an unknown distance.

Billy stares at the page. He wants to add captions, but he is a long-time comic book collector. Nothing he can think of sounds right. He hears the voices of the YouTube channels, and his uncle in his head but they are too stiff. It won't play. It's better without explanation, the terrified child abducted by the semitic devils, dragged to the tunnels beneath the city. They will find the tunnels, he knows. Once he's made his move. Once *The Last Patriot* is discovered, and published, they will have to look. They will invade the temple and follow the paths beneath throughout the city, and beyond. They will find the lost children. He is less certain about the lizard men, but it's not out of the question. He adds this at the end of the 3.3 description: "glowing reptilian eyes line the tunnel walls in the distance, or maybe just flecks of reflected light."

He's plotted the story in his head and has the gist of it scribbled in the back of an old spiral notebook. He's filled dozens of them with notes, facts, ideas for comic scripts. Some are completed scripts, but he's never sent them anywhere, or shown them to anyone. Not even Uncle Bob.

At first, he was just nervous that they weren't good. He did not like to be made fun of, and he also didn't want to get in any more trouble for hurting others who laughed at him. He was a little too old to get away with the boys will be boys routine, and though he had the right to remain silent, time had taught him that he lacked the ability. He had a purpose, a goal he needed to reach, before he could let the words out into the world. He was pretty sure he'd miss their launch, but it was necessary. It was what The Last Patriot would do.

He had never written so much at once. He knew there would be errors but felt that they would bring a human element to the script, that others would patch the holes in the story. He dreamed of a famous artist being called in to do the inking, another to color. He imagined comic bookstores across the nation with life-size cardboard stand-ups of The Last Patriot, his own name blazoned across the base as creator.

The final script was twenty-three pages long, one more than necessary. He read it over several times but could not see a way to shorten it. It would have to do. Maybe they could use the last page for a bio of the real Last Patriot, Billy McFarland. The one who didn't talk on YouTube, or rant on social media, but took matters into his own hands. The one who made a difference and struck a blow against the evil threatening to taint pure blood, who took a stand for the missing children. It wouldn't be easy to get that into a single page, but it was all he could offer them.

He removed the twenty-three pages carefully, trimmed the spiral binding edge, and placed them on his scanner. He punched the button that would scan to e-mail and send them to Uncle Bob, and to dozens of news outlets separately. It was late evening, and he knew he only had a small window of time to prepare. In his mind he tried to imagine the soundtrack—if his life became a movie. He hoped they wouldn't go with AC/DC because Iron Man, in the end, served the deep state. He'd embraced the worst in humanity. Maybe Ted Nugent would have something for him. Maybe a new track, something special. The thought made him smile.

He left his office, and hurried down a dingy hall to the other, slightly larger bedroom that had belonged to his parents. His mother had left when Billy was twelve. She wasn't a believer. Things had gone bad after she left. His father's anger at the world had only Billy for an outlet. Then, a sudden aneurism, and the old man was gone.

Billy had done his best to keep the place up. He avoided alcohol, even though Bob and all the others drank. Billy had tried it, and each time he'd felt less, as if the alcohol dragged him down toward complacence, where complaining about the far-left terrorists was enough, where posting memes about arresting former politicians who were never going to be arrested was forwarding the cause. Uncle Bob had an excuse; he couldn't leave his bed. Billy didn't intend to search for an excuse of his own. He was going to be part of the solution. For his father, for his uncle, and for so many others he'd met who talked a good fight but were clearly never going to step over any line that made a difference.

Billy didn't have a car, but the city had a decent transit system. He knew the schedules, and he'd planned this route months in advance. He had a job as a mechanic and spent very little on the utilities and upkeep of his father's home. Tech gadgets were among his few indulgences. He knew people like Bill Gates were using them to take over society, but he was careful. He'd downloaded the apps his uncle recommended and removed as many connections as possible without losing his service. His footprint on social media was that of a ghost. He went to work, collected his check, talked to as few people as possible, and recorded his thoughts and dreams in the myriad notebooks he'd collected. When he could, he visited Uncle Bob, but when he did, he mostly listened. Bob, and Bob's friends, were clearly compromised, but they had a lot of good intel all the same. It was just intel they would never act on.

The Deep State was insidious, leaving the shell of your mind intact, but using their chem trails and their signals embedded in the cell-phone signals to manipulate it. A lot of Uncle Bob's associates thought the radiation itself was the problem, but Billy knew how signals worked. Anything could serve as a carrier. If there was something at the far end of the signal to strip that carrier out, data could be transferred. That was where the chips came in, for the others. Billy wasn't so sure. He thought it was more likely they just installed them in smart phones, computer monitors, personal wireless assistants. They called it "The Internet of Things," but Billy knew it was more likely a huge mesh of communications devices, passing God knew what across the airwaves and infecting everyone and everything it touched.

Aluminum foil hats and carefully configured firewalls were just smokescreens. They were false-flag protections to bring down their guard. There was only one solution. The enemy had to be eradicated, pod by pod, leader by leader. The unclean had to be cleansed from the Earth and there were few, so very few, who would act. Billy would act. He would shift the balance, and others would see. Some would even understand, and if they read *The Last Patriot*? They would act.

Before he left, he returned to his office and spun the old desk lamp's flexible stand around so the bright light from the single bulb illuminated the Nazi flag. "This is for you, dad," he whispered. The turned made his way through dingy hallway to the door and stepped out into the night.

As he walked, he mentally inventoried his backpack. Billy owned several guns. He had practiced creating explosives, and even driven into the desert to test them. No one knew. His uncle knew about his .45 caliber service revolver. Billy's father had given it to him on his sixteenth birthday. It had come from a gun show where everyone knew everyone else. Billy had looked at shinier, flashier weapons, some chrome plated, even an old, beat-up Ruger, but his father had insisted, and he'd been paying.

"Was good enough for me in the Navy," the old man had said. "It's good enough for you. You learn to break it down, clean it, hit something with it, you can pick the next one."

He'd bought others, after his father passed, but only when something fit a need. He'd outlined dozens of operations and gathered everything necessary to pull off each of them. They'd all been flawed. They were detailed in previous issues of *The Last Patriot*, but he had disassembled the supplies, sold some, traded others, and waited. The news, such as it was, had taught him one irrefutable law. You get one shot. If you plan poorly, or act recklessly, you are removed from the board and forgotten. Another talking point on social media, defended by people pretending to care who would use you to further their various agendas, and vilified by the deep state and held up as an example of the worst of humanity.

All of that was going to happen anyway, but before it did, Billy was going to make a difference. His moment would be *his* and not assimilated into some pointless theory or used to scare school children. He would be remembered for making a difference. It didn't matter that the unenlightened would think his actions were an abomination, only that he was remembered, and that his actions performed a cleansing. That was the name of the final issue of *The Last Patriot*. "The Cleansing."

He had the .45 and two clips. He did not intend to use it, but it was symbolic. His father was with him. He had C-4 that he'd stolen from a stash Uncle Bob had told him about after two or three too many bourbons. Billy had been very careful, a little bit at a time over a span of weeks. He'd gotten the detonator from another gun show. One a hundred miles away where he hadn't known anyone. No one had questioned him. No one ever did. The gun shows were packed with the various brotherhoods. They knew the signs; they knew the right questions and answers.

The backpack was capable of removing most of a city block. All he needed it to do was to seal the tunnels. He had to get in, he had to make sure no children had been taken that night, that he would not kill the victims to erase the unclean demons who were stealing them away. But if it came down to it, he had to close the tunnels.

He caught the bus at Forty-Second and Kennedy, dropped a token into the slot and took a seat near the front. He wasn't worried about anyone noticing him. No one ever noticed him. No one knew he existed. Yet.

The temple was lit brightly. Men, women, and children made their way through the doors. Billy stayed in the shadows and watched, waiting for a moment. He was almost ready to take a chance, duck his head and try to slip in, when a man hurried to the door. He was carrying a bundle, child sized. There was an urgency to his movements, and when he spoke others gathered. As a group they turned and hurried inside.

Billy crossed the street, splashing a friendly smile across his face. He wore the yarmulke he'd picked up online. He reached the door, and an old man, bent and gray, smiled up at him. He smiled back.

"I'm new in town," he said. "I passed by here yesterday. I hope you won't mind. I am hoping to make this neighborhood my home."

He had practiced sincerity in front of mirrors. He had recorded himself, over and over, adding just the slightest inflection to his accent. He kept his eyes downcast and shuffled his feet. The old man barely gave him a second glance.

"Welcome, welcome," he said. "Come in, make yourself at home. I hope we will see you again, and often."

Billy only nodded. Anything he said was a gamble, so silence was his best defense. He slipped inside and was happy to find the old man did not follow. He knew the layout. He had blueprints. He knew that the stairway leading down was inside the main body of the temple, and to the right. He looked around carefully turning his gaze to the left first, scanning the interior of the temple and then glancing right, just in time to see two men disappear below. One held the bundle he'd seen from the street. The other held the door. The man at the door glanced around, as if to see if they had been spotted, and then disappeared after his companion. Billy didn't hesitate. Walking as if he'd been there a thousand times before, he made his way to the door and slipped through.

The stairs were carpeted, so he made no sound. There was light below. He scanned the walls, and then, thinking just for a second about lizards, he glanced up sharply, turning to be certain the ceiling over his head held no threats. As he turned, the toe of his boot caught on a loose thread of carpet. He felt himself tilting and reached to the wall, but there was no banister. He tried to turn back and get his hands out in front of him. He bit back the scream that threatened to give away his position, but he was falling, far too fast and without any way to break the fall, tumbling down into the tunnels below.

His shoulder struck first, and he tried to roll. He bounced once, came down heavily and his head struck the wall. Then it hit again on a step below, and he slid and banged his way downward, fighting to remain conscious. He struck bottom and lay very still. He heard voices, and footsteps approaching rapidly, but he could only make out vague shapes, and none of the words made sense. He felt someone release the strap on his backpack. He tried to reach for it, but even that small motion brought too much pain.

Later, as his mind cleared slightly, he heard new voices. There was a rough moment of agonizing pain, and then something solid pressed to his back. Straps bound him to it, and he was turned to face the ceiling. Faces peered down at him, wide worried eyes.

"Don't worry," a soft voice said. "They will take care of you. We will check on you soon."

The words made no sense, but it didn't matter. He was lifted suddenly, and he had the pain to deal with as he was carried back up the stairs toward the temple. He heard the voice a last time.

"Your bag," it said. "I have given it to the ambulance attendant."

Billy closed his eyes. Someone shook his shoulder. He blinked.

"What's this?" an angry voice demanded. Billy found he could turn his head, just slightly. A uniformed officer held his backpack. It was open. Billy closed his eyes again. It couldn't be happening.

"Cleansing," he muttered.

"What?"

Billy didn't reply. He kept his eyes closed and found that they had injected him with some sort of pain killer. He followed it into darkness as somewhere in the distance a voice droned on.

In Billy's office, the nail holding the upper corner of the Nazi flag slipped free. The flag was old, and heavy. It folded down toward his desk, draping over the face of the rusty lamp. A few moments later, a blackened spot formed, and began to spread, smoldering. Smoke rose. Ten minutes later, the blaze was out of control.

Billy's bag rested on the desk of Detective Michael Stone. Michael, 'Big Mike' to his coworkers, was sorting through the evidence and shaking his head. The bomb squad had cleared the C-4. The detonator was gone, as well as the .45 and clips. The rest of the stuff in the bag was just strange. There was a folded packet of papers. He'd opened it, spread it carefully.

The words were arranged, like a tv script or something. Mike saw a Nazi flag scribbled in one corner of the page. There were other symbols he'd seen. He smiled, then glanced around to be sure no one noticed.

"What a joke," he said loudly. Officer Markum, at the next desk, turned and raised an eyebrow. "This kid," Mike said, waving at the papers on his desk. "He thought he was some sort of fuckin' Nazi super soldier. It's all here. Blow up the temple, close the tunnels underground and save stolen kids. There's even a lizard man, can you believe it?"

Markum held his gaze a moment, then shook his head. "Underground huh?"

Mike glanced back at the paper. Under his breath he whispered, "Damn shame you were too stupid to pull it off."

Before he bagged the pages, he slipped his phone out of his pocket and snapped a quick picture of the first page. He knew some Internet sites that would love this shit. Punk kid trying to take down the Deep State. As if it was that easy.

He bagged and checked the evidence in, then headed out to the street for a smoke. There was no one around, so he pulled his phone out. Grinning, he opened the photo. He pulled another phone out of his pocket. He transferred the shot of the script page and deleted it from the work phone. No one was liable to check, but he cleared it from deleted items by habit. You couldn't be too careful with all the left-wing, antifa bleeding hearts carrying torches around to burn good, God-fearing men.

Mike typed a quick message. "The Last Patriot has fallen." He inserted an eyeroll emoji and then that of the brotherhood. He punched SEND and chuckled. He tucked the burner phone away and headed back inside.

#THELASTPATRIOT trended on Twitter within an hour. Multiple sources leaked bits and pieces. Talk show hosts and media outlets snatched it up hungrily. CNN portrayed Billy as a dangerous product of right-wing brainwashing. Fox News claimed he was misunderstood. Artists everywhere drew panels from the script. All of them portrayed the author as either a scared kid, or a joke. Three weeks later a group of armed men were caught trying to break into the temple basement where the accident had happened, looking for tunnels.

In Iowa, a young man named Scott had printed out the script and pinned it to a corkboard in his bedroom. He'd sketched in details, and he'd changed the name of the temple. It was surrounded by articles about missing children. When Scott closed his bedroom door, it hid the corkboard, and he kept a school banner dangling across the front. The plan wasn't perfect, but it was a start. Scott was a pretty good artist, and he had a plan. Someone had to stand up. It was going to be him.

Wayne's World

(For Wayne Allen Sallee)

I stood alone among the crowds that had gathered outside the prison, watching in ways they could not, and waiting. I was celebrating the death of John Wayne Gacy, but not in the manner that the rest of them were, or not in the manner that I *assumed* they were celebrating. I assumed that they were happy because they felt, foolishly, a bit safer. I assumed, as well, that it was a moment of control for them, a moment in which the evil of the world could be labeled, restrained, and would in due time be erased—wiped out forever.

This latter idea amused me. The "moment of control" theory is one of the prevalent ideas on the motivation of sociopathic killers. It makes sense. It also makes a hell of a mirror for these people to look into if they ever realize why they came down to witness this killing. A sociopathic society?

The control angle is a fantasy. The evil had been diminished not one bit by John's departure from their midst, whatever they might believe. The good guys were not winning. The good guys *couldn't* win. If there were no bad guys, there wouldn't *be* any good guys. Try and explain that to your average citizen, lost in his own little empty-headed world. Try and explain that to anyone, for that matter. Lord knows, *I've* tried.

But that's what it's all about, isn't it? Our own little worlds. Every one of them is different, separate, and distinct. Don't fool yourself into believing otherwise; it's a waste of time. You live in your world, I live in mine, and never the twain shall meet. Period.

Gacy had his world—right up until the end, he had it, wrapped tightly around him like a cocoon. They've been studying him for several years now, psychologists, psychiatrists, penal reformists; none of them seem able, or willing, to see the truth of it. They are trying to analyze an alien landscape by referencing the only thing they have to reference: their *own* little world. That's right. They can't see the light for the trees, so to speak—their own trees.

Sometimes a whole group of worlds seem to align. This is what they call a society. It isn't a true picture, either, but it lets the weak and unimaginative sleep better at night. When a group of people truly believe that what they see and what their neighbor sees in any given moment are the same, they have deluded themselves. If you give the same coffee, morning paper, and bus-ride to work to twelve different people, the entire scheme of events, actions, and reactions will be absolutely different in each case. Different worlds. Odds are, the criteria you use to ascertain this will be based on your own world, so I wouldn't trust your data much on this, either.

Take that newspaper we just mentioned, the one our "control" group read over breakfast. Let's say there's an article covering a killing on the front page—top center, headline in bold print. "Police Apprehend Alleged Kidnapper/Slayer of Three." This story will not contain facts—not by pure definition. It will contain the impression that society has agreed upon as fact—the majority opinion.

It will not tell you why the killer's world required that these people be abducted and killed. It will not tell you how the police intersected their own reality with that of the criminal and brought him to justice, not really. It will tell you what fits into the pseudo-world of society, and you will believe it. It is the path of least resistance.

John's world is about to come to an end, as he knows it. The others, those who have studied, hated, died, and reviled it—they will never know it at all. You can't enter another man's world. Therein lies the rub. Even now, as I pontificate from my own, I know that every reaction to these words will be different, and that no two people will read them the same way, or with the same outcome. The difference is that I accept this—to a point.

It hit me when I was still a child. Nobody really understood me. I was riding in the car with my mother, watching the houses go by, and it hit me like a sledgehammer to the center of the forehead. There were people in each and every one of those houses. Each of them lived a separate life—most of which would never, in any way, interact with my own. Each of them loved, hated, lived, and lied—alone. That was fine, as far as *they* were concerned, but that wasn't the end of it. It meant that *I* was alone as well.

Even in that car, with my mother—the closest human being to my universe to ever exist—I was absolutely alone. I accept this now, as I've said, or at least I've come to somewhat of an understanding with it, but to a six-year-old boy it was a staggering revelation.

I tried to talk to my mother then, tried to explain the fear this concept had caused me—tried to get her to explain it away and make things better. Wasn't happening. First, she smiled at me, told me I was being silly. Then, when I continued to pester her with it, when I couldn't let it go—she got angry. One car, two worlds. It felt as if the carpet had been yanked out from beneath my universe.

I was scared witless, frightened as I'd never been before. In the face of this, after hearing what had frightened me in my own words –or my explanation of those words as interpreted through the lens of my mother's world—she felt amusement, then anger, but no fear… no understanding.

A friend of mine once recounted a similar experience. He was an artist, or could have been, if he'd stuck with it. He could draw like you wouldn't believe, and he could make the things he drew seem real. He was also obsessed, had been since *he* was a child.

He'd been drawing along, pretty as you please, forming vases, walls, and doorways, learning the magic of perspective, when it hit him. There were no lines in or around the things he was drawing. On the paper, everything was separated from everything else by the dark borders of his pencil outlines. There were borders. There were limits. On the real wall, or around the real vase of flowers he'd been drawing, there were none.

"How can I draw," he wondered, "if there are no lines? If there are no lines, what keeps me from being part of that vase? What makes me different from the floor, or the pencil in my hand?"

Of course, his mother laughed. Of course, she next got angry—very similar world to my own mother, I'd say, though I'd of course be wrong. None of them are the same.

So, there he was—by the time I met him, 21 years old—still trying to figure out how to draw without using any lines. He also still had the anxiety attacks that came with the knowledge that if there were no lines, there was nothing keeping things out of one another. I tried to explain to him that all of those things he wasn't separate from were in his own world anyway, and that as long as they were part of *his* world and not someone else's, it was nothing to worry about. Of course, he didn't understand. He never will, not the same way that I do.

There are certain moments that I remember more clearly than others. I read a lot—mostly about people who seem caught up in their own little worlds. Serial killers are all like that. Sociopaths, they call them. I call them realists. They understand that nothing beyond their own world matters. They understand that no matter how safe a society might seem, it only takes a small slip from the "norm" before they begin to hound and persecute you out of their own insecurity. A part of them knows the society is bullshit, but they mostly have that part locked away pretty deep inside. To look at them, you'd think they really *did* see the same things.

I read a book recently by a man named Straub, writing as a man named Underhill, writing about characters that may or may not have existed in the lives of one or the other of them. Worlds within worlds. In it, he mentions a photograph, front page of the New York Times the day after Ted Bundy was fried. I was obsessed, so I went and looked it up, and there it was. Louise Bundy, communicating for the last time with her son before his execution, their last connection immortalized.

That photograph is a perfect illustration of my concept. She was calling him from her own little world, of course, and in that world, she believed that none of the places where her son's world and that of society had meshed were real. She believed that she could turn back the hands of the clock to the time when he was her "good boy."

He was never that person. That person was a figment of her own imagination, a construct that took the place in her own world inhabited by the world that was her true son. I wondered if he'd seen the houses along the road, as I had, or if he'd tried to draw the vases without lines. Maybe he just saw doorways into other people's worlds, and he went through them at will. He certainly seemed to be able to gain their trust. I think that Ted found a way out, if only for a little while, a way into other worlds. I think John found one too.

My own world becomes stagnant, at times. It would be refreshing to enter another, to understand how someone else understands, if you get my meaning.

Even if Louise Bundy could have maintained complete contact with her son throughout the execution, she would never have seen his world. No telling what might have happened in hers, though. Maybe old Teddy would've come waltzing in for the first time, face to face with his creator—maybe he'd even have said "Heeere's Johnny!" I'd like to know for sure, but then, my impressions would never be quite the same as his, or hers, would they?

That same book I read, by Straub/Underhill/whoever, held another insight for me. All of the introspective writers have that quality. They make you think. Things could be different. In Vietnam, says Underhill, he met a man named Dengler. The world they walked through over there, endless jungles, short little men who looked different and didn't operate in the "American" mode of "society," ate away at them. The "world," their term for reality back here at home, faded slowly into the background. The Earth itself made noises. Dengler said, "I think that's what happens when you're out here long enough. The edges melt." Maybe he should have met my friend—he could have found out that it's okay if they melt; there are no edges—no lines, either.

The lines melt too. When you separate yourself long enough, concentrating on the only world that matters, your own, the lines on the vases disappear, the relationship of time to reality becomes less important, and the barriers melt away. Your world, in my world, is different. Your world in my world is mine. This is the fundamental truth that I have discovered in over thirty years of research, the fundamental truth that I can't even explain to you, but that is no less true. In my world, I am God. In my version of your world, I am God, still. John knew.

In John Wayne Gacy's world, the tiny universe of a man named after a big, slow-talking actor who drank too much and didn't like black people, John Wayne Gacy, was God. He even constructed his own hell, beneath the floor of his home. That is one of the things that make me believe that he knew. I wonder if he stole the clown thing from Stephen King.

I read a lot, sorry to digress. I just wonder—when the bodies were pulled from beneath his house, bloated and rotting—did they hear a sinister, Tim Curryesque voice floating up through the drain?

"Down here, we bloat... we all bloat."

Writers fascinate me. Within their own worlds, they create others, worlds within worlds, and they share them. We can't do that with our true worlds. When someone kills thirty-three people and gets caught, they fry him and celebrate. When someone creates a serial killer in his mind, imagines that killer's life and thoughts as his own, if only for a short time, and puts it on paper, he is paid the big bucks and labeled as a genius. A creative talent.

Maybe it's just a payoff. Maybe they read about killers that can't hurt them, and they thank the writer for capturing the "evil" on the paper and not releasing it into "society." Maybe they just envy the writer his release. Or maybe they have just a hint of the desire that I have, the desire to find a way into other worlds.

One question about these writers remains, for me: do the edges melt when they write? Are they fully in their own world then, or do they create a new one that they can slip into at will, enjoying freedoms there that they are denied by the concept of society? Do the characters have lines, or do they blend one to another? Is each character in "his" own little world? Gods in a pantheon? Good questions.

I tried writing myself. Thought I'd push the boundaries a little, see what came of a little creative hack and slash on the old keyboard. Nothing came of it. Either there is no magic there of the type I sought, or I just don't have the talent to bring it forth. Not that my plots were lacking. It was just that, whenever some creation of mine began to put his fingers around some young woman's throat, or to bash a particularly innocent young man's face against a wall, I did not want my fingers on the keys. I wanted my fingers wrapped in soft skin or banded like steel across a pliant throat.

Description falls short of reality every time, and the visions in my head only screamed the louder for release as my fingers and mind failed to bind them to paper. The lines did not melt, they solidified. My characters were trapped within them, and even I could not set them free. I couldn't reach them at all. I was still stuck in my own little world, no help for it there.

For every question, I am told, there is an answer. I would modify that to say that for every question there are as many answers as there are people, or worlds, but it is sufficient to know that there *is* an answer for me. The question? How can I get into another man's world—how can I become his God? It is possible that this only happens at the moment of death, but somehow, I believe there is another way. I am going to find out today—tonight.

I've been working off that death angle for several years, and while it is satisfying in its own way, it is incomplete. I can become another man's God by destroying his world forever. This I know. I have seen it in their eyes, felt it seeping from wounds and rattling through throats on the heels of proverbial last breaths. In that moment, that final moment where they look into my eyes and truly *see* me, our worlds collide. That is also the shortcoming of death—it is only a final *moment*. I want more than that.

That is why I stood there, watching, and waiting, moving with the crowd as it lived and breathed a separate life of its own, a temporary bonding of all those souls who just couldn't keep away. It is a life-form more closely aligned with Gacy's own world than they might believe. They have all come here expecting—praying, even—for one thing. They want a man to die. They want to be the pantheon that rules his world. They want it for their own.

Granted, he was a dangerous man by any standards, particularly those of "society," but a man, nonetheless. A man with vision beyond their own. Watching the hungry looks on their faces as they waited, I was reminded of the gladiators in Rome.

There's a visual for you. Gacy and Dahmer at forty paces, silverware to the death—battle until the second course is served. It might help pay for all those people languishing in the prison system, their own worlds shrinking in around them until they take up no more space or energy than a parking space. It might also prove another interesting study into the way those who gather to watch executions react to violent entertainment.

In two hours, give or take a minute or two, John Wayne Gacy will cease to exist. I will not. His world will be vacant, or what his world represents in my own, and I will step in. I have already done so. That simple. Gacy is out, I am in. The sequel.

It's taken a lot of planning, but, hey, what have I got but time? The house wasn't so tough. His plans were on file with the city, just like any others, and the diagrams in the magazine spreads and the paper made re-creation of the "hell" beneath it all a snap. Since hell is in place already, I'll put a little effort into heaven—for the truly good ones, of course. It's a thought.

Stagnancy is not the goal. I believe he was on the right track, making progress, and I plan to pick up where he left off. It will be my interpretation of his world, of course, but I've been pretty thorough, and I believe it will be close enough. I think I can work myself in before everything snaps shut, before his world is banished to the ether. His world, my insight—the sky is the limit.

I find that the folks in the Jaycees are a friendly bunch. They took me right in, especially when they saw how many hours of volunteer service they could wring out of me. Upstanding citizen. Fund raiser. Not a family man, yet, or a father, but I have all the time in the world—John's world. He won't be using it. I thought about sending him a thank you note, but why ruin his last few hours? Let him die the God he was in life—if I'm right, he'll know soon enough—he'll be with me, and he'll be out of life.

The crowd surged forward near the end, but I hung back. Nothing to see from the outside, anyway, and I have other things to do, other worries. I've been careful with the paint, base coat of white, big red balls for cheeks and three colors of blue lining the outside of my eyes in stars (always wanted them to say I had stars in my eyes). My face is even registered—painted on an eggshell and registered as mine, and mine alone. They do that for you when you graduate clown school. Not an easy thing to do, in reality. There's more to the world of a clown than most people realize. Certainly more than I realized. Everyone might love a clown, but they don't necessarily love themselves. Not all the frowns on clowns are painted on, believe me. More of those masks are really hiding something than not. Another revelation.

Another insight as well. A new face, a new world? Construction worker face—society world. Clown face, surreal world. John's "real" face? Only dead men can explain that one to you, dead men, and John himself, and he's still claiming innocence.

Some of the people brought their children to the execution. Pretty tacky, I say, but what the heck? What's the lesson here, it's bad to kill? It's fun to watch people die? Beware the Boogey Man? I don't really care what their motives were in making it a family affair; It gives me a chance to practice. Maybe you saw me on the news the day after. I was carrying a sign—there were other clowns there besides myself, we all had signs. Mine was painted bright orange and red. Clown colors. "Clowns Make People Laugh, John," mine says. Nobody is laughing at John. The children smile when they look my way, but nobody is really laughing at me today, either. That's fine.

My little hell is waiting at home, and there is plenty of time. They will see me, and they will laugh. When I wear the clown face, live in the clown world, they will find me funny as hell. Others will come to me, and they will work with me at the little construction firm I've started—only a sub-contracting business, so far, but with plans for expansion. They will trust me, and they will drink with me in my construction worker world, and when I put on the paint and prance for their children, they will laugh at me too.

In the end, I will steal their worlds. I will be their God. It will be simple—everybody loves a clown.

The Devil's in the Flaws

It was shaping up to be the strangest New Year's celebration of Jeffrey White's life. Far from home, alone, in a crappy hotel room staring out over the streets he'd grown up in, wondering why the hell he was there, and, at the same time, glad that he was. He was in a thoughtful mood, something he'd developed to something of an artform during the two years of the pandemic. At the moment, he was thinking about the entire notion of celebrating a new year.

New Year's Day has always been a lie. An arbitrary check mark on a calendar created so long ago that most of those using it have no idea where the names of the months came from. Few of them care. The media, as in all things, applies false labels and pokes at whatever emotional buttons will draw the most attention. A time of rebirth, of new beginnings. A time when you can shed the problems of one 365-day period and make a fresh start. A time to create new goals that will change your life.

Older civilizations were more honest. They celebrated rebirth in the spring, when farms and forests rose from seeming death to brilliant life. When creatures that had slumbered, or huddled, or buried themselves deep in the mud wandered the fields, sunned themselves on logs, hunted, and lived. They did not set goals. They did not confess the sins of their past. They were part of a cycle so old it spawned the very calendar that made New Year's Day possible. They were that grain of truth you hear is behind every legend, or folk tale.

The modern truth is that January first falls in the middle of the coldest, deadest part of the year. It draws people together for warmth. They celebrate to banish the emptiness, they drink so they can believe, just for a little while, that their goals and resolutions and dreams are somehow changed by the flipping of the page on some cosmic calendar. They see others lifting glasses and laughing, and believe themselves part of a greater whole, while deep down they understand that the ties binding them to those people are as fragile as the hours of a day, ticking away and breaking like icicles as the hands of time grind past midnight.

Jeffrey sat alone in a metal chair overlooking the streets from the tenth floor. He couldn't even remember the name of the hotel. He had a small patio outside sliding glass doors, a round metal table and two chairs. There was a single liquor store within walking distance of the hotel, the front door and windows covered by heavy bars, and those bars coated with advertisements, flyers, and graffiti. Their stock had been surprisingly varied, rotgut vying with hundred-dollar bottles of bourbon for shelf space, and the expensive stuff behind the counter, protected by more bars, and the ever-present spit guard gifted to retailers by the recent and ongoing pandemic.

The hotel's ice machine sported an out-of-order sign so yellowed and faded it looked more like it said, "Out of odor," the letters splashed with melted ice and unidentifiable fluids. Better not to think about it. On the table beside him two fingers of Elijah Craig glittered, reflecting the flashing neon across the street. There was no ice, and the bottle was down a third, or more. The television was on in the room behind him, reruns of some '90s sitcom populated with twenty-something pretty people living above their means and apparently doing so without actual jobs. The laugh track ebbed and flowed with the flickering action and setup jokes, but Jeffrey ignored it.

Next to the bourbon bottle, a single sheet of paper covered in tiny, cramped script, lay open, riffling slightly in the breeze that in no way offset the heat. The air conditioner inside was struggling, leaking water down the wall, but with the sliding glass doors open, it was an impossible battle. He could not remember a New Year's Eve more surreal.

The sheet of paper was a letter. It had been delivered to him in North Carolina, accompanied by a single faded Polaroid. It was such a Lenny thing to do, an actual letter, hand-written, and the original photograph. Anyone else would have scanned the image and sent an email, but somehow this seemed right. The photo showed two old men, seated in straight-backed chairs on a street two blocks from the hotel where he sat. One wore a yarmulke, the other a kufiyah. They were smiling. Both men were smoking thick cigars, and Jeffrey could, if he closed his eyes and drifted, still smell the acrid scent of the cheap tobacco.

Jeffrey,

I never thought I'd write this letter. I've kept it in the back of my mind all these years, thinking we'd just get drunk someday and laugh about it. I won't insult you by asking if you remember our oath. I know you do. I know you'll come. I didn't want to ask, but a lot of things have changed in the neighborhood. None of the changes are good.

You were with me the day I took this photo. My father and Jamal, his friend. How many hours did we spend listening to them, wondering if they were mad or brilliant, deluded or some sort of weird street prophets? An Arab and a Jew, smoking and drinking and discussing the world. Things were so different then. The neighborhood was filled with strange characters, but they got along. They co-existed. None of that is true now, and my grandfather is dead.

There is no diversity here now. What were once shops and cafes, bars, and brothels, are only tiny kingdoms, protected as well as possible from all others, chained and barred, and barren of life.

I would have left long ago, but, as you know, my parents have also passed on. My father left me the pawn shop, and things have become very strange. I have learned things I didn't want to know about my family, about my heritage. I find that facing this alone is more than I can bear, so I am calling in your debt.

I'll see you soon,
Lenny

Jeffrey didn't need to read the letter again. He'd read it so many times the words were burned into his mind. The flood of memories it had caused had haunted him from the moment he'd sliced the envelope open. He wasn't surprised that the letter had come. He was relieved. There were a lot of childhood promises and dreams that had faded to dust, but there were promises, and then there were oaths. He smiled, very slightly, at the Taylor Swift reference.

He remembered the day they'd sealed their oath like it had happened a few moments in the past. He'd run it through his memory so often it felt like a scene from a favorite movie. The kind of movie that left you in tears, wondering how the characters could ever move on. The kind of memory you used to shore up your confidence and form a foundation for the face you present to the world. The kind of oath you didn't break.

He hadn't called Lenny when he'd arrived. In the morning, he'd walk to the pawn shop and step through a door into his past. He knew it would be changed, maybe beyond recognition, but he thought he would know the scent of the place. He thought he would feel something, and he wasn't certain how he'd react. And then there was whatever Lenny meant by things having changed. Jeffrey wasn't sure what he was bringing to the table, and he didn't even know what was on the table.

He'd already witnessed some of the changes. The liquor store was a small sample. Most of the shops had been closed. He'd seen very little that he remembered, and even less that he understood. He'd left behind a community, and come back to a war zone, tiny islands separated by wrought-iron bars, chain-link, and padlocks. It was easy to forget just how many years had passed. The stronger the memory, the easier it was to conjure, and his memories of the neighborhood were among the most powerful he possessed.

He downed the last of his whiskey, grabbed the bottle, and headed back inside. Tall and lanky, his blond hair retreating on both sides, one last combed-over lock remaining to curl across his forehead, he felt the years weighing on him. He needed to call Barbara, and he needed rest. The last two years had brought a forced isolation from the rest of the world that neither of them had ever experienced, and he was pretty sure the idea of his heading off to the city for a while, even over New Year's, had been a relief. Neither of them had caught the virus. They'd isolated, masked, been vaccinated as soon as possible, and waited it out. That said, there were only so many shows and movies streaming, and for some reason, even though there was more time than ever available, the list of things he'd intended to do had grown longer, not shorter. He knew their relationship was solid. It let him concentrate on the moment, and on the past.

He closed the door and felt the slight shift in heat and humidity. He thought that if he listened closely, he would hear the AC unit groan. He put the bottle and glass on the dresser, stripped down to his underwear, and lay back across the lumpy, worn-out mattress. He propped himself up with the two shapeless pillows and picked up his phone.

Barbara answered on the second ring.

"Hey," he said. "I didn't wake you?"

"Not a chance. I'm just in bed, reading. I have two of the three cats here."

"Sandy out laying on my chair?"

"Of course. She's barely been out of it since you left."

"Stupid cat."

"She loves you. Me too, you know?"

"Yeah. If you are in the mood for a story, I thought I'd tell you one. From my past. I left in kind of a hurry, and you didn't question it, but heading off to fulfill oaths sort of seems like the kind of thing that needs an explanation, and really, I'd like to get it off my chest."

"Of course," she said. He heard her closing her book, imagined her slipping the bookmark carefully in place and straightening the dustjacket.

"Imagine, if you will," Jeffrey said. "A world where I'm only four feet tall." Drifting into memory, he told his story.

Even when they were children, the neighborhood had had boundaries. There were places where you could go and play, a small park, a basketball court. There were businesses it was safe to visit, even when your parents, or grandparents, were not with you, but in a city, borders aren't solid. They waver. Sometimes you find that you are standing in a place you've stood a hundred times before, and it is suddenly on the far side of some invisible, imaginary line between light and shadow.

That was where Jeffrey had been the night Lenny found him. A new family had moved in, not in their neighborhood, but a few blocks beyond. There were several children, but one in particular was big. His hair had been so blond that, in the pooled illumination of the streetlights, it seemed white as snow. His eyes were set very close together, and blue, like chips of ice. Every time Jeffrey had seen him, something had felt off. Wrong in an indefinable sense. The boy never smiled. He'd never talked to the other kids in the neighborhood, or at least none that Jeffrey was familiar with. His name had been Friedrich.

That night Jeffrey had gone to the store for his mother. She needed milk for breakfast, and his father was working late. It was only a few blocks, and it was a straight line down the sidewalk. No one was out, at least, no one he could see and though it was dark, and he was alone, it had been like any other night. He'd felt safe.

Old Mr. Fitzgerald, who ran the corner market, had been counting his daily take and readying to close when Jeffrey ducked in and grabbed the last carton of milk from the cooler. He dropped the money his mother had given him on the counter, and Mr. Fitzgerald smiled.

"You are a good boy, Jeffy," he said. "You hurry and get that home to your mother while it's cold."

"Yes sir," Jeffrey said. He tucked the milk under his arm and turned to go.

"You be careful," Mr. Fitzgerald called after him. "It is late, and it is dark. These are bad things for a boy at night. Either he is making trouble, or in danger of facing it. Remember that."

Jeffrey had not answered. The words were strange and ominous, and, being a boy, he'd paid no attention to them. A few blocks and he'd be home. The milk would be tucked away in the old, rattling Frigidaire, and he would be off to read comic books by the light of a flashlight in his bedroom.

Except, that one night, the borders had shifted. He hadn't

noticed; how could he? The market was a place he was allowed to go. The blocks between were a neutral space he traveled through every day. When Friedrich stepped from the shadows to block his way, it felt as if all the light drained away. Nothing existed but the cold, damp weight of the milk carton under his arm, and those ice-chip eyes that were staring straight through him.

Jeffrey had shifted left, trying to pass around the bigger boy, but Friedrich blocked the way with a quick sidestep. Jeffrey thought the boy's lip had curled slightly farther than usual. There was still no emotion or recognition in the gaze that pinned him in place, but there was purpose. An energy that rippled over the boy's features and made his fingers twitch. Jeffrey was pretty sure the kid didn't know who he was and might not be aware of what he was seeing, but it was clear Friedrich knew what he was doing. What he wanted to do.

Jeffrey took a step backward, then a second. He knew the neighborhood, and he was fast. He was trying to judge his chances of darting back the way he'd come and making it around the block and home before Friedrich could catch him.

No chance. Without warning, the bigger boy drew something bright and glittering from his pocket. He lunged forward, much more quickly than Jeffrey would have believed possible. The world tilted, as he fell back, trying too hard to backpedal and losing all sense of balance. Friedrich dropped after him, his arm drawn back, and Jeffrey closed his eyes. His shoulders struck the sidewalk, and then the back of his head and everything went bright white.

In that last flashing moment, he heard a sound, a scream of anger and rage. He saw a small figure dart from the shadows, and suddenly Friedrich's weight was no longer on him. It was tumbling away toward the street. Everything went black and hazy, he thought for just a moment. When he opened his eyes again, though, he saw a face, leaning down over him.

It was Mr. Fitzgerald. There were sirens approaching. Lights flashed. Despite the old man's protests, Jeffrey sat up. Beside him on the sidewalk Lenny sat, his face as white as death. He was clutching his shoulder and Jeffrey saw that blood had soaked his friend's shirt. There was a towel wrapped around it tightly.

"Jeffy," Mr. Fitzgerald said, shaking him gently. "Jeffy, are you okay? I have called your mother, and the ambulance is on its way."

Jeffrey didn't answer. He turned first, toward the road. Memory was flooding back, and he needed to know.

In the road, face down, lay Friedrich. Off to the side, a glittering blade glistened with light captured from the streetlight, and then the approaching flashing lights of the ambulance and the police. A bright pool of blood had formed around the boy's head. The expression on his face, twisted toward Jeffrey at a very wrong angle, bore the same expression it had in life.

"My god," Barbara said, when he finally fell silent. "Why have you never mentioned this?"

"It's not the kind of thing that comes up in casual conversation," Jeffrey said. "And it was a very long time ago. I'm past it, it's not a lingering issue, but Lenny saved me that night. I have no idea why he was there, but if he hadn't shown up, you would never have met the man of your dreams."

"Very funny. You be careful, and you take care of your friend. I need to meet him now, you know? I'd like to thank him."

"Count on it. When this, whatever it is, is over, I'll be inviting him for a visit with less drama attached."

"What will you do tomorrow night? What do they do in your city for New Year's Eve?"

"I have no idea," Jeffrey said, laughing. "No big ball to drop, no central park safe enough for bands or celebrations. At least not in this part of town. We always stayed home. Lenny and his family would come over, or we'd go over there, and our dads would watch sports and complain... just family stuff."

"That sounds wonderful."

"It was. Next year, maybe we can invite Lenny over and create our own version. Surely the world will have opened up a little by then."

"Get some sleep," Barbara said. "I'm going to try and read another couple of chapters, then it's lights out. Try and have some fun."

"Will do. I'll call again when I know more."

"Night. I love you."

"Love you more..."

The line went dead, and Jeffrey stared at the screen for a moment. He emptied his drink in a single gulp and turned off the light. He figured he would lay there until morning, just like that, but in moments he was fast asleep.

From the street, it was hard to visualize the shop he remembered. The same bars and gates protected the doorway as he'd seen on all the other businesses. There were sales and advertisements, some on the outside of the grating, and others on the window behind. A flashing neon sign above the door read, simply, "Pawn—We Buy Gold."

It was difficult to swallow. His memories warred with the reality he faced, and he nearly turned away. He'd come back to help a friend, to pay a very old debt, but he hadn't counted on his entire worldview shifting. Where he lived, where he worked, there was none of this. He had chosen rural North Carolina because there was space. Because the worst traffic was not as bad as a five-block commute in the city. Because, despite the allergies and the farmers with their big-ass equipment blocking the road, the rednecks with four-foot-tall tires on trucks that sounded like jets, it gave him space. The city, this one, not the one he'd left behind so many years before, was like a different dimension, a place where none of the rules he understood applied. How had the span of so few years wiped away generations of history? Or had that history just cordoned itself off, hiding behind the bars, chains, and grates, digging in for the long fight?

Jeffrey pushed through the door and heard the familiar ding of the old bell. The bars on the door might be new, but that sound was as old as his childhood, and it shifted time. The scent was there, as he'd expected. Old cigars. Leather, polished brass, spices and candles and oddities of every imaginable shape and purpose. The shop had always been dimly lit, but Jeffrey found that the closed-in nature of the current situation caused that dim lighting to seem brighter. Different objects glinted and caught his eye. Things he might have missed were centered in their own small spotlights. And he had to smile when he realized how many of the items on display had been there all along, had never sold or moved on. There were new things aplenty, but the bones of his memory held true.

No one was behind the counter, so he turned and started browsing, letting his mind sift back to other times. There were lamps that might have lit the tents of sultans. There were clocks that might have been ticking when Abraham Lincoln walked the halls of the White House. There were ageless tapestries hung on the walls. And then, there were new things. Watches, radios, stacks of records piled beside CDs, DVDs, Laserdiscs, all with a small pile of players that would bring them to life. Time had marched on, but at each mile marker it had left tribute. Every tick of the clock was recorded in these cabinets, shelves, cases, and corners. Jeffrey could not help but think that, even though Lenny's grandfather was gone, the heart of this shop was still beating.

"It can be overwhelming."

The voice came from the shadows behind the counter. Jeffrey spun and saw Lenny leaning on the door frame behind the cash register, the same old lopsided grin, dark curls, and deep-set eyes. There were more wrinkles around those eyes, and the smile lacked some of its brilliance, but he knew his friend immediately.

"It's like I closed my eyes and stepped into the past. It's different, but so much the same," Jeffrey said. "I don't recognize all of the things, but I recognize how they connect with time. And some," he turned toward one of the clocks, "I know as well as I know you."

"Plus ça change, plus c'est la même chose," Lenny said, straightening and starting across the room. "Rush got that part right."

The two met in a deep hug in the center of the room. Everything faded, just for an instant.

"Thank you for coming," Lenny said.

"You knew that I would, but you're welcome. I'm not sure why it's taken me so long to visit."

"The world moved on," Lenny said, "and so did we. It would have been great to see you, but now? Now I need you. Two very different things."

Jeffrey stared at his old friend. "You said you'd learned things. I remember those days so well that I have to wonder what. A lot of it is a blur, but that's because we were kids."

"Those were the best days of my life," Lenny said. The conviction in his voice tugged at Jeffrey's heart because it sounded so bleak. He remembered those days fondly, but it was obvious that his own life had grown in ways his friend would probably not even understand. He loved his life, and his wife, and he had few regrets about leaving the city behind.

"What happened to the neighborhood?" he said. "I've been to Washington, D.C., and this reminds me of that now. Where are the people? The children? Where are the families and when did people stop selling on the streets?"

"Most of those questions have different answers," Lenny said. "The old families moved on to better places, and others moved in. Robberies increased. The streets got dangerous, and then we welcomed in the pandemic. Everything just collapsed in on itself. There aren't very many here you'd remember, and those who stayed have changed."

"What about you?" Jeffrey asked.

"Oh, yeah. I've changed; everything has changed. Maybe the differences in me aren't as obvious as others, but... I have some things to show you, and then I have other things to tell you. As bad as things are in the neighborhood, none of it would have been enough for me to call in the oath. The shop is doing well enough. I'm not in any physical need."

"I wondered about that. I wasn't sure what I could do about," Jeffrey turned and scanned the barred windows and the street beyond, waving his hand vaguely, "this."

"Nobody can fix the city," Lenny said. "It's not just here; it's everywhere now. Things are breaking down; old patterns are rearranging. It's not the first time the world shifted and changed. It won't be the last, though I'll tell you straight up I hope it's the last time during my lifetime. I've seen things in the last couple of years that remind me too much of my grandfather's stories of the old country. I remember words in our history classes, statements like, 'this will never happen here,' and 'we will never forget,' but they forgot, and the world is a mess."

"I would drink to that but..."

Lenny walked to the door, flipped the OPEN sign to CLOSED, locked the door, and headed toward the back of the shop. Jeffrey followed, and they rounded the counter, stepping through the door beyond to a world that Jeffrey had only dreamed of.

When they'd been children, Jeffery and Lenny had concocted wild plans for sneaking past the outer shop and into Lenny's grandfather's private chambers. The shop was big, but the building was deep. They knew there were rooms beyond, that there was more than just an office. Storerooms? Secrets? They had devised intricate strategies to slip in and explore, but none of them had come to pass because, no matter how much they both loved the old man, and the shop, they were also frightened of him. He knew things or seemed to know things that went beyond what they learned in school. His friend Jamal was the same. For every hour the two boys had spent listening to the two old men pontificate on everything from politics to magic to life and romance, there had been two hours where the two were locked away beyond the sales counter in the shop.

Now it was an open door.

Lenny stopped just before stepping through. "It's a bit much," he said. "I know you watched Dr. Who, so you'll understand when I tell you—it's bigger on the inside. There are treasures beyond this door that my grandfather considered too important to put on the floor. He may have had a private clientele that they were targeted for, but it doesn't feel that way. Things appear to have been the same for a very, very long time. And there is more, of course. I wish there wasn't, but..."

He pushed through the door then, and Jeffrey followed.

The chamber that opened was, as promised, much larger than Jeffrey had ever imagined. If he had come in from the rear of the building, the shelves and cases, counters and displays might have seemed like the shop, and the door leading out the far side might have seemed like the access to an office, or a storeroom. It was at least as big as the main room, and it was enough to take his breath away. It was very much the same, and, at the same time, absolutely different.

While the outer shop was filled with intriguing antiques, things with stories, things with a past, it felt like a five-and-dime store beside what now surrounded him. The room was lit by ancient, glass-shaded lamps. The floor was covered, wall to wall, in deep, plush rugs and carpets that swallowed his feet, and that he felt vaguely guilty for stepping on. The windows were curtained, and so little light seeped through that he knew there must be solid shutters on the outside. The same bars, or stronger, that he'd seen throughout the city. If Lenny had turned and told him his grandfather had placed kabbalistic wards to seal the place off from the world, he would not have doubted, because that was how it felt.

"A lot to take in, right?" Lenny said. "The first time I came in here, I only made it as far as that chair over there. I remember thinking, I should not sit on this. It's probably a thousand years old. I'll break it, and even though he's gone, he'll know. Then, I fell back into it as if my legs could no longer support me, and, of course, the chair was fine. In fact, I'd never sat in something as wonderful. I sat there, dazed, and I just looked around, trying to take it all in. That, of course, was impossible.

"Since then, I'm back here as often as I can be. There are books, some journals my grandfather kept, and other more personal items up front by the counter. I've been going through them, learning more about my family and my culture than I ever dreamed existed. When I inherited this place, it felt like an anchor, and now I can't imagine any other outcome."

"It's...a lot," Jeffrey said. "But nothing feels out of place. If anything, you seem at peace. Why did you call me?"

"Take a walk around here," Lenny said. "I'm not going to talk while you do. Take it all in and tell me when you see it."

Jeffrey shrugged and slowly wandered around the big room, stopping to touch a strange sculpture, running his fingers over polished furniture, standing mesmerized by what appeared to be a very old, very intricate clock with all its gears visible through crystal windows in the frames. There was no face, no hands existed to indicate the hour, and he frowned. He felt an odd sensation each time he touched one of the objects, and none of them had the sort of familiarity of the inventory in the outer shop. Most of it only vaguely made sense, the shapes and designs somehow wrong or off. It took a long time to make his way through it all, because each piece felt important. They whispered to him, and he heard them. Every touch held the sense of a future promise. Each time he gave up on translating those promises and moved on.

Then he reached the desk. It was the first piece in the back room, other than the lamps and carpet, which seemed real. It was massive, like something out of a movie about Spanish royalty, so deep that you could sit behind it with someone across from you and feel as if they were in an entirely different room. It had a leather surface covered in glass and huge, ornate drawers. Dinner for a large family could easily have been served on it, or a boardroom meeting held with plenty of space for folders and notebooks. The surface was almost bare. There was a small file organizer, and a laptop, closed and silent, and this only served to enhance the overwhelming sense of size.

Then, as if invisible fingers had pressed on his chin and lifted, Jeffrey glanced up at the wall beyond. It was bare, except for one grand tapestry. There were sconced lights at the upper corners, angled slightly so they lit the entirety of the vast image. In the background there were mountains, lined in gold from a brilliant sun. Roads wound down from the top and grew larger as they curved toward the center and down. The colors were subtle, and then bold, perfectly blended. It was far too much to take in with a single glance, and then, as he scanned more slowly, his mind nearly went blank. It was too much for a single anything. He had the dislocated thought that he could stare at it endlessly, day after day, and never grasp it. Never really catch the details or the intent. It seemed impossibly perfect. And then...

There was a single patch near the bottom right that caught his eye. It wasn't the way something beautiful calls to you and arrests your attention. It was sudden, sharp, and dark. It snagged his gaze like a fishhook. It was so different from the rest of the tapestry, so out of place, so wrong, that it hurt. He felt as if his mind had been slapped, and he took a step back, staring. A wave of utter revulsion washed over him, and he stumbled back farther. His heel caught on the edge of an antique chest, and he started to topple.

Lenny caught him, a strong arm around his shoulder steadying him until his mind cleared. He shook his head, turned, and gasped.

"What in the hell was that?" he asked. "Why would someone? How...?"

"I know," Lenny said. "Believe me, I know. No one was here when I saw it for the first time. I nearly got a concussion hitting the floor. This is only the shallow surface of something so deep I'm afraid I'm drowning."

"But it's just a tapestry?"

"It is a tapestry, yes. It is the most beautiful thing, and the vilest, that I've ever seen. But that's far from all that it is. I don't even know if I can begin to explain what I believe to be true, what I know, and what I don't know. There are things I'll only be able to show you, but first, I think we'd better head back out into the main store and have a drink."

Jeffrey nodded. "Damn straight. Maybe you can try to tell me before you show me. I'm not sure if I'm ready for something like that again any time soon."

"When I'm finished, you're going to wish for something like that."

Lenny turned and stepped through the door, back into the public shop.

He turned left and headed to the corner at the end of the counter. Jeffrey followed, and then stopped. Everything had been cleared out of that area. No shelves or bookcases lined the walls. There was just a squat table, two ancient metal chairs and, on the table, a bottle of bourbon. Beside the bottle were two faded glass tumblers, and a wooden box with the pieces from a chess set. The table's surface was old and cracked, and the checkerboard pattern had faded to the point where you would need good light to differentiate dark from light.

Lenny caught his shocked expression and grinned.

"We can't sit out in the alley anymore," he said. "The stench would drive us batty, and the odds of us surviving more than an hour without getting mugged or arrested for dealing something we don't have aren't good. When I took over the store, one of the first things I did was to bring it all in here. To preserve it. I was afraid someone would break the table, or steal the chess set. I didn't want to lose it."

"You mean, you didn't want to lose them," Jeffrey said. "So now it's our turn. No one here to listen to us as we explain the secrets of the universe."

"Good thing," Lenny said. "I don't know any of them, and I've reached a point where I wish to hell I'd listened more closely and understood more of what I heard. I always thought they were just talking, going on about old stories, or shared fantasies. Now…" He waved his hand at the table. "Have a seat. I'll pour, and then I'll tell you what I know, and what I don't."

"Weller," Jeffrey said. "Must have cost you. We can't even get that back home unless we order it at three times retail off the Internet."

"I was related to a guy who knew a guy," Lenny said. "You would not believe what my grandfather had in his bar."

"Got any ice? I wouldn't want to water it down, but it's always better cold."

"Sure," Lenny said. "I have to go upstairs to the apartment to get it. I'll bring down an ice bucket. Maybe I'll get some newer glassware too. Those held up a lot of years, but I think I'd rather start fresh if it's our table now."

Jeffrey watched his friend disappear through another door behind the counter, then sat back and closed his eyes. It was too surreal, too much to take in all at once. When he'd been a boy, Lenny's grandfather, Caleb, and his friend, Jamal, had been neighborhood icons. The two boys had had special access, almost constant contact with the two old men, but everyone in the neighborhood stopped by now and then to listen or be part of the conversation.

As he slowly relaxed, the shop faded. He shifted through

time. Suddenly the memory became his reality, the scents of the shop became those of the alley, and he shrank in on himself. He was aware of all of this, but unable to control it. Moments later, that other time came into sharp focus. He heard voices. At first, he shook his head, trying to clear it and come back to reality, but it was no use. The voices he heard became clearer. He felt the brick wall at his back, sensed Lenny at his side. The memory flooded in with absolute clarity.

"The world is so much larger than we believe," Caleb said. He took a puff off his pipe and closed his eyes for a moment, expelling smoke through his nostrils and drinking in the taste and scent of the tobacco. "And that is just this world, eh? There must be so many others. If we could but find the doorway, yes? If we could find a way through whatever separates them."

"You are a dreamer," Jamal replied. "There is one world, and it holds enough wonder and secrets for many lifetimes. Why would you want more? Why would you not be satisfied with what you have?"

"So, you are satisfied, then? You are happy with what you know and learning nothing more, happy to exist as you have always existed and then, when your moment comes, to cease?"

"There is nothing else. What is important is how you use what you've been given. If you spend your existence seeking more, you will pass on to another world with too many questions and no answers."

"There is no reason for this life," Caleb countered, "if there are unanswered questions, and you are satisfied without answers. What? I should ignore the mysteries and just play chess until I die? I live because there is more to know. There is no other reason."

The two fell silent for a moment and Jeffrey, leaning silently against the wall of the alley, his back to the cold bricks, waited. He didn't know why, but he wanted to know who would win this debate. He wanted to believe there was more. Their small neighborhood was cut off even from the rest of the city. Other than school, he knew family, a few friends, and the blocks that were safe from the gangs in other neighborhoods.

"I have a thing to show you," Caleb said at last. "It came in last week. I have been studying it, but I am not sure that I understand what I have uncovered. I am not sure that I want to understand, but you think differently than I. While I dream, you scheme, while I wonder, you ponder, yes? Perhaps together we can find an answer to it."

"It? You are speaking in riddles, and you know I love riddles. What is this new wonder you have uncovered? A magic lamp? Will there be a genie, do you think?"

"No genie," Caleb said, "but a doorway? Possibly. At the very least, there is a mystery to uncover because, I will tell you, I have never seen anything like it. I have heard of things similar, of a concept that is realized in this object, but I have never seen it rendered, and I would never have believed it could exist in such a complete form. I admit, as much as I wish for answers, there are times that I wonder if the questions should be asked. It is too late for this one. It is a cat out of the bag, as they say. I have seen it, and I have to follow what I have seen to the end."

"Well then," Jamal said. "There is no time like the present."

Jeffrey looked to his left, where Lenny should have been seated, but found that he was alone. The two old men had risen, oblivious to his presence, and turned toward the back door of the shop. Quietly and carefully, he rose, and he followed.

The back room of the pawn shop was very similar to the way he had seen it earlier, with Lenny. Jeffrey was aware that it was impossible that the two older men were present, but incapable of denying the reality of the vision. The tapestry he'd been studying earlier was hung, just as he'd seen it. He avoided glancing at the lower right corner. Most of the room was open space. There were palettes and crates, piled boxes where he'd seen the strange, disconcerting antiques. He didn't want to look at the tapestry again. He already knew what he'd see. Instead, he ducked into the shadows along one wall and watched. He wasn't certain if they were aware he was there, or even if it was possible that he was. He might be flashing back to an actual memory he'd suppressed, though that suggested other possibilities he wanted no part of. He was aware that he was far shorter, that he was dressed differently. None of it felt strange, though a voice deep in the back of his mind was screaming that it was crazy.

"You see it?" Caleb asked.

There was no need for Jamal to answer. Just as Jeffrey had done earlier that day, the old Arab had started at the top of the tapestry, wound his gaze down in slow, sweeping arcs, as if under a spell. When he reached the final corner, it was as if the expression on his face was glass, and the image before him shattered it. He staggered back, not losing his balance, but averting his eyes quickly.

"You know what it is?" Caleb asked.

"It is an abomination," Jamal said. "It should not exist."

"No, you are wrong," Caleb replied. "It is so perfect that it had to be controlled. So beautiful that it had to be marred, because only God, Allah, whatever you name Him, or Her, or it…only God can create perfection."

"This was purposeful," Jamal said. "That does not suggest respect for an all-powerful deity. It suggests deception. It is a means of hiding a truth. If someone can create a thing that is perfect, that is a gift. To disrespect that gift in such a manner is an abomination."

"It is a protection," Caleb said. "It is a means of preventing attention, of avoiding discovery. It is a secret, and a wonder. You could imagine, if you believed, that it was woven by an angel. I have read many times of weavers and rug makers who introduce a poorly wrought thread, or a color that is not right. Here in America, Native Americans have employed the same tactic. It is a ward against…something."

"But why? And why do you have it here, hung upon your wall? If it is obscuring a secret, what?"

"That is more than one question," Caleb said. "I am not sure I can answer all of them. It is here because I found it for sale, and I brought it back. It is on my wall because it is a wonder, and a mystery, and I would solve it. What it protects, and why it has been flawed? That is why I brought you here. I believe I know how to find out, but I don't want to do so alone."

Jamal shuddered. "I would like to meet the man, or the

woman, or whatever creature wove this," he said. "But that? That abomination?" He pointed at the offensive corner. "I am certain that I do not want to meet the one responsible. And what can you do? How can it be fixed? Should it be fixed? I don't know why I am here."

"Because I am an old man," Caleb said, "and I have found something remarkable. I have no idea what it is, what it might do, or whether it's important. I am fascinated, and I am terrified. You are here because you are my friend—possibly my only friend. You are a wise man, and I cannot face this alone. You are here because I need you."

Jamal closed his eyes. It was hard to tell if he was just thinking or if he was praying, but a moment later he glanced at Caleb, and he nodded. "That is a good answer," he said. "I have tried to find a hole in it, and failed, so, what shall we do? I have many skills, but weaving is not one of them."

Caleb smiled. He crossed the room to a table in the corner. He reached out and unlatched the lid of an orange, polished wooden box and raised the lid. He stood very still for a moment, then he reached down and lifted out an odd, metal device. It was rectangular in shape and very ornate. The center of it was crystal, some sort of prismatic lens. He turned and presented it to Jamal.

"This came with the tapestry," he said. "I have no idea what it can do. It is a great deal to ask, but I am asking. Will you stay?"

Jamal nodded. Caleb closed his eyes, and then, moving slowly, he approached the tapestry. He held out the lens of the device to the strange, malignant patch on the tapestry. As it covered that vile disfigurement, there was a sudden, incredibly bright flash of light. Caleb stepped back with a cry. Jamal moved to steady his friend, and Jeffry, unable to withstand the brilliance, closed his eyes. Something in the room shifted powerfully. He pushed back and found himself tipping.

Something stopped him from toppling backward and he took several gasping breaths. Then he rocked slightly forward and felt the legs of the chair he sat in strike the floor. Strong hands gripped his shoulders, not tightly, but firmly. He shook his head and turned.

"What...?"

"I was about to ask you the same thing," Lenny said. "Where were you? What did you see? You were about to fall away from the table when I got back. I was barely quick enough to catch you."

"I must have dozed," Jeffry said. "I had a dream. A vivid dream, like a memory. I was in the alley, with your grandfather and Jamal. I don't think they even knew I was there, but they never really did, did they? I followed them inside, and they were looking at the tapestry, Jamal for the first time."

Jeffrey turned quickly. "Have you found a carved wooden box? It was polished wood, almost orange. There would be a device in it, some sort of viewer. It had a lens like crystal. I saw them place it against the tapestry, against the broken part, I don't know what else to call that. There was a flash of light."

Lenny stared at him.

"I have no idea what you're talking about, but there are so many things in the shop. In the front, in the back, so many cases and boxes, I've seen nothing like that, but I didn't know to look."

"Sit down," Jeffrey said. "I need to get my thoughts straight, and if there's something in that back room to match the vision I just had, it's not going anywhere. If anything, it seems that the tapestry, or something, wants us to know a secret. I'm going to go out on a limb and suggest that not only will we approach that secret more calmly if we drink the bourbon, but that even if this is not the case, we are meant to find it, and we will enjoy the bourbon. The universe can spare us a few moments to sit, drink, and talk.

"It was very strange to see those two old men, to hear them talk about things beyond the normal. We heard so many stories and now I wonder how much of that we wasted by either not understanding or not paying attention. The vision I just had didn't feel like a revelation, it felt like a memory. You weren't there, and that was odd, but what if they're speaking to us? What if they knew this moment would come?"

"Like spirits? Ghosts? And they brought us here," Lenny said, "so that we could face this together?"

Jeffrey nodded. "Yeah, I know. It sounds like something out

of a particularly cheesy science fiction movie. You going to pour that whiskey?"

Lenny took a seat, uncorked the bottle, and poured two fingers into each of two tumblers.

"Why don't you start at the point where I left for ice and tell me what in hell just happened?" Lenny said. He raised his glass and took a slow, appreciative sip of the bourbon.

"I sort of dozed off, I guess," Jeffry said. "It didn't feel like a dream, though. At least, not like any dream I've ever experienced. I was there—the alley out back. Your grandfather and Jamal were talking. I don't believe they were aware of me. Maybe, on that actual day, I wasn't really there. It's fuzzy.

"I followed them inside, and your grandfather showed Jamal the tapestry. He had the same reaction that I did, and I assume you did as well. That piece on the bottom corner seemed to physically assault him. Before the vision faded, your grandfather opened a wooden case. He pulled out a rectangular device with a crystal lens. I think he was going to use it to view that corner of the tapestry. I'm sure, in fact, that he did, because when he handed it to Jamal, they both leaned down toward that corner. The vision ended before I was able to see what happened."

"I haven't found anything like that," Lenny said, "but it makes sense. That corner feels so wrong it physically hurts to look at it. It's obviously hiding something important. In fact, without some device or key, I can't imagine a better defense. I've tried to study it, but any amount of time even looking at it makes me so ill I have to leave the room."

"I don't know where the viewer is," Jeffry said, "but I know where it was. I know what it looks like."

"Are you sure you even want to find it?" Lenny asked. "I called you back here because you owed me a favor. This goes way beyond any sort of childhood promise. It may be dangerous. In fact, if it wasn't, why would that hideous seal be on it at all? Why would it be locked away, and why would my grandfather be so adamant that my father pass this place on to me? They both knew I wanted out. I wanted to be away from this city, from all the ties and struggles. The family is scattered now, and the neighborhood doesn't even exist in any form we could recognize. I'd be lying if I told you the entire thing didn't scare the hell out of me."

Jeffrey raised his glass, then took a sip of the whiskey and smiled.

"That is the biggest pile of bullshit I've heard in a very long time," he said. "You called me here, because you knew I was the only person in the world that might just accept this, that might understand and believe. I know you're afraid because I am. I love art. I've loved it all my life. Music, paintings, novels that transcend the mundane have called out to me since I was a kid. In all those years, I have never experienced such a physical, overwhelming reaction. Not to art, not to love, not to anything. I could no more leave here without knowing what that is than I could will myself to stop breathing. You knew that before you called. It's not a pleasant reaction, but it's a reaction to something someone created. How could I not see this through?"

Lenny lowered his gaze.

"It's okay," Jeffrey said. "Jesus, if I knew you had this—whatever the fuck it is—here and didn't let me in on it, I'd have hated you for the rest of my life. Do you know how long I've believed in this sort of experience, and been denied any proof?" He laughed. "You do, of course you do. I told you. I told you so long ago that if you stacked us one on top of the other, we would not be as tall as you are now."

"Guilty, of course," Lenny said. "Still..."

"Still nothing. Drink your whiskey, and let's get to it. We don't have to use the thing today, but we ought to at least try and find it. I'm going to need to get back to my rooms and get some rest eventually."

"Not at all," Lenny said. "Let's go get your things first. I have three extra rooms upstairs. I tried to tell you that before you left home. You have to stay here, and we'll see this through to whatever. The neighborhood may be shot to hell, but business is actually good. The sorts of things my grandfather gathered are in demand, and I've expanded sales to the Internet."

"Give up my half-dead air conditioner and rickety balcony view of the city?"

"Don't make me angry," Lenny said. "You wouldn't like me...when I'm angry."

They both laughed. Jeffry raised his glass and they clinked both together before draining the whiskey.

"As long as you have more of this here," Jeffrey said, "you'll have a hard time keeping me away. It's only a few blocks to my hotel. We can get there and back with my bag and my bottle of inferior bourbon and get settled. I don't suppose there's anything worth eating here?"

"There is not," Lenny said. "Thankfully, the one thing that has not disappeared from the neighborhood is the variety of cuisine, and almost everyone delivers. We can figure out what we want once we get back."

"Sounds like a plan," Jeffrey said.

The two rose and headed out the front door. Lenny locked it behind them, and they started off down the block. Once outside, walking down the familiar street, Jeffrey finally felt the nostalgia he'd expected. He caught the smell of Thai food, something that was probably Mexican, and they passed an Indian restaurant where the scent of curry hung heavy in the air. The bars were in place on all the windows, but there were pockets of life. He had missed them walking to the pawn shop earlier in the day. Everything felt different. Alive, and connected.

On their way back they stopped at the Indian place and took dinner back to the shop. It felt good, and comfortable. For just a little while, it was just two old friends remembering good times. They got Jeffrey settled into one of the empty rooms over the shop and didn't mention the tapestry even once. It was like the calm before a storm. They didn't know what kind of storm, and for the moment didn't care. Just that one night, their dreams were their own.

When Jeffrey woke, had showered, dressed, and left his room behind, the scent of freshly brewed coffee drew him down the hall. The apartment was sumptuous. The furniture was a mix of several centuries of design, each piece carefully selected to fit a pattern. The carpet was deep and soft, and should have been faded, but somehow was not.

He found Lenny in a brightly lit kitchen. The coffee awaited in a large French Press centered on the table. Eggs and bacon were frying in a pan on the stove.

"Good morning," he said. "You were up bright and early."

"I never sleep long," Lenny said. "I'm a deep sleeper, and when I wake, it's over. I've tried staying in bed and forcing myself to rest, but it's no use. I find that if I get up, eat, have my coffee, and then sit quietly for a while, I am able to run back through all of the things that I need to accomplish, and all of the questions I'm trying to answer. I supposed it's a form of meditation. Today, I am meditating over eggs and coffee, because we already have a plan, and I don't want to be distracted."

"Sounds about right," Jeffrey said. "At the very least, we shouldn't face whatever is waiting downstairs without eating something first. But what about your shop? Won't people notice if it's closed up again?"

"Business is spotty at best. I do more online and with my grandfather and father's contacts than I do with street traffic. Honestly, it's a relief not to have to worry about a robbery. It's not the city it was when you left."

"So you keep saying."

Jeffrey sat. Lenny served the eggs and bacon, and they emptied the carafe of coffee. As on the night before, they avoided the subject of the tapestry. It hung in the air, the elephant in the room, but they managed to ignore it, and to enjoy the food. Finally, it was time.

"I'll rinse these dishes," Lenny said, "and we can get started. I don't imagine what we're looking for will be in the outer shop. It's going to be in the back room, and I suspect it's not going to be hard to find. I think it's a secret that wants to be discovered. Also, if my grandfather or Jamal left it, they intended it to be found."

"Agreed. I can't believe that the vision I had, or dream, or whatever the hell it was, just 'happened' for no reason. Someone, or something wants us to figure out what is up with that tapestry, and I have to say, as nervous as it makes me, I would be hard pressed to walk away from this, and probably haunted for the rest of my life. So, thank you for that."

Lenny laughed. "You're welcome, I think. I hope you don't end up hating me for it. On one hand this feels like a weird wild goose chase through our childhood. On the other, it seems dark, dangerous, and like a very bad idea."

"Nothing ventured," Jeffrey said, downing the last of his coffee. "Let's get to it."

They deposited the dishes in the sink and headed out and down the stairs. At the bottom, there were two doorways. One led to the shop and the other to the back room. They turned left and did not look back.

"I'll start at the corner by the old table," Lenny said. "You start in the far corner and work your way toward me. If we meet in the middle before we find it, we'll cross and spread out to the two remaining corners."

"Sounds like a plan," Jeffrey said. "Remember, the box is wooden. It was highly polished and sort of orange. It's hard to explain because I don't know of any sort of wood colored that way."

"Got it," Lenny said.

They set to work. It was hard not to get distracted as they worked their way through the inventory. There were ancient books, their leather, whatever hide they had been crafted from so soft and supple they seemed somehow ageless. The pages were filled with figures and characters that might be some ancient language, or something else entirely. None of them were legible. There were statues, odd devices, clocks, and an endless number of perfectly preserved hats, vases, and pieces of furniture. There must have been hundreds of cabinets, drawers, dark corners, and alcoves, all filled with a dizzying array of things that, under other circumstances, might have caused one or both of them to wonder if Caleb had been involved in some sort of black-market antiques scheme.

In the end, they found the box tucked underneath the front counter. If they had simply walked around to the far side, they would have seen it, and once they did it felt obvious enough to send them both into gales of laughter.

"Who would have thought," Lenny said, "that he'd keep the

key to the tapestry in the cabinet directly under it."

"We would have found it sooner," Jeffrey said, "but I wasn't really hoping to get that close. Is it just me, or has that thing been looming over us the whole time?"

He pointed to the tapestry, and Lenny nodded. "Not just you, man. Feeling a little silly, but hey, this place is amazing. I'm glad to have gone through it. Did you notice anything strange?"

"Other than the fact that things that should be old, worn, and aged look as if they were just created?"

"That, but there's more. I've been around things like this all my life. I've seen antiques, I've listened to my grandfather, and then my father, go on and on about ancient devices, books older than this country. More things than I could describe, really. Some of this?" He gazed around the room and shook his head. "There are things here I can't explain. Things I've never seen and that I'm pretty certain, if you were to try looking them up in an antique guide, or scan them with Google Lens, you would find that they don't exist."

Jeffrey stared at his friend, then turned and glanced out over the room. He remembered an odd brass device he'd assumed was something used for navigation, maybe before colonial times. Now he wondered why he'd thought that.

"It's sort of like there's something hiding it," he said. "You noticed it, but I think that might be because you've been here longer, and you have more context. Now that you've said something, I see it, but I swear I thought I knew what every one of those things was."

Lenny nodded. "Then there's this."

He lifted the lid on the wooden box and withdrew a silk-wrapped object. "It's heavy," he said. He laid it on the counter and pulled aside the silk. What was revealed was an odd, metal-framed lens. It was rectangular and, once Lenny turned and lifted it in front of him, it matched up with the bottom-right corner of the tapestry, about the same size as the offending glitch in the pattern. He started to move it closer, and then hesitated.

"You ready for this?" he asked? "I'm honestly freaking out. I have no idea what this is going to do, and I'm absolutely positive that it's going to do something."

"Same," Jeffrey said, "but if not, then why are we here?"

Lenny took a deep breath and pressed the lens in close to the tapestry. As it neared the surface, a bright white glow washed over the thing. For just a moment, the offending corner of the tapestry simply disappeared. Then, in the time it would have taken for a camera flash to go off, it came into focus. The tapestry was no longer marred, the lens revealing the perfection beneath, and the entire thing started to shimmer.

Jeffrey gasped and took half a step back, but Lenny was locked to the lens in his hand, encased in the growing brilliance of the light. The image, already nearly perfect, expanded. What had been a beautiful, colorful picture of a place that might or might never have existed expanded into other dimensions, taking on mass and form. Lenny stepped forward and Jeffrey, seeing this, lunged after him.

"Wait," he said.

It was too late. He grabbed Lenny's shirt as he toppled forward and was pulled along in his friend's wake. They tumbled into what should have been a wall, and was, instead, a pool of darkness. He thought, at the last second, to cry out, but that too was swallowed.

And then his mind cleared. Or at least he thought it had cleared. He glanced around the room. Lenny was sprawled on the floor. He cradled the lens, and he was staring back past Jeffrey with an expression of abject horror on his face. Jeffrey stepped forward, blocking his friend's view of whatever was behind him, and leaned down, prying the lens from Lenny's white-knuckled grip. He was not staring at the tapestry, but at a nearly identical room to that he'd stumbled out of, stretching off into the distance. Except all of it was wrong. The furnishings were off. Some too tall, some too thin. Nothing was quite right, and it caused his head to ache, so he tore his gaze away from it and turned to Lenny. His friend's horrified stare had not wavered.

"I don't know what you see," he said, "but look away."

Lenny didn't move. Jeffrey, careful not to turn or look back, stepped forward and slapped his friend hard across the face.

"What?" Lenny tumbled back, pressing his hands to the

floor, and glanced up, breaking the spell of whatever it was that he'd been staring at.

"Pull yourself together," Jeffrey said. "I don't know what's behind me, and until it's time for us to leave, I don't want to know. We are—where? I don't know."

Lenny turned and stood slowly. The two of them studied the room. It was so familiar, and yet totally alien, that it was hard to focus. The air was thick. Every scent was unfamiliar, but not like a new tobacco or a strangely scented candle. The odors felt impossible. Colors rippled in patterns and hues that they were seeing for the first time, as if the frequency of light itself had warped.

Jeffrey stepped forward. There was a wooden table, like a nightstand. On top of it was a vase, or a bottle, but that bottle had a solid center, and the portion of it that would hold liquid, or whatever, was beyond that core. There were boundaries to it, but they seemed ethereal. He picked it up.

At the first touch, he nearly dropped it, turned, and ran. It was so cold that it seemed to burn, but it wasn't the sensation of heat, or even extreme cold, that he was familiar with. It was like the scents in the air, everything else about the place. It felt as if it was burning him, but it was simply overloading his senses. Some energy within it, some essence so unfamiliar the sensation of touching it was painful. He gripped it more tightly, fighting for breath and control. He felt Lenny come up beside him and steady his arms. Lenny did not touch the vase.

"What in the hell is happening?" he asked. "Where are we?"

Jeffrey swallowed, fighting off the sudden nausea brought on by the familiar touch of a human hand on his skin while holding that...thing.

"We need to leave," he said. "We need to open whatever we opened to get here. We can take this with us, whatever it is, but the longer I stay here, the more my head pounds, the less I can see, or at least see the way I did. We shouldn't be here."

Lenny nodded. "We're going to have to look at the tapestry. You aren't going to like it. Think of that corner. Think how it made you feel. Here? That's what the entire thing is like. I don't know this for sure, but I think what we have to do is to concentrate on that corner. It will be the one piece that looks the way our tapestry looks. We'll have to jam this into place and dive."

Something moved behind them. They whirled, and saw what appeared to be a man, or a blurred bit of air where a man might or might not be, moving rapidly toward them. The figure was horribly out of focus. Its face appeared to be fracturing, jagged bits of flesh completely separated from the whole. The eyes were dark, and it clearly struggled to press through the thickened air. They heard a sound, like a scream, but at the same time it was a word. The closer the figure came, the more its form tore apart, and the louder the screams, pinpoints of light spread from the center of the eyes.

Then it stopped. Before they could turn and dive for the tapestry, it spoke.

Not exactly words, but close, as if forming the sounds was nearly impossible, but being overcome by force of will. The thing stretched out a hand toward Jeffrey.

"Trrrrrrrrrrradddddde," it said.

"What?" Lenny choked out, before he could stop himself.

He and Jeffrey backed toward the tapestry, keeping the thing clearly in sight. It moved another step closer, and then again. "Traaaaaaade," it said.

"What is it saying?" Lenny asked.

"I'm not sure," Jeffrey said. "It sounded like trade."

"Jesus, look out!"

Behind the form, sparks of energy had formed along the walls. Shadowy forms skittered about the room and what might have been tiny bolts of lightning flashed between them. They were closing in on the figure in front of them, whatever it was.

The creature grew more agitated. Then it sparked and began splitting apart. It splintered, bits and pieces of its form ripping apart. It screamed again, and the two of them spun as one, lunging toward the tapestry.

With a sound so high pitched and discordant that the room shimmered and nearly lost focus entirely, the creature dove at them. As Jeffrey, who had the lens, pressed it to the tapestry, unable to miss one quick glance at the entirety of it and nearly passing out from the sudden jolt of nausea that single glance induced.

"Run," he cried.

"Nooooooooooooo!" The creature behind them reached Jeffrey before he could pass through the suddenly open portal and slapped the vase from his hand. It was all he could do to hang on to the lens, and there was no time to think.

As he fell back into his own world, the thing screamed at him so loudly that the force of the sound drove him face first into the floor. He knew he would have a bruise, and that his nose was probably bleeding. In the depths of that scream, he heard the word again.

"Traaaaaade."

It was a little bit clearer...then it fizzled, the world snapped back to what he had always considered normal, and that was too much. He lost his balance, curled himself around the lens to protect it, and dropped to the floor, only barely managing to roll and catch himself on his shoulder before his head struck the thick carpet and all conscious thought departed.

Hours later, seated at the old table again, the bourbon open and poured, the two friends stared at one another. On the table rested a brass device the size of a small clock. It had several finely machined levers, and the interior mechanism, gears, and a central rotor gleamed as if they'd been created only that day.

"What does it do?" Jeffrey asked at last, sipping his drink. "Have you tried the levers?"

Lenny nodded, and then shook his head. "I have. I've turned it every which way. I've pushed and pulled all the levers. Now and then one of the gears moves a notch. There's a dial of sorts embedded in the corner of one side. You can operate the mechanism to change the position of the pointer, but none of the possible positions causes anything noticeable to happen."

"And yet, I can't believe it's some beautifully crafted Rube Goldberg machine. I mean, no one exerts that level of craftmanship without purpose."

"So, I think we're in agreement," Lenny said. "It's not that it doesn't work. It's that it doesn't work here."

Jeffrey took another drink, as if it might wash the thought away, but in the end, he nodded. "And I'm going to suggest," he said, tapping his wristwatch with the rim of his tumbler, "that if I had tried to check the time over there, it wouldn't have worked. Would have meant nothing. That the physics we know and learn are not the only physics that exist."

Lenny nodded. "But who was that?" he asked. "Whoever it was, whatever it was, it didn't seem to belong there. It was as if the effort to communicate with us, to reach our consciousness, was tearing it—him—apart."

"That's a very important question," Jeffrey said. "As far as we know, the only two men who knew about this," he reached out and tapped the wooden case that held the lens, "were Caleb and Jamal. I know that Caleb died, and you told me Jamal was gone. To where? Where did he go? Is he also dead?"

"I don't know," Lenny said. "No one ever told me if he did. If there was a funeral, no one mentioned it. When my grandpa died, I asked my father why Jamal wasn't there, and he only shook his head. No one seemed to know where he was, or what he was doing."

"Then we have to consider the possibility that we know that answer," Jeffrey said.

"But if that's Jamal, why is he there? How is he there?"

"I have no idea, but if that was Jamal, he knocked me silly trying to prevent me bringing that vase, or whatever it was, back with me. He screamed that word at us over and over. I'm convinced it was trade. I think, though I'm not sure how it helps, that there are rules. I just wish one of the two of them had bothered at some point to write them down."

"Maybe they did," Lenny said. "Maybe we just haven't found them yet. One seems to be clear. If you bring something back, you have to leave something there."

"We can start with that," Jeffrey said. "It makes sense, and it helps to explain all of this," he tipped his glass at the room full of oddities. "I'll have to think about it for a while to see if it applies to whoever that was. If it was Jamal, what did he do? What did he fail to trade? Or did he stay too long, and that place wanted a trade for him?"

"Maybe he made the trade," Lenny said. "What if someone or something from that other place is already here?"

Jeffrey glanced around uncomfortably. "And they are where?"

"How would I know? I'll tell you what I think. If they slipped over here, and got a good direct look at the tapestry, they may have run. They might be fighting for their sanity. They might have abilities we don't understand, and I can't imagine that experience has made them very sympathetic to us. It makes sense that if their side makes us ill to the point of catatonia, our side does the same to them."

"If they are here, and they're trying to get home, they'll need the lens. If they're aware that we found and used it, we may be on a short timeline here."

"To what, save him? Save Jamal, or whoever that was? Stop him from..."

"Yes, yes, and if there is a reason, yes. This portal didn't just happen. If Caleb and Jamal simply found this, and didn't create it in some fashion, it follows that whoever or whatever is on the other side did. If that's true, the existence of the lens here means someone tried to stop whatever they planned, and we have the key."

It was Lenny's turn to gulp down some of the bourbon.

"I guess this means another trip through," he said. "We take something, we grab something, make the trade and get out?"

"That is absolutely the last thing I want to do," Jeffrey said. "So, of course."

Lenny laughed. "Of course."

"You realize there's an entirely different possibility."

"What?"

"That your grandfather never took anything through that tapestry to trade it. That whoever is on the other side, whatever is on the other side, was coming here. If that's true, there may be a reason why they chose, for instance, this—whatsit." He pointed to the brass mechanism on the table. "What if there's a plan behind it? What if all of this," he waved his arm to indicate the entire back room, "is being gathered for some purpose? Something we have no chance of understanding. Maybe the only thing Caleb and Jamal traded for and brought back, was the lens?"

"You mean someone on the other side was bringing things all that time? Seems like a stretch. My grandfather would not have simply sat and watched that room fill up, wondering where his inventory was disappearing to. It had to have been them."

"That doesn't mean that whoever, or whatever, is on the other side didn't manage to place the items they needed in such a way that they became the trades. Just something to think about."

They sat quietly for a while, thinking, and sipping their bourbon.

"There are a lot of questions," Lenny said. "I think the only way we get answers is to make a plan, test it, and see what we can learn. For one thing, we have to guard that lens with our lives. If we were on the other side and lost it, we'd never get back."

"We also have to figure out what to trade," Jeffrey said. "We can't let it be anything that would be harmful to us, or to others. Something inanimate and ornamental."

"What if you can only trade a device for a device, and a decoration for a decoration? I suggest we try the latter first. I don't believe we can be too careful."

"That sounds like a good start. I wonder, what if we took a video camera over there? If we traded it for something that looks similar and left it running, then went back and traded something from this room, something not from here, to get it back? Do you think it would operate, since we know how it works, and it works here, and that they would not be able to figure it out? It might be just like this thing on the table to them, buttons and a lens, but no function. I have a bunch of cameras that attach wirelessly to the security system. They don't require being plugged in, and the batteries are amazing. They last for weeks at a time."

"That sounds like a pretty good idea. If it doesn't work, at least we'll have tested the first trade, and then, a second trade of something of theirs for something of ours. Maybe we send back something already here on the second trade. If there is a plan, our changing the items out may buy us more time."

"And if not, we'll still know more than we know now. We're really doing this, aren't we? I mean, the smart thing to do would be to break that lens into a million pieces and burn the tapestry, then go on with our New Year's celebrations. But I can't see myself doing that."

"Nope. Grandpa couldn't stop himself, and I guess I can't either. I'm going to go and get one of those cameras. This time, I'm not looking back at that tapestry, and I don't think either of us should, except at that one corner, right when we're headed back through."

Lenny rose, downed his bourbon, and headed for the front of the store. Jeffrey sat for a few moments longer. He took a sip of the bourbon, then tipped the tumbler back and downed it. He hated to hurry it, because he only got bourbon of this quality on special occasions, but he thought his time would be better spent looking around at the other items and seeing if there was some sort of pattern."

If he took the notion of all of it working together to form some single device or condition, then the thing to do was to treat it like a puzzle. He wandered down the aisles, mentally pressing one piece to the next, then to the next, looking for any sort of a match. On the third item, a table with a lid that opened to reveal a cabinet, he noticed something. There was a tag on it. It was a simple yellow label with a four-digit number. On top of the table was a smaller box. He lifted it and tipped it over. On the bottom was another label.

"Thank you, Caleb," he said softly. He hurried across the room to the counter and began going through the drawers behind it. In the third one he found a stack of ledgers. He pulled out the top one and opened it. A long column of four-digit numbers ran down the first column. The second held a date, and those dates stretched back decades. The main entry for each was a description of each item. Hundreds of items. In yet another column was a separate number, these containing five digits, but with a letter A at the beginning of each.

When Lenny returned, Jeffrey was deep into the inventory, glancing around the room to try and associate descriptions with the pieces on the floor.

"What is it?" Lenny asked.

"This ledger," Jeffrey said. "It's a catalog of the items in this room, with dates and vague descriptions. There are also these," he spun the ledger for Lenny to see, "a second set of numbers with a letter prefix."

Lenny glanced at it and nodded. "That is the numbering system for the inventory of the shop. Each of those will correspond to the main ledger of sales out front. Do you think these are the items that were traded? Or taken?"

"It seems so. It's good your grandfather was so attentive to detail, but it doesn't appear he intended the records to be useful to others. At least not in a practical way. There's no indication here whether things were taken, or given, or both."

"Wait," Lenny said. He spun and headed back to the outer shop. He returned with an even larger ledger and set it beside the one Jeffrey had been perusing. "There are a lot more details in the main ledger. We have to keep track of who we sold what in case there is ever a legal question. Pawn shops are one of the first stops the police make when things go missing. Let's see if we can match some of those numbers up with items in the main ledger and see what he wrote."

They flipped back through the pages, years of sales, notes about customers, some from the neighborhood, some they recognized. Then they saw it. The first number where the entry made no real sense. It was recorded as a sale, but there was a notation that it was a "sale for goods tendered," and there was no amount listed for the sale. It was a null entry. Probably for taxes, as much as anything.

"Here," Lenny said. He pointed to the final column of the listing. "Lamp, unknown provenance, inoperative." There was a code next to it. "That is a location code for the back room. "We can find this item there, and we know what date the item in the front office disappeared. What is the date for the arrival of the piece in the other ledger?"

Jeffrey ran back through the numbers until he reached the matching entry. He glanced up. "No help. It's the same date. Either he wanted the records to match in case he ever got audited by the IRS or he traded the item himself, or for some reason, he didn't want to record the truth. In any case, it leaves us with a little more knowledge, but no real answers. I think we're going to have to figure it out ourselves."

"Plan is back on, then," Lenny said. "We pick something, take it through to the other side, and we bring something back. We guard the lens as if our lives depend on it, because, probably, they do. And if possible, we make some kind of weird contact with whoever or whatever was on the other side. Are we in agreement that the object we take is a security camera?"

"I think it's the best option, and one that your grandfather didn't have. I'm not convinced that the technology will work over there, but what about this? What if it actually does, and when we bring it back here, we can see what it was doing? But if it were there..."

"The levers would just move a notch on the dial, and nothing would happen." Lenny finished. "Or the on-off button and the light that shows the camera is on, I mean."

"Exactly. I can't shake a very real sense that all of the things in this room work exactly as they are intended, that if we took them to the other side and traded, we might see—over there— what happens when you push a lever or open a lid."

"This is making my head hurt. I think I need another bourbon, and then, I don't see how we are going to sleep tonight if we don't make that first trade."

"Absolutely. I'm not going to feel right about anything until I know we've got a better idea what's going on here. Whether we've stumbled onto something amazing and can finish something that has been going on for a very long time, or whether we need to burn the place to the ground. How often do you get to walk into an Indiana Jones movie?"

"Once is more than enough. Seriously. And everything Indiana Jones tried to touch was a trap. You remember the boulder? Now that you mention it, I'll be waiting on a boulder to squash us the entire time we're over there, or an arrow to fly out of one of the walls."

"Probably the best frame of mind to attack this with. I don't know about you, but that was easily the most terrifying couple of minutes in my life, and we're planning on heading right back into it like a couple of idiots. I wonder if we shouldn't leave something behind, like a note? It will sound crazy, but assuming that lens ends up here, no matter what happens, we should do what we can, right?"

"So, we write it down, and then, we go in."

"Do we need a fist bump?"

Lenny laughed. "We don't need it, but I'm in." He raised his fist, and Jeffrey tapped his own against it. "Stupidest bargain in the history of ever. Sealed."

It only took a few minutes to write the note. They didn't really know anything, and what they did know would just sound crazy. In the end they took a photo of the lens, and a second of the top part of the tapestry. Lenny printed them out in his office, and they scribbled a hasty note beneath the shot of the tapestry.

Under no circumstances look at this tapestry with the lens/device attached. It will cause irreparable damage to one of the most valuable items in the world.

"You have to figure," Jeffrey said, "that if something happens to us, eventually someone will get in here. If it's someone with the police, they aren't likely to mess with the tapestry. If it's someone else, they won't risk damaging something they can steal. They'll just pull down the tapestry and take off."

"And they probably won't take that lens, even if it looks valuable, because they won't want someone accidentally damaging their haul. They may even think, seeing the shape of that monstrosity on the bottom corner, that someone already looked at it once and caused the damage."

"Let's hope all this turns out to be is something we laugh about when we're as old as Caleb and Jamal were. Writing the note seemed like a great idea, but now? It's like we've made the danger more real. Jesus, Jeffrey, we're leaving a damned suicide note."

"Nope," Jeffrey said, laying his hand on his friend's shoulder. "Suicide is a decision. This is a precaution. We're not leaving the note so people will know what happened to us. We're just protecting them."

"I wish I felt qualified. Let's get this over with."

Lenny fished a small white cylindrical object with a base from his pocket. He set it on the counter, aimed the lens at the wall. Then he pulled out his cell phone, unlocked it, and opened an app. He turned the screen so Jeffrey could see it. It was a clear, high-resolution image of the wall. You could read the text on a framed print. The name of the photographer, Ansel Adams, was printed at the bottom.

"That's a good image," he said. "That must have cost some money."

Lenny laughed. "You need to spend more time on the Internet. It's 1080p high definition, the battery lasts a month, and it's under one hundred dollars. I have them set up all over the place: the apartment, the street outside, and the alley out back. I've never had a break-in, but I'm not stupid. This isn't the neighborhood we grew up in. I have a camera for answering the door, all of the windows on both levels have alarms that will go off if they are opened or shattered, and the cameras are activated by motion, if not set, like this one, to be on all the time. If it works over there at all, it will record what happens. I doubt we'll be able to see it from here."

"Probably not, but man, when this is all over, you need to visit me and show me this setup. We use a local company, but I've never been comfortable with the fact that it is installed and monitored by guys making minimum wage."

"Deal," Lenny said. "I've been wanting to meet the woman who settled you down, and after stealing you away like this, seems like the least I can do."

Jeffrey held up his fist again. "This one is personal," he said. "It's going to happen."

Lenny nodded and tapped his fist against his friend's. "Word."

"Don't..." Jeffrey said with a laugh. "Don't ever say that again. Seriously."

They stood in front of the tapestry for several minutes. Neither of them glanced down at the lower-right corner. Instead, they took in the beauty of the rest of the image, the perfect symmetry. It was easy to get caught up in the artistry. Whatever this thing was, it was a nearly flawless work of art. It was capable of shifting a person's thoughts, showing the perfection that was possible. It was mesmerizing, and though they were aware of its charms, they still allowed a few moments of appreciation before moving ahead.

"Remember," Lenny said. "We have to find something similar in size and apparent function to the camera. We don't know that it's important, but it makes sense. We need to place that camera where it will take in the biggest segment of the room, and we need to get out before anyone, or anything notices. Ready?"

"Absolutely not," Jeffrey said. Then he lifted the lens, aimed it at the corner of the tapestry, and they stepped forward into the sudden void.

The shift was no less debilitating than the first time they had passed through, but both were ready for it. They fell to the floor on the far side and shielded their eyes. Neither of them shifted their gaze until they were certain they weren't facing the far side of the tapestry. They were close together, and Lenny reached out, gripping Jeffrey on the shoulder.

"You have the camera?" Jeffrey asked.

"Yes. See if you can find something that looks like it. I'm going to find a place to put it that isn't too obvious."

The air was thick, as Jeffrey remembered, and there was an audible hum, more a vibration than a sound, some frequency beyond normal hearing. It rattled his teeth and caused little shifts in his vision. He saw sparks randomly lighting the walls and running along the floor. He glanced around the room. It was basically the same as the back room of the pawn shop, but at the same time it was totally alien. None of the things he saw made sense. There was a piece of furniture he believed had to be a counter, or the central point of the room, but its angles were out of proportion, and the surface slanted back toward the rear of the room. He scanned the room slowly, taking in the benches, tables, and displays. Then he saw something that caught his attention.

It was basically the same size as the camera. It was impossible to know what the material was, but it had an opening on one side like a lens. He stepped forward, grabbed the thing, and turned back.

"I have something," he shouted.

Lenny had just turned back toward the tapestry. He kept his eyes averted until the last moment and pulled up the lens. He didn't hesitate. He pressed it to the corner of the tapestry and both of them dove forward, launching through the suddenly open portal into their own world. As soon as they were through, the lens now pointed away from the tapestry, there was an audible snap of energy, and the air grew lighter and easier to breathe. The silence was almost unnerving.

It all happened fast, but despite the sparks and the sound, there had been none of the crackling electricity, and if the figure that had assaulted them on their first visit had appeared, neither of them had noticed.

"Either 'trade' was the key," Jeffrey said, "or that thing just didn't have the energy to confront us again. It seemed to be fighting something just to appear the first time."

He rose, careful not to bang the object in his hand on anything and lifted it to show Lenny. "There's a button on the side. I can't tell in this light if there's anything in the opening, but it might be a lens. Might be a light? Some sort of meter?"

"I think we'd better assume it's not a coincidence you found it, and that it's similar in size and shape to the camera. Let's put the thing inside a box and aim it toward a wall. If our experiment works, we don't want to be sending back anything useful. Maybe we'd better trade something completely different when we go back?"

"Bring that out to the table," Lenny said. "I'll find something to seal it up in."

Jeffrey carried his prize to the old table, and Lenny returned a moment later with an old metal box. It was ornate, with a brass clasp to hold the lid closed. He placed it on the table and opened it. Jeffrey put the thing he'd brought back inside, and they sealed it quickly.

Returning to the back room, they took it to the farthest corner from the tapestry and placed it on a cabinet, the side where they knew the lens-like opening faced, aimed at the wall.

"I wonder if we should cover it with something more?" Jeffrey said. "We could put the box in another box..."

"I think it's fine," Lenny said. "It will work, or it won't, and I doubt another layer of protection from our world will change the outcome one way or the other. It doesn't seem to be doing anything."

The two returned to the front of the store and the old table. Even with nothing happening, they felt safer out of the back room and out of sight of the tapestry.

"See if you can pick up anything on your camera now," Jeffrey said. "If it works, we might catch something important."

Lenny pulled out his phone. The app opened, and he clicked on the icon for the cameras. Jeffrey glanced at the screen as he did and whistled.

"You weren't kidding when you said you had a lot of cameras."

Lenny grinned. "I might be a little obsessive." He tapped on the first camera in line.

The window that should have displayed the camera's image opened. At first, it seemed as if they might pick something up. The phone's screen lit, but it was nothing but static. Then, very suddenly, it cut off. All that remained was a dead black window, and a warning that said the signal had been lost.

"So much for that," Lenny said, closing it down.

"Not a bust until we get the camera back, right?"

"Hard to say," Lenny said. "The camera has a small internal hard drive so it can continue to operate if it loses the signal. Whether it can record over there, or whether the battery will even power it, we can't tell for certain."

"We should spend some time deciding what to take over next. Did you see anything over there that looked intriguing or odd? We weren't there very long."

"Nothing I can recall, but if we get that camera back and it has anything on it that's useable, we can see what's there in more detail and work from that."

Before Jeffrey could reply, the lights flickered. For just a moment they went out completely, and then, just as suddenly they came back on.

"What the hell?" Jeffrey asked. "Does that happen often?"

"Never that I can remember," Lenny said.

They hurried to the back room and did a quick walkthrough. Everything looked as it had when they'd left, and they were about to write it off to a power surge when Lenny suddenly grew very still. He raised his arm and pointed.

Jeffrey followed his friend's gaze to the box where they'd stored the device. The box stood open, its lid tipped back. The mechanism stood on the cabinet next to the box. The opening in its side was now aimed out into the room. There were no lights. There was no indication if the thing was operating, recording, or transmitting, but it was not where they'd left it.

"What the...?"

"Quiet," Lenny said. He turned very slowly, scanning the room. Jeffrey wasn't sure what he was listening for, but he kept quiet and waited. Lenny started toward the cabinet and the camera. As he drew closer, he leaned in and tilted his head to the side. Then he stopped, straightened, and turned. "It's humming," he said. "Whatever the hell this thing is, it's humming, and it's working. If it really is a camera, something, or someone, is watching us."

"What should we do?"

"It did not hop out of that box by itself. What I don't know is... who is watching it? Who will look at the recording on the other side, if we take it back, and what is happening to our camera over there? What I do know is that the answers to all these questions are important."

"Should we put it back in the box?"

"I don't know. If we do, we'll have to lock it somehow, and I'm wondering if doing so wouldn't result in someone, or something, on the other side damaging our own equipment. It might be an attempt at communication."

"Yeah, and it might not," Jeffrey said. "It's pretty clear that something is here with us right now. Something we don't understand and apparently can't detect. Something that can make things happen on our side. It might be trapped. It might have come with a purpose. I don't know how we're going to figure it all out."

Then the lights dimmed again, and there was a screech of static. The thing they had crossed over with shot a brilliant bolt of energy directly at the tapestry, in the upper-right corner.

"What the...?" Lenny lunged at the thing, banging off of cabinets and sending several objects crashing to the ground. Jeffrey stood still, watching. The beam did not seem to be cutting or burning, but something was happening. The images on the tapestry rippled and shimmered, and then he staggered back, ducking away from the sight. "Stop it! he screamed. "For fuck's sake, stop it!"

He tried to stumble after Lenny but couldn't bring himself to open his eyes. He couldn't risk another glance at the abomination he'd just seen. The image on the tapestry had begun to shift, to change and rearrange into what he'd seen, just for a second, on the other side. Then he heard a crash, and Lenny's voice raised almost to a scream. Then another crash, and silence. The rippling beam was gone. Slowly, as if the thing had been soaking in the power in some strange way, the lights flickered, and returned.

Jeffrey steeled himself and glanced up at the corner of the tapestry. It was unchanged. No damage. Whatever that thing had done, it wasn't permanent, or it had been incomplete when Lenny had gotten to it.

Jeffrey took a deep breath and crossed the room to where he'd last seen his friend. The cabinet that had held the strange device was a shattered mess. The wood, if it was wood, hadn't splintered normally. It sprang out at odd angles as if it had unwound, somehow. Lenny rose, very slowly, from the floor beside it. He held a solid, lamp-shaped object in one hand, gripped by its slender base like a club. His eyes were wide, but he seemed to be unable to get his bearings. He stood, then staggered and nearly fell. Jeffrey dove forward and caught him.

Lenny swung the thing in his hand, and Jeffrey ducked.

"It's me! Stop it. What's wrong?"

"I, my eyes. I can barely see. It was so bright and..."

Lenny dropped whatever the thing in his hand was and slumped against Jeffrey.

"Let's get you to a seat," Jeffrey said. "You need to clear your head. Where is that thing?"

"It's on the floor. I think I broke it, but I can't be sure. We need to get it out of here."

"You aren't getting anything anywhere right now. We'll seal it in something and as soon as you are a hundred percent, we'll take it back."

"You think our camera will be there?"

"I guess we'll find out. Just not quite yet."

Lenny nodded. "You're starting to come back into focus. I can make it to the table. Go back and make sure that thing is smashed. See if you can find something, maybe a copper-lined humidor or something in the shop. Whatever you do, don't let it point at the tapestry."

"I'm on it. Sit down, pour us a drink. I'll be there as soon as I've done everything I can to put that thing completely out of commission."

Lenny walked slowly off toward the table, supporting himself on whatever was available. Jeffrey turned back to the smashed cabinet. He took a moment to study the alien nature of the material, so much like wood, and so much not like wood. He reached out, as if to touch it, then yanked his hand back.

On the floor there were bits and pieces of the cabinet, and, canted over on its side and dented in so that the gap he'd considered to be a lens was nearly closed, was the weird mechanism. He lifted his leg and slammed his foot down on it. It was solid, but a soft metal. The gap closed further. He reached down and grabbed it by its base, careful not to let the slitted opening point toward the tapestry. He carried it to the outer shop and, just as Lenny had suggested, dropped it into a large humidor and slammed the lid closed. He waited, but there was no sign of the strange energy, and the lights remained bright and steady.

Still, he glanced around the shop. Nothing in the outer room seemed out of place. He walked carefully back to the rear of the shop, sweeping his gaze over all the shelves and rows of merchandise, looking for anything out of place or odd. There was nothing. He wound through the back room to the desk, up near the tapestry. He risked a single glance up at the corner where the thing had been transmitting its strange beam. Nothing had changed. With a shrug, he turned and headed back to the table, where Lenny was waiting.

"Well," he said. "That happened."

Lenny pushed a half-full tumbler of bourbon across the table and picked up his own. "It felt like we were set up," he said. "I mean, we took that camera across, and we brought that—whatever it was—back, but now I have to wonder if it was our idea at all. Did you see what it was doing?"

"I did," Jeffrey said. "If you hadn't stopped it, it would have ruined another corner of the tapestry. Maybe all of it."

"I get the sensation this is not the first time. Maybe that bad patch on the bottom of the tapestry wasn't always there. I wonder if maybe my grandfather didn't cause it. Maybe it was perfect at one point, but somehow, they got their hands on that lens."

"Maybe...but I don't think so. Your grandfather may have known what caused it, but it just doesn't track. Remember the vision I had. That glitch, or whatever it is, at the bottom has been there. He saw it, and he knew it was wrong. That's why we're involved in this at all."

"You're probably right," Lenny said. "It makes you wonder though, who made the tapestry, and how did it become flawed? Why? What is the end game?"

"It's bad," Jeffrey said. "The end game is bad, and sorry for the Earth, but I think we are the only things between our reality and whatever is assaulting it."

There was a sudden musical ringing, and both men jumped to their feet, spinning. Then Jeffrey started to laugh. He reached into his pocket and pulled out his cell phone. He glanced at it.

"It's Barbara," he said. He turned and raised the phone to his ear. The sound, and the fact someone was contacting them from outside the shop, drained the tension from the air like a popped balloon.

"Hey," he said. "I was about to call you."

"Sure you were," Barbara said. "Who did you kiss when the ball dropped, big boy?"

He stared stupidly at the phone, and then turned and stared at Lenny as if seeing him for the first time. How in the hell had he forgotten it was New Year's Day?

"Only you," he said, trying to keep his voice steady. "Lenny's a great guy, but he has bony legs, and he needs a shave."

Barbara laughed. "I sat with the cats and watched old Twilight Zone episodes until the fireworks stopped. They took it pretty well, but none of them left my side."

"Lucky cats," Jeffrey said. "I'm going to be here a few more days. Some things have come up Lenny can't handle on his own, but I should be back by the weekend."

"I miss you."

"You, too. I would not be lying if I told you this city is not the one that I remember. When they say you can't go home again, they mean you shouldn't."

"Sounds like you're having a grand old time. Just help your friend and get back here. And tell him he owes us a visit now. At the very least, I need some young Jeffrey stories."

"Will do. See you soon. I love you."

"I love you too," she said.

Jeffrey hung up, took a deep breath. "Well," he said. "We have until the weekend."

Lenny started laughing. "Great. I'll just step in there and explain it to the alien energy beam trying to reweave our tapestry."

"We need a new plan," Jeffrey said, "and it needs to be more than 'let's take a camera over there and find something that looks like it.' Whatever is there, it knew. We were looking for something a certain size and shape and didn't even question it when just about the first thing we saw was exactly what we were looking for. We were set up, and I think we dodged a major bullet, but barely."

"We may have broken it, but that thing goes back. We'll still need to trade something, but what? They may have moved the camera, and I think it's time we tested whether the trades need to seem similar at all. How do we choose what we bring back?"

"Not sure, but I think, maybe, one of us needs to make that decision, and we should definitely not talk about it. Not here, and possibly not anywhere. We don't know that if something made it through to our side that it's anchored to this place. We might be eating dinner on the other side of town and have it sitting in the middle of the table, watching us."

"Right then, plan is no plan." Lenny said. He glanced around the room. "You don't think just taking back that thing we smashed and grabbing the camera will work?"

He stared at Jeffrey as he said this, and his expression was strange. Jeffrey was about to ask if he was constipated when he got it.

"That would be taking a big chance. What if a broken thing can't be traded for something that's not? What if the camera isn't even there? Maybe we should leave it here, in the outer shop, and take over the humidor. Another test. Can they hear us here, on this side of the shop, or only when we're nearby, or standing in the middle of all the things brought over from their side?"

Lenny nodded. "And we should move further into the room, take something not obviously offered to us. Something less expected. Something that looks nothing like a humidor. Of course, that eliminates a lot of things—anything that is a small box, for instance."

"You choose," Jeffrey said. "I'll grab the camera; you take the humidor. That's our first move. Then we'll try something completely different, but I'll choose, and I won't tell you what I'm thinking."

He winked, and he saw Lenny's lip twitch. He knew his friend was about to laugh, and that it would not be good if he did. He rose quickly and downed his drink. "Let's do this then," he said. He headed off to retrieve the humidor, and as he did so, broke the moment. Lenny didn't laugh. Instead, he rose, returned to the back room, and started glancing around as if he was studying the inventory and lost in thought. Then, very suddenly, he started wandering up and down the aisles, lifting first one thing, then another, opening cabinets and boxes, and remaining on the move.

Jeffrey came in from the other room, carrying the humidor.

They locked gazes, just for a second, and then turned toward the tapestry. They moved as quickly as possible, Lenny grabbing the lens and Jeffrey gripping the humidor tightly.

"Now," he said.

Lenny pointed the lens at the tapestry, and the image wavered, then became perfect and clear. They lunged through. As they went, Jeffrey ditched the humidor, tossing it behind him and hoping if it was valuable that he hadn't damaged it too badly. He stepped into that other place, shadowed and dark, and reached into his pocket. Lenny stood at his side, just for a moment, then dove for the camera, which was sitting right where they had left it. He grabbed it and turned.

The room flickered, and both knew that something was gathering energy, but they did not give it a chance. Jeffrey pulled his hand from his pocket. He drew back his arm and threw the smashed lensed device as hard as he could. It made a satisfying crash against something out of sight in the shadows. The two turned, placed the lens, and tumbled back to the other side, feeling the strange portal close behind them with a snap.

The humidor was lying on the floor, tipped over on its side, and Lenny scooped it up. He handed it to Jeffrey, and they spun, placing the strange gleaming device to the tapestry again and diving through.

This time there was movement. Shadows flitted around the room, and crackles of energy snaked around the walls and the edges of the ceiling. As they tumbled in, Jeffrey rose and stood, scanning the room. Lenny had spotted what he was looking for the first time through. He dropped the humidor as gently as he could and grabbed a square object off the front table. As he did so, the energy in the room shifted.

Jeffrey felt the same sensation he got when water had clogged his ears or if he stood too quickly. His heart hammered. The world was utterly silent. Everything was focused and centered directly on him, and he lacked the strength to react. His mouth opened, but no sound came out.

Then Lenny smacked him on the arm, and he ripped his gaze free from the sparking, rippling energy.

"Go!"

It still felt as if he was trying to push his way through a sea of mud, but Jeffrey turned and pressed the lens to the one bearable spot on the tapestry. It rippled, and they pushed through. He sensed something bearing down on him from behind, something fast and powerful. He wanted to glance back, but he ignored the urge. Something brushed his ankle and then there was a huge crackle of static. Above that sound they heard a single word.

"No!"

Then they were free, and the portal was closed. Both of them lay still on the floor, eyes clenched, waiting, but nothing happened. The lights remained lit, there were no strange sounds. Very slowly, Jeffrey rolled over onto his back. He cradled the lens to his chest. He kept it flat and very carefully avoided letting it lift to any position where it might bring the tapestry into focus.

Lenny rose to his feet and stared at the box in his hand.

"Do you think...?" Jeffrey said.

Lenny shook his head. He pointed to the door leading to the outer shop and headed there on unsteady feet. Jeffrey stood up, placed the lens in its case, and tucked it under his arm, following.

Neither of them spoke. Lenny grabbed a pad of paper and a pen and wrote quickly. "I think it worked. It proves they've been watching, though. They knew what we were after the first time, and it was right there waiting for us."

"That box you grabbed was right there too," Jeffrey wrote, glancing up at his friend.

"Yes, but it was there the first time too. They didn't move it, and it wasn't something they positioned for us to grab. It might not be important, but I don't think it's dangerous. I don't believe they suspected we were coming back through, and we may have actually made it out with something useful."

Then he pulled the camera out of his pocket and placed it on the table. The blue light that meant it was active was lit, just as it had been the last time they'd seen it. He pulled out his phone and opened the app. At first, all he saw was the wall of the shop, but he clicked off the live view to the motion-detected history recordings. There were dozens. He glanced at Jeffrey.

"You ready for this? I honestly have no idea what to expect."

"I'm just glad it works off a battery," Jeffrey said. "I have the feeling if you had it plugged into the wall, there would be issues with the power again."

"Still might be. Maybe better to watch while the phone is sitting on the table?"

Lenny nodded and placed the smartphone in the center of the table. He picked up the pencil he'd been writing with and turned it, jabbing the eraser down on the "play" icon.

At first there was nothing, and it wasn't clear what had set off the motion. Then, as they had on their second visit of the night, shadows began moving about the room. They were only visible because they were darker than the rest of the room, and sparks of energy outlined their forms. Tall, slender, and twisting strangely. Jeffrey was reminded of the balloon men outside car dealerships. The movements were elongated, and sharp, not fluid. One of the figures approached the camera and wavered, sliding in close, but appeared to either not be able to tell that the device was functioning or not to care.

None of it was focused, and there was no sound other than a light hum of static. Objects were lifted, moved, and carried about the room. Several times the figures gathered, or met at a single point, leaning in close to one another. All of it was ordered and quiet, reminiscent of their own movements through the shop when there was no imminent danger.

"Do you think they're talking about us?" Jeffrey asked. "I wish I felt like we could contact who, or whatever, has been helping us. Something grabbed at my ankle on our second trip. I think it might have caught me and pulled me back."

"I heard," Lenny said. "Then I heard that voice again, and there was no doubt what it said this time. 'No.'"

"They seem to be able to contact whatever made it over here. I think we need to find a way to detect it."

"Maybe work out a trade?"

"I'm thinking. Might be a good time for some flames and a hammer if we pull it off."

"Probably better not to talk about it, but yeah. Let's get through the rest of the videos. Maybe our guardian angel over there left us a message, or, if not, maybe we can find a clue on who or what is stranded over here."

Nothing new surfaced in the rest of the recordings, just more of the same odd shadows, the energy sparks, but nothing in focus that gave them any new insight. That left the box they'd brought back. They had carried it out of the back room with them on the chance that proximity to the tapestry, or even a line of sight to it, was necessary for anything crazy to happen.

"I guess maybe we're about to find out if we're as clever as we think," Lenny said. "If we are, they had no idea we were going to take it. If not..."

"We'd better be ready to duck and run again," Jeffrey said. "It's all we've got, so I don't think we have a choice. That thing in there, that portal, or door, or tunnel to—where? We can't just leave it. I'm not sure breaking the lens would be enough—you saw what happened with that projector thing. Whatever is over there is trying to find a way through, and they are relentless. In all of those videos, they're in constant motion. Like sleep, or rest, or maybe even time the way we understand it doesn't apply."

"You're just drinking the bourbon, right? You didn't sneak something stronger in?"

Jeffrey took a swipe at Lenny's head. "I'm serious. We have to stop that thing. As the old saying goes, we may not be the heroes the world wants..."

"But apparently, we're the idiots it needs."

They both laughed, but there was a hint of darkness in it.

Lenny spun the box 360 degrees, examining all of the sides. There were no obvious cracks, no lid, no handles. Unlike the other device they'd studied, there were no levers or buttons. There was nothing obvious that moved. It seemed to be a solid block of some strange material. Not wood, as it had appeared, but maybe something similarly organic from the other side. It was polished and shone in the dim light of the shop.

Starting on the lid, he ran his fingertips over the surface, tapping and pressing, testing each bit of the design. He covered all of the top and sides, but if there was a hidden lever, he could not find the trick of it. He stepped back and stared at it, frowning.

Jeffrey stood and gripped the thing by the sides. He flipped it slowly, as if afraid the top might just fall off, despite their failure to open it, but nothing happened. He placed it upside down on the table, and they both stared. On the bottom, clinging to the surface with some sort of sticky substance, was a bit of paper. On the paper, in shaky script, was a four-digit number: 0198.

Beside the four-digit number was the corresponding five-digit number with a letter designation: J01934.

Nothing on any of the other items in the back room had writing or characters that could be understood. There were strange glyphs and weird mathematical formulae on a few, but nothing that they could read, except for the tags that Caleb had affixed to them over the years. This was different. Crude and less defined.

"Get the ledgers," Jeffrey said.

Lenny hurried to the other room and brought back the ledger his grandfather had used to catalog the strange collection he'd accumulated. He also brought the second book they'd been comparing it to. He laid them open on the table, flipped through the pages, and stabbed his index finger on a single entry.

"Container, electronic. 1960s, exotic. Inoperable."

"What was traded for it?"

Lenny scrolled through the entries in the other ledger and found J01934. The corresponding number from the back-room journal was there, but no description. No exchange listed.

Lenny glanced up.

"What do you think that means?" he asked.

"I don't know, but I think we'd better find this electronic container. Your grandfather's records are impeccable. I went through a lot of pages, and I didn't see any other blanks. It has to mean something."

"Whatever is over there that screamed at us may have planted the number," Lenny said. "It's the only thing that makes sense. The words it spoke were in English. These numbers, they are legible. Unless this piece has been on this side before and returned, there is simply no way it's marked with anything we'd understand."

"It may be the key, then. But let's not get ahead of ourselves. They've already played us once, right? We can't assume anything on that side of the tapestry is on our side. It could all be tricks, and a lot depends on figuring that out."

Lenny glanced down at the ledger again, then headed into the back room. Jeffrey followed. They wound through the aisles, checking numbers and scanning shelves, cases, and cabinets. In one of the far-back corners, tucked away behind a bookshelf, they found a tall, cylindrical device resting on a tripod-like stand on the floor. The top was capped with what appeared to be a tightly screwed lid. Small metal rods jutted out from it in all directions. There were no switches visible. The surface of the cylinder glistened like chrome.

Lenny knelt close to it, but he didn't touch it. He held out his hand, his palm a few inches from the thing's surface. Then he pulled it back sharply.

"What?" Jeffrey asked.

"I don't know," Lenny said. "There is something off about it. Something wrong. The closer my hand got..."

Jeffrey knelt beside him and reached out as his friend had. He felt it. Something cold, and wrong. Something dark. He pulled his hand back. Lenny started to say something, but Jeffrey shook his head. He nodded toward the outer room. Lenny nodded and turned away. He had to catch himself for balance on a bookshelf as he passed.

When they were out of the back room, Jeffrey gestured toward the door. The two of them headed out into the street.

"Let's get some food," he said, once they were free. "And another drink. We have to figure this out, and this might be our last chance to do it. We got close enough to that thing to touch it. Somehow, I think it's aware. They may be aware."

Lenny nodded. "That has to be the source. But what do we do about it? I can't imagine actually touching it."

"We have to figure that out, and fast. I don't think we have much time now. Whoever planted that number for us has changed the level of pressure, I think. They have been doing this for decades, but now that we're involved, the possibility we might not stay, that we might simply report it or destroy the place, has to have occurred to them. I would feel better if I knew whether that worked in our favor, but it's all we've got."

"One more trip, then?"

"Yes, I think so. But it's going to be different. What I think may be correct, or it might not be. We could be trapped. We might open a gate to their world and let them in. We might just die."

"Happy New Year to you, too," Lenny said. "Don't know about you, but I'm not planning on any of that."

"The first thing we need is a way to touch that thing. Just getting close nearly made me lose my breakfast, and I have an idea that this one is more than a knick-knack. Either they—or it—will be aware if we mess with it. Might already be aware for that matter. If we sensed something, we probably set off alarms at the same time."

"So, we're on a short timeline. Probably for the best. You can't stay here forever. I don't want your wife to hate you, and I can't live much longer knowing what's in that room, beneath where I sleep and one wall away from the shop."

Jeffrey nodded. "Most of what we've seen seems electrical in nature. Maybe not exactly as we perceive it, but definitely sparks and energy beams. I think if we hit a hardware store, we can get some of those thick, insulated gloves. I'd say if we could put it in something, it might help, but that makes any sort of trade harder. And do we look for a thing like that on the other side? Is our savior over there trapped in the same sort of thing, or just there? Do we have to bring something back?"

"I think we have to risk that we don't if we want to bring whoever that is back with us," Lenny said. "I think we take this over there, we leave it, and we run. Whatever happens, happens, but if that thing is what I think it is, keeping it on the other side at whatever cost is vital. If we can break their contact to this plane, or dimension, maybe we can trap them over there."

"You think one of them is inside it?" Jeffrey asked. "I mean, is it just some weird antenna, or did they send someone over here? Some *thing*?"

"Your guess is at least as good as mine. I just know it belongs over there, and we're the ones to take it."

"As long as we get back," Lenny said.

"We'd better get out then and get some things. Is that hardware store still open over on Forty-Second Street?"

"Louie's?" Lenny grinned. "It is. And it's still as shady, run-down, and interesting as it ever was. They don't stock everything; nobody in town does. There are just things you need in an urban environment that aren't useful here. For instance, there are a lot of locks and security systems, but not so many lawnmowers. The guy who runs it now, Sam, is Louie's brother."

"What happened to that old guy?"

"No idea. For all I know, he's retired to a room above his store and making his brother's life miserable. I don't know how many times he chased us out of there, and even after I grew up, he watched me like he thought I was shoving tools under my belt or running off with the rat poison."

"I bet there's still plenty of that. Some things in the city never change."

They closed the ledgers, flipped the box right side up again, and headed for the door. "We might as well get something to eat while we're out," Lenny said. "I don't see either of us sleeping before this is done, and I don't feel much like cooking."

"Might need to refresh the bourbon too," Jeffrey said. "I have a feeling that whatever comes next is not something you want to face completely sober."

The old bell rang as they left the shop behind, and the door closed and locked with loud click.

They returned less than an hour later, arms full. When the door closed behind them, locking them in, it felt ominous, and final. There were few lights on, and Jeffrey was nearly certain he caught a flicker of sparks from the doorway leading to the back room. He hoped it was all in his head but decided to proceed as if it wasn't.

In the end, they'd stuck with necessities. Two heavy pairs of rubber insulated gloves and a bottle of bourbon. There was no Weller to be found in the neighborhood, but they'd settled on a small batch bottle from the same distillery in Kentucky.

"It's not like we're going to be sitting around sipping and reminiscing over old times," Lenny had said.

"My dad would say, 'whatever gets the job done.'"

They had covered the details of the plan on their walk. It seemed unwise to discuss anything in the shop, even the outer part. If they were right, it wasn't just another dangerous piece of equipment or weird ray-gun. It was the thing that powered them. There was a connection between the two sides of the tapestry, and if the warning that had been sent through was correct, they were about to try and send it home. It seemed simple in principle, but neither of them trusted it. Whatever they were faced off against had been working for a very long time to reach an end. They had been aware of it for a solid two days. Even with a plan, and the help of whatever had aided them on the other side, it felt like a very bad idea.

"No reason to put this off," Jeffrey said. "In fact, we do that, I might not be able to manage it at all."

"No hesitation," Lenny said. "Seriously. We hit that door, and we move. No time to think, no time to slip up or give ourselves away. All or nothing."

"You really need to work on your pep talks. And you need to let that 'all or nothing, we might not make it back' crap go. Don't make me start up with the high school fight song."

Lenny laughed and stood. The two of them pulled on the gloves, then took a roll of duct tape and wrapped the tops of the gloves tightly so they couldn't slip loose. One thing they'd agreed on, they couldn't afford to accidentally leave something behind that they didn't intend without a trade, and there was likely no time for that. That included gloves and safety equipment. They were already pushing what they knew to be the rules because, trapped or not, they weren't bringing item 0198 back. Hell, or high water, they were dropping that thing on the far side and diving for the portal without it. The hope was that whoever or whatever was trapped over there, if it really wanted out, would follow.

There was a plan B, but neither of them was ready for that, particularly Lenny.

"I'm trying to think of the right movie quote for this," Jeffrey said, "But I've got nothing. See you on the other side."

"That can be the quote when we write the script," Lenny said. Then he turned and raised his hands, the black gloves looking ridiculous, and headed for the back room.

Jeffrey was unable to contain a grin as he followed. Jesus, he thought. We are idiots.

Lenny headed for the back of the shop and the weird cylinder. Jeffrey went straight to the front. He flipped up the cover and grabbed the lens, holding it close to his chest and watching.

He saw Lenny lean down, and a second later rise, the strange container held tightly in his gloved hands. His friend started forward, and Jeffrey held his breath, but nothing happened. He turned toward the tapestry and lifted the lens, but before he could finish the motion, Lenny cried out.

Jeffrey spun and saw that his friend was now running toward him. The strange energy they'd seen before crackled over the cylinder and around his gloved hands. It was working back toward the point where the duct tape secured the gloves. Lenny's eyes were wide, and his movements had grown jerky, but he pressed on.

"Now," he screamed. "Open that thing now!"

Jeffrey did. He spun, placed the lens, and waited. Lenny came up behind him like a steam train and dove into the portal. But not through. Something seemed to have gripped him, either pushing back, or the energy itself pulling. Lenny was stuck halfway through the tapestry, screaming as if his heart was being ripped out. His feet scrabbled for purchase, and he jammed them against the floor, but he was barely holding his own.

"Fuck this," Jeffrey said. He held the lens tightly in one hand, leaned down, and drove himself into Lenny's hip. He felt pressure, resistance like he would not have believed, and something hot licking at his shoulder. With every ounce of strength he possessed, he wrapped an arm around Lenny's waist and drove him through, following as if suddenly sucked into a vacuum.

Where there had been resistance, now there was the opposite.

It felt as if he were being drawn into a huge wind tunnel. The air crackled with lights and bolts of energy. One struck his leg and he screamed. It felt as if he'd been flayed to the bone. He reached down but couldn't feel anything through the gloves. He was still able to stand, so he gazed around wildly, trying to find Lenny.

He followed the bolts back to their source and saw his friend, huddled on the floor. He gripped the container with both hands, but there was nothing now between him and the energy. The gloves were still securely in place, but the lines of light had spun and wrapped around him, twisting into a strange vortex that threatened to block him from sight. There was no sound, but Lenny's face was a rictus of pain. His eyes were open far too wide, and his features had stretched, as if unseen fingers gripped his flesh and were attempting to tear him apart.

Jeffrey staggered to Lenny's side, tucking the lens awkwardly into the waistband of his pants. He knew they were going to have to cut off the source of that energy, or he'd never get them back, never even get Lenny off the floor.

He gripped the protruding metal bars circling the top of the cylinder, ignoring the sudden bite of cold and the pain that instantly began inching up his arms. He threw his strength into it, but the lid wouldn't spin. He tried again, trying to unscrew the thing. Nothing. Then, as if someone had whispered a secret in his ear, he reversed his effort, turning it clockwise. At first, he felt only the slightest sense of motion, but that was all it took. With a scream of rage, terror, and anger, he spun the thing with everything he had left. The top of the cylinder spun off crazily, and a booming white flash that might have been lightning shot out of the opening, blasted onto the ceiling of the strange room, and washed down the walls.

It lit the scene in a macabre, chiaroscuro wash of brilliant white and draining darkness.

"Let it go!" Jeffrey screamed. He tossed the lid aside, heard it bang off of something, but kept his gaze on Lenny. "Let it go!"

Lenny tried to speak, but no sound came out. He shook his hands helplessly, tugging first one way and then the other, but he could not release the container, and the energy threatened to engulf him. Jeffrey reached down, gripped Lenny's wrist, and threw his weight back. As Lenny's hand was yanked from the cylinder, the connection shattered, and Lenny fell away. He crashed into a table and sent it toppling backward. The cylinder flew to the side, the last crackling streams of whatever had been released spinning like a brilliant white-hot tornado into the darkness.

Then it was gone. Lenny blinked, but all he saw were afterimages, strobed outlines of shadowed furnishings.

"Lenny! Where are you?"

At first there was nothing. Then he heard a crash and a groan. "Here. I hit my head. I..."

"Stand still," Jeffrey said. "Keep talking."

"You still have the lens?"

"Yes," Jeffrey said. He pulled it out of his belt. "Are you okay?"

"My head is killing me, but I'll live. Can you see?"

At that moment, Jeffrey's groping hand touched Lenny's arm.

Lenny screamed and Jeffrey gripped and shook him. "It's me. We have to go."

"Great, but where? I can't see a thing. Either there is absolutely no light here now, or that flash blinded me. Either way, we have to find the tapestry."

There was a scrabbling sound near the rear of the room or off in the distance. There was no way to tell if it was a room at all, or just an endless stretch of darkness. All traces of the weird energy had dissipated. It was an odd sound, like something sliding across the floor. A broken wire? Live with that energy? Something else?

"What was that?" he said.

Lenny stepped closer, keeping his voice low. "I don't know, but we don't want it to find us. Do you have any idea which way to go?"

"Not really. When we came through, we were moving straight in a single direction away from it, but when that thing started sparking and I opened it... I'm not sure. I nearly fell, and you disappeared in that flash of light."

The sound repeated. This time it was louder and seemed to be coming from more than one point. Whatever was in the room with them was growing closer. Something crashed, and there was a strange hiss, maybe pain. The sound withdrew just for a second, and then began moving again.

"It's looking for us," Lenny said. "I don't think it can see. Maybe it can't hear, either at least not like we do. It's only a matter of time though. Either there are a bunch of them, or whatever is back there is big. It's getting closer."

"If it's coming from that direction," Jeffrey said, "the tapestry must be in the opposite, right? I don't know why but it feels like it would be coming from the back of whatever this is..."

"I don't have a better idea, but we still have a problem. If we can't see the tapestry, how do we place the lens?"

There was another crash, closer this time. Whatever caused it did not retreat a second time. Jeffrey turned away from the sound, keeping his grip on Lenny's arm and clutching the lens in his free hand. He shuffled forward, one small step after another. He didn't want to bang the lens on something and drop or break it, and he couldn't afford to trip and lose his bearings. Lenny followed jerkily.

"What happened to those shadow things?" Lenny asked. "Are they still here? There was always some weird light..."

"They were here when we came through," Jeffrey said. "There was light, and I could see, but then it all seemed to concentrate on that cylinder. It must have been the source."

He stopped suddenly, jerking Lenny toward him, and nearly dropping the lens, despite his care. A single soft tone broke the silence."

"What the hell? Stand still." He let go of Lenny's arm and shoved his hand into his pocket. He pulled out his phone. The screen glowed dimly, and there was a message icon. A text.

"We have to go! Now!"

"What...?"

"My phone! It has a signal. Something is happening. Grab the back of my shirt." Jeffrey didn't wait for his friend to act. He swiped his thumb up and flipped through the pages of ridiculous apps on the phone. The screen flickered, but he had a signal. He found what he wanted and pressed down hard to open it. A small beam of light shot out from the far side of the phone, and three feet ahead of them the tapestry loomed. The design was sickening, but the level of discomfort had dropped from inducing vomit to simply looking wrong. Like it had lost some integral segment of the design.

The corner was still brilliant. It flickered, as if separate from the design, but it was also dimmed. You could tell there was a difference, but the significance wasn't as immediate. Nothing clutched at his chest as he stared at it. He reached out and pressed the lens against it. At first it seemed that nothing had happened, and then everything before them went dark. Jeffrey dove, and Lenny gripped his shirt, tumbling after. They stretched through the dark opening and then, as if hitting a brick wall, they stopped. Jeffrey felt something resisting his forward motion. He was off balance, but he dug his feet into the floor and leaned, driving with all his strength. Jeffrey slid his arms around his friend's back and clutched him tightly.

"Something has my leg," he screamed. "Something big. Like a snake. It's strong."

"Don't let go," Jeffrey said. He leaned further into his forward progress. He tossed his phone and the lens ahead of him and heard them clatter ahead, but he was only partway through the hole, and Lenny was dragging behind. He closed his eyes and focused on a moment in his past. In high school, both he and Lenny had played football. Lenny had been a defensive back, quick on his feet and nimble, but Jeffrey had always been bigger and stronger. He'd been a fullback, the guy they called on when there were two yards to gain and not a lot of hope of making them. He bunched his muscles and drove forward. It seemed as if he would make it, that he would drag them both free. But again, they stopped. He kept his eyes closed and dug deep. It was a standoff. He felt Lenny clutching him and felt, as well, that his friend was pulling now, adding his strength, feet pressed to the floor, but they were barely holding their own.

Something shifted behind them. There was a high-pitched hum drowning out any other sound. He had no energy to speak, but he felt it building. Another shift, and he was able to drive a foot forward, and then another. The hum rose in pitch, like a siren, until it filled his thoughts and erased everything beyond the press forward and the resistance.

Then, in a sudden burst of what might have been static, and might have been words, whatever was dragging them back slipped, then slipped again, and he surged forward. He felt Lenny nearly pull free of his grip. He clutched his friend more tightly and followed. There was something else. It was strange, but there was still a weight, a resistance that grew weaker by the second. With a scream of anger and pain and determination, Jeffrey dove forward and heard a loud pop! behind him. He fell forward, raising his hands to break the impact. He hit a solid floor, slid forward, and rolled into a ball for protection.

Lenny had lost his grip, but not until after the sound and Jeffrey was sure his friend had made it through. There was something else, but he had no energy to spare. He ducked, rolled, and came to rest against something solid. He didn't open his eyes. He clenched them tightly and braced for whatever impact might come next. There was nothing. He waited a little longer and then, very cautiously, he opened his eyes and uncurled. The lens had lay where it had landed when he'd thrown it. He reached for it instinctively, then stopped.

Lenny lay between him and the tapestry. His friend was face down, but after a couple of seconds of watching, Jeffrey caught the slow, up-and-down motion of his breath. The glove on his friend's hand was a torn, ripped mess, bits dangling from the remnant of the duct tape. The shirt above the gloves had burned away to the collar. The skin was blackened, no way to tell how badly they were burned.

He lifted his gaze. The tapestry hung as it always had. The colors were dim because there was little light, only what seeped in from the outer shop. Something had changed. There was something subdued about the image. It was no less beautiful, but the shimmer that had captivated him the first time he'd seen it was gone. His mind fought him, but he trailed his eyes downward, seeking that bottom corner. Seeking the ugliness, the wrongness that marred the thing's perfection.

What he saw was not that, but a completion. A correction. Still, the accomplishment of that did not bring the satisfaction it should have. The image did not come to life. The villages and roads, the mountains, were finely crafted silk, but no more than that. It was just a tapestry. Jeffrey had difficulty swallowing as an odd emotion rose from within. Tears welled in the corners of his eyes, but he didn't look away. He couldn't. He heard Lenny stir behind him, heard his friend rise, fall back, then rise again, but he didn't turn. A moment later the two stood side by side, lost in the intricate needlework, shocked beyond thought by the evening's events.

Jeffrey finally tore his gaze from the tapestry and glanced down at the lens on the floor. He knew he should let it rest. Knew, in fact, that he should be smashing the heel of his boot through the center of it and crushing the crystal, or glass, or taking a sledgehammer and pounding the metal frame into twisted, unrecognizable junk. It felt foolish, and important. He turned, stepped over to it, and leaned down.

His fingertips nearly brushed it when he saw something reflected on its glistening surface. Something moving. A face, he thought, far away. He leaned closer, but before he could touch the frame, a final brilliant spark of light crackled out from it, spreading in all directions along the floor. He stepped back, blinded, and would have fallen, but suddenly Lenny was there, catching him and holding him upright.

As before the light was too bright. He blinked, holding his hands out in front of him, though there was nothing to catch. Lenny held on to him, but staggered back, sending them both off balance. Somehow, they came to rest against the counter and Lenny caught hold. He cried out when he did, and Jeffrey knew the burns were not good. They were going to need a doctor.

"What the hell?" Lenny said, steadying them both.

"I think maybe I wasn't supposed to touch it again," Jeffrey said.

"What?"

"The lens. I was trying to pick it up. I saw something move. It should have just been reflecting my face, I think, but..."

A groan floated in from the outer shop, and both of them froze.

Jeffrey closed his eyes tightly and counted to ten, then opened them and turned very slowly. Lenny had released him and had already spun toward the sound. They left the back room behind and entered the slightly brighter light of the main shop. It was hard to make anything out in the gloom, but they could both see someone was seated at the old table. The figure was slumped forward in one of the old seats, collapsed across his crossed arms.

Lenny started forward. Jeffrey followed, but more slowly. He still didn't trust that the portal was closed, or that the danger had passed. He didn't know who or what was sitting at that table, but he wasn't going to rush forward and find out it was another trap, a mistake.

Lenny didn't hesitate. He stepped up to the table, gripped whoever was seated there by the collar, and lifted their head. Both stared. There were more lines than they remembered, and some scars. The hair was brilliant white, where it had been so dark it seemed black, but they knew the face. There was no way to mistake it.

"Jamal?" Lenny said. He leaned in closer, sliding an arm around to lift and support the old man. He didn't seem so much older than they remembered.

The old man lifted his head. His eyes were bright and deep.

"I knew that you would figure it out; such clever boys," he said. "I thought they would win, that my life would be in vain and your grandfather…" Jamal bowed his head. "I thought that he would die forgotten. We were so arrogant, such fools. All of this," he sat up, waving a hand vaguely at the room behind them. "We thought we would change the world, that we would bring back treasures and use them to build a better place. The tapestry was so beautiful. It had to be a sign, a symbol of a better future. In the end, we were blind. We let them in, brought their vile devices across to this world, and, in the end, gave them the power they needed. I could not have made it back if it had not been for you."

"It was you who told us we had to trade," Jeffrey said. "You knew we were there."

Jamal nodded. "Yes, yes, but it was so hard to speak, almost impossible. I was not a captive—they were never able to figure out how to do that—but I was in their world, and there was no one here to come and trade. Once we brought that demon, that thing across, their strength grew. All of their power was drawn from that source."

"But wasn't that just one of the shadow creatures?" Lenny said. "Didn't they just trade one of their own for you? Like an agent on this side?"

"Oh, no. That was what they wanted to set free. They brought it forth and trapped it in that... thing... but it was no more like them than it was like us. They needed its power. They needed it to transform the portal so they could move through. They would have cast it back when they were finished, into that shadow world."

"They were controlling it?"

"No. They were afraid of it. I could not fully understand them, but I caught snippets. They do not communicate as we do. They share images. Wherever they found it, that thing, they hated it. They were able to contain it by some odd ritual, something I could sense but not understand, but they were terrified it would break free, or that they would lose control. When you freed it, I sensed they were simply gone. Either they fled back to whatever place they came from originally, or..."

"Or it took them." Jeffrey whispered. "But how...?"

He fell silent as thin, white veins of light rippled through the old man's hair. It flickered, died, and returned, stronger. The hairs on Jamal's hands stood on end and thick, bushy brows had come to a life of their own. The old man stared down at his arms on the table, then lifted his gaze once more.

"Is it...?" Lenny started.

Jamal shook his head. "No." His voice was lower, wispy, as if fading in and out of phase. "It is simply my time. I am a very, very old man, Lenny. I should not exist, and I fear my own energy was also being drawn from that... thing."

"But what should we do?" Lenny asked, moving forward. "All of this," he waved an arm vaguely at the room, and turned. "And that tapestry?"

"You must..." Jamal whispered. Lenny reached out again and placed a hand on the old man's shoulder, but this time the contact appeared to break whatever spell, circuit, or anomaly had allowed him to be there at all. Jamal fell away in a fountain of sparks, dissipating before they even had a chance to strike the floor. There was a brief, strobed afterimage from the flash, and then he was simply gone.

"Must what?" Jeffrey said.

Lenny only shook his head. They stepped through the doorway and turned toward the tapestry once more. Whatever magic or otherworldly technology had animated it was gone. Despite the magnificence of the design, it looked dead, draped over the wall like a trophy from some crazy big game hunt.

Jeffrey picked up his phone, and Lenny retrieved the lens. He held it up, as if considering glancing through it at the corner of the tapestry, then thought better of it. The case was still open on the counter. He dropped it in and slammed the lid hard enough to rattle the countertop.

They turned and left the room.

"I can't stay here," Lenny said, leading the way up the stairs toward his apartment.

"You're welcome to come visit us for a while," Jeffrey said. "Barbara is already on me to invite you."

Lenny stopped and turned, hand on the rail. "No," he said. "I mean, I'm done. This place, this city, I think. I'm going to find a way to destroy or dispose of all the stuff in that room. I think I'm going to burn the tapestry, just in case, and smash that lens. It will never be enough. If I'm upstairs, and I know what was down here, and has been here all this time, I'll always wonder. Did we close it forever? Did we get all of that thing out of here? The room feels different now. It's better than it was, but now there's no life to it. Everything feels dead. I don't want to be around if it changes its mind.

"And Jamal. He just disappeared. Or did he? Is he going to show up in the bathroom mirror writing notes? Was that him at all, or something lingering trying to throw us off? I mean, what even happened? What was that place? It felt like a void, like some in-between trap, the gooseneck in a drain. And those things... how long have they been there? How did they trap that power, that being? What was it, and what would have happened if it was set loose?"

"But it's done now," Jeffrey said. "You see that, right?"

"No. It's not done, and it never will be, and I'm pretty sure you know that. I believe we stopped something. I believe we closed off a doorway. Do you?"

"Of course," Jeffrey said, "but..."

Lenny held up a hand. "If we closed off a doorway, there are more. If there is a place that isn't here, it's still there. If there are other creatures, creatures trying to break through into our reality, and we've peeked through that window, there's no way to unsee it. I don't know if I'm ever going to sleep deeply again. God help me if I'm outside and there's a lightning strike, or some electrical wire goes haywire while I'm too close. I'll scream like a baby. I think you will too."

Jeffrey remained silent for a moment. Then, very slowly, he answered. "You stood up to something unknown. You didn't run, you didn't hide. Look at your arms. You went through a small hell in there. Why? Because you were strong. I'm not spending my life being afraid of some unknown lightning monster. I'm spending mine knowing that all of the things I hoped were true when I was younger are true. I didn't know then how absolutely terrifying that knowledge would be, but I know now. I know to watch. I know I can count on you, like you counted on me."

Lenny held his gaze for a moment, then turned and continued up the stairs. Jeffrey stood for a moment, lost in memory.

"Hey!" Lenny called from the top of the stairs. "Are you okay?"

Jeffrey clutched the rail for a moment, shook his head to clear it, and started up after his friend. "I'm good," he said. "Just thinking."

Lenny waited until he reached the top of the stairs, as if afraid he'd faint and fall back down, or be suddenly snatched through the solid walls, but he made the top without incident.

"I think we should have a drink, and then try to get some sleep," Lenny said.

"That sounds right," Jeffrey said, taking a slow, deep breath and fully clearing the old memories. Then he stopped, reached out, and took Lenny by the shoulder.

"I'm going to stay until we get that stuff out of here," he said. "Together. If we have to, we can smash every bit of it. I have some real-estate contacts, and I think what's in the outer shop would do well at auction. I was thinking, if you moved closer, maybe we'd both sleep better. Maybe if something that doesn't fit distracts one of us, the other could just be there? I mean, this is the first day of a new year. Might as well make it the first day of a better one."

Lenny smiled. "That's the best idea I've heard in a very long time," he said. "What will Barbara say?"

"Barbara is the real-estate contact," Jeffrey said, laughing. "This neighborhood may not be what it once was, but part of what it is now is valuable. She'll jump at the chance to see it and help you sell it. We can clear out the back room and then send for her. We could have you out of here and moved to our spare room in a couple of weeks."

Lenny stared, just for a moment, and then nodded. Then they walked slowly down the hall to the kitchen in search of whiskey and ice. There were only a few hours until morning, but neither felt like they were likely to sleep. Behind them, a light flickered, just for a second, then blinked out. They did not look back.

About the Author

David Niall Wilson is a *USA Today* bestselling, multiple Bram Stoker Award-winning author of more than forty novels and collections. He is a former president of the Horror Writers Association and CEO and founder of Crossroad Press Publishing. His novels include *This is My Blood, Deep Blue,* and many more. Upcoming works include the novels *Tattered Remnants* and *Into Nothing*. His most recent published work is the novel *Jurassic Ark*—a retelling of the Noah's Ark story . . . with dinosaurs. David lives in way-out-yonder NC with his wife Patricia and an army of pets.

You can find information on his novels, collections, and more at his website: www.davidniallwilson.com

You can connect with David on Twitter at @CrossroadPress or on Facebook at: www.facebook.com/DavidNiallWilson